Karin Schaefer lives in country New South Wales, Australia. She is author of the pony books, Dawn Ride and Winning. Karin is intrigued by the relationship between humans and horses. Many people around the world share their lives with horses, as does Karin herself. To some, they are creatures of beauty and refinement, superior athleticism or enormous monetary value. To others, they are healers, spiritual guides, creatures of the mythos or simply friends. Karin uses fiction to explore these relationships, bringing her knowledge of horses and horse owners together to evoke both laughter and contemplation of what, to her, is one of life's great mysteries and joys.

BlueBuckle

Karin P Schaefer

First published by RedHat Publishing in 2020
This edition published in 2020 by REDHAT PUBLISHING

BlueBuckle

EPUB: 9781925786880
POD: 9781925786897

Cover design by Red Tally Studios

Publishing services provided by Critical Mass
www.critmassconsulting.com

To Miss Moo, who opened my heart
to everything I didn't know about horses.
This tale is for you.

When I bestride him, I soar, I am a hawk:
He trots the air; the earth sings when he touches it;
The basest horn of his hoof is more musical
Than the pipe of Hermes.

WILLIAM SHAKESPEARE – HENRY V

WHO'S WHO & WHERE'S WHERE

PEOPLE PEOPLE	
Ben	- DJ son of the owners of the Highlands Hunt Ball venue.
Buckley brothers	- Lucien Blythe's guests for the Highlands Hunt opening meet, along with their wives and one of Buckley sisters.
Charlie & Maddie Vilanders	- Hosts the Highlands Hunt at their property Colo. Charlie rides with the Hunt.
Dick and Sandy Bowers	- Friends of Highlands Hunt Joint Master and Huntsman Simon Sinclair. Attend the opening meet.
Digger Fahey	- Sydney publicity guru and racehorse breeder and owner.
Christie Fahey	- Much younger wife of Digger, newsreader for a top television network.
Donnacha Keogh	- Irish manager of Whistlejacket Thoroughbred Stud in Burragong. Rides Whipper-in for the Highlands Hunt. Lives in the manager's cottage at Whistlejacket.
Eleanor Lonsdale	- Young Kiwi partner of Simon Sinclair. Field Master for the Highlands Hunt. Lives at Gwynedd with Simon.
Garry Hume (Rowdy)	- Burragong local, comes to work at Gwynedd for Simon.
June (the Fairy)	- Garry Hume's mother. Miracle cleaner-up of celebrity tips.
Jack Mariner	- Lucien Blythe's guest for the opening meet along with partner Dion.
George Manning	- Hong Kong racehorse trainer, friend of Lucien Blythe's.

Opal Manning	- George's daughter.
Gill Findlay	- Owns Blooming Beautiful flower shop in Burragong and mare Hester. Member of the Highlands Hunt.
Nicholas Findlay	- Gill's husband, university lecturer.
Olivia Findlay	- Gill's and Nicholas' teenage daughter. Goes to school in Burragong. Best friends with Hazel Teo.
Oscar Findlay	- Twenty-three-year-old son of Gill and Nicholas. University dropout, living somewhere in Mongolia.
India Ann Levy	- Twenty-four-year-old granddaughter of Grace Levy, schooled at northern tablelands boarding school, studied art at the Slade School of Fine Art in London. Ambition is to be a portrait painter.
Grace Levy	- India's deceased grandmother, lived in her later years on a small acreage outside Burragong, Mars House. Founding member of the Highlands Hunt.
Janet Reedhead (Mrs R)	- Whistlejacket's housekeeper.
Beef (Brian) Reedhead	- Janet's husband, all duties man at Whistlejacket.
Julie Rice	- Burragong cat and garden obsessive. Sold Blooming Beautiful flower shop to Gill Findlay, looked after Grace's rescue greyhound, Jeffrey, after Grace died.
Lillian Bickham	- Julie's partner, member of the Highlands Hunt. Ex-diplomatic corps, rides identical buckskins called Passionfruit.
Kevin and Martin	- Lady Blythe's support team. Duties include buttling, chauffeuring and looking after Lady Blythe's dachshunds. Kevin also

	is Lady Blythe's and Whistlejacket's accountant and manages the Whistlejacket website.
Leila Caffrey	- Mid-twenties, in charge of foaling-down and yearling preparation at Whistlejacket. Interned at the National Stud in Ireland.
Lenny	- Drinks waiter at the Bombay Duck. Studying dentistry.
Lesley Bond	- Whipper-in for the Highlands Hunt. Breeds and runs pigs free-range with her husband.
Lucien Blythe	- Son of Lady Blythe and Jonno Blythe (deceased). Born in England. Moved to Australia with his mother after his father died. Co-owner of Whistlejacket Thoroughbreds with his mother. Joint Master of the Highlands Hunt.
Lady Blythe	- Mother of Lucien Blythe, widow of Jonno Blythe. Lives in Burragong at Le Manoir. Plays bridge at the Burragong Bridge Club.
Jonathon (Jonno) Blythe	- Deceased third husband of Lady Blythe, father of Lucien.
Margot Apsley (Villon)	- English wife of Pan Villon.
Nelson Cherry	- Veterinarian. Equine specialist.
Pan Villon	- Born in England to a teenage mother and Greek father. In his early days lived with an aunt on a small farm. Schooled in England and Switzerland. Economics degree. Worked for a London bank and was briefly married to Margot Apsley before buying a property in the Highlands, Big Hill. Has studied and worked with esteemed horse trainers and animal communicators around the world. Works

	with problem horses. Rides with the Highlands Hunt. Midseason Whipper-in.
Pinkie	- Whistlejacket's Office Manager, Pauline Bowen. Highly efficient and popular with Whistlejacket clients. Has semi-styled herself on the rock singer Pink. Lives in Burragong with her parents.
Scott Page	- Dressage rider and instructor. Lives with partner Stephan on their horse property Tarlo on the Sydney side of Burragong. Dressage instructor at Garton House and Whipper-in with the Highlands Hunt.
Stephan Olsen	- Scott's partner, co-owner with his sister Yolanda of the popular Burragong restaurant, The Bombay Duck. Master chef.
Yolanda Olsen	- Scott's sister and co-owner of the Bombay Duck.
Simon Sinclair	- Founder with his now deceased wife, Rebecca, of the Highlands Hunt. Joint Master with Lucien Blythe and Huntsman. Lives at his Burragong property Gwynedd. The hound kennels are at Gwynedd.
Vivienne Teo	- Owner of a chain of hairdressing salons, including the exclusive A Cut Above in Burragong. Has two children, Hazel and Toby.
Hazel Teo	- Teen friend of Olivia Findlay. Rides with the Highlands Hunt.
Toby Teo	- Hazel's older brother. Surgical Registrar at Sydney's Royal Prince Alfred Hospital.
Xavier Swift	- Burragong local. Very successful real-estate agent.

DOG PEOPLE	
Benzo, Beret, Ghillie, Sadie	- Pan Villon's dogs. Benzo – a rescue greyhound with very specific ideas about where he should pee, Beret and Ghillie –hunting obsessed terriers, Sadie – a black Labrador of impeccable loyalty.
Jack	- Simon Sinclair's Jack Russell terrier.
Jeffrey	- Grace Levy's rescue Greyhound.
The Cairns	- Gill Findlay's Cairn terriers
The dachs	- Lady Blythe's dachshunds, Pavarotti and Caruso.
Sorrows	- Donnacha's woolly Jack Russell.

HORSE PEOPLE	
BlueBuckle	- Kentucky stallion purchased for ten million AU$ to reinvigorate Whistlejacket's sire roster.
Chopper (LutePlayer)	- An ex-racehorse Pan is working with. So named after tearing off a stable hand's ear.
Elvis	- Eleanor Lonsdale's chocolate coloured warmblood. A present from Simon.
Expresso	- Olivia Findlay's hunter.
Frenchie (FrenchTartin)	- Chestnut thoroughbred rehabilitated by Pan and now permanent resident at Big Hill.
Hester	- Gill Findlay's hunter.
Looking for Love (Looky)	- Xavier Swift's hunter.
Mockingbird	- Dark brown thoroughbred mare bred at Whistlejacket.

Monash	- Scott Page's ageing dressage horse.
Oyster	- Donnacha's hunter, an obliging strawberry roan Percheron thoroughbred cross.
Dorothy	- One-eyed pony mare owned by Hazel Teo.
Passionfruit	- Lillian Bickham's two Buckskin hunters.
Stanislas, Speed, Birdie	- Whistlejacket's stallions.
Pharlap	- Big Hill's security guard. Sow bred by Lesley Bond, spared death as a piglet because of her human eyes. Gifted to Pan Villon as a housewarming present by Lesley.

PLACES	
A Cut Above	- Vivienne Teo's exclusive Burragong hair salon (one of five).
Big Hill	- Pan Villon's Highlands property.
Blooming Beautiful	- Flower shop in Burragong on the high street owned by Gill Findlay. Previously owned by Julie Rice.
Burragong	- Beautiful village in the New South Wales Southern Highlands, location of multimillion-dollar houses and properties.
Colo	- Maddie and Charlie Vilanders' property – setting of a Highland Hunt's winter meet.
Garton House	- Burragong's most exclusive school.
Gwynedd	- Simon Sinclair's property.
Jottings	- Multimillion-dollar Highlands property purchased by Digger Fahey.
Le Manoir	- Lady Blythe's Burragong home.
Mars House	- Grace Levy's house and ten-acre property, twenty minutes' drive from Burragong.

Tarlo	- Scott and Stephan's horse property just outside Burragong.
The Bombay Duck	- Popular Burragong restaurant owned by Stephan and Yolanda Olson. (Nothing to do with the Mumbai fish "Bombay dax", often Anglicised to "Bombay duck".)
The Burragong Arms	- Burragong's local hotel, known as The Barmy.
Tulameen Berry Farm	- Location of the Highlands Hunt Ball.
Whistlejacket	- Boutique thoroughbred stud farm owned by Lady Blythe and her son Lucien. Other than Donnacha, Janet Reedhead, Beef, Leila and Pinkie, staff are the predominantly overseas farmstay workers with horse experience known as the dorm team.
Wirral	- Location of the Highlands Hunt's opening meet.
Yarra	- Property for sale near Gwynedd.

1

'Come on Jeffrey, out.' India Levy gave Jeffrey's collar another tug and with a deep sigh the old greyhound tumbled out of the car and onto the grass. At the front door of Mars House, however, his years fell away. He impatiently bumped India's calves with his nose as she fumbled with the keys and the door at last opened, he pushed past and disappeared into the gloom of the hallway.

India followed reluctantly. The air was still and smelt of cold wood ash and dust. Everything was much as she remembered. In the living room, the cavernous fireplace, mystical Aboriginal desert paintings, the sofa placed to catch the warmth of the fire. In the dining room, the long oak table, her drawings and paintings, professionally framed worthy or not forming a frieze on the wall. She picked a pair of reading glasses up off the keyboard of the laptop open on the table and quickly put them down. The glasses, the laptop, the horse magazines on the sofa, they all told the same lie – Grace, her grandmother, had just gone out to feed the horses, or to Burragong for the weekly shop. She would be back any minute, clucking for her glasses, making the rooms of Mars House feel small with her long stride.

India recoiled from the thought. Grace was dead and dead meant gone, no longer, extinction. Mars House was now just a shell, an empty shell.

She flicked a light switch. Nothing. She went to another. The same. She sat down on the edge of the sofa. Come night, she would be sitting in the dark with the cold cutting through her and she would be even more hungry. She had planned to stay at a B&B while she organised the house sale, but that was before she had been landed with Jeffrey; it hadn't crossed her mind that the friend of Grace's who had taken him in wouldn't want to keep him.

She rose and went to the pantry, hoping to find some dog biscuits, but there were none. She would have to drive back to Burragong.

There was just enough wood in the basket by the fireplace to get a fire going. In the garage, however, stacked against the wall on the other side of the horse float, there was enough for a few weeks at least. She began loading the wheelbarrow.

When the fire was at last throwing out some heat, she drew the firescreen and went to find Jeffrey. He was in Grace's room, on her bed. Her eyes averted, she covered him with a blanket: the solicitor who had contacted her in London said that Grace had died in her sleep.

The road to Burragong wound through lightly timbered grazing country. The cattle were chunky, the horses rugged to their ears. Iron gates and tree lined driveways flashed past, along with glimpses of sprawling houses, tennis courts and riding arenas. Amongst such opulence, Mars House was a poor relation.

But even a poor relation in the Southern Highlands was worth far more than she'd imagined, India discovered as she studied the windows of the real estate agent offices on the Burragong high street. She would have enough money to buy a decent sized flat, or maybe a bedsit and a cottage in a village like Burragong so that she could escape when London oppressed her. She'd be able to give up her job and paint fulltime, hopefully until the commissions started coming in.

Thankyou Grace. Thankyou.

She found everything she needed on the bustling high street. A supermarket for candles, cheese, fruit and wine and biscuits for Jeffrey, a bakery for pastries to quiet her stomach, a café for a much-needed coffee. In the Op Shop she bought a woollen beanie and a thick tweed overcoat that smelt of mouldering leaves.

The shopping stowed in the hire car, she cocooned herself in the coat and gulped down the latte. Jetlag was making her feel rubbery, but she had thought that while she was in Burragong, she should get some flowers for Julie Rice, Grace's friend who'd been looking after Jeffrey. If Julie knew that she was going to sell Mars House, she might take Jeffrey back or help find him another home.

2

Gill Findlay left the callistemon stems she'd been working into an arrangement and went to the front of the shop. A tall, pale young woman with long ribbons of ivory coloured hair as dubiously clean as her coat was studying the buckets on the floor. There was something familiar about her. Perhaps she'd been in a fashion magazine or on TV. Young things that looked like they'd just come from a photoshoot or music video set were not uncommon in Burragong.

Feeling double her almost forty years, Gill hid her reddened hands behind her back and nodded at the bouquets in the fridge.

'There are those too. Or I can do you up something if you'll be about the village for half an hour.'

The young woman glanced at the fridge then returned to scrutinising the buckets.

Not much money, Gill thought. She pointed at a bucket of Oriental lilies. 'They're good value. They smell divine and they'll keep at least ten days with some care.'

The young woman lifted a bunch of the lilies out of the bucket and cupped her palm to catch the drips from the stems.

Gill took them from her and led the way to the counter. 'Do you want a card with them?'

The young woman thought a moment then said in a very English voice, 'Thank you, yes. To Julie from Jeffrey.'

'Julie, Jeffrey? The voice.' Gill stared. The arrow-like eyebrows, the elegant jawline – it must be, it could only be. She smoothed her apron and attempted to push her ratty bob into some sort of shape.

'You're Grace's granddaughter, India. I'm Gill, Gill Findlay. Welcome to Burragong.'

'Actually, my name's Ann.'

'But you are Grace's granddaughter?'

The young woman nodded and put some money on the counter.

Gill pushed it back towards her. 'Don't worry about it. You must come for dinner as soon as you're settled. My daughter Olivia adored Grace. We all did. She was a great friend.' Gill wrote her mobile number on a shop card. 'But in the meantime, call if you need anything. Anything at all.'

After India had left the shop, Gill returned to her workbench. But it was impossible to concentrate. Everyone had assumed that India would return after Grace's death. But when she had not and the weeks passed, it had seemed that she had no intention of ever returning. Mars House stood empty and would remain so, the grass getting longer, the garden wilder.

But now ...

Gill threaded fronds of wattle through the fire engine red blooms of the callistemon and set the arrangement in a wide necked tube so she could adjust the stems. Grace's death had come as a shock. No one had known about the cancer. No one except Grace. And India, Julie Rice firmly believed. But Julie firmly believed many things: that her cats were reincarnations of Egyptian gods and priests for one.

The phone rang and presuming it was Julie calling to say that India had been to pick up Jeffrey, she answered it saying, 'Doesn't she look like Grace.'

'Grace?' came the nasal voice. 'Who looks like Grace?

Gill mouthed a silent 'fuck'. It was not Julie Rice but Janet Reedhead, Whistlejacket Thoroughbreds' housekeeper.

'Sorry Janet. I was talking to a friend and the line dropped out. I thought it was her ringing back.'

Janet Reedhead was not put off so easily. 'You were talking about Grace Levy, weren't you?'

'No, no. About my friend's goddaughter Grace. Now, flowers. What do you need? I'm flat out.'

Her tone telling that she knew she was being falsely served, Janet Reedhead turned to the business of her call; she was after all a busy woman with heavy responsibilities.

'Twelve arrangements, six for the house and six for the guest rooms and cottages.'

'A full house for the opening meet then. I don't suppose we're giving out names?'

'I don't suppose we are,' Janet sniffed.

'Oh well, I'll see them all at the meet anyway,' Gill said cheerily, unable to help reminding Janet that while she might be the owner of a lowly flower shop, she was on the right side of the divide.

'And I'll need everything tomorrow,' Janet said. 'Brian will be in at ten. He'll be pushed, so don't keep him hanging about.' Brian, Janet's husband, was Whistlejacket's all-duties man.

'Serves you right,' Gill told herself as the line went dead. She hated snobbery but Janet Reedhead brought out the worst in her. She added Whistlejacket's order to the book. Twelve arrangements! She ought to be grateful for the business, but with an already lengthy list of orders for the weekend and a wedding, she'd be lucky to be awake during the opening meet. Not that she'd really mind. If she hadn't been on the hunt committee and her daughter Olivia not counting down the days to the meet, she'd have happily given it a miss. The hunting she lived for began when the social hunters faded away. Grace had been the same.

The phone rang again. She ignored it and went to the stock refrigerator. The ringing stopped and her mobile started. She veered from the fridge to the workbench and filleted her phone out from among a tangle of smashed stems and soggy ribbon and checked the caller ID in case it was Olivia.

But this time it was Julie Rice. Despite having decided that she now couldn't afford a minute's idleness, she answered and listened a while before agreeing. 'Oh, she picked Jeffrey up earlier. She must have come back into town then. He wasn't with her. I couldn't help staring either. Yes, stunning. Well, except for the turnout. But she's an artist. Yes, yes, funny about the name. Grace only ever called her India. But anyway ...'

She broke off as Julie described the sketch of Jeffrey India had only just minutes ago left with the flowers. 'I didn't see it,' she said, disappointed. 'Yes, I know she's a portraitist. No, I didn't get the impression she was peering at me. You did? Oh, I doubt it. Do you think she's planning to do animals as well? I wouldn't mind getting her to do the Cairns while she's still affordable.'

Again, Gill paused, listened and then replied. 'No, I don't think she's come for the opening meet. There's nothing planned anyway. And as far as I know, she doesn't ride. Must go. Bloody Janet Reedhead just rang. Whistlejacket's got a full house for the meet and Janet wants the flowers tomorrow morning.'

3

India peered in Blooming Beautiful's door. The front of the shop was in darkness but there was a light on at the back. Hopefully Gill didn't leave it on for security. She knocked again.

After a minute Gill appeared. Her salt and pepper bob was awry and her apron and the wrists of her sporty hoody were soaked. She looked like she'd been battling her way up a blustery beach.

'Oh, hello,' she said as she opened the door. 'I thought I heard someone knocking. People don't usually want flowers this early, but I do get the occasional frantic husband who's suddenly remembered it's his wedding anniversary.'

'We've been for a drive,' India said, gesturing at Jeffrey. 'My body clock's all out. I saw the light and wondered if I could charge my mobile and computer?'

'Of course,' Gill said.

The back of the shop was a mess of buckets, headless flowers, stripped stems and bits of ribbon, foam and wire. India slid her laptop and phone out of her tote and set them on the table while Gill cleared some space on the desk and juggled with the powerboard to make room for a couple more plugs.

'That's a very smart coat,' Gill said, admiring Jeffrey's bright blue woollen coat.

'I think Grace knitted it,' India said. 'There's a cupboard full of them at Mars House.' Last night, just before she had passed out, she had attempted to struggle into a mohair number, thinking it would keep her warm in bed and not realising it was a dog coat.

'Grace was a great knitter,' Gill said.

'I suppose it passed the time.'

'Time was something Grace never had enough of. She knitted jackets for rescued penguins and premature babies too,' Gill said, her voice even more crisp. 'Sorry, that sounded ratty. Not enough sleep, I'm afraid.'

India pointed at the orchids on the workbench. 'Those are amazing.' The flowers' white throats were streaked with what looked like tiny rivulets of fresh blood.

'Aren't they. I'd love to meet whoever or whatever it is or was that came up with the idea of flowers. Though what you'd say to such an extraordinary intelligence I can't imagine. "Hi, I like your work" wouldn't quite cut it.'

Gill admired the flowers then said, 'I don't suppose you could get us a coffee? You'd be saving my life. Jeffrey can stay and keep me company. Pregos'll be open. Up the high street and left into the first lane. It's the best coffee. Better make mine a double shot.' She produced a bed for Jeffrey from under the workbench and got some change out of the till.

Glad to have something to do, India headed out into the new morning.

Despite the early hour, Pregos' outside tables were mostly occupied. The coffee must be good. She quickened her step and then stopped, her stomach tightening. Van Morrison's "Moondance" was coming from the café, the Irish balladeer's peaty voice clear and distinctive in the still morning air. An image came into her mind, a photo, her "naming" in a friend of her parents' yurt. Her mother, cradling her, had flowers in her hair and her dress clung to her braless breasts. Her father's collarless shirt had pointed sleeves that hung down over his hands like a jester's and his feet were bare. It was 1998, the age dawning not that of Aquarius but of a new millennium. The revolution had fizzed out decades ago, a small fact that her parents had chosen to ignore. "Moondance", their anthem, had probably been playing at the so called naming.

She pushed the image from her mind and her balled hands into the coat's gritty pockets and continued towards the café.

When she got back to Blooming Beautiful, Jeffrey raised his head and slapped his tail against the side of his bed.

'He's certainly much brighter, Gill said. 'Happy to be home, I expect. He was wretched after Grace died. Some say animals don't grieve, but it's rubbish. Lillian wanted to put Jeffrey on Prozac but Julie wouldn't. The fact that he was suddenly living in a cattery can't have helped either. If you didn't notice, Lillian and Julie's house is overrun with cats. Egyptian Maus. I don't generally mind cats, but those give me the creeps. They hide behind things and stare and you get the feeling that they're trying to hypnotise you. I'd have taken Jeffrey myself, but my two torment him. They get either side of him and bark until he doesn't know where he is. Grace had to leave him in the car when she came over.' Gill took a sip of the coffee. 'This is heaven. I might have to send you back for another.'

Well that counted Gill out as a possible home for Jeffrey, India thought. She'd had no luck with Julie Rice, either. The ferocious faced little woman had grabbed the flowers and sketch of Jeffrey and disappeared back into the house before she'd had a chance to say anything more than 'thank you'.

'I was wondering,' Gill said, 'if there was any chance you could do the shop for a few hours this morning if you haven't got anything planned? I'm desperately behind with the orders.'

India thought for a moment then said, 'Yes, I could.' There was still some time before the real estate agents opened and Gill might look after Jeffrey while she went to see them.

Gill rattled off a volley of thanks and following her instructions, India began putting buckets of flowers about the polished concrete floor. Jeffrey wandered along behind her, catching her gaze and pressing against her legs when she stooped to place price cards beside the buckets. This done, they started on the chaos around Gill's workbench and it was suddenly time to open the shop.

At mid-morning, after a smiley man with a huge stomach had left with arms full of native flowers, the doorbell jangled and the cry of 'mum, mum' filled the shop. Two teenage girls appeared, one fair, tall and athletic looking like Gill and the other dark-haired and stocky. They were identically dressed in skinny jeans and oversized tshirts and waving mobile phones.

'My daughter Olivia and her friend Hazel Teo,' Gill told India. 'They've got a pupil free day.' She pulled a face at the girls. 'Another one. Hello. Let me finish these roses and I'll introduce you.'

Olivia Gilbert gave India a dismissive glance then seeing Jeffrey, now back in his bed, rushed over and knelt beside him. Hazel followed more slowly.

'Mum, it's Jeffrey,' Olivia said. 'Has Janet dumped him? Is he coming to live with us? What about the Cairns? They'll drive him mad.'

'Jeffrey's back at Mars House,' Gill said. 'This is Grace's granddaughter, India. Sorry, Ann. Stand up and say hello.'

Hazel smiled at India. 'Hello,' she said politely. 'I thought your name was India.' She started to giggle.

Olivia stood up and said to India, 'Jeffrey's breath smells. I bet Julie's been feeding him cat food. Grace only gave him chicken necks. She believed in them absolutely. Unlike mum, who gives ours any rubbish that's on sale.'

'Liv,' Gill said sharply. 'You're being rude. You too, Hazel.'

Olivia met her mother's stern gaze with an equally fierce one of her own, then her face crumpled as she too began to giggle. 'Sorry India, we've been doing assertiveness training at school.'

'It's not even a subject, Liv,' Hazel protested.

'Dad rang,' Olivia said to her mother. 'He's not coming down. He said that between the shop and the opening meet you'll be a nightmare. And he's got a lot of papers to mark.'

'More likely he's got a date with one of his students,' Hazel said under her breath. '*Multum in Parvo.*'

'That's so not funny,' Olivia said.

'You don't even know what I said,' Hazel giggled.

'I so do. It's Latin. Hazel's very screwed up,' Olivia said to India. 'She's got no father and Mrs Teo wants her to be a judge.'

'Come on Liv, we've got to go,' Hazel said. 'Mum's doing our nails,' she explained to India, waving her fingers like a Bollywood dancer.'

'In a minute,' Olivia said. 'Are you coming to the opening meet?' she asked India.

'India's only just arrived from London and I'm sure she's got lots of other things she wants to do,' Gill said. 'Now buzz off. If I don't get these orders finished, we won't be going to the meet either.'

Olivia rolled her eyes. 'Bye AnnIndia. See you at the meet. Jeffrey'll be looking forward to it. Grace always brought him. And don't forget about the chicken necks. Grace went to the butcher next to the Sourdough Bakery.'

Olivia put her arm through Hazel's and dragged her towards the front of the shop. The bell jangled and everything went quiet. Very quiet.

'Sorry,' said Gill, threading ribbon through the yellow rosebuds she had worked into a posy. 'Olivia's not always so bolshy. Fourteen's a terrible age. One day they're mini adults with all the wisdom and the weight of the world on their shoulders and the next they're like two-year olds in a supermarket. Do you know how many kids are on anti-depressants? Over a hundred thousand, if you can believe it.'

India did believe it. She taught drawing in a school favoured by celebrity parents. 'It's the same in the UK.'

Gill removed a less than perfect petal off one of the buds with a pair of tweezers. 'And I bet a lot of the parents are on the same drugs. Being a parent's almost as complicated as being a kid these days. Though some seem to manage okay. Hazel's mother's pretty much brought up Hazel and her brother Toby on her own. Toby's doing medicine and Hazel's aiming at law, hence the Latin.' Gill laughed. 'We don't know what she's saying half the time. If you want a spectacularly good haircut, her mother's salon's the one. A Cut Above. It's just off the high street.'

India checked the time on her now charged phone. The morning was getting on.

'I was wondering if you'd keep Jeffrey for an hour or so while I visit some real estate agents? I'm selling Mars House.'

'Oh,' Gill said. 'What a shame. Poor Jeffrey. Sorry, I'm being as rude as the girls.'

4

Fingers keeping beat to Pink on the steering wheel, Lucien Blythe motored down the highway towards the Highlands and Whistlejacket, towards home. The Hong Kong trip had been a success. With his friend George Manning he had gone to pre-dawn gallops and race meets, toured stables and dined with Hong Kong Jockey Club execs. And with George's daughter, Opal, he had done other equally satisfying but far more exciting things. And to cap it off, two Whistlejacket bred horses had had big wins on the track.

He smiled at his reflection in the rear-view mirror, his face was as photo ready as ever. If George had found out about the frolics with Opal, however, the picture would have been not so pretty. He might even at this moment be feeding the crabs on the bottom of Victoria Harbour. Just as the horses in George's multi-storey stable were trained for Happy Valley and Sha Tin's richest purses, so too had Opal, his only daughter, been prepared for the rarer richer reaches of Hong Kong's establishment. But like all young thoroughbreds, Opal thrilled quickly and had a mind of her own and she was determined that her gilded cage be filled with trinkets of her own choosing. Watch this space, Lucien thought, putting on the indicator for the Mittagong exit.

His mobile rang and IDing the caller, he listened for a moment and said, 'See you in about twenty. Don't wash those fingers.'

A short while later, he pulled up at the Burragong Cricket Museum. The museum was having a busy day – despite it being a

Friday, there were at least three tourist buses and numerous cars in the carpark. He entered through the side door for which as a board member he had a key and after letting himself into the office, sank into one of the armchairs and allowed himself to be lulled by the muffled narratives of the interactive displays coming from the museum's main hall.

And then here was Christie, bare legs Barbie doll long in pink Louboutin pumps. He slid her white linen shift up over her thighs and pulled her against him so her hands, fumbling to undo his jeans, were sandwiched between their groins.

'Hi,' he said into her ear.

Christie freed her hands, slipped her dress off over her head and undid his shirt and rubbed her breasts against his chest.

Thinking about Opal's hard little breasts, he turned her round and bent her over the desk.

'Missed me, did you?' Christie said a few short minutes later.

He put a finger to his lips. A friend had been caught using this same office for a similar purpose and been booted off the board. He pulled Christie against him, her heels putting their groins at equal height, as perhaps had been the designer's intention.

'Of course,' he lied softly into her very blonde mane.

Minutes later they were dressed and standing in the carpark beside Christie's Mercedes. Christie's mobile rang and she waved him away, slid into the car and took the call.

He was halfway to Burragong when her name appeared again on the caller ID, her voice once more that of a prime-time newsreader.

'See any good horses or Chinese pussies in Hong Kong?'

'Both,' he answered. 'How's Dig?'

Christie was married to Digger Fahey, a Sydney advertising scion.

'Creaky, but still making squillions.'

'I hope he's planning to send me some mares this season.'

'You've already got his best,' Christie said.

Lucien laughed and cut the call.

A short time later, as the gates to Whistlejacket Thoroughbreds swung open, he let out a contented sigh. Home. He drove along the avenue of Ash trees past the homestead and towards the stables. The housekeeper, Janet Reedhead, who believed herself closest of all the staff to the throne, would be getting sourer by the minute but he wanted an update on the new stallion, BlueBuckle. The stallion, purchased from a Kentucky stud, had arrived from quarantine as he was setting off to Sydney for the flight to Hong Kong. Whistlejacket's manager, Donnacha Keough, had hurriedly backed the prize horse off the truck and everything appearing to be fine, he'd gone on his way a happy man. Not long after, however, in Donnacha's words, things had gone 'completely to shite'.

Donnacha was on the phone in his office in the hospital stableblock. Lucien caught his eye and looked pointedly at his watch. Donnacha drew a circle in the air, signalling that the person on the other end was going on. His usually lank dark hair looked like it had had the Vivienne Teo treatment and, as if tickled by the memory of something sweet, a smile played about his lips. Things must still be going well with Leila, Lucien thought. Pity. Leila should be setting her sights higher, a lot higher. Though her build was all about work, her open, freckled face and sweet chin and thick chestnut hair made her worth a second look. And there were those long thighs, made for cradling a man's hips. She had also done an internship at Ireland's National Stud – it was probably there that she'd developed the unfortunate taste for tricky Irishmen.

Donnacha ended the call. 'Feed merchant's changing the brand of foal mix. Wanted to go into every detail in case we had any concerns.'

Lucien was not interested in foal mix. 'How's the stallion?'

Donnacha shook his head. 'Starting to look like an RSPCA case. Lucky he's up at the old yards.'

'Has Nelson seen him?' Lucien asked. Nelson Cherry was Whistlejacket's vet.

'A couple of times, from outside the yard.'

'Let's go and look at him, then. We'll walk,' Lucien said. He'd been sitting for the better part of twelve hours and needed some air in his lungs.

They headed off through the stables, Sorrows, Donnacha's woolly terrier following at a safe distance; Lucien intensely disliked dogs about his heels.

'The dorm crew are doing some work for a change,' he said, pointing to the swept floors and clean stalls. Whistlejacket's labour was mostly supplied by visa workers, some on gap years, others working their way around the world. Their accommodation was a converted shearing shed known as the dorm, hence they were called the dorm crew.

'A couple of the new Germans are handy,' Donnacha said.

The old stallion yards were at the end of a laneway that ran between the weanling paddocks, colts on the one side, the fillies on the other. Lucien and Donnacha were still some distance from the yards when they heard the pounding of hooves.

'Sets up when anyone's headed that way,' Donnacha said. 'Buggered how he knows. You could understand if it was someone in a vehicle but not when it's someone on foot.'

The pounding grew louder. A chill went down Lucien's spine.

'I see what you mean about an RSPCA case,' he said as they reached the yard.

The stallion's blue-grey coat was black with dried sweat and every rib was visible. Seeing them, he stopped for a moment then came at the fence with such speed that they both stepped back.

'Shit!' Lucien said as BlueBuckle slid to a halt, reared and struck out in the direction of their heads. 'No wonder Nelson wouldn't go in the yard.'

BlueBuckle dropped back onto his feet, wheeled, galloped around the yard and came at them again.

'Did you speak to quarantine?'

'I did,' Donnacha said. 'They said he was testy and needed an experienced handler but that's nothing out of the ordinary. The horse transport company said the same. Cherry did say something about a brain tumour. We'd never get the hoss to the surgery though, and even if we did somehow get it into the yard the mobile xray's not likely to give a good enough image.'

'Stop his water. The hay too.'

'The hay won't be a hardship,' Donnacha said with the hint of a smile. 'He just tramples it anyway.'

Bloody Irish, Lucien thought. The worse a horse behaves the more they like it. 'And make sure nobody else comes up here. If anyone asks, BlueBuckle's still in quarantine.'

BlueBuckle reared again, his nostrils livid caverns, his eyes the dark of murder.

'You fucker,' Lucien said setting off back down the laneway. He'd been months searching for a stallion to upgrade the Whistlejacket stallion roster, one the stud could afford to buy outright, and now it seemed that he'd bought a ten-million-dollar lunatic. Fuck, fuck and FUCK.

5

India woke with Jeffrey's back pressed against her side. She lay for a while enjoying their shared warmth. Strange – she would never let a lover stay over or if the bed they'd ended up in was his she'd be gone from it not long after the sex, but she didn't mind Jeffrey's company while she slept.

She dozed off then her eyes sprung open. A real estate agent was coming at eight thirty and another at ten. She ought to tidy the kitchen and living room at least, and maybe cut back the shrubs around the path to the garage if there was time. The agents were bound to want to see the yard as well and it was a fight to get to the garage and the paddock beyond.

She slid reluctantly out of bed. The air was icy; even inside the tweed coat she was still cold. But at least now she could make tea. By some fluke, she'd discovered that the gas to the stovetop hadn't been turned off. How much gas was in the bottle was anybody's guess, but she'd worry about that later.

The tea drawing in the pot and there being no plug for the bathroom sink, she put an enamel bowl from the laundry into the sink and poured in the remaining hot water. The smell of leather soap rose on the steam. She could hardly meet the estate agents smelling like a saddle! She opened the cupboard over the vanity. Chanel Body Lotion. That would do it. She added a few drops to the water, dropped the coat on the floor, stripped off her pyjamas and set to work with the flannel, avoiding any glimpse of her naked body.

Cleanish and dressed, she dampened the hairbrush and forced her hair – it needed washing – into a semblance of straightness, braided it and flicked it over her shoulder out of immediate sight.

Where had the time gone? The first agent was due in half an hour. She stowed Grace's computer and glasses in the pantry, along with the horse magazines from the sofa. In the living room, she noticed for the first time the doghair on the sofa, the drifts of dust and Jeffrey height smudges on the walls. Oh well, whoever bought Mars House would likely gut it anyway. She looked around with a feeling almost of regret; as a child she had thought Mars House a palace.

She took her plate and wine glass from last night to the kitchen and was about to boil some more water to wipe a few surfaces when the doorbell made its funny growling.

'Rob Marks,' said the fifty something man on the doorstep. 'Argyle Real Estate.' He gestured at the door. 'The bell sounds like it's got a nasty disease. Ringtones are the thing these days.'

'I used to think there was a fairything living in there when I was little,' India said, dizzy from his aftershave and the clashing colours of his olive and lilac shirt. 'My grandmother fed it after I'd gone to bed. It liked potato chips'

'Lovely time, childhood. Sorry for your loss. Of your grandmother, I mean. Grace wasn't it. Let's get started. Weekends are my busiest time. I've got an open house in an hour and an auction.'

But suddenly Jeffrey was between them, bony bottom butting Rob Mark's shins, eyes fixed on India's face. Rob Marks swatted him away. 'Not a fan of dogs,' he said, fussily brushing the knees of his trousers.

India steadied Jeffrey and then beckoning him to follow her, settled him on the sofa in the living room. He couldn't know that Rob Marks was here to sell Mars House, could he? It was possible. Grace believed that animals knew much more than humans allowed and shared many of the same feelings. She stroked Jeffrey's ears. 'Sorry,' she said guiltily. 'I'll work something out for you, I promise.'

Rob Marks was in the first room off the hallway.

'Good size,' he said.

She looked around the room, unchanged since she had claimed it for herself when she had come to live with Grace. She'd been eight and had chosen it not only because it was clean, but because it was the room closest to the front door, to the outside, to safety. She stepped back into the hallway.

They went quickly from room to room, Rob Marks stopping to scan ceiling, walls, windows, floor, fittings and furnishing. In the dining room he stood in front of her drawings and paintings. 'Some of these aren't bad.'

India left him and went and joined Jeffrey on the sofa. There was the sound of cupboards being opened and closed. Sniffing. The laundry door banged.

'You knew my grandmother?' she asked when Rob Marks reappeared.

'Not me, my sister. She's horsey as well. Now, the paddock. There's a path through the garden I believe. That's if we can find it. Common problem with these deceased estates. Before you know it, the garden's a jungle and the spiders have taken over the house.'

'I don't mind spiders,' India said.

'Animal mad like your grandmother, then,' Rob Marks said, making it sound like a disease.

Swatting away the shrubbery with the same determination with which he had gotten rid of Jeffrey, he led the way to the garage then the paddock.

'It's about ten acres, I think,' India said, finding his aftershave even more oppressive in the outside air.

'Shame it's not subdivided.'

'Subdivided?'

'Turn this into two, ten blocks and you'll quadruple the value of it as a single lot. Possibly more than quadruple. With Burragong prices the way they are, buyers are looking further afield. The blocks'd sell in a flash. Subdividing costs, but what you have to think is that one block is going to cover the outgoings and the rest is profit.' Rob Marks paused to give India time to absorb this. 'But if that's not the way you want to go, tin tacks, I'd be putting the place on the market for …'

A huge amount.

Rob Marks drummed on the top of the gate with his fingers. 'Your grandmother had a lot of stuff. It'll all have to go. Burragong loves a garage sale. Some'll come just to stickybeak, but you'll be surprised what they'll buy if the price is right. My sister could help with the horse gear and she could do something with the Aboriginal paintings as well. She's got connections in Sydney. And don't forget the Op Shops. Burragong's takes furniture. I'd get a dealer in first. Your grandmother had some nice pieces.'

Rob Marks looked at India to make sure he still had her attention. 'But I'd give subdividing some serious thought.' He handed her a business card. 'I'm in the office in the mornings. No need to make an appointment, just drop in.'

He was gone, at last.

India sat back down beside Jeffrey, careful not to disturb his what looked to be exhausted sleep. She had thought that selling Mars House would involve agreeing on a price, signing a contract and handing over the keys and then waiting for the money to hit her bank. She hadn't given a single thought to what was in the house. The saddles and bridles in Grace's office, the racks of Jeffrey's coats, the furniture, Grace's clothes and books – it hadn't occurred to her that they were also something she would have to deal with.

The doorbell grringed again. Jeffrey woke and his tail thumped the cushions.

'Stay here,' she told him.

A lithe young man, glowing with cleanliness, stood on the doorstep. He held out a hand.

'Xavier, Xavier Swift.'

Fearing to dirty the manicured hand, India brushed the air near it with her own. 'Ann Levy.'

'I thought your name was India.'

'It's Ann.'

'But you are . .?

'Grace's granddaughter? Yes.' India looked over Xavier's shoulder towards the road. 'I'm expecting a real estate agent.'

'That's me,' Xavier said brightly. 'You called in at our office yesterday.'

India held the door open. 'I'm afraid I haven't done much to the house,' she said, thinking about Rob Marks' disparaging looks.

'Glad to hear it. It wouldn't be Mars House without dust and doghair.'

Jeffrey's tail thumped even harder when Xavier sat down beside him.

'Hi gorgeous. I bet you're pleased to be home.' Xavier looked up at India. 'He didn't eat for days after Grace died. I would have taken him but Julie Rice got in first. He was a rescue dog, you know. Those scars along his spine are from cigarette burns.'

'She was happy enough to see him go,' India said, remembering Julie Rice shoving Jeffrey into the hire car.'

'He'd started snapping at those Egyptian cat things, that's why. They used to pounce on him when he was asleep.'

India pushed her fist into her stomach as it rumbled loudly. 'Sorry. I haven't had breakfast.'

Xavier patted his own very flat stomach. 'Me either. I was at the gym at six. Let's go to Pregos and have a feed. You're probably living on stale bread and celery. The power's off of course.'

'You don't want to look around the house? At the paddock?'

'Know it all inside out. Anyway, you don't really want to sell. Why would you? Anyway, you can't. It's Jeffrey's home.' Xavier stood up. 'Come on, I'm panting for a coffee. Do you think Jeffrey's warm enough? It's freezing in here.'

The thought of food was too much for India to resist; the last proper meal she'd had was two days ago on the plane. She'd talk to Xavier about the house and Jeffrey when her stomach wasn't making a fuss. And when she was sure he really was an estate agent – he seemed too young, in his pristine white shirt and black trousers, a schoolboy still.

Xavier's shiny black BMW, numberplate XAV-LFL, made her think this suspicion had been wrong. The car was way too much of an expensive toy for a schoolboy.

'Looking for love,' Xavier said, explaining the numberplate as he held open the door for India. 'My horse's name.'

He slammed the door and in a short minute they were flying towards Burragong, Xavier pointing out properties he had sold and so often murmuring 'friend of Grace's', causing India to crane her neck to catch some detail of a disappearing house or farm.

After some fifteen minutes, Xavier pulled off the road and killed the motor in front of an imposing pair of wrought iron gates. The ironwork was shaped into feathers and India could see that when it opened, the gate would give the impression of a pair of wings rising on the air overhead.

'Whistlejacket Thoroughbreds,' she read from a plaque fixed to one of the massive sandstone gateposts.

'Home of the most beautiful thoroughbreds in the Southern Highlands and the most beautiful shit in Burragong,' Xavier said. 'Excluding myself, of course. Tragically though he's straight as time's arrow. We'll be putting a guard at Mars House when he gets a glimpse of you.' Xavier waved at the camera on one of the gates. 'Morning, Lucien.'

The trees lining the driveway were streaked with crimson, as if a drowsing god had knocked over his wine, sending its lees falling to earth. India took out her phone to capture the iron feathers, the wine splashed trees, but noticing the outline of a rearing horse on the plaque, she stopped.

'That's Whistlejacket.' The stallion painted life-size for its owner more than a century ago by the equally famous equestrian artist George Stubbs. The etching on the plaque was Whistlejacket's exact outline.

Xavier nosed the car back onto the road. 'Grace sent me a post-card of it when she was visiting you once. She said Whistlejacket looked so real she wanted to give him a carrot.'

'It's an extraordinary painting.' It was in a room of its own at the National Gallery. Grace had gone to see it every time she came to London.

The car picked up speed, and the countryside was once more an olive blur. But what were those people doing? India looked back but the car had rounded a bend. She searched her mind for any remnants of what she had seen. Nothing. She must have imagined it: the bush clearing, the circle of huddled figures.

'Lucien's father,' Xavier was saying, 'had a stud farm in England called Whistlejacket. When the old man died, Lady Blythe, Lucien's mother sold and set up in Burragong with some of the mares. Lady Blythe's Australian, but the Blythes are supposedly related to the

Marquess of Rockingham who owned the original Whistlejacket. The horse, I mean. That's how come they can use the name.'

They found a table outside Pregos and were soon sipping coffee. After bracing for more Van Morrison, India was relieved to hear a violin concerto coming from the café.

Xavier put down his latte. 'It's just come to me. Saddle soap and Chanel. I smelt it when you got in the car. You smell like Grace.' His brown velvet eyes misted with tears and his pretty mouth drooped. 'This morning's the first time I've been back to Mars House since … It's shitty that she's gone, totally shitty. She taught me to knit. She used to say knitting was her contribution to world peace. Less idle hands to do the devil's work. I thought maybe she was trying to stop me masturbating. You know, idle hands, the devil's work and all that.'

The waiter came with their breakfast. Visibly cheered, Xavier said, 'Best don't look. I'm a pig when it comes to food.'

But though rapidly consuming three poached eggs, a wad of smoked salmon and Turkish toast, Xavier's face and the front of his white, white shirt remained pristine.

He pushed his plate away and signalled the waiter for more coffee. 'Grace helped me through one of the worst times of my life.'

Her plate still more than half full, India dipped a corner of toast in a pot of tomato relish. 'Tell me.'

'My parents had me when they were older. I mean much older. They'd been wanting kids for years but had given up. Then I came along, the reward for years, an almost lifetime of serving the church. The old church, the church that doesn't do gay. I was suicidal. Grace helped them come to terms with it. She saved my life. I'm only sitting here because of her.' Xavier squared his shoulders. 'Mum and dad don't know that she's gone. They'd be devastated. But they can't remember from one moment to the next, so I don't feel bad not telling them. They're in a nursing home.'

And who, where … what would I be if Grace hadn't adopted me after my father's overdose India thought? An adult stuck in childhood? A handmaiden to her whale-serenading guru mother?

Going from one man to another, trying and failing to find in them her father? She pushed her plate away and pulled her coat more closely around her.

Xavier rubbed his stomach, which showed no sign of the enormous feed he had just consumed.

'Are you coming to the opening meet tomorrow?'

'The opening meet?'

'It's the first hunt of the season. Always a big deal. Grace would have been there with bells on.'

India shook her head. 'I've got to start sorting out Mars House.'

Xavier picked up his phone. "Don't bother about that. I'll just call Gill. We'll take her a coffee. She's so pleased you've turned up in Burragong and that Jeffrey's been rescued from Julie Rice. It was weighing us all down. Triple shot it is,' he said into the phone. 'See you in a tic. India's with me.'

'Ann,' India reminded him. Though she really didn't mind India, it was a hippy name, a fake hippy name.

'Breakfast's on me,' Xavier said.

India shook her head. 'I'll pay.'

He gestured at the tweed coat. 'Where did you get that?'

'The Op Shop.'

'My point exactly. You can buy the breakfast when you start getting commissions.'

The tray with Gill's coffee held out in front of him, Xavier slipped through the shoppers on the now bustling high street with the efficiency of an eel threading its way through water grass. Outside Blooming Beautiful, India stopped him as he was about to push open the door.

'What do you think about subdividing gran's paddock?'

Xavier looked pained. 'You've been talking to Rob Marks.'

'He came earlier. Before you.'

'Rob Marks says to everyone with anything over an acre that they can doubly-quintuple their money by subdividing. What he doesn't say is that it does the same to his commission. And what he also doesn't say is that subdividing involves a lot of costs. For everything from specialised kerb and guttering to snow-load rated bus shelters.'

Xavier stepped back to let a woman with a yellow Labrador into the shop. 'And he doesn't give a fig about green spaces or habitat. If it was left up to him, the Highlands would become a giant housing estate stretching all the way to Sydney.'

'Does that mean you'll sell Mars House as it is?' India asked. 'I'd rather that anyway. I want to get back to London as soon as I can.'

6

In the direct light, Jeffrey's eyes appeared milky pools and India wondered how much he could see. She stood at the paddock gate and watched him bound in slow motion towards the trees. What was she to do with him? At the rate things were progressing, however, he might be dead before Mars House was sold. Every time she'd tried to talk to Xavier about selling, he changed the subject and Rob Marks had made everything seem so difficult she didn't know if she could face him again.

But there had to be someone that would sell Mars House without making a drama of it. On Monday morning she'd start again with the real estate agents on the high street.

Jeffrey ambled back and they returned to the house, and each in their coats, settled on the sofa, sitting close for the extra warmth. The woodpile was already visibly diminished so she would light the fire later, when it was getting dark.

She retrieved her sketchbook and pencil from under a cushion and began to draw. The prostrate juniper that lapped the garage wall, Rob Marks' harried eyes, Xavier's long hands, the little huddle of people in the bush clearing – together they made a path that showed where she had recently been, and where she might yet go.

Jeffrey woke and pricked his ears and a minute later, the doorbell grringed.

It was Olivia Gilbert and her friend Hazel. Hazel's eyes were red and she was making whiffling noises. Olivia pushed her down the hall and into the living room and pointed at the sofa. 'Sit there,' she ordered. 'And stop crying. You'll upset Jeffrey.'

Hazel sat where she'd been told and Olivia positioned herself in front of the fireplace.

'We need tea.' Olivia said. 'Tea with brandy. The bottle's in the pantry.' She held out a plastic carry bag. 'Xav said to give you this. He drove us here. Mrs Teo's picking us up.'

Hazel let out a sob. 'She's going to kill me!'

'I keep telling you,' Olivia said, 'she'll never see it. The last time mum saw my bum was when I was in nappies.'

Hazel moaned. 'She will. She sees everything.'

'I'll make the tea,' India said.

'But you haven't asked what's wrong,' Olivia said. 'How very heartless. Are you sure you're related to Grace, *Ann*India?'

'She wouldn't be here if she wasn't,' Hazel hiccupped.

Olivia looked at India beadily. 'Xav said you're painting his portrait. I hope you're not fantasising about having sex with him. Everyone in our class wants to lose their virginity to him because he drives a BMW but he's totally gay. The dumb slags, they wouldn't know their virginity if they trod on it. Lucien Blythe's having mine. Why don't you draw us? Then we'll know if you really are who you say you are.'

'Lucien Blythe is revolting,' Hazel sniffed, her eyes filling with tears. 'Mum's going to kill me. She won't believe that you made me, Liv.'

'You wanted a tattoo as much as I did,' Oliva said.

'I didn't,' Hazel shrieked. 'And you said it wouldn't hurt.'

'I'll make the tea,' India repeated and headed for the kitchen.

'Don't forget the brandy,' Olivia called after her. 'Grace always gave us brandy when we were upset. And fruitcake. Homemade.'

India filled a saucepan with water and opened the carrier bag and took out a book. "Eucalypts of the Southern Highlands". She had asked Xavier the name of the massive, white-trunked gum trees that dotted the edge of the road to Burragong, but he hadn't known. She put the book on the bench reluctantly and the water on the stove to boil.

All was quiet when she returned to the living room. But all was not right. Stripped down to bra and knickers, Olivia and Hazel were showing off the tiny tattoos on their left buttocks.

Olivia wiggled her bottom. 'Take a photo, AnnIndia.'

'Not on my phone,' Hazel said quickly. 'Mum checks it.'

'It'll have to be yours, then,' Olivia said to India. 'My battery's dead. Hurry, before we freeze.'

'Put you clothes back on,' India said.

Olivia twisted round and regarded the tiny inking with satisfaction. 'At least tell us what you think. They're our star signs. I'm Leo and Hazel's Sagittarius. We're both fire signs. Grace always read her stars. And Jeffrey's. She was Aquarius. That's why she could always calm us down. Cool waters etcetera. Jeffrey's Cancer. Aquarius and Cancer are highly compatible. What sign are you?'

'Star signs are hippy rubbish, please put your clothes on,' India said, the thought of Hazel's mother turning up and finding her daughter not only partially dressed but also tattooed adding an edge to her voice.

Olivia rolled her eyes. 'You're definitely not Aquarius.'

In seconds, however, the girls were back in their jeans and rugby tops and parked on the sofa either side of Jeffrey.

India handed them a mug of tea. 'No cake.'

Hazel took a sip of tea and pulled a face. 'No brandy.'

'Grace wouldn't have put brandy in your tea,' India said. 'It would have tasted foul.'

'Like Lucien Blythe,' Hazel snorted. 'My bum hurts. I wish there was some cake.'

Olivia smiled sweetly at India. 'I bet you really are Aquarius. Look how much better Hazel is. Even without brandy and cake. We did always used to come here to Grace when we were upset. And when we weren't.'

Hazel gazed at India frankly. 'Mum's going to want to do something with your hair. And your nails. She used to do Grace's hair.'

'She does everyone's hair,' Oliva said.

'Everyone that matters.' There was a note of pride in Hazel's voice.

'Mum wants you to have dinner with us at the Bombay Duck tonight, AnnIndia,' Olivia said. 'She's worried about you sitting here in the dark with nothing to eat. You can't say no. She's already booked ...'

'Tell the truth, Liv,' Hazel interrupted.

'Why, you never do?' Olivia said.

'Mrs Findlay already had the booking,' Hazel said to India. 'But now Mr Findlay's not coming home there's a spare seat. Liv was scared Mrs Findlay would cancel because Lucien Blythe's always at the Bombay Duck with all his mistresses so she told her to ask you.'

The salon closed for the day, Vivienne Teo took a mini Moët into her office and having poured it into a chilled glass, sunk down into the sofa.

Hairdressing had not been on her parents' list of desirable occupations for their only child, but it had been her first and only choice. Her small child's hands had reached not for the brightly coloured toys her parents had indulged her with but for their hair. Her teenage passion was not boys but fashion magazines and on the way home from school, she would stand by the door of the local salon and when it opened to let a client in or out, inhale the scents of ammonia and manufactured botanicals as if they were smoke from precious incense.

When she had told her parents that she wanted to be a hairdresser, however, their faces showed such hurt she decided to wait for a more auspicious time before fulfilling her ambition. But her aspiration had lowered her star. At least that was how her parents saw it. She had not gotten the marks for law or medicine but instead had to settle for accountancy.

While her parents believed they were preparing her for a new, albeit lesser destiny of a partnership or financial controller in a major firm, she was gathering information about running a small business. In her third year, she told her parents that she had been offered a part-time job at a salon near the university. They made no comment and she took their silence as permission. Looking back, she realised they had been too spent to oppose her. The dedication that had seen them not only leave their own families in China and work almost every waking hour to send their only child to a top private school and to university, had sapped their spirits. They had given more than they had to give.

The salon position was lowly. Much as Hazel begged to do now, after school she swept hair up off the floor, balled and binned the cut squares of foil used for highlights and made tea and coffee for the clients. After a time, she could take out the rollers from the pensioners' perms.

Her degree completed she started a hairdressing apprenticeship and finishing this, spent six months with a top Los Angeles colourist and a similar term in a London salon, where the price of a cut and colour made her almost stop breathing. Since then, she had bought and renovated six salons, four of which she had sold for a hefty profit.

She sipped the Moët and stretched the muscles in her neck and shoulders. Yes, beginning with the parents she'd been born to, she had had luck. But to earn it, she had done the work and lived the life of two. And not all the luck had been good, either. She had married, borne a son and a daughter and buried their father after the cancer in his liver had finally taken him. Not long after, she had buried her father and watched her mother dement and then also die.

But the worst of the luck was not these deaths but the fact that her parents never got to appreciate the blessings their love had brought her. She closed her eyes.

Most beloved father,' she prayed. *Most beloved mother. Your daughter thanks you for your sacrifice and wishes you peace and pride in your hearts. Your grandchildren continue to do well with their study, and it is their mother's prayer that your grandson will find a cure for the illnesses that robbed him of his grandparents and father and your granddaughter will fulfil the ambition that you had for your daughter. With humble love and gratitude, the daughter of your heart, Vivienne.*

She opened her eyes. It was time to collect Hazel and Olivia. She was looking forward to meeting Grace's granddaughter. Very much in need of a makeover Xavier said, but still very much like Grace.

She rose from the sofa. Maybe she'd ask India to paint her portrait. Maybe in the nude – Lucien was always saying her body was better than that of a twenty-year old's. And that was about how old she felt as, hips wriggling at the memory of Lucien's loved-up tongue, she set the security system and strode through the salon towards the lift.

7

Through the window over the sink, Leila saw Donnacha crossing the lawn. She went to the oven and took out the chicken pie she'd made them for lunch.

What made you fall for someone? Chemistry – pheromones meeting pheromones? Fate, if you believed in it? The attraction of opposites, of the similar? The fact that someone appeared in your dreams the same night as you appeared in theirs? Timing, being the right place at the right time?

Whatever it was, she had fallen for Donnacha Keough in a major way.

Though conscious of his dour good looks, his smoky green eyes, she had thought him a snob at first. When he had looked at her during her interview, it had been down his hoity nose. Lady Blythe, on the other hand, he had fixed on attentively during her stupid questions about the schools she'd gone to, if she'd met this or that person at the Irish National Stud. Questions more suited to a dinner party than an interview for a foaling-down and yearling preparation position.

The back door slammed and Donnacha came in with Sorrows.

'I'll go wash,' he said, sliding his hands down her arms.

She served the pie onto warmed plates and put them on the small round table that took up almost half of the kitchen. Sorrows followed on her heels, ready to catch any straying morsel.

Her stomach rumbled and she drank a glass of water to keep her hunger at bay. The workday started at six, when, it not being the foaling season, she joined the dorm crew for feeding and stable cleaning. After morning tea, the weanlings and yearlings claimed her. Several of the yearlings were entered in an upcoming sale and they had to be ready to travel and cope with different environments, not to mention muscled and polished. She had also been getting some horses ready for Lucien to hunt, Whistlejacket bred ex-race-horses with ex-racehorse bodies and minds.

Donnacha joined her at the table, sitting to the side so he could stretch out his legs. For a while the business of the moment was the pie, but every so often their eyes would collide. Though they had been living together in the cottage now for over a month, they still felt like children playing grownups.

'I think Blythe's gone and stopped BlueBuckle's water himself,' Donnacha said, his plate now nearly empty.

Leila frowned. When Donnacha had told her about Lucien ordering him to stop BlueBuckle's water she'd begged him not to. Dehydrating horses to calm them was a cruelty that belonged to the old ways, the bad days when a horse had to be broken before it could be of service.

'I don't think the hoss is drinking anyway,' Donnacha continued. 'It's like he's got a death wish. I've not seen anything like it.'

'What about getting Pan Villon to look at him?' Leila asked. 'He'll be at the hunt tomorrow.'

Donnacha pushed his plate away. 'Blythe wouldn't have him on the place. Pan found him beating his hoss when it wouldn't jump a creek last season and knocked him off it in front of half the field.'

'We could show him some film from the yard,' Leila persisted. 'He's worked with the best in the world.' She said the names of some of the horse trainers and animal communicators Pan Villon had studied with.

Donnacha raised his eyebrows. 'You've been doing your homework.'

'Grace told me. Pan doesn't have to come here. We could just show him some of the yard footage for a start. Lucien wouldn't have to find out. I'm sure Pan wouldn't tell him.'

Donnacha shook his head. 'Going behind Blythe's back is not something I'd do.'

Leila left it there, for the moment. She reached out and stroked the inside of Donnacha's wrist, letting him know she was on for a lunchtime quickie.

He caught her hand and held it. 'Blythe's in a mood. Nothing to say he won't come up here with some new idea about the stallion.'

The thought of Lucien walking in on them doused Leila's lust. She began clearing table. 'Did he say if I was coming out with you tomorrow?' She had asked Lucien if she could take one of his horses to the opening meet, one that he didn't plan on taking himself.

Donnacha rose from the table. 'He didn't say. Digger Fahey and that missus of his'll be down for the breakfast though, so he might be in a charitable mood. Mrs R says he's having a thing with the missus.'

Unlike most of Whistlejacket's staff, Leila had no interest in Lucien Blythe's personal life.

'Do you know which horse he's taking, then?' she asked. 'I hope it's not Mockingbird.' The mare Mockingbird's career ending barrier stall accident had left her claustrophobic and panicky, but she had great movement and when her mind was calm, she learned quickly. A few minutes with Lucien on her back, however, and the trust she was beginning to build would be gone. 'What if I bandage one of her legs and say there's been some heat in the tendon?'

'I wouldn't,' Donnacha advised. 'If Blythe thinks someone's putting obstacles in his way, it makes him more determined. Best act like you don't care which horse he takes.'

Leila leaned against Donnacha's chest and let herself be soothed by his closeness, his smell of horse and linseed.

'He's more like to take one of the geldings anyway,' she said. 'Mockingbird's a bit small for him. I've thought about asking if she might be for sale. By the way, I'm waitressing tonight. Yolanda called earlier. The roster's suddenly fallen apart.'

Donnacha's arms stiffened and he went and hit the switch on the kettle. Leila tried to read his expression, but his face was mostly hidden. He couldn't be mad because she was waitressing. She'd had the job at the Burragong eatery, the Bombay Duck, almost since she'd started at Whistlejacket. She'd always had a second job, and Donnacha knew that too. He also knew that every cent she earned at the Bombay Duck went to the mortgage on the flat she'd bought in Brisbane a few years ago, and that she was determined to pay it off as quickly as she could. Maybe he was worried that she'd wake him when she got home – he was not the best of sleepers. Or maybe he was worried that if Lucien did say she could go to the meet, she'd be tired and not at her best.

That would be it.

'I won't wake you when I get home,' she said. 'And if I can hunt tomorrow, I'll be fine. I've hardly done a thing today.'

Donnacha shrugged and headed for the door. 'Whatever. Thanks for the pie.'

BlueBuckle stood in the far corner of the yard, rump pressed against the rails, head hanging down between his knees. His lips were drawn back in a grimace and his head looked like of a shaft of blackened bone.

Leila aimed her phone and took a photo, then another from a different angle. BlueBuckle remained where he was, motionless, eyes fixed on the ground. While he'd been in quarantine, waiting to come to Whistlejacket, Donnacha had shown her footage of his Kentucky win, of him prancing to the winner's circle, bowing to the cheering crowd lining the rails. He'd looked fresher than before his mighty race. He was glorious and he knew it. No way you'd think that now. Rock still in his corner, he appeared a spent force.

She made a kissing sound and BlueBuckle raised his head a fraction.

She knew she shouldn't – only Donnacha and Beef attended the stallions – but she slipped the chain and let herself into the yard.

She'd taken only a couple of steps when he came at her, teeth bared, neck outstretched, head snaking and hooves striking the ground then the air like the fists of an angry god. The ground shook, the sky disappeared and just as he was about to crash down on her, to drive her into the dirt, he dropped back down onto all four hooves and turned, swivelling on his haunches so hard and fast it sucked the air out of her.

Some part of him, his shoulder, knee, or perhaps it was the centrifugal force of his turn sent her backwards into the gate. She dragged herself up and fumbled the chain loose. BlueBuckle lined her up and pinning her with his eyes, charged again. But again, he turned just before he was on top of her and somehow, amongst the noise and his scalding slipstream, she managed to stumble out of the yard.

Her hands shaking and pain searing her shoulder, she felt for her phone and finding it still in one piece, set it to film and propped it on the railing as BlueBuckle charged again.

8

'I can't thank you enough,' Yolanda Olsen said as Leila dropped her coat over the back of the chair in the Bombay Duck's tiny office. 'Everyone under twenty-one is going to some concert in Sydney.'

'Most of the dorm crew are going as well,' Leila said. 'Hopefully enough will make it back for feedup in the morning. Full book?'

Yolanda nodded. 'Two sittings and the phone's still ringing.'

The Bombay Duck, co-owned by Yolanda and her brother, Stephan, was one of the Highlands' top eateries. Located in a long, high ceilinged room that was part of an antique storage ware-house, the restaurant's dark green walls were hung with paintings of leashed macaws and leopards and young women in high-necked gowns posing against jungle backdrops and shaded by parasols held by boys in loincloths. A display of antique hunting horns sur-rounded the fireplace and the windows, draped with deep blue velvet, looked out on a courtyard decorated with urns of ivy. Like the decor, the menu was of rich taste. Stephan, the restaurant's chef, was obsessed with spices.

Stephan appeared with coffee. Pro-basketballer tall but without an athlete's muscling, the deep lines around his eyes told of hours squinting against fluorescent light and steam.

He propped against the desk and leered at Leila's black-stockinged legs.

'Haven't you got a jus to reduce?' Yolanda told him.

He gave Leila a stagey wink. 'Come and see me later. I've got something special for you.'

'I bet you have,' Leila said, waving him away. Stephan's banter was innocent; his partner, Scott Page, a dressage instructor, was the love of his life. She pressed her hand to her shoulder where it had taken the impact of the railing in BlueBuckle's yard. Christ it was sore. Maybe she should show Scott the film of BlueBuckle on her phone. He'd had years of experience with hyper dressage horses, stallions included. But she quickly dismissed the idea. Scott was a Whipper-in with the Highlands Hunt and if he accidentally said something to Lucien, she'd lose her job. And possibly the job at the Bombay Duck as well. She turned away and pressed her shoulder again, wondering if the bone was chipped. It very much felt like it. Loading and unloading trays was going to be torture, and if Lucien did say she could hunt tomorrow she'd be riding one handed.

'Stephan's running on adrenaline,' Yolanda said, breaking into her thoughts. 'He was here all last night putting together hampers for the hunt breakfast.

'When's Stephan not running on adrenaline?' Leila said. 'Now, where do you want me to start?'

'Maybe with the table settings,' Yolanda said. 'I'll go through the specials when the others arrive.' Besides Leila, she had managed to gather four other wait staff. She would look after the seating and the wine would, as usual, be the department of the much-inked Lenny, who was putting himself through dentistry at a Sydney university. 'I love your top by the way.'

'Thanks,' Leila said. The cream satin shirt had sheer chiffon sleeves and wide satin cuffs. She'd found it in the Op Shop and hadn't been able to believe her luck. It was gorgeous. Shame Donnacha didn't think so. When she'd gone to tell him that she was leaving for the Bombay Duck, he'd looked her up and down and walked off without a word. What was it with him? What had she said or done, or not said or done?

She went from table to table, moving a spoon here, a glass there. She was only passing the time – the table settings were immaculate. The heavy silver cutlery was perfectly polished, the knives engraved with the letters BD. The white dinner service was also high-end, and on each side-plate lay a dark green napkin which, when opened, would reveal the wood-blocked outline of an imperiously posed Indian Runner duck. The glassware too had been chosen for quality, the water and wineglasses pleasingly shaped and generously sized. Yolanda and Stephan were amazing. No matter how long her day at Whistlejacket, she always got a charge out of being around them.

Yolanda appeared carrying a tablet with the bookings. 'Lucien has a full table. Which one's the current squeeze?'

'Probably all of them.'

Yolanda laughed. She pointed to a pair of names on the screen. 'I'll get you to look after these two. They're considering distributing Stephan's Bombay Duck pâté. It'd be such a boost for him. Scott's got his eye on some horse that costs more than a house in Burragong.'

Gill and Olivia were dressed in knee length skirts, buttoned up denim jackets, flats and bright scarves. They followed India down the dark hallway to the living room, which was lit by candles.

'You still haven't got the electricity on,' Gill said. 'The place is an icebox.'

'It's not worth lighting the fire if I'm going to be out,' India said. And it certainly wasn't worth getting the electricity on if she was leaving Burragong soon.

Olivia squatted next to Jeffrey. 'He's shivering.'

'He's not at all,' Gill said, peering at Jeffrey, who appeared to be wearing two large rashers of mohair textured bacon. 'He couldn't be in that coat.' She gazed about, taking in what she could in the flickering light, remembering the unmoored feeling that had come over her when she'd been told that Grace was dead. Perhaps it was better that Mars House was sold – visiting it was worse than visiting a cemetery.

'Come on,' she said. 'Let's get going.'

'If you had electricity, AnnIndia,' Olivia said, having kissed Jeffrey on the top of his head, 'You could run the reverse cycle like

Grace did when she didn't want to light the fire. Then you wouldn't have to always wear that coat and you could have a bath and wash your hair.'

'Olivia!' Gill snapped. 'That's so rude. Apologise or I'll take you home.'

'Sorry, AnnIndia,' Olivia pouted.

Gill also apologised. 'We're both a bit ratty. Liv wanted to wear a skirt that showed her bottom and …'

'My darling mother cut it up and put it in the rubbish,' Olivia interrupted. 'So here I am about to have dinner in the same restaurant as Lucien Blythe and I look like I'm going to an audition for the school choir.'

'If we don't get you fed and into bed,' Gill said, 'you'll be falling off Expresso tomorrow and that definitely won't impress Lucien. And anyway, you don't need to audition for the choir, you're already in it. Come on now, hurry or we'll lose our table.'

'We'd better not,' Olivia said, setting off for the front door while India put out the candles.

The flashlight on Gill's phone revealed the outline of a battered Prado parked on the grass next to the gate. 'Sit in the front with me,' Gill said to India.

The car smelt of dog and jasmine and a cello concerto started up with the engine. They'd been driving a while when Olivia leaned forward and said in India's ear, 'Mum made me leave my mobile at home, too. She's losing it. I can't take the pressure.'

India turned and said softly, 'Did she like the tattoo?'

Olivia fell back against her seat with a thump.

India pointed as a long, pale shape flashed by. 'That was a White Topped Box tree. Some of them are over a hundred and fifty years old.' She had found much to interest her in Xavier's book.

'The same age as my mother,' came the bleak mutter from the back seat.

'And I can tell you now, she feels it,' Gill answered.

The Bombay Duck was already half full. Yolanda greeted them warmly and thanked Gill for the centrepieces she had recently made for the high-profile footballer's wedding breakfast that had taken place at the restaurant.

'Those peonies were divine. Perfectly suited to the bride. You know …' Yolanda cupped her hands in front of her chest. 'Your mother really is clever, Olivia.'

'Clever at stuffing things up,' Olivia said, her head swivelling as she searched the restaurant for Lucien Blythe. 'Look what she made me wear.' She tugged at the denim jacket.

'Yolanda,' Gill said over this further rudeness, 'this is Grace's daughter, India. Sorry, I mean Ann India.'

'Welcome to Burragong,' Yolanda said. 'We were always happy to see Grace here. She was an incredible horsewoman, I believe.'

'AnnIndia's selling Grace's house,' Olivia said. 'It's inhuman.'

'Burragong's not for everyone,' Yolanda said diplomatically. She gestured to the grey-haired couple at the door that she was coming and after a quick, 'Enjoy your evening,' was gone.

Gill sat back in her chair with a happy sigh. 'Isn't this just gorgeous.' She sniffed the air. 'And the smells – heavenly.'

Olivia pushed back her chair. 'I'm going to the bathroom.'

'Sorry about Liv,' Gill said. 'She's not coping with the fact that her parents' marriage is falling apart.' The words came out in a rush. 'Well, truth tell it probably has fallen apart, but we're stuck pretending it hasn't for Liv's sake. It's like revving a car in neutral. Lots of noise and fumes but going nowhere. Nicholas is through and through city and I'm through and through country. We were in Adelaide with his work for a spell, then Brisbane and then Sydney. Always in the city. I nearly went mad. Nowhere to ride unless you paid a fortune for city stabling or travelled for miles and the dog parks were crowded. I thought Burragong would be a good compromise. An hour from Sydney, a regular train service. I grew up here and after living here and there it was like coming home. I started to feel sane. But Nicholas hated it. Hates it. The silence is too noisy, the streets paved with yokels and animal hair etc, etc.'

Gill sipped her water. 'If it weren't for Liv and Oscar I wouldn't mind as much. Oscar's Liv's brother. He's in Mongolia, living in a monastery. He dropped out of uni. Nicholas blames me. It's all very well for opposites to attract, but when the attraction palls, things can get pretty tricky.' Gill took another sip of water. 'Sorry, I didn't mean to dump all that on you. Oh god!'

India followed the direction of Gill's stare. Olivia was mincing towards them, so much makeup on she looked clown-like.

'We're going to have to leave,' Gill said.

'Pretend you haven't noticed,' India said.

'I don't know if I can.'

'She's creating a scene to get a reaction. If she doesn't get one, she'll be forced to think, and that's just what she needs to be doing. Getting things straight in her head. But it's something she has to do on her own.'

'Okay,' Gill said doubtfully. 'I'll try.'

'Where I teach drawing,' India said, 'some of the girls are so screwed up they make Olivia look well-adjusted. Which I'm sure she is really,' she added quickly. 'You wouldn't believe the things the girls draw.'

'What things?' Olivia said, smiling at them through layers of lipstick. 'What things do they draw?'

'Elephants,' India said. 'Tigers and elephants.'

Olivia giggled. 'Do you know that elephants produce enough dung in a day to fill the inside of a Volkswagen?'

The drinks waiter, sleeveless tshirt showing off his elaborately tattooed arms, came up with the wine list.

'Hi Lenny,' Olivia said. 'Want to examine my teeth?'

'You've got lipstick on them,' Lenny said.

Olivia jumped up and set off back to the bathroom, saying over her shoulder, 'Mine's a Peach Cruiser.'

Lenny grinned at Gill. 'Looks like she's had a few already. I suppose she's got herself done up for Lucien Blythe.' Lenny's younger sisters went to the same school as Olivia and had told him about her answer to the virginity survey. 'Don't worry, Mrs Findlay, Lucien's booked for the second sitting. Now, what can I get you to drink?'

Gill introduced India and checking she was happy with red, ordered a cab sav from a local vineyard and a mineral water and bitters for Olivia.

'I'll tell her it's a vodka and tonic,' Lenny said, seeing Olivia heading back to the table with even more lipstick and eyeshadow on her face. He shook his head. 'Though I'd be surprised if she can open her mouth with all that muck on her lips.'

The restaurant was now almost full. Fragrantly steaming entrees and mains had started appearing from the kitchen. Watching the door for Lucien, Olivia pushed away the menu and announced she would have the Bombay duck.

'What about you, India?' Gill asked.

'AnnIndia,' Olivia corrected. 'She'll have the Bombay duck too.'

It would have to be an entrée, India thought. Tempting as it sounded, the Bombay duck would be too big a hit on her remaining funds.

'The Bombay duck,' Olivia repeated.

India looked at her. 'I bet you're a Sagittarius. No, a Leo. I bet you're a Leo. I always thought the Leo symbol would make the cutest tattoo.'

Olivia narrowed her eyes and India narrowed hers back, saying, 'You've got lipstick on your teeth again.'

Olivia leapt out of her chair and headed back to the bathroom.

While she was gone, Lenny returned with the drinks and Leila.

'I didn't know your gran for long,' Leila said to India, 'but she was such an inspiration. An incredible horsewoman. I hope I'm still hunting when I'm in my seventies.'

'Are you coming out with us tomorrow?' Gill asked.

'Fingers crossed,' Leila said.

'The opening meet's chaos anyway. When you can organise a day off midweek we'll go together. You can ride Expresso. Olivia won't mind'

'I'll take you up on that,' Leila said. 'Hope to see you again,' she said to India. 'I'll send over your waitress. You must try the Bombay duck.'

'I saw Leila,' said Olivia, having returned from the bathroom some minutes later with a spotless face, her damp fringe and reddened cheeks telling that it had been scrubbed with some force. 'I'm going to ask her to get me a holiday job at Whistlejacket.'

India pursed her lips, signalling to Gill to ignore Olivia's changed appearance.

'I'm starving.' Gill said. 'Choose whatever takes your fancy, India. Dinner's on me. Liv, how about some of those pea pastries you like?'

'Only a fool would go past the Bombay duck,' Olivia said, taking India's menu.

9

Lucien's guests had all now arrived. The Buckley brothers and their wives and one of the Buckley sisters were settled in the homestead, Jack Mariner and his eventer partner, Dion, in one guest cottage and Digger and Christie in the other. They gathered in the living room, redecorated by Lucien when his mother had moved into Burragong, with red and white toile curtains, rust velvet sofas, a marble and wrought iron side table and an 18th century French oak armoire.

The fire crackling and Lucien the lordly host, they drank the champagne and ate Janet Reedhead's canapes, caught up on gossip and talked horses and soon enough, it was time to think about dinner.

Only Lucien, Christie and Digger were going to the Bombay Duck, the others opting for Janet Reedhead's lamb shanks and an early night so that they'd be up in time to give their horses some light work before the opening meet.

Lucien refused Digger's offer of a lift into Burragong, saying that he needed to return some calls. He pulled out behind the silver Merc and checking the rear-view mirror, saw that Christie was watching him. This morning he had been anticipating sneaky feel-ups and risky fucks but now she was getting on his nerves.

'Get your calls made?' she asked as they met up on the footpath outside the Bombay Duck.

He nodded. 'Almost.' And without saying anything further, he led the way into the restaurant.

Waiting for Yolanda to show them to their table, Lucien saw that his other guests, Joint Master of the Highlands Hunt, Simon Sinclair and his much younger Kiwi partner, Eleanor Lonsdale, along with Simon's friends Dick and Sandy Bowers, were already seated. Eleanor's turnout was perfect as usual. Her short golden hair fell in a thick wave over one side of her face and her creamy shoulders were just a little bared by her close-fitting blue dress. Their eyes met and she flushed prettily. How Simon, a jolly monk type with a messy mop of white curls and plump cheeks and stomach, managed to keep such a woman was beyond him. Though Simon was nicely fixed, so was Eleanor as well.

He looked at his watch impatiently. Where was bloody Yolanda? Christie had been clocked by the other diners, the women busy calculating the cost of her jewellery – a hundred thousand at least – the men, the length of her legs and though Digger had her firmly secured to his side with his arm, the thrust of her pelvis told that she was turned on by the attention.

At last Yolanda came to show them to their table.

He took the seat opposite Eleanor and ignoring Christie as she slipped into the chair beside him, reached across the table and helped himself to Eleanor's wine glass. He scanned the restaurant and his gaze fixed on a fair, statuesque girl talking to Gill Findlay by the door. The baggy overcoat was totally wrong, but she could have been dressed in a space suit for all it mattered. Shit! A hand was crawling across his thigh. Christie's. He shot her a look and the hand stopped but remained on his thigh.

'Should be a good scenting day tomorrow, Lucien,' Simon said across the table. 'Weather's on our side.'

'As long as we get some decent runs,' Lucien said. 'Jack Mariner's coming out and he likes it fast. 'The Buckley's, too.' Last season, the cost of keeping the hounds having risen considerably, he'd become Joint Master and in his opinion, Simon paid too much attention to the hunting and not enough to the enjoyment of the subscribers.

'The runs will be what they be,' Simon said.

'Where are you planning to cast, Simon?' Dick asked.

'A hill not far from the yards,' Simon answered. 'There's been some new lambs dragged up there.'

Lucien took a sharp breath as Christie's fingers closed around his balls. 'Too steep,' he said through gritted teeth. 'If hounds put a fox up there, there'll be no chance of a run.' Christ, Christie was trying to sterilise him!

'I dropped in at Whistlejacket while you were in Hong Kong, Lucien,' Eleanor said. 'Leila's done a great job with the horses. They look fit enough to go all day.'

Digger pointed to the next table, where Leila was handing out menus. 'Lovely Leila's looking pretty fit herself.'

Christie gave a tight smile. 'That shirt's a Sass and Bide. You're overpaying your staff, Lucien.'

'I wasn't looking at the shirt,' Digger said roguishly.

Christie rapped his knuckles with the flat of her knife. 'A randy seventy-year-old is not a good look, darling.'

'Oh, I don't know about that,' Eleanor, ever tactful, said.

Sandy Bowers smiled at Christie. 'Nor's a randy fifty-year-old.'

Lucien almost choked as Christie's nails sunk viciously into his thigh. He sat up in his chair and beckoned to Leila.

She came straight over. 'Good evening. The specials are on the board by the fire. The …'

'Mixed entrees and the Bombay duck all round,' Lucien said. 'And tell Lenny to bring a couple more bottles of whatever Simon and Eleanor are drinking. Is the kitchen running to time?'

'Perfectly. I'll go and catch Lenny now.'

'Tell him we're waiting,' Lucien said.

'Thank you, Leila,' Dick Bowers said. 'Just when you've a moment. I can see you're run off your feet.'

Eleanor retrieved her now empty wine glass from Lucien. 'Is Leila coming out with us tomorrow?'

Ignoring her, Lucien said to Simon, 'Leila's moved into the cottage with Donnacha.'

Simon beamed. 'That's grand. Donnacha's one of the best Whips I've ever hunted with. Ears and eyes as sharp as a fox's. Knows every hound by their voice and which way they'll head the minute their noses go up or down. Watches their sterns like a hawk.'

'Sterns?' Christie asked.

'Tails,' Dick Bowers explained. 'Hounds' tails are called sterns.'

Lenny brought the wine, topped up everyone's glass and slid away with the smoothness of a *Dancing With The Stars* contestant.

Lucien took a deep swallow of wine. Christie's hand was creeping about his thigh like a spider. If she thought that she was turning him on she must be insane.

Leila appeared and began placing plates of steaming naan bread and silver bowls of dips, dahl and rose scented pastries about the table.

Sensing Eleanor was waiting for him to ask her to the meet, Lucien instead began discussing the renovations at Sydney's Royal Randwick Racecourse with Sandy. Having chosen the servant over the master, there would be no special privileges for Leila Caffrey he had decided.

Christie removed her hand from his thigh and began loading Digger's plate like the good wife she was not. His thoughts returned to the girl that had been with Gill Gilmore. She reminded him of someone. Maybe one of the Victoria's Secret models. But whichever beauty it was, she clearly wasn't one for putting it out like Christie.

The entrées demolished and the dishes cleared away, they waited for the feted Bombay duck.

Digger pinged his glass with his fork. 'Christie and I have an announcement to make.'

The restaurant fell silent.

Eleanor looked at Christie, her face shocked. 'You're not are you?' Simon started to giggle, and she held a silencing finger to her lips.

'What's she on about?' Digger asked Christie.

'She thinks I'm pregnant.'

'Oh dear,' Sandy said, also starting to giggle.

'Shut up,' Digger told them. 'I've bought Jottings. Signed the contract today. Me and Christie are going to become Highlanders.'

Mutters came from the surrounding tables. Jottings was one of the Highland's most expensive properties.

'Wow,' Eleanor said. Then remembering her manners, added, 'Congratulations.'

Digger beamed. 'Scone is too far from civilisation for my darling wife. But you never mind coming down here, do you darl. Must be the Bombay duck.'

'Are you selling Scone, then?' Dick asked. Digger's Scone farm, north of Sydney, was over a thousand acres and sometimes when he couldn't sleep, he tired his brain by imagining what he'd do with such a holding.

Digger looked coy. 'One thing at a time, Dick.'

Simon raised his glass. 'Great to have you in the neighbourhood, Digger. Great to have you both. We'll have to put Jottings on next season's fixture.'

'Wonderful, Dig,' Lucien croaked as Christie's fingers again gripped his balls. 'It'll be fabulous to have you around more. You and your mares.' Christie's fingers relaxed.

'You better walk out that new stallion before we go tomorrow, Luce,' Digger said. 'Jim's working out the nicks.' Jim Speer was his breeding advisor and their partnership regularly produced six figure horses.

'He's still in isolation, I'm afraid,' Lucien said. 'It'll be another week before anyone can go near his yard. Some new biosecurity rule.'

Digger sounded annoyed. 'We'll look at the yard footage then.'

'Dig's got cameras everywhere,' Christie smirked. 'Even in my lav.'

Sandy Bowers' eyebrows shot up. 'I'd have thought some things were better not shared.'

Lucien pushed back his chair and stood up, shaking off Christie's hand. 'I'll get Lenny to dig out something special, shall I?'

Christie smiled around at the table. 'Sydney's getting insane. I'll be able to hop in the helicopter and before you know it, be in my own little oasis.' She looked dreamy. 'I've already booked some riding lessons. I'm absolutely determined to join the Hunt.'

The long, white, stiff cravat was designed to be wound around the neck several times to stop it from breaking in the event of a crashing fall. Donnacha put it back on the bed. His first hunting tie wouldn't have protected him from a fleabite, let alone a broken neck. It had been a limp affair, and grubby, a tossout from one of his brothers. But at six years old and about to have his first ride with the Ballymacad Hunt, his appearance was the last thing on his mind.

His brother Larry, nearest to him in age and already a bully, had shaken him awake and ordered him to be at the bottom of the stairs in exactly one minute. The cold had shocked his eyeballs and instantly numbed his hands. In the dim yard light, his other brothers were pouring buckets of oats, molasses and chaff into the horses' troughs and kicking away the terriers whose litters their father was always tossing in the river. His mother and father were snarling as usual, at each other, at their duff sons, at the dogs and at the horses, his father sipping from his silver flask which, unlike his wife, never left his side. Just like the pups he frequently dispatched, Martin Keough's own five could have been sired by any one of the studs in the county.

An hour later, the dawn broke, grey, damp and as still as a fox watching a hen. His father, looking like he had a fever, raised his flask to the new day.

Hunting took you like that, like a fever. Or a fixation. One of the Ballymacad huntsmen was buried standing up so as to forever be able to see hounds heading out for their day's work. Then there was a kennelman laid to rest in the earth beside the kennels where hounds could daily cross his grave. Indeed, hunting could take you like a fever or a fixation. Much as some women could. But when a woman got in their blood, men did far dafter things than having themselves buried standing up or where hounds could cross their grave. They did things like slitting the throat of their wife's horse. Things you'd never speak about.

Donnacha touched the gold fox mask tie pin Leila had given him for his recent birthday. She'd only had bits of his story of course. Carefully selected bits that made it sound like he too had had a regular childhood. And that was all she'd ever get.

Sorrows nudged his leg and he reached down and scratched along his back. 'I know, man. I need to tell her what an eedjit she's gotten herself tangled up with.' But how could he tell Leila that the moment she'd moved into the cottage his father had moved into his head? And that sometimes, like this afternoon when he'd seen her looking utterly gorgeous in that blouse, he didn't know in whose voice his thoughts were talking – his father's or his own.

He closed the door of the spare bedroom so that Sorrows couldn't jump up on the bed and lay on his kit. There was a football game on tele, AFL, which he enjoyed, but he couldn't settle to it. His last round not for another hour, he headed out anyway.

The air smelled of the sweet breath of stabled horses. All was in order: the feed and tack rooms tidy, aisles swept, the lights dimmed. A couple of the youngsters, in because of a cut or scrape, were walking their stalls, but the older hands snoozed contentedly, their bellies full of the best feed money could buy.

Lucien's guests' horses were in the last stableblock. They too, despite the unfamiliar surroundings were settled. He checked their rugs and water and then clipping on Sorrow's lead so that he wouldn't disappear into the dark, set off for the old stallion yards.

Three quarters along the lane he heard him. Thud, thud, thud. Jesus, the hoss'd burst his heart if he didn't take a break.

Sorrows planted. 'It's all right, man,' he told him, tugging his lead to get him moving.

'What's with him, do you think?' came a voice out of the dark a few minutes later.

He turned the torch in the direction of the voice. Beef Reedhead was near the yard but well away from the rails. He ran the torch beam over BlueBuckle. The stallion's eyes flared red as he spun and took off for the back of the yard.

He switched off the torch. 'Nelson Cherry said it could be a brain tumour, but I don't know, it doesn't fit. The hoss's balance'd be affected, surely?'

'Blythe's not happy,' Beef said.

Donnacha picked up Sorrows and held him against his chest. 'He's stopped the hoss's water. For certain it'll bring him to his knees but where's the benefit in that?'

'I'd say Blythe's already thinking about the insurance.'

Donnacha stared into the yard, his eyes fixed on the maliciously moving dark streak once again thundering towards them.

'Unless the hoss suddenly comes to his senses, he's going to go down anyway,' he said gloomily. 'I've got the yard camera feed on my phone so I can call Cherry when he drops.'

'Blythe's okay with that?'

'Haven't said anything to him. But the hoss should be given a chance don't you think? Even if it's only the chance of a humane death.'

Beef nudged the six-pack at his feet with his toe. 'Beer?'

Donnacha shook his head. The mood he was in, one beer would turn into five and then some.

10

Lucien stretched out his arms and legs, toe by toe, foot by foot, thigh by thigh, finger by finger, and imagined them heavy and sinking into the mattress.

An hour later, he was still awake, his breathing shallow, his arms and legs twitching, his heart racketing like a hundred-year-old engine. If he didn't get to sleep soon, he'd be in a stupor at the opening meet.

He turned from one side to the other then back again. Because of all the wine he'd drunk – buckets of it in the end – a sleeping pill wasn't an option. But perhaps that was the problem, the wine? But it wasn't, he knew. The problem was that no matter what he did to relax, he remained on alert for any sound that Christie was in the house.

Why had she talked Digger into buying Jottings? Was she angling to become a permanent fixture? He groaned into the pillow. As soon as the moment presented, he'd tell her it was over. Sooner than later and hopefully in time for Digger to pull out of Jottings, the poor bloody turkey.

But for the moment sleep was what he needed, sleep and only sleep. He got out of bed and padded downstairs. In the kitchen, he warmed a mug of milk in the microwave and added a good slosh of Janet Reedhead's cooking brandy (Courvoisier!!). But instead of returning to bed, he carried the nightcap to the little sitting room his mother and Janet Reedhead sometimes used for their tete-á-tetes. It had a sofa that pulled out into a bed and Christie would never think to look for him there.

Asleep in his basket under the window, Sorrows too seemed oblivious to her return. She slid into bed and moved her arm so that it lay against Donnacha's back. He flinched away. Bastard, he was awake. She turned on her side, her back to his, an empty strip of bed, a wasteland, between them.

She had been certain that she would come home to a welcoming pair of arms. That the darkness that had come over Donnacha like a black fog rolling down a hill would have lifted. And she'd been just as certain that Lucien, seeing an opportunity to look even more gilded in front of his friends, would have let her ride one of his horses at the opening meet. The bastards! Donnacha and Lucien – they were both deaf dumb and blind to anything that wasn't in front of their noses. Her eyes filled with angry tears.

India sat on the back step, gripped by the darkness, the silence. Except for Jeffrey, she was alone. She could stretch her arms, her senses, the reaches of her mind out in every direction and touch no one; no wonder Grace had loved Mars House. Yet despite living in such an out of the way place, her world had been full of people. People who knew things about her about which she, her flesh and blood, had no idea. Her star sign, that she read Jeffrey's horoscope and kept homemade fruitcake in the pantry. That out hunting she jumped wire fences. That her favourite flowers were heritage roses and that she subscribed to the New Yorker magazine and Vivienne Teo cut her hair. That she smelt of Chanel and saddle soap, knitted not only dog coats but tiny suits for stillborn premature babies and rescued penguins.

She pulled the tweed coat around her against the cold. It was as if there were two Graces: hers and the Burragong Grace. Her Grace had made the drive to her school every second weekend and then spent more road time taking her to further flung country towns. School holidays meant galleries, concerts, films and plays and the opera; back then there had been a Sydney base, a tiny flat in Manly. Her Grace had said the occasional word about horses and hunting but nothing about teenagers coming to Mars House for cake when they were upset, nothing about friends with Egyptian cats. Such conversation as there was had been about schoolwork, drawing, the exhibition or play or film they had just seen. It had been the same when Grace visited her in London after she'd been accepted into the Slade School of Fine Arts.

She rose and called for Jeffrey.

The old dog watched as she lit the candles and a fire and when she sat down on the floor, he stretched out beside her, his back pressed into her thigh. She rested her hand on his side. The candlelight turned the desert paintings into distant nebulae, their dots not exploded or newly birthed stars, but the words of story without beginning or end, and for a while she lost herself there.

Then she reached under the sofa for her sketchbook and turned to a new page. She worked fast – Gill, Xavier, Olivia, Hazel, Julie Rice, Yolanda – Grace's pathway, the road she had travelled and that she, her own flesh and blood, had not known existed.

11

Five thirty. Leila turned off the alarm and sniffed the air. Bacon and eggs and, bliss, coffee. Donnacha had made them breakfast. They had argued, that was all. It was always going to happen, that first argument. Arguments were just something to be figured out like bathroom smells and who cleaned the oven. What did it matter that she had no idea what the argument had been about?

She swung her legs out from under the doona and sat on the edge of the bed. Her shoulder ached nastily, but her heart was as light as an escaped balloon. She combed her hair back with her fingers and smoothing her nightdress down over her thighs, rose to meet the day. Hunt day.

The kitchen was empty, the table bare. On the bench beside the sink was a single plate and knife and a coffee mug, each rinsed.

Tears burned her eyes. 'Bugger you Donnacha Keough. Bugger you!' She wasn't having it. Whatever his problem was he could keep it. She'd move out of the cottage. This morning, while he was at the meet.

She was at the sink washing the dishes after making and forcing herself to eat an omelette when she heard the back door and Donnacha came in, looking pale and tired. Worse than she felt.

'You've got a bonny day for your meet,' she said coolly. 'And just to let you know, I'll be gone by the time you get back. I don't believe in leaving notes.'

'Gone? Gone where?'

'From the cottage. From here.'

'Why would you want to do that?'

'Isn't it what you want?'

'No, it 'tis not.' Donnacha came and stood next to her 'It's just … I get jealous.' He avoided her eyes.

She stared at him. 'Jealous? What have I done to make you jealous?'

Donnacha ran the backs of his hands down her arms. 'Nothing. It's in the blood. My father,' he said, then stopped.

Her breathing deepened. She'd watched him soothing cranky mares with just the same touch, stroking and calling them 'derrlin' and 'missus' until the crabbiness went out of their eyes and their lips went slack. It was magic to watch but even more so to be so soothed.

What made you fall for someone? The fact that when they stroked you it was like being rocked in a cradle of clouds.

His phone rang. He checked the screen and cut the call. 'Blythe. I'll have to go.'

But this time when he spoke, he looked in her eyes. She nodded. 'Okay.'

His phone rang again and this time he took the call, saying, 'Just getting my tie. I'll be down in a minute.' He pulled her close and rested his chin on her head. 'You didn't mean it, did you, about moving out? I'd truly hate that.'

She breathed him in, filled her lungs with him, filled her heart. 'I was confused. I'm sorry.'

A short while later, scrubbed head to toe and dressed against the morning chill in jeans and a navy Whistlejacket hoodie, she headed for the stables. So much drama and the day only just begun! At least she didn't have to spend it shifting her things out of the cottage. It wasn't a good idea to make threats like that, she told herself. What if Donnacha had taken her up? When she got up-set and angry, like her mother, she was unable to see the trees for the burning bushes and then, whoosh, suddenly the whole forest was on fire. Thanks mum. Maybe it was time to tell her parents about Donnacha. Not that her mother would be thrilled. In her current opinion, men were responsible for all the world's evils, war, chemical fertilizers, space junk and overpopulation and her father would judge Donnacha "not officer material". But that was them and she mostly loved them and had long ago stopped caring too much about what they said.

And maybe she was going hunting after all. Donnacha had come good so who was to say Lucien wouldn't? She was ready if he did give the word. Her breeches and black woollen jacket, both eBay bargains, hung on the wardrobe door next to Donnacha's and she'd been polishing her boots, also from eBay, for weeks.

She went straight to Mockingbird's stall. The mare nuzzled her cheek with her lips. 'Hello girl,' she said, stoking her shiny dark neck.

Edmund the Black, the horse she thought Lucien should and would ride, stuck his grey head out from the next-door stall and pulled a threatening face.

'He's all bullshit,' she told Mockingbird as the mare nervously retreated.

Along the aisle, Donnacha came out of the tack room with an armful of bridles.

'Hi,' he said. 'Can you take a look at Oyster? He hasn't touched his breakfast.'

Leila let herself into Oyster's stall. A massive roan Percheron thoroughbred cross, he was the perfect hunt horse: tireless, strong and outwardly phlegmatic. Qualities all shared with his master. His feed, a mix of oats, chaff and vitamin loaded horse nuts was untouched.

She felt under his rug. He wasn't hot. Maybe he was just wound up inside. He would know the day was special. Animals knew far more than it was ever allowed that they knew. She stroked Oyster's speckled face.

'What do you think?' Donnacha said from the stall door.

'He's not sweated up. Want me to try him with some hay?'

'Ta, that'd be great. I need to check I've loaded all the gear. Blythe'll go spare if anything's missing. He's like a tin soldier this morning.'

'Has he said anything about me coming?'

'Sorry love. Not a word. And he's got a mean eye on him, I'm afraid.'

Oyster went to the door and watched Donnacha head out of the stables. Leila ducked under his neck and let herself out of the stall. In the feedroom, she broke a biscuit of lucerne hay into a tub and drizzled molasses over it. Oyster needed to eat not only to have energy for his day's work, but also to protect his gut: horses ridden hard on an empty stomach were at risk of painful ulcers.

'Well, old man,' she said as she returned with the hay. 'Looks like there's no hunting for Leila today.' She couldn't deny her disappointment, but she'd spend the morning making Donnacha a fine lunch and take it to the meet. And she'd definitely find out if Mockingbird was for sale. Maybe she'd be able to keep her with Oyster and she and Donnacha could hunt together. Now wouldn't that be a dream come true.

Donnacha was in the tackroom, loading a bag with bandages and veterinary supplies from a cabinet behind the door.

'Which horse is Lucien taking?' she asked.

'Mockingbird.'

Her heart hit the ground.

'Sorry love,' Donnacha said. 'I'll do my best to keep an eye out for her.'

A heavy engine started up outside the stable and they stepped apart.

'Sounds like the Buckleys are getting ready to load,' Donnacha said. His phone buzzed and he looked at it. 'Blythe's on his way.'

She set off out of the stables, but it was too late. Lucien caught up with her outside the office. 'Wait, would you.' He went up to Donnacha. 'Gear all in the truck?'

Donnacha nodded. 'And the hay.'

'Get the horses on then. Jack and Dion are pulling out and Lindsay and Brad are almost loaded. I'll see you at the meet.'

Coming back down the aisle Lucien said, 'I want you to keep an eye out for Digger, Leila. I've told him that BlueBuckle's still in quarantine but he's allergic to the word "no". Janet's putting Viagra in his coffee and there's a bucket of it in his bathroom so he should be busy until it's time to leave for the breakfast. But if he does surface and it looks like he's heading for the old stallion yards, turn him off. And if he wants to see the yard camera footage, tell him you don't have the password for the computer.'

'What will I say if he does head for the yards?'

His eyes went from her face to her breasts. 'I'm sure you'll think of something. You're on overtime until he and Christie have gone.' And with this, Lucien strode off.

Wanting to be as far away from him as was possible in that moment Leila went quickly in the opposite direction. Her phone buzzed. A text from Donnacha: **whas ws thit abrut?** She put the phone back in her pocket. The phone buzzed again. She ignored it.

Only when she had reached the lane to the old stallion yards did she stop to catch her breath. The sky was cloudless, the blue deepening. The paddocks either side of the lane were carpeted with vivid green grass. Empty now, when the season started in August, they would hold the mares newly served by the Whistlejacket stallions Speed, Birdie and the ageing Stanislas, the testosterone bank Blue-Buckle had been purchased to revitalise and rebrand.

She leaned against the fence and turned her face towards the sun. A magpie landed nearby and eyed her. She stared back and it cocked its black and white head, showing its savage beak to full advantage, and began to warble. On it sang, piping its ode to the morning, to the sky, or perhaps to her. Then it fell silent and she could hear the song of others of its kind. Her companion opened its wings and flew off.

Her spirits restored, she checked her phone. A third message from Donnacha. **XXALOVERD.** She smiled. Donnacha had the thumbs of a drunken sailor when it came to texting.

Caps now LOL she messaged back. **Look out for Mockingbird, XXXL.**

The gate at the end of the laneway had been shut and padlocked. She hauled herself over, her bruised shoulder making the movement awkward.

BlueBuckle was at the back of his yard, hindquarters pressed into the rails, head in its usual place between his knees. His eyes were hollow and his coat, darkened and dulled by dried sweat, was the grey of an angry sea. The dry droppings around his feet and his look of having shrunk inside his hide told that he was dehydrated.

'Poor fella.'

She walked slowly around the outside of the yard. BlueBuckle didn't raise his head, but a minute shifting of his weight signalled that he was clocking her movements. The water trough was bone dry. Lucien must have turned off the water himself as Donnacha thought. Maybe he was in a mood because he'd found out that Donnacha hadn't.

She frowned. To open the valve, she'd have to go into the yard again. But hang on, Lucien wouldn't have gone into the yard. No way. He'd have turned the water off at the laneway inlet. That would make things much easier. Then she realised that she had no idea where the valve key was kept. Donnacha and Beef would, but it was unlikely they'd tell her.

What to do? There was nothing she could do. She hadn't been able to protect Mockingbird and now she could do nothing for BlueBuckle. And with the valve off at the laneway, the water wouldn't flow into his trough anyway.

There was a flurry in the air and her magpie friend, or some relation, landed on the top rail of the yard near the trough. BlueBuckle's ears twitched. Great, she thought. Now he'll get stirred up again and dehydrate faster.

The magpie organised its feathers and looked for all the world like it was settling in for a show. 'No show,' she told him. 'Show's over.' Then she had an idea. The trough was close enough to the next-door yard for her to get water into it with something with a spout. A watering can. She'd have to find one and haul some buckets of water from the nearest working trough and give BlueBuckle only a little at a time – too much and he might colic – but so what if she spent the morning at the yard? She didn't have to leave for the hunt breakfast for some hours and she'd said nothing to Donnacha about making lunch. And anyway, be buggered if she was going to hang around keeping an eye out for Digger Fahey.

12

Gill hit the brakes and the Prado and float swerved and slewed dangerously. Holding her breath, she lightly pressed the accelerator and both vehicles righted themselves. The float rocked, telling her that the horses were still up and were now rebalancing themselves. Her breathing returned to normal.

'Olivia what's the matter?'

'I left my mobile at home.'

'You nearly got us all killed because you haven't got your phone? You're a wreck. You should have gone to bed early like I said.'

Olivia sniffed loudly. 'I wanted a photo of me and Expresso for dad. And Oscar.'

Oh dear, Gill thought. I've handled things badly. As usual. 'Sorry love. I got a fright when the float swung like that. You know I hate towing. I'll take a photo and send it to dad.'

'He won't look at it when he sees it's from you.'

Gill grimaced. He probably wouldn't either. 'Hazel will have her phone. And Mrs Teo. They'll get some photos for dad and I'll get one for your brother.'

'When's Oscar going to get in touch?'

'I don't know,' Gill said. It had been nearly two months since Oscar's last postcard.

'There's no point in taking a photo for him anyway. He disapproves of hunting, like dad.'

'They're entitled to their views,' Gill said with a cheeriness she didn't feel.

Another loud sniff followed, this one moist.

'Oscar could be dead,' Olivia said. 'He could have been dead for months.'

Gill stared at the road. The same thought woke her up in the night. But someone from the embassy would have been in touch if he was, surely. And surely, she, Oscar's mother, would know if her son was dead. Surely.

'Oscar's fine.' He had to be. If he wasn't, their already fragile world would shatter. 'He's in a monastery, remember. With all that chanting and meditating and carrying water, there wouldn't be much time for writing.'

Glancing at Olivia, Gill saw she was biting the tip of her thumb, a sign she was genuinely upset. But at least she wasn't crying.

'You can listen to your iPod, if you want,' she said. 'And there're mints in the glovebox.'

'I forgot that as well,' Olivia said, getting out the mints and putting one in her mouth and handing one to her mother.

'I'm sorry about your dad,' Gill said, after a while. 'I know you wanted him to come today. And I'm sorry about Oscar as well.'

'It's not your fault,' Olivia said flatly. 'No matter what dad says.'

'Thanks, angel,' Gill said. But she couldn't help feeling that it was her fault. Nicholas told her often enough that it was.

They drove on in silence, sucking mint after mint. As they neared Wirral, where the meet was taking place, they joined a line of floats and trucks headed in the same direction.

The colour returned to Olivia's cheeks and she started jiggling her legs and tapping her knees. Seeing Xavier's float ahead, she bounced up and down. 'Bugger dad. Hunting's the best.'

I really should tell her off for that, Gill thought. But, well … bugger Nicholas. Why shouldn't she and Olivia be doing what they loved? Olivia's first word had been "horse" and her first outing with the Highlands Hunt when she turned twelve. She'd quickly learned to bridge her reins on her pony Expresso's neck so that she didn't pull on his mouth and to gallop standing in the stirrups to save his back. She'd also learned the ins and outs of hunting etiquette and, to her father's disgust, on the days leading up to a meet talked about little else. Just like her mother.

'Do you think AnnIndia'll bring Jeffrey?' Olivia said. 'It'll be surreal not having Grace with us.'

'Sad,' Gill said. 'Surreal and sad. I miss her.'

Olivia put a comforting hand on her thigh and she covered it with her own.

A few minutes later, she eased off the accelerator. Expresso and her mare, Hester, began to stomp impatiently. Olivia put down her window and stuck out her head. 'Steady on you fools,' she yelled. The truck travelling behind beeped its horn. Olivia waved. 'Debbie Harmer,' she told her mother.

They slowed to a crawl and Gill followed the vehicle in front through the gateway, over a cattlegrid and onto a rutted dirt road. After about a kilometre of slow, bumpy passage, a sign marked with a red arrow pointed the way to a paddock already half filled with horse trucks and floats.

Gill found a parking spot near some weathered timber yards and slotted the float into it. 'Right,' she said. 'Let's get to it. Xavier is just over there.'

'I can't see Hazel,' Olivia said. Hazel and her pony, Dorothy, travelled to the hunts with Xavier.

'Don't worry about Hazel,' Gill said. 'Horses first.' She jumped down out of the Prado and stood for a moment taking in the air. Was there anything better than a hunting morning? If there was, she couldn't think of it.

'Horses first, of course, of course,' Olivia chanted as she flipped the bolts on the tailgate.

Expresso and Hester unloaded briskly. Gill and Olivia tied them to the side of the float, next to each other. All about them, excited horses neighed and pawed the ground while their owners tried to give them a last polish or tighten their girths. Some riders were already walking and trotting their horses in and around the vehicles while others fuelled themselves with hot drinks and sandwiches.

'I love it here,' Olivia said.

Gill nodded. Opening meet or not, there was always a good turnout at Wirral. The property's owners, Margie and Nigel Tippet, were on the hunt committee and their seven hundred acres, with its huge granite boulders and breathtaking views, had an airy magic.

Expresso and Hester were saddled and bridled. Gill secured Olivia's hunting tie with the white gold and ruby pin she had given her on her first hunt.

'They'll be sorry,' she said as a late truck pulled into the paddock. There was nothing worse than having to rush to get a horse ready; horses were not good at haste.

'Can I go and see Hazel now?' Olivia asked, watching Gill wind her own hunting tie firmly around her neck and start its complicated fold.

'Okay. Tell her and Xavier to come for a cup of tea. We're going well for time.'

Like Olivia, Hazel was wearing a tracksuit over her cream breeches and shirt and vest to stop them getting dirty. Xavier, however, had chosen to protect his kit with a green and purple onesie with a wave ridged tail.

Olivia stared. 'You look brilliant, Xav. Expresso'll go berserk when he sees you.'

'He's already terrified dozens of horses,' Hazel said. 'Dorothy doesn't seem to mind him.' She rubbed her pony's neck lovingly. 'Though maybe she hasn't seen him yet.' A chunky liver chestnut with a bell-shaped blaze high on her dark brown brow, Dorothy had lost an eye in a polo match.

'What sort of animal is he?' Olivia asked Hazel as Xavier lashed her with his purple and green tail.

'Poof the Magic Dragon,' Hazel giggled.

Olivia grabbed the tail and yanked it. 'Dare you to get on Looky and ride through the floats.'

'Don't do dares.' Xavier said. 'Give me back my tail.'

'Mum said to come and have a cuppa,' Olivia said. 'We've got banana cake.'

'She can do up my tie,' Hazel said. 'Xavier's hopeless at it. He did an excellent job with Dorothy's plaits, though. He could get a job at the salon. Mum should be here soon. She had to do Lady Blythe's comb-up first.'

'I adore Lady Blythe,' Olivia said as she inspected the buttons of hair along Dorothy's neck – the Highland Hunt did not allow loose manes. 'Very tidy, Xav.'

Xavier put a velour arm around her shoulders and said in her ear, 'I think you should stick with Hazel today.'

'No way,' Olivia said. 'Dorothy can't keep up with Expresso.'

'I really think you should,' Xavier said. 'Hazel's scared she's going to come off and end up in hospital and her mum'll find out about a certain picture on a certain part of her.'

Olivia pushed him away. 'She's just looking for attention. She never comes off. Dorothy's as sure footed as a cat. It's probably something to do with only having one eye, a compensation thing.' She pointed at a massive float a few rows up. 'Look, the bloody Harts are here, of course.' Daisy Hart was the same age as her and Hazel, her sister, Matilde, a couple of years older. Both were mega thin, mega pretty and like their parents, mega competitive riders with mega expensive horses. Most irritating of all, however, their parents doted on each other.

Daisy Hart caught Olivia's eye and waved.

Olivia gave a half smile and turned away. A horrible thought came to her. If Mrs Teo found out about Hazel's tattoo it would give her the perfect excuse to move Hazel to Garton House, Daisy and Matilde's school. She hit her forehead with the flat of her hand. What had she done!

'Hazel's my bestie,' she said to Xavier. 'Of course I'll ride with her. Why wouldn't I anyway? You piss off and do your thing.' Her eyes roamed the onesie. 'Whatever that is.'

A while later, Gill, Olivia and Xavier mounted their horses and joined the forty or so riders, the field that would follow the hounds, on Wirral's lawn. The hounds were out of the truck and Simon Sinclair was talking to Salty, who, in kilt and sporran, would lead the hunt out with his bagpipes. Eleanor was with them.

Gill greeted Nigel Tippet's mother, Jo, took a cup off the tray she was holding up and sniffed it appreciatively. 'Smells gorgeous.'

Jo whisked the tray out of Olivia's reach, saying, 'I don't think so,' with a thin smile.

Xavier took one of the cups. 'Not a bad drop,' he said, sipping the warm, spicy wine as Jo moved away. 'Should have got two. What about Digger Fahey buying Jottings?'

'I hear it hadn't even been advertised.'

'It's a seller's market at the moment,' Xavier said. 'Jottings wasn't with us, though, sadly.'

Gill patted Hester's neck. An off the track thoroughbred re-trained by Pan Villon, the mare was nicely relaxed, unlike many of the other horses on the lawn.

'Jottings is massive. Too big, really. I did the flowers for a wedding there. The ceilings are so high I felt like a dwarf. I ...' Gill stopped as one of the Whippers-ins took off towards a corner of the garden screened by Rhododendrons. 'Oops, looks like someone's made a break for the chook house.' Minutes later the Whipper-in, Lesley Bond, appeared driving a shame-faced hound before her, back to the rest of the pack.

'Naughty creature,' Gill laughed. She looked happily around at the big old trees, oaks, weeping elms and maples that bordered the lawn. Behind them, a series of terraces led up to the homestead, a Spanish style hacienda designed by a much feted 1930s architect. 'I'd much rather something like this than Jottings.'

'Dream away,' Xavier said. He pointed. 'Simon's on the move.'

Simon Sinclair rode his big white horse, Polar Bear, into the centre of the lawn, the hounds and Whippers-in a short distance behind.

Silence came over the lawn.

Simon looked about with obvious pride. 'Morning all. It's a pleasure to be here with you on the first meet of the season. As most already know, I'm Simon Sinclair and along with Lucien Blythe, your Joint Master. I'm also greatly privileged to be your Huntsman. Today we're hunting twenty-three hounds, eleven and a half couple. Tradition has it that it's the single hound that gets the fox, so keep your eyes sharp if you're interested in how hounds go about their work. In the pack also we've four young hounds that are out for the first time. If you see a hound off on its own, it'll likely be one of these new entries. I'd be grateful if you'd stay with them and get the attention of one of the Whips so that they don't get really lost.'

Simon turned around, beamed at the hounds then continued his speech.

'For those of you out for the first time, Eleanor over there on the big, dark horse is your Field Master. You must always stay behind her.' Simon raised his hunting whip at Eleanor, who in turn acknowledged him and the field with a tip of her black bowler.

'Thank you, Eleanor. Our Whippers-in today are Donnacha Keough, Lesley Bond and Scott Page.' The three Whips tipped their helmets and Simon continued. 'I shouldn't need to remind you that hunt staff and hounds have right of way at all times, and when hounds are working to keep your voices down. If you see a fox, raise your cap in the direction of its travel and call out "tally ho" as loud as you can. No paddocks with sheep are to be entered and gates must be closed by the last one through.

'I'd like to thank our host and hostess, Maggie and Nigel Tippet for their hospitality. Their sons Jude and Angus are having their first ride with us today. Raise your hands boys so everyone knows who you are and can look out for you.'

The Tippet twins, eight years old and mounted on the smaller and older of their parents' stockhorses, put their gloved hands in the air.

Simon smiled at the boys. 'Now, I know you're all as keen as I am to be done with the chit chat, but there's one last thing I have to say. A few months ago we lost one of our founding members, Grace Levy. Grace, no matter where you're calling home these days, I know you're with us today.' He pulled a roll of black tape out of his pocket, broke off a piece and wound it around his upper arm, tossed the roll to Donnacha and raised his flask.

'To Grace.'

Gill's eyes filled with tears. 'To Grace,' she murmured.

'All on,' Donnacha cried, telling Simon that all the hounds were present. Salty stepped out, cradling his pipes. Simon followed, the hounds, flanked by the Whips, at Polar Bear's heels. The sound of the pipes cut the air. Eleanor raised her arm for the field to follow.

'Let's go,' said Gill, bridging her reins on Hester's neck. She looked across at Olivia, admiring her calm as she prepared Expresso to canter. Seeing her daughter so happy, so confident, more confident on horseback than she ever was on the ground, made the long hours at the shop worth it. And her rotten marriage? Yes, that too.

She touched her cap briefly in a salute to hunting and stepped Hester into a canter.

13

The front wheel of the Land Cruiser went into a deep rut. Chopper kicked out hard at the side of the float. Pan slowed to a crawl and held his breath. There was no more kicking, no scrabbling, anything to tell that Chopper was in a panic. He relaxed and checked the rear-view mirror. Bloody hell! Chopper was leaning back on the tie rope. He accelerated off the road and was out of the vehicle in a heartbeat.

Chopper's hindquarters were bunched over his splayed back legs. His neck was stretched to its limit, the halter cutting into the soft flesh behind his ears and making his eyes bulge. He was dragging in air in ragged snorts.

Pan stepped up into the front of the float and leant his forearms on the chest bar next to Chopper's head. 'Hey big man, you're okay. It was only a rut and we're out of it now. Back on solid ground.'

The desperation in Chopper's eyes faded a little. He shifted his weight minutely forward and some of the tension came off the tie rope.

'That's better. No doubt you're a good fellow. Very smart.'

And with this and a small hop, Chopper rebalanced himself and his head now free of the straining rope, he gave an almighty shake from ear to tail.

Pan let out a long breath, which Chopper, lifting his head, appeared to take in through his still livid nostrils. Moved, Pan resisted an urge to stroke his nose.

But what now? There was still a kilometre at least of dirt road and another setback might be too much for Chopper to cope with, a further cruelty that he neither needed nor deserved.

Perhaps he should ride him the rest of the way? Tack him up here and leave the float where it was, off the road?

Half past ten. The hunt would be well away. Not that it mattered. Getting Chopper onto the float and travelling to the meet and, if he was calm enough, riding him at the back of the field was all he had planned. If Chopper achieved that it would be a triumph.

Decision time.

If he rode Chopper the rest of the way he would have to leave early or wait until most of the other vehicles had departed. But that was a minor consideration. The trickier problem was what to do with Chopper when they got back to the float? He would either have to leave him tied to the fence while he turned the float or load him straight away and risk him losing it again. Turning a float was challenging enough on flat ground, but on rutted dirt with a panicking horse onboard it would be suicidal. But then leaving Chopper tied to a barbwire fence might be equally so.

'Right, this is how it's going to play,' he said to Chopper. Horses might not understand words, but if their minds were calm, they could see the picture that came before the words.

The plan communicated, he stepped out of the float, shut the door and climbed back into the Land Cruiser. He checked the rearview mirror. So far so good. He turned on the ignition and eased the vehicle forward. The float jolted but that was it. Keeping the vehicle to a steady crawl, he leant over the steering wheel to better see any dips or holes that he might be able to manoeuvre around. On the seat beside him, his Lab, Sadie, copying her master, put her pudgy black paws on the dash and brought her nose up to the windscreen.

The last of the journey passed without incident. He turned into the paddock where the floats and trucks were parked and drove to the furthest row so that Chopper would be facing the open country when he unloaded. He had not seen so many vehicles since his last race and the sight might be another challenge.

But once out in the cool morning air, Chopper looked about with interest rather than concern. He had survived the earlier terror in the float, the bumpy ride, and his confidence had grown a little more.

Sadie headed off to sniff out some fresh manure, her favourite breakfast. Pan undid the straps of Chopper's travelling sheet and a watchful eye on his head and his left arm ready to protect himself, began brushing him. It was weeks since Chopper had had a go, but it would be foolish to think that the fury that had earned him a suspended death sentence was not still lurking in his new calm. Even Grace had been taken aback by his savageness. But she had not doubted his goodness. There had been a time in his short span of years when he had looked at the world kindly. When he had been known by the gracious name LutePlayer rather than the ugly moniker attached to him after he had started swinging his head with bone crunching force and snapping his teeth like a rabid dog.

He tied the now saddled Chopper to the float and went to find Sadie. She was lolling on the tailgate of a nearby truck looking smug and well-fed. He hunted her back to the Land Cruiser, settled her on the front seat and put the windows down far enough so she could put her head out but not escape.

Now dressed in his hunting kit, he mounted Chopper and walked him round the vehicles, both to loosen him up and so he could get a proper look at things. Chopper stayed relaxed, a sign that he was truly healing. He loosened the reins: trust begets trust. Chopper propped a few times but moved on without a fuss after some reassuring words and a rub on his neck.

At the paddock gate, he asked Chopper to stand. He took Grace's hip flask out of his pocket and rubbed his thumb over the inscription on its base – *The best of my fun I owe it to horse and hound.* Tears pricked his eyes. He unscrewed the cap and took a sip of the buttery whiskey port that had been Grace's hunting tipple then capped the flask and returned it to his pocket.

'Come on big man,' he told Chopper. 'Let's get some air into our lungs.'

Chopper didn't move.

14

Resplendent in a scarlet coat appliqued with felt foxes, Jeffrey sat bolt upright, his legs trembling. India caught a glimpse of cars, floats and small trucks.

She slowed the car. 'We must be nearly there. According to Olivia's map there should be a gate …'

And there it was, an open double gate, the stencilled sign "WIRRAL", the cattlegrid and dirt road as they appeared on the map.

The road was so rough she wondered if she should turn back. But with the edges where they merged with the furrowed paddock even more rutted, she pressed on, praying that one of the rocks they were rattling over wouldn't rip a hole in the underneath of the hire car.

'Sorry,' she said to Jeffrey as they lurched through a pond-sized pothole and his head bounced against the roof.

At last they found the vehicles she'd glimpsed. The paddock was almost as rutted as the road and steering carefully, she parked at the end of a row of trucks. Jeffrey whined as she turned off the ignition. Her heart cramped, hoping that he wasn't expecting to find Grace here.

It was a relief to be out of the little car. There was no one about except for her and Jeffrey. She walked to the fence and gazed across the paddocks. The hills were the colour of beach sand and the air smelt of dried grass and animal manure and unfettered winds. She closed her eyes, imagining herself the wind skimming the tops of the hills, filling the wings of a hawk or an eagle.

When she opened her eyes, Jeffrey was gone.

She began walking back towards the car calling his name. He hadn't gone far. He was heading towards a horse. She called him again and he broke into a run. The horse leaped sideways. The rider jumped down off its back as she reached them.

'Sorry,' she apologised. 'I should have had Jeffrey on his lead.'

The man looped the reins over his arm and knelt beside Jeffrey. 'Hey, I thought it was you. You've escaped from Julie and Lillian. And you've got your hunting coat on.' He rose and took off his cap. 'Pan. Pan Villon,' he said, introducing himself.

'Pan,' she repeated. Pan. Someone Grace *had* mentioned. She looked at him as she would a subject or a painting. Late twenties, tall, loose limbed, dark blond hair brushed back from his brow and tucked behind his ears and flattened to his head by his cap, which had also marked his brow with a red line. Slightly hawkish nose. Expression ... unreadable.

'The woodland god. You were a friend of my grandmother's.'

'And you're India.'

'Ann,' she corrected. It was as though all the while she had been away at school, living in London, someone called India had been living in Burragong. She too, it seemed, like Grace, had a life she knew nothing about. She receded further into the coat. 'I prefer Ann.'

'Grace said you disliked India,' Pan said. 'But she thought it a good name for an artist. One that people would remember.'

'I'd rather they remember my work than my name.'

'She'd be pleased you're here today. That you've brought Jeffrey.'

She put out her hand to touch the velvety skin of the horse's nose, but Pan pulled its head away.

'I should be getting on,' he said to Jeffrey.

She watched him trot his horse through the gate. High in the pale sky a cloud, something of the shape of a hand, seemed to beckon them towards the horizon. The horse picked up speed.

Simon rode up to Donnacha. 'Check?'

'I'd say so,' Donnacha said. 'Hounds'll appreciate a breather.' He raised his arm to get Eleanor's attention and pointed ahead to a flat corner of the paddock. Eleanor waved to say she had gotten the message.

He put Oyster into a canter and Simon and Polar Bear set off alongside, the hounds following.

'Good job with the kangaroo,' Donnacha said over the thud of hooves. A kangaroo had bolted across the line the hounds were working, but they had kept to their job. It wasn't always the case.

'Goose thought about giving it a run.' Simon stood in his stirrups and turned and pointed his whip at a big speckled hound. Feeling the sting of his master's gaze, Goose dipped his head.

Donnacha pulled Oyster to a sudden halt. 'Bloody shite. What's Lucien doing?' Mockingbird was thundering down the hill and in a minute would be on top of them.

'She's in a bolt,' Simon said. 'Lesley's on it.'

Behind them, Eleanor and the field had also stopped and on the top of the hill, the vehicles following the hunt also. They watched with bated breath as Lesley galloped up alongside Mockingbird and leaned out of the saddle and hit her across the shoulders with her whip, knocking her off stride. Mockingbird stopped suddenly, pitching Lucien up her neck.

Donnacha rode over to them. Sweat dripped off Mockingbird's belly and her face and neck were flecked with bloody foam.

'You take Oyster,' he told Lucien. 'I'll walk the mare back to the truck.'

Lucien shook his head. 'She'll be right now she's got that out of her,' he said, loud enough for everyone to hear. 'I've no idea what spooked her, but she's certainly got some acceleration. I might have to put her back onto the track.'

Donnacha shook his head and rode off.

Olivia was gazing at Lucien and Mockingbird with admiration.

'That was so cool. I don't know how he stayed on. We'd all have been mangled or dead.'

'Spooked rubbish,' Gill said in a disgusted voice. 'The mare was trying to get free of his hands.'

'I don't know why you hate him, mum,' Olivia hissed.

Gill swung off Hester, loosened her girth and led her over to Hazel and Xavier. With a last longing look at Lucien, Olivia followed.

'Bloody Lucien,' Xavier said. 'I thought he was going to ride over the hounds.'

'You hate him too, Xav,' Olivia said. She gulped from her hip flask. 'You all hate him.'

Xavier grabbed the flask, took a sip and then poured the contents onto the grass. He passed the flask to Gill. 'Vodka and raspberry cordial.' He held out his hand to Hazel. 'Give me yours.'

'Don't,' Olivia told her.

Hazel gave Xavier her flask. He sniffed it and turned it upside down, sending pink liquid glugging out onto the grass. He raised an eyebrow at Hazel. 'I was wondering why your mum's cocktails had lost their sting. You know there's a test you can do to check how much of the bottle is vodka and how much is water.'

Hazel trembled. 'There's not.'

'It works for gin as well.'

Olivia looked scornful. 'You're such a liar Xav ...'

'I think you girls should walk your ponies around,' Gill interrupted. 'You haven't even loosened their girths.'

Xavier pointed. 'There's a trough over there if you're thirsty.'

'Phew,' Gill said as Olivia stomped off, Hazel following. 'I didn't think to check the flasks. Vivienne would have shaved my head if Hazel had ridden in half cut.'

'How much for my silence?' Xavier joked.

'Name your price,' Gill said. She sighed happily. 'Hasn't the hunting been magic? Simon's got the hounds just right.' She lowered the reins so that Hester could pick at the grass. 'Shame you emptied the girls' flasks though. I left mine in the car.'

Xavier raised his eyebrows. 'Vodka and raspberry cordial, really?' He handed Gill his own flask, filled with weak black tea and a jigger of ginger wine.

She took a swig. 'Yum.'

'Have some more.'

'No thanks. There's nothing worse than galloping on a full bladder.'

'Except maybe jumping.'

They laughed, then Xavier said, 'It's not the same without Grace.' His arm drew an arc over the paddock, the clusters of horses and riders, Simon and the hounds, Donnacha and Lesley leaning against their horses and sharing a flask. It's like ...' Xavier searched for the right words but couldn't find them. 'It's just not the same.'

Across the paddock, Lesley tilted her head and said angrily. 'I don't believe it. But then maybe I do.'

Donnacha followed her gaze to where Lucien and Eleanor were clearly sharing a dirty moment, their horses shielding them from Simon.

'Crash that party as well do you think?' Lesley said.

Donnacha held out his hand for Lesley's reins. 'Sooner than later. Give us your horse.' Fucking Eleanor. Fucking Lucien fucking Blythe. Bad choice of words. 'Get a hurry on.'

He positioned himself between Oyster and Lesley's little Appaloosa and took out his phone, holding it close to his stomach so he couldn't be seen. The world might be an endless chorus line to Lucien Blythe but for him there could only ever be one woman on the stage. And right now, he wanted to hear her voice.

Leila answered after a couple rings. 'Hey, how's it going?'

His tongue was clumsy. 'Hounds are working well. Ground's a bit hard. Scent's probably gone for the day. How's it going there?'

'I've been dodging Digger. Jesus he's an old goat. He and Christie have just left. They're going to Jottings first. Digger's bought it.'

'More helicopters coming and going. The Highlands'll sound like a fecking war zone soon.'

'How's Mockingbird?'

Donnacha cursed. Eedjit! He should have had an answer ready. A toe connected with his knee, knocking him into Oyster's legs. It was Lesley, saving him, for the moment.

'Got to go, love,' he said quickly. 'Been busted by Lesley.' Phones were forbidden out on the hunt, even for hunt staff.

Lesley nodded to where Eleanor, now alone, was repositioning Elvis' saddlecloth. 'I said someone in one of the vehicles was filming them.'

'Should be the end of it then,' Donnacha said, not believing it for one minute.

Lesley stared at the phone as Donnacha slipped it into his pocket. 'I didn't see that.'

'Thanks,' Donnacha said. He looked over at Simon, who was now doing up Polar Bear's girth. 'Looks like we're moving off.'

'Simon wants to draw that paddock next to the wetland,' Lesley said, tightening her horse's girth. 'Sometimes foxes lay up there after their night's dirty work.' She stopped. 'Look. Pan's brought Chopper out. Amazing!' Her property was on the same road as Pan's and they were good friends.

Donnacha watched Pan ride towards Simon to tell him he'd just arrived, a required courtesy. Pan's horse, a big bay gelding, was walking out on a loose rein and Pan, relaxed in the saddle, was letting him look around.

'Nice hoss.'

Lesley swung up into the saddle. 'You wouldn't have said so a few months ago. He was totally screwed up. Bit someone's ear off and had had a good go at the poor bugger's chin before they managed to drag him out of the stall. That's why he's called Chopper. First day at Pan's he smashed up his stall and the stall next-door the day after. Pan ended up repanelling the whole stable block.'

Donnacha narrowed his eyes at Chopper, now standing calmly next to Polar Bear while Pan and Simon chatted. If the hoss had been half as bad as Lesley said, then maybe Pan was BlueBuckle's only hope. He set off after Lesley, who was riding over to Pan.

'Morning, Pan,' he said, reaching them. 'Nice hoss. Lesley was telling me he'd come to you with a few troubles. You wouldn't think it now.'

Pan touched the brim of his cap. 'Morning, Donnacha.' He rested a gloved hand on Chopper's neck. 'So far so good. A bit of a hiccup in the float and he wouldn't go through the gate, but he went through later without a fuss.'

'Looks relaxed enough now.'

'Is he going back on the track?' Simon asked. He'd also heard Chopper's story from Lesley.

'No, he's staying with me,' Pan answered. 'Owner's gifted him.' He rubbed Chopper's shoulder. 'There's a lot of heart here. He's rolled over the panels and his canter's a song. Eats up the ground.'

'Sounds like he might have the makings of a good hunt horse,' Simon said.

'Could well,' Pan agreed – when midweek hunting started, he often rode Whipper-in, Donnacha and Scott Page being usually unavailable.

Simon turned towards the hounds. 'Time to get the show back on the road,' he said, raising his horn.

'Are you staying for the breakfast?' Donnacha asked Pan.

'Depends on this fellow,' Pan replied as, at the sound of the horn, Chopper shot backwards.

15

The noble rank had come to Lady Blythe not through birth but through marriage and as life is, it had been quite some journey.

The passage of upward nobility had begun many years before the grand arrival. She had been baptized Lynette, Catherine, Ladybird, Resnick. Lynette after her father's mother, Catherine after her mother's grandmother and Ladybird after the wife of the American President her parents had met on their honeymoon. One day, however, it struck her that she had never come across a Lynette in the captions under the enthralling photos in her mother's *Vogue* magazines. She was the kind of girl that noticed such things.

Because she got on well at school, kept her room tidy and was polite to their guests, her parents thought her preoccupation with her name was a stage and indulged her, calling her Catherine as she wished. But by the time the now Catherine started secondary school, even they had forgotten that she had once been Lynette and her younger sister and brother knew her only as Catherine.

And she was Catherine to first husband, barrister Denis Brenner. It was on the marriage certificate and divorce papers both. Her second husband, Tory politician Richard Lowe (she had settled in England after her divorce), however, called her Kitty, which she thought suitably caption-like. Until she discovered that, believing his nursery years, including, revoltingly his potty training the best of his life, Richard nurserified everything. Luckily, however, not long after this revelation, Richard went off with his new secretary, an Eton mess like himself. If divorce was a career, she had it well and truly nailed.

The almost last leg of her journey to the noble ranks began, fittingly, in the Royal enclosure at Ascot. She had become separated from her group and was on her own, excited because for the first time she had made a large wager. The race, as she was never to forget, was the Diamond Jubilee Stakes. As the bell rang to signal that the horses were nearing the final bend, the man standing next to her pitched forward and though a third of his weight, she put out a hand to steady him.

'Name's Jonno Blythe,' he said. 'Now I've got your attention, let's go and have a drink and you can tell me yours.'

She had assumed from his burliness and the puffiness of his handsome face that he was a footballer, but Jonno Blythe turned out to be the breeder of an earlier winner, a mare named, prophetically they both agreed, Colonial Lass.

When she produced her birth certificate for the marriage licence, Jonno declared she would be Ladybird to him. With her wasp's waist and almost Scandinavian fairness she was the furthest thing ever from a round red spotty little bug and that tickled him. And he liked being tickled very much. It also tickled him that, like his good friend R Sangster, he now too had a pretty Australian blonde to flaunt trackside and at the sale rings.

The Blythe base was the Berkshire thoroughbred stud, Whistlejacket, established by Jonno's parents. His parents both dead and he an only child, Jonno had continued the business, breeding from American as well as English, Irish and French stallions and producing some remarkable gallopers. When the great jockey Frankie Dettori was asked to drop a ride for a Blythe horse, he didn't hesitate. HM, herself, owned several Whistlejacket mares.

The new Mr and Mrs Blythe attended race meetings and sales about the world. There were trips to Japan, Hong Kong, Dubai, America, and Australia and between take offs and landings, parties at the Nunnery and five-star hotels in the world's capitals. Three years into the marriage there was also a son, Lucien, a blueprint of his father. Like the mare Colonial Lass, gifted to her by Jonno on their engagement, Ladybird was having a dream run. She and

Jonno were one of racing's golden couples. Racing royalty. Which was not to say that Jonno's forays outside the golden cage did not draw blood from her heart, but there was always their golden son to turn to for comfort.

But like all dream runs, Ladybird Blythe's came to end. At fifty-six, the exact same age his father had expired, Jonno died suddenly and similarly of a heart attack. Ladybird was forty-one, Lucien, thirteen. Her widow's lot was a string of broodmares and racehorses and an art and property portfolio that before the first handful of dirt fell on Jonno's casket, saw her swamped by suitors.

A year later she returned to Australia. Three marriages had been sufficient, and her heart was raw enough to make running into Jonno's spring flings in the enclosures of the world's racecourses an ordeal.

For her new home, Ladybird Blythe settled on the parcel of Highland acres that was to become the new Whistlejacket and it was not long after that she achieved the noble ranks. The hon's title was bestowed on her by her Highlands hairdresser, Vivienne Teo, who at their first meeting misheard her name. And why correct her? Like the right sized cap or glove, the title fitted snugly, and Jonno had been in line for a knighthood in any case. It might have been a long line and he might have been nearer its tail than its top, but she was certain he was in it.

And thus so, Lynette, Catherine, Ladybird Resnick became Lady Blythe. Jonno Blythe might have been in line for a peerage, but of the couple, the wife was much more the deserving.

The Australian Whistlejacket was founded with the Berkshire Whistlejacket mares and quickly became a quiet star in the Australian thoroughbred world. Lucien learnt to be a man among men at St Paul's, where he boarded during the week, despite proximity to his home, to Whistlejacket. When not at school, he continued his education in thoroughbred breeding and being the beautiful son of a beautiful widow. When he turned twenty-five, Lady Blythe moved out of Whistlejacket's stately stone homestead into Le Manoir, a charming two-story villa on the outskirts of Burragong. It was time for Lucien to find his feet.

Le Manoir sat at the end of a curved gravel drive lined with white agapanthus. With its faded red render and wrought iron window planter boxes, Lady Blythe's Burragong home would not have looked out of place in the South of France.

Vivienne Teo parked and headed towards the porticoed front door. Lady Blythe's late-night call meant that her own day had started at five. She never skipped her morning workout, Hazel had to be ready for Xavier by eight and she had a list of things to organise for the hunt breakfast, including Toby. But seeing Lady Blythe's number on the call screen and knowing that it meant an unscheduled visit, it had not crossed her mind to refuse. Aside from the cachet Lady Blythe's patronage bestowed on her business, being her secret lover's mother, it could be said that she was also her secret defacto mother-in-law.

The front door was opened by Martin, one half of the dour couple that served Lady Blythe around the clock.

'She's waiting.'

Vivienne swiftly climbed the stairs to the salon, where the masseuse and manicurist also attended Le Manoir and performed their magic.

Lady Blythe was seated at the basin, her frost coloured hair flowing in perfect little waves.

'Morning, Vivienne. Splendid day for the opening meet.' The crystal pings in Lady Blythe's voice told just how far up the ranks she'd travelled. (Jonno's voice had been sadly nasal and he'd had a habit of dropping in accents from *Neighbours*, which he'd started watching with his nanny.) 'Martin is bringing up tea. Though I'm inclined to have him open a bottle. Would you care for a sip?'

'No thanks. I've still heaps to do. Toby's home. He's coming to the meet for the breakfast.' Vivienne unfurled one of A Cut Above's signature lotus print capes, draped it over Lady Blythe's shoulders and began laying out combs.

'And how is Toby?'

'Working night and day,' Vivienne said with not a small amount of pride. 'He's got into the surgical program. It's very competitive.'

She pursed her lips and studied the strand of Lady Blythe's hair she now held between her thumb and index finger.

Martin appeared with a tray set with a rose petal pink tea pot and matching teacups.

'I've decided on a sippet,' Lady Blythe told him.

Martin raised an eyebrow. It was not unusual for Lady Blythe to have a glass of champagne mid-morning, but nine was early, even for her. His back stiff, he poured Vivienne's tea and picking up the tray and unwanted cup and saucer, left the room without a sound.

'I never see Toby these days,' Lady Blythe said, watching in the mirror as Vivienne misted her hair. 'Tell him to come to lunch next time he's down.'

'I'll make sure he says hello at the breakfast,' Vivienne promised. But it was a promise she had no intention of keeping, just as she had no intention of passing on the invitation to Le Manoir. On Toby's last weekend home she had come across him and Martin and Martin's partner Kevin, sharing a table at Pregos and the way they were laughing had made her uneasy.

'Thank you my dear,' Lady Blythe said as Martin reappeared and handed her a crystal flute.

'Stephan's hamper has arrived,' he said.

'Put it in the Rolls,' Lady Blythe told him. Her eyes met Vivienne's in the mirror. 'Did you get a hamper, Vivienne?'

Vivienne twirled the scissors. 'Stephan's bringing it to the meet.' She snipped a single hair near Lady Blythe's ear, put the scissors down and began fussing with a comb out of sight of the mirror.

'Still moving Hazel to Garton House?'

'Yes. Your reference was perfect, thanks.'

Lady Blythe lost herself for a moment in the fluttering of Vivienne's fingers over her crown. She put her head on the side, admiring the way her layered bob kept its shape despite the disturbance.

'I expect Hazel is excited.'

Vivienne frowned. Hazel didn't know the change of schools was imminent. When she had tried to tell her, she had gotten so upset that the conversation had lasted only a few minutes.

'She's not happy about leaving her friends. Especially Olivia Findlay.'

'She'll make new friends,' Lady Blythe said bloodlessly. 'Nice ones. What if you bought her a new horse? That pony is getting too small for her. Scott Page is the riding instructor at Garton House. Hazel could start dressage with him.'

Vivienne reached for the now cold tea. It wasn't a bad idea. 'What would I be looking at for a dressage horse?'

'Eight, ten thousand. Maybe twelve. She'd need a schoolmaster, but nothing too old. She'd want to get a few years out of it.'

'Hmm,' Vivienne said noncommittally.

Lady Blythe took another sip of champagne. 'Someone at the bridge club said Grace Levy's granddaughter is in Burragong.'

'Yes, she is. I've met her. I picked Hazel and Olivia up from Mars House. They went to visit Jeffrey.'

'Don't tell me that disgusting hound is still alive.'

Vivienne positioned the hand mirror so that Lady Blythe could see the back of her head. 'I don't know what India's planning to do with it. She's selling the house and going back to London.'

Lady Blythe waved vaguely at her head. 'Thank you my dear, I'm ready to face the world again. Back to London? I must send Martin to invite her for a drink sooner than later, then. The gal will no doubt be missing her grandmother, like we all are.'

16

BlueBuckle showed no sign that he had heard his name. Leila's heart lurched. She thought he might have picked up a little from the earlier drink – the bottom of the trough showed only a slick of moisture. But he hadn't colicked so he could now have a decent one. But not from the trough. From the bucket.

She quietly slipped the gate chain, stepped into the yard and did up the chain with her spare hand by feel.

BlueBuckle did not move.

Murmuring softly and avoiding looking in his eyes, she walked slowly towards him, her body language passive.

A few meters from him, she put the bucket on the ground and stepped back. BlueBuckle continued staring at the ground.

She picked up the bucket and took another step closer.

Still, BlueBuckle did not move.

Perhaps he would drink if she went away. But if she left the bucket, she would have to retrieve it before Lucien or anyone else came across it.

'Come on BlueBuckle,' she pleaded. 'Come on fella.'

Leaving the bucket wasn't an option. She wouldn't care so much if she lost her job, but Donnacha might lose his as well, and who knew how that would play out.

In two steps she was standing in front of BlueBuckle. She put the bucket down in front of him. 'Come on fella.'

For a moment nothing happened, then, with a rush of air that filled her ears like the sound of a jet engine, BlueBuckle swung his head and hit her with such force she was knocked to the ground. She lay stunned, waiting for the lethal thud of hooves on her body.

The ringing in her ears faded a little. She lifted her face up out of the dirt. BlueBuckle had resumed his dejected pose but was watching her.

She began edging back on her stomach, and after an age, reached the gate and dragged herself up, fumbling the chain to let herself out.

Her neck was stiff, her jaw aching fiercely. She could feel the start of concussion and there was ringing in one of her ears, the left or right she couldn't tell. But all she could think about was getting to the hunt. She had to see Pan. BlueBuckle could have killed her but he had shown mercy and that was as good as a cry for help.

She made her way dizzily back down to the cottage. The beanie she found to hide her swelling jaw and cheek looked like a Christmas stocking crocheted by a drunk, but it did the job, almost. And it made her head feel like it wasn't going to split in two. She searched a while for her sunglasses and remembering that they were in the Forrester – thinking was getting harder by the minute – she grabbed the keys and headed off.

The road to Burragong buckled and twisted but she managed to stick to it. Stephan's van was parked at the back of the Bombay Duck and she pulled in beside it, hoping a break would settle her head a bit. Enough for her to get to Wirral and find Pan. She didn't care what happened after that.

Every centimetre of the Bombay Duck's kitchen was covered with hampers – goodie filled cardboard boxes of different sizes wrapped in green and white gingham and tied with hessian strips. The red rims around Stephan's eyes and the line of empty coffee cups told that he'd been up all night.

'Blythe didn't offer you a horse for the meet?' he asked.

'No.'

'He's an arsehole.'

She sipped a glass of water. The thought of Lucien made her head feel worse. And her shoulder, where she'd been driven into the yard rails the other day, was also now aching again.

'How many orders did you end up with?' she asked, changing the subject.

'Enough to make a profit,' Stephan answered. 'We priced them from thirty to a hundred and fifty, depending on the menu selection and how many they're to feed. What do you think about the labels? Scott did them.'

She examined one of the brown cardboard tags, which had the purchaser's name and an outline of an Indian Runner duck on the front and a list of the hamper's contents on the back. Even with her on and off blurring vision, the stylish dark green ink writing was easy to read.

'Very smart. I didn't know Scott could do calligraphy.'

'He's my man of many talents,' Stephan said smugly.

She peered into one of the larger cartons waiting to be wrapped in gingham. Even though her stomach was fizzing, her mouth watered at the feast of pork pies, mini quiches, sourdough baguettes, tubs of beetroot hommos, tabouli, olives, custard tarts and chocolate truffles.

'Yum. Do you think they'll take off?'

'I sure hope so,' Stephan said. 'I'm planning to do functions as well and mini hampers for working lunches and kids' parties. Yolanda's doing a website for me.'

Leila stood reading the names on the tags while Stephan finished tying up the last of the hampers. It might have been the strain of making out the words on the tags or the bright kitchen lights but suddenly her head began to throb sickeningly. Her knees buckled and she grabbed the bench to steady herself. Maybe she shouldn't be driving? She straightened her back. It was only concussion.

'Are you okay?' Stephan asked.

'Late night.'

Stephan gave a tired smile. 'Know all about that. Scott thinks you should get yourself a horse and keep it with us, then you wouldn't have to be begging Blythe for rides. What about that mare you were telling him about?'

'Mockingbird.' She picked up her bag and keys. Another reason to get to Wirral sooner than later.

'Any chance of Blythe selling her?'

'I'm going to ask.'

Stephan pointed to a small carton next to the sink. 'There's a couple of pork pies in there. Grab some truffles as well. If he's anything like Scott, Donnacha'll be starving when he rides in.'

Martin slid into the driver's seat of the Rolls-Royce, next to Lady Blythe. Are you sure we shouldn't be going by Whistlejacket and swapping the Phantom for one of the Land Cruisers?'

'I do think an 800,000-dollar motor can cope with a couple of kilometres of dirt road, don't you?' Lady Blythe looked across at Martin. 'Are we going, or not?' Some of her friends never sat next to their driver. How silly and affected. And that besides, the back of most men's heads had the charm of faux fur.

His lips a thin line, Martin hit the start button and eased the Phantom towards the front gate.

'I was thinking about the dust,' he said, after they had travelled a while in silence.

'Rodger will wash the car tomorrow. I'm sure he's not beyond that simple task.' Rodger was Le Manoir's ancient gardener. In answer to Martin's cynical sniff, Lady Blythe continued, 'My dear, none of us are getting any younger,' she said, her tone suggesting that Martin himself should take a good look in the mirror. And indeed, she had more than once offered to arrange an appointment with her Bondi Junction man.

She closed her eyes and let her thoughts drift along with Mozart's *non pui andrai*. She had wondered if she herself was not feeling the touch of time's grasping hands. The race meetings that had been to her religious observances – the Queen Elizabeth Stakes, the Dubai World Cup, the Golden Slipper, the Kentucky, Curragh, and Epsom Derbies – she was now just as happy watching on Sky as through binoculars. The grand hotels, those laps of luxury she so adored nestling in, had also lost their magnetism, as had the sale rings and fashion shows that for years had been her favourite entertainments.

But it was not the robber hands of time filching her pleasures. It was the equally thieving fingers of fear. The golden son was turning into his father. While waiting in the Rolls for Martin to attend an errand and idly turning the pages of his *Telegraph*, she had come across photos of a duke and cabinet minister friend of Jonno's. The pictures were grainy but the man snorting cocaine off the prostitute's breasts and enjoying other nastinesses with her companion, was unmistakably His Grace. She and Jonno had been at his wedding and his children's christenings. He had spoken at Jonno's funeral. And now here he was wearing one of the revolting girls' bras and doing what he was doing while he was meant to be in cabinet. But more terrible still, it could have been Jonno, had he still been alive.

She had thought about ringing Electra, the Duke's wife, but decided that it was better she didn't. Who knew on what heads the storm that would follow the story would break? Best keep hers low.

The days had passed and the awful images and thoughts the story had induced began to fade. Unlike Electra, she had had a lucky escape and it almost put her in the mood to celebrate. That was until she came across a photo of Lucien in the front row of a Victoria's Secret parade.

Her eyes snapped open. 'Is that slutty newsreader going to be at the breakfast?' she asked.

'Christie Fahey? She and Digger stayed at Whistlejacket last night, so you'd expect they'd be there.'

She fretted with the platinum and jade bracelet she had chosen to dress up her Chanel suit. 'I suppose that means they'll be eating with us.'

'They've bought Jottings, you know.'

Lady Blythe's mind raced. 'Surely they're not planning a move to the Highlands?'

'I can't imagine why else they'd buy the place. It's a bit big for a weekender, even for someone with Digger's money.'

<h1 style="text-align:center">17</h1>

'Now stand.' Lucien pulled Mockingbird's head in until her chin was almost touching her chest and then spurred her in the sides, making her leap up in the air. Leila had been letting the mare get away with murder. She'd totally lost respect for the bit, not to mention the person on her back.

He took his phone out of his pocket and grinned at the photo of Opal Manning on the message screen. There was another photo and then, even better, much better, a minute of film.

Suddenly uncomfortable in the area at the front of the saddle, he leaned back to ease the pressure and messaged, Planning a film career? He returned the phone to his pocket and swung down off Mockingbird and deftly rearranged things so that he could stand with comfort. His phone vibrated again. I hear you're a good director, Opal had returned.

He turned off the phone and stood watching the hounds as they spread out over the side of the hill. Simon, Donnacha and Lesley, also off their horses, were conferring and Eleanor had the field gathered up some distance away. It was a pretty scene. He looked at his watch. One. They had been out now for over three hours. Simon was likely deciding to blow Going Home. A minute later, Simon raised his horn.

A short note, then a much longer one, almost a moan signalled the day's work was done. As one, the hounds turned their heads and looked towards Simon, who, remounting Polar Bear, called them to him with another blast of the horn.

Lucien gathered up Mockingbird's reins, readying to mount. Mockingbird swung away but with a quick hop he was in the saddle and finding the other stirrup, he spurred her into a gallop.

Simon and hounds in the lead, the field arranged themselves behind Eleanor for the ride home. Olivia and Hazel rode alongside each other and behind them, Gill and Xavier, like Olivia and Hazel, standing in their stirrups so their weight was off their tired horses' backs, did the same.

In the parking paddock, Jeffrey, curled up on Expresso's travelling rug, raised his head at the sound of the horn and clambered to his feet. India stowed her sketchbook in her bag.

'Want to walk for a while? We'd better put your lead on, though.'

Jeffrey set off purposely. A van with the Bombay Duck's Indian Runner duck stencilled on its door passed them, followed by a battered four-wheel drive and a Rolls-Royce. At the gate to the open country, Jeffrey pushed his way through the gathered knot of people and stood with his chest out and his head high. In the distance, a man in a red coat on a large white horse was cantering towards them, followed by a line of hounds. More riders came into sight, some waving.

Jeffrey started to shiver. India knelt and put her arms around him. He whimpered and pressed his head into her shoulder. The horses pounded past, making the ground shake. India thought she heard Olivia calling hers and Jeffrey's names.

Eleanor tied Elvis up to the baling twine on the side of the truck, loosened his girth and stepped into the tack compartment. The meet had gone perfectly. No broken bones, no delinquent hounds and except for Lucien (what did you expect!), everyone had behaved well. And now there was a yummy breakfast to look forward to; she was surprising Simon with one of Stephan's hampers.

'Time for a quickie?'

Lucien's lips were caressing her neck, his fingers unpinning her hunting tie.

'I might for the right person.'

Donnacha pulled Polar Bear to a stop. Lucien Blythe was walking away from Simon's truck. Seconds later, Eleanor appeared at the door of the tack compartment, patting down her hair and checking the buttons on her shirt.

He clicked Polar Bear into a trot and reached the truck just as Eleanor stepped out.

'Hope it was worth it?'

A look of fear crossed Eleanor's face, then she shrugged. 'Time will tell.'

'It usually does.' Donnacha thrust Polar Bear's reins into her hand, flinching as their fingers touched. 'Simon wants the hoss rubbed down and rugged.'

On the way back to the Whistlejacket truck, he saw a tall, fair girl with a dog in a red knitted coat. Jeffrey? It had to be. His mood lifted a little. He went to them.

'Hey, Jeffrey,' he said, patting Jeffrey's head and introducing himself to the girl. 'Donnacha, Donnacha Keough.'

'Ann Levy,' the girl said.

'Grace's granddaughter, of course. Great of you to come. Grace'd be chuffed you brought our friend here. He never missed a meet.' He smiled at Jeffrey, now pressing himself against his muddy boots. 'Wonderful to see you, fella.'

'We were just going,' India said. 'Jeffrey got upset when every-one came in on the horses. I think he was expecting Grace to be with them.'

'No, he knows she's gone. Animals know about death. He's just missing her. Like you, I imagine. You're not staying for the breakfast?'

'I told Jeffrey I'd take him home.'

'Best be off me, too. Have to see to the horses. Grand of you to bring Jeffrey.'

Whistlejacket's truck was only a few rows ahead. He quickened his step. Leila would be here soon, and he needed to get Mocking-bird cleaned up and settled.

He hurried around Xavier's float and stopped dead. Leila was here already. She was with Pan. His arms were around her and she was leaning against him. And bloody Sorrows was with them.

He wanted to run at them, smash Pan with his fists, throw Sorrows in the air, put his face in Leila's face and tell her he'd known all along. But he didn't. He turned on his heel and did what he always did. Went to the horses.

Mockingbird was sweat as thick as glue from ear to tail. Lucien hadn't even bothered to loosen her girth. Oyster too was looking, not miserable, but ready for a rub down. Which horse should he start with? If he hadn't just seen what he'd seen he'd have begun with Mockingbird. And what did he care if Leila started carrying on about the state of the poor beast. But for all the boiling blood in him, he couldn't leave her as she was. He stripped her down, got the thermos and emptied the steaming water into a half bucket of cold.

Losing himself as he did day after day in the smell of horse, the push of muscle against his own, the throbbing under his hands of the nobler of the kingdom's hearts, he drove the image of Leila and Pan Villon out of his thoughts. 'You'll be right, deerling,' he murmured to Mockingbird as she flinched away from the sponge. 'You'll be right. Let's get you sorted. I'll make you a mash when we get home.' The mare's lips were bloody and swollen, too sore for stalky hay.

'The truck's got Whistlejacket on the side,' Christie told Digger. 'And the rearing horse.'

'I know the frigging truck. My mares have been on it often enough. Hate to think what it cost to use the image,' Digger grumbled, trying to keep an eye on the road while looking out for Lucien's truck. 'Total waste of dosh. The agency could have come up with something for a poofteenth.'

'Lucien's related to Whistlejacket's owner,' Christie said. She had no idea if this was true, but it was impossible that someone as good-looking as Lucien could have come from ordinary stock.

She gasped as the Mercedes lurched though a deep rut. 'Christ, Dig, you'll do an axle.'

Digger checked the rear-view mirror to make sure that the Jack Russell and the child chasing it he had swerved to miss were still in one piece. They were, and better still, the child, wearing a Barbour jacket that came down to the tops of her gumboots, was now holding up the dog and kissing its nose.

Christie pointed. 'There's the truck.'

Noting the pretty flushing of her cheeks and the brightness of her eyes, he wondered how she would react when he said he thought it was time she had a kiddie. His other wives had all had at least one and with his grandchildren now popping out onto the scene every other day, Christie would have plenty of other young and youngish mothers to share the joy with.

'There's the Rolls,' Christie said, reaching into her bag for her compact.

'Only Lady B would drive a Phantom around a paddock,' Digger said approvingly. With her neat calves, sharp little suits and equally sharp claws, Lady Blythe reminded him of the first and undoubtedly the best of his wives.

Christie ran a critical eye over her face and hair. 'Careful,' she snapped as Digger braked as she was adding a touch of gloss to her slightly chaffed lips. Digger had insisted on a blow job before they left Whistlejacket and then again at Jottings. He must have had some Viagra stashed somewhere that her searches had failed to find. She snapped the compact shut. Lucien was opening the Rolls' door for his exquisite mother and she was out of the Merc almost before Digger had turned off the engine.

'Lady Blythe, what a pleasure.'

'Hello Christine,' Lady Blythe said, thinking that in her Hunter gumboots, baby pink twinset and diamonds Christie looked like an extra in a *Hello! Magazine* country spread. 'You found the property without any trouble?'

'Digger knows his way around a satnav like he knows his way around ...'

'A Kings Cross tart,' Lucien drawled. 'G'day, Dig.'

'G'day Luce.' Digger made a show of tipping the brim of an invisible hat. 'And g'day to you, Ladybird.'

Lady Blythe's smile was genuine: not only was Digger vastly older than her but he had put millions into Whistlejacket's coffers over the years.

'Digger, my dear. I hear you've bought Jottings. The house is seriously lovely and I hope this means we'll be seeing more of you.'

'You can see as much of me as you like,' Digger leered. 'Just say the word.'

Christ, Lucien thought, Mrs R must have put a bucket of Viagra in his coffee.

'How was the hunt, Luce?' Digger was asking.

'Mockingbird went like a dog. Leila's completely ruined her.'

'That's appalling, Lucien,' Christie exclaimed. 'You should sack her.'

'Might not be the horse's fault,' Digger said. 'Could be down to the sire. Those Commands can be a touch fiery. Great racehorse, though. Shame he turned up his toes when he did. There's only two of his colts about. Skilled and …'

Christie laid a silencing hand on his arm. 'It's too early in the day to be talking bloodlines, darling.'

'Never,' Lady Blythe said. 'It was me and Jonno's favourite breakfast topic.'

Christie attempted a placatory smile. 'I agree it's fascinating knowing who's out of whom …'

'Not to mention who's up whom,' Digger interrupted.

Christie raised her voice over Digger's and Lucien's laughter. 'But when Digger gets going, things can take a nasty turn, as you can see.'

'Where are we eating, darling?' Lady Blythe asked Lucien.

'With Simon and his lot,' Lucien answered, wondering if Eleanor would be able to meet his eyes. He put his arm around his mother and turned her until she was facing a dry-stone wall and some wide steps of similarly weathered stone. 'Up there on the lawn.'

'Perfect,' Lady Blythe said. 'I just love what Maggie and Nigel have done with the garden. It's so manageable.' She pushed Lucien's hands away. 'Do keep your distance darling. You smell like a bear pit.'

Lucien's phone rang and he looked down at the call screen, ready to switch off if it was Opal, who was clearly in a party mood. But it was Donnacha. Apologising, he turned away and took the call. A minute later he ended it.

'Donnacha's heading back to Whistlejacket.'

'Shame,' said Christie, who thought Donnacha lush.

'Rushing home to lovely Leila, I expect,' Digger said.

'Leila's here,' Lady Blythe said. 'I saw her.'

'He's asked for a couple of days off.'

'He probably wants to put some space between him and Leila,' Christie said. 'After seeing how Mockingbird went today, he'll know she's not the horsewoman she claims she is.'

Gill put her hand on India's arm. 'Stay and have some lunch.'

'You can't just drive all this way and then drive back,' Olivia said. 'Jeffrey'll get carsick.' Her eyes were vivid with adrenaline and wisps of her hair, freed from her braid floated about her face as she hopped from one booted foot to the other. 'I want to tell you about the hunt. Expresso was brilliant. We didn't have to go through one gate. He jumped everything.'

Gill smiled. 'You both did really well.' She patted Jeffrey's head, telling India, 'You can let him off the lead. The hounds are back in the truck.'

'I know all their names,' Olivia said. 'Every single one.'

'That's going a bit far,' Gill said.

Olivia glared at her. 'I do so. And the names of the ones in the kennels as well.'

'Jeffrey won't upset the horses?' India asked.

Olivia shook her head, making her braid whip around her head, loosening even more hair. 'They'll be pleased to see him. They're all old friends.'

India unclipped Jeffrey's lead. 'We met someone called Donnacha who knew Grace, and Jeffrey settled right down. He was a mess before that. I thought he might have been thinking he'd see Grace.'

'I certainly was,' Gill said. 'Every time someone rode up beside me, I thought it was her.'

Olivia took India's hand and pulled her over to Expresso, who was tied up next to her mother's mare, Hester. 'This is my horse. I've had him for two years, seven months, three weeks and five days.' She dragged Expresso off his hay and turned his head towards India. 'You can pat him if you like.'

India put out her hand and brushed Expresso's black nose.

'Careful,' Olivia said, as Expresso opened his mouth to sample India's fingers. 'He thinks you've got a treat.'

India withdrew her hand. 'I don't know much about horses.'

Olivia sniffed. 'I'd have thought they were in your blood. Didn't Grace teach you anything about them?'

India watched as Jeffrey licked Expresso's nose and Expresso blew gently out his nostrils into Jeffrey's face. 'There wasn't much opportunity. I was away at school and Grace and I used to go on trips in the term breaks. Or I went to camp or stayed at school.'

'I'll teach you to ride,' Olivia said. 'You can paint me and Expresso's portrait. Riding lessons are expensive, you know.'

Xavier and Hazel joined them, Hazel carrying folding chairs and Xavier an enormous Esky. 'India's painting me first,' Xavier said.

'I am?' India said.

Xavier put the Esky down with a sigh of relief. 'We can start tomorrow. I'll fill myself up with Nurofen and drape myself over Grace's chaise longue and be your best sitter ever. Mercy, I'm stiff.'

'Me too,' Hazel said. 'I'll have to get a note for school.'

'Me too,' Olivia said.

'It's always the same at the start of the season,' Gill said to India. 'A couple of weeks and we'll be hardened.'

India studied Gill's horse, trying to see the hidden musculature that gave her neck its look of power. The horse turned her head and met her gaze, hers as soft as felt.

'I'm starving, mum,' came Olivia's wail. 'It feels like breakfast was days ago.'

'I'll have to find out where Stephan's parked,' Xavier said. 'I ordered a hamper.'

'Mum was picking ours up on the way here,' Hazel said, her cheeks pink from the sun and the wind.

Olivia sighed. 'I wish we'd gotten a hamper. The Harts'll have a ginormous one. And one for their smelly dogs as well.'

Xavier poked her in the ribs. 'Hampers are for people who can't cook.'

Olivia watched her mother drag a worn wicker basket off the Prado's back seat. 'Hampers are for people who can afford them.'

'Mum can't even boil an egg,' Hazel said. 'One of the hairdressers at the salon makes my school lunches and does casseroles for our dinners. They're very tasty.'

Olivia prodded her. 'Come on. We want to be somewhere we can see everyone.'

'She means Lucien Blythe,' Hazel said to India under her breath.

18

Wirral's lawn was dotted with picnic tables and folding chairs. Ties off and shirts open at the neck, the hunters stretched their booted legs out in front of them and refreshed themselves with beer, wine and champagne. The sky was now a perfect crystalline blue. Magpies and parrots provided a steady stream of background song and chatter while an assortment of terriers and bitsers fought over food scraps and rumbled children that had escaped their parents' watch. Stephan's hampers were everywhere.

Olivia had found a spot with an unobstructed view of Simon's table. With Hazel looking out for her mother and brother Toby, her own mother unpacking the picnic basket and Xavier busy opening champagne, she undid another button of her shirt and pulled some more strands of her hair out of its plait and began arranging them around her face.

'I feel useless,' India said to no one.

'That's because you are,' Xavier told her with a grin.

She reached into her tote and brought out a wheel of brie and a punnet of strawberries. 'Maybe not completely,' she said and put them on the table. 'I nearly forgot these.'

'Gorgeous,' Gill said, immediately starting to hull the strawberries for the champagne.

'Thanks,' India said, accepting a glass from Xavier. She leaned back in the chair and gazed about the lawn at the people Grace had been joined to by horses.

Catching sight of her mother and brother, Hazel jumped to her feet and waved her arms. 'Over here, over here Toby.'

India studied Hazel's family as they made their way through the tables. In black jeans and cowboy boots and a bright yellow cardigan over a navy shirt, Hazel's mother looked as sharp as she had when she'd picked Hazel and Olivia up from Mars House. A pair of amber earrings broke the surgically straight line of her hair and jaw and her look was completed by one of those totes that cost as much as a small car. Hazel's brother had the same dramatic cheekbones, dark hair and light brown skin as his mother, but was closer in height and build to Hazel. He too, however, in a navy jumper and jeans and carefully draped camel scarf was sharply turned out.

Gill rose to greet them, signalling Olivia, Xavier and India to do the same. Xavier made room for the chairs Toby was lugging, along with an enormous hamper.

'Lady Blythe's hair looks nice, mum,' Hazel said, pointing at Simon's table and at Lady Blythe.

Vivienne took a quick peek at Lucien and then at Lady Blythe, whose hair looked exactly the same as it had when she'd arrived at Le Manoir this morning. Toby gave Hazel a hug, said 'How do you do,' to India and then he, Hazel and Olivia began going through Stephan's hamper with cries of delight.

Across the lawn at Simon's table, Lady Blythe said to Lucien, 'Who's the gal in the overcoat sitting next to Vivienne? 'She gestured at Gill's table. 'She looks familiar.'

'I don't know, ma,' Lucien said. 'She was at the Bombay Duck last night.'

'I didn't see her,' Christie said.

'She has to be a model,' Digger said. 'I wonder which agency she's with?'

'She looks grubby,' Christie said.

'She might be Toby's girlfriend,' Eleanor said. 'She's about the right age.'

Lady Blythe frowned. 'Toby doesn't have a girlfriend. He's giving all his attention to his studies. And Vivienne would have said if he was bringing a friend down.'

Sitting between Toby and Xavier, Olivia, thinking that Lucien had finally noticed her, loosed some more hair and sent hot stares in his direction. Following her gaze, Xavier noticed that Lucien, while appearing to listen to Digger Fahey, had his eyes on their table, on India. Watching some terriers fight over a bread roll, India seemed completely unaware. He shook his head. Had someone looked at him like that he would have burst into flames.

Leila couldn't believe it, the Whistlejacket truck was gone. She pulled out her phone and texted Donnacha. Where r u? She stood staring at the phone. The screen remained blank. She shuffled her feet, looked up at the sky, around at the trucks and floats and back at the screen. Nothing.

She squatted down next to Sorrows, who looked at her questioningly with his little black eyes. 'I don't know where he is,' she said. 'Maybe Lucien told him to take the horses home.' It was the only reason she could think of that he might have left.

She sat down on the grass next to Sorrows, her head again swimming. Pan had been nice when her legs had gone, but when her legs were steady again, she'd been so busy apologising and reassuring him she was okay she had missed the chance to tell him about Blue-Buckle. He was wanting to get his horse settled in the float for the trip home and much as she had wanted to, it had not felt right to keep him any longer.

After what seemed like an age, her phone chimed.

Heading bk

? Lucien told you to

Not in mood for fahlahdah

I'm coming back too

Don't bother going t gorge

Call me!!!!!

She put the phone in her lap and sat staring at it. The gorge, about an hour's drive from Burragong, was where Donnacha went to get away. She had gone with him once, spending an exhausting day on a rough narrow track that led down, ever down through rugged bushland to the river that, over millions of years, had created the spectacular slopes of the mighty gorge.

They had spent the night beside the river, their camp at the foot of a massive grey, water worn rock. In the morning, she had woken tight chested and anxious, feeling that for all its machines and technology and notions of progress, humanity was of little, if any, consequence. Clearly happy on the other hand, Donnacha had been bathing in the freezing river, the dark hair on his chest forming hard little curls.

Sorrows rested his muzzle on her thigh. If she left now, she might catch Donnacha before he took off. He'd be an hour at least unloading and settling the horses and unpacking and sweeping out the truck.

But what was the point?

She stood up and for a moment thought she was going to black out. She staggered towards the Forrester. It was warm in the car. Sorrows settled on the seat beside her, she leaned the seat back, closed her eyes and went to sleep.

Giving in to Hazel's and Olivia's nagging, Toby rose from the table. 'Okay, okay. We'll go and see the hounds. Want to come, Xavier?'

Xavier shook his head. 'I've seen enough of the hounds for today.'

Hazel took India's hand. 'You'll come, won't you AnnIndia?'

'She will,' Olivia said briskly. 'Is your phone charged, AnnIndia? You'll want some photos. They're very handsome. You might want to paint them. We'll go and see the horses too. I've saved Expresso a piece of banana cake. He's crazy for it.'

'My phone's dead again,' India said.

'Hopeless,' Olivia said. 'She's got no power at Mars House,' she told Toby.

'What make is your phone, India?' Toby asked. 'I've got a million car chargers in the glovebox.'

'Come on!' Hazel said. 'Before the truck goes.'

'Make sure you tell Toby and AnnIndia the name of all the hounds,' Gill said to Olivia.

Olivia looked at her nastily. 'If you don't believe that I know all their names, why don't you come and see for yourself?'

'Piss off, Liv,' Xavier told her.

Olivia, Hazel, Toby and India headed off. Gill sipped her champagne. 'I shouldn't have said that, but it's hard to resist winding her up sometimes. She never stops doing it to me.'

'It's such a difficult age,' Vivienne said, thinking that she had never seen Gill looking so tired and Olivia so out of control. Hazel was definitely due for a friend upgrade. 'For some girls,' she added.

Xavier patted his chest. 'Boys are so much easier.' He eased himself into a more comfortable position. 'It's fab to be back hunting, but I really am bloody stiff.'

Vivienne laughed, 'I didn't realise hunting was so exciting.' Xavier slapped her on the arm. 'You should come to Pilates,' she told him. 'It's brilliant for suppling the muscles. I've a routine I do every day.'

'I don't know how you find the time,' Gill said. 'Some days I'm flat out getting a minute to brush my hair.' She lifted her glass, refilled by Xavier, and took a large swallow. When she was transporting the horses, she usually only allowed herself just the one drink, but today ... She looked at Vivienne's sleek outline and smooth hair and skin. Maybe if she did a bit more with her appearance, Nicholas might be more interested in spending some time with his wife.

'But you've got the horses as well as the shop,' Xavier said, knowing that as the hunting season approached, Gill was up at five every morning to exercise Hester and Expresso.

Another bugbear of Nicholas', who claimed that her early morning starts cost him an hour at least of extremely vital rest. At least that was the excuse he often used when he rang to say he was staying in Sydney for the weekend, or, more recently, the semester break.

Gill downed the rest of her drink. 'Come on Xav. Let's go and find Toby and the girls.'

They were in a knot around Expresso, being lectured on his finer points by Olivia. Expresso, who had heard it all before, was giving his hay net his complete attention and Jeffrey was snoozing on a rug on the float's tailgate.

Seeing her mother, Hazel called out, 'Take some photos of us, mum. I'll get Dorothy.'

While Hazel fetched Dorothy, Olivia dragged Expresso off his hay and Vivienne took her phone out of her handbag and read her texts and email. Olivia prodded Toby. 'You and AnnIndia get in the middle. Stand close so we'll all be in the shot.'

'What about Jeffrey?' Hazel said, appearing with a rushed looking Dorothy.

'Get Jeffrey,' Olivia yelled at Xavier, still a little way off with Gill.

Xavier refused. 'He looks perfectly comfortable where he is. Anyway, he's asleep.'

'Come on,' Vivienne said impatiently.

At last everyone was lined up to Olivia's satisfaction, the unamused ponies positioned as bookends.

'Take another one,' Hazel instructed her mother as Vivienne went to put her phone back in her bag.

Vivienne raised her phone and then froze as a desperate shriek came from nearby, followed by the sound of pounding hooves and shouts of 'loose horse, loose horse'.

'Shit!' Xavier leaped sideways as a chestnut horse, the straps of its rug tangled around its back legs, galloped towards him and Gill.

Further spooked, the panicked horse propped and wheeled and trying to save itself from falling, lunged forward, catching Gill with its thrashing hooves.

Olivia and Hazel screamed.

Xavier jumped at the horse's head and latched on to its halter and dragged it away from Gill, now lying motionless on the ground.

Olivia ran to her mother, joining Toby, who was already kneeling at her side. 'Mum, mum. Are you okay?'

'I think I've broken my leg,' Gill managed to gasp.

'Keep still,' Toby told her. 'Call triple zero,' he yelled at his mother.

'Mum,' Olivia shrieked, tears running down her face.

'Get a lead rope so I can tie this bugger up,' Xavier said to Hazel. The horse, having kicked off the rug, was now standing quietly, blowing out through its reddened nostrils and resting one of its hind legs.

'Your mum'll be okay,' Toby told Olivia. 'But we all need to stay calm.' He put his hand on Gill's shoulder. 'Mrs Findlay, you need to lay still until the ambulance gets here. Completely still.'

'I'm calling dad,' Olivia told her mother.

Gill reached for her hand. 'Truly, angel, except for my leg I'm okay. And I'm sure that's nothing really bad.'

'Dad should've been here,' Olivia sobbed. 'It wouldn't have happened if he'd been here. I'm going to call him.'

'No,' Gill said, struggling to take back her hand, which Olivia was holding onto with both of hers. The jolt that ran through her body caused white hot pain to flood her leg. God, what if it was really damaged? What if she couldn't ride anymore? 'Don't ... don't call your father,' she moaned, then fainted.

Olivia screamed.

'We need a blanket,' Toby said urgently.

'I've got a space blanket,' Xavier said and set off at a run for his float.

Having made sure that Jeffrey was safely tied up, India went to Olivia, and with a brief glance at Gill's grey face, gently but firmly pulled her to her feet.

'Come on, Toby's a doctor. We'd better keep out of his way.'

'An ambulance is coming,' Vivienne said. 'We need someone at the gate to show them where to turn. 'We'll go,' said two women who had rushed to help.

'See if one of you can find out who owns that bloody horse,' Xavier said, tossing Toby the space blanket.

'Is Gill okay?' Vivienne asked Toby.

Toby tucked the space blanket around Gill. 'She's gone into shock.'

19

Leila pulled up in front of Whistlejacket's gates and rummaged in the door pocket for the remote control. Staff were supposed to only use the back entrance, but last season in a moment of confusion caused by trucks from different studs arriving at the same time, Beef had given her a control. Beef had never asked for it back and she'd hung onto it because the gates fascinated her. But she had never used it. Now, however, she was just in the mood and if she was sacked for it, all the better.

Seeming to rise and spread like the wings of an angel, the gates opened soundlessly. She drove out of their shadow and into the crimson tunnel of the Claret Ash trees. She drove slowly, taking in the sight of the homestead and its manicured surrounds, the stone pillared pergola, the planters of olive trees and sandstone seated pool. It was like a movie set; if this was her last day at Whistlejacket she would at least have this memory.

The driveway split and without having to think, she veered towards the cottage. Donnacha's ute was gone. She scooped up Sorrows and squeezing him past the steering wheel, dropped him out onto the ground so he could have a pee. But instead of relieving himself, he sniffed about where the ute was usually parked and headed briskly for the cottage.

She climbed stiffly out of the Forrester and set off in the direction of the yards.

Oyster was pushing around a biscuit of lucerne in his paddock. He wandered over and positioned himself alongside the fence for a scratch. She looked about for Mockingbird in case Donnacha had turned her out with Oyster. Oyster was on his own.

She found her at last in the hospital stable block, pressed against the back wall of the stall, the corners of her mouth badly swollen, her eyes black with fear and bewilderment.

'You're okay,' she said, gently undoing the stable rug chest strap. 'You're okay.'

But Mockingbird was far from okay. Her flanks were a mess of welts and ripped and broken skin. Blood and serous fluid oozed through the salve that had been liberally applied and the muscles around the wounds twitched as though under attack from biting insects. Her eyes had not told the whole story.

The whiteboard in the stable office read:

STALL 11 BAY MARE
- Penicillin 5 d commenced today pm
- Bute 5ml am pm 3 d
- Lacerations flanks bd clean, Neocort, lips Vaseline
- Stall rest 4 d, Cherry review if off feed or sign of wound or other infection.

<u>LUCIEN BLYTHE NOT TO GO NEAR</u>, she added with the whiteboard pen.

Sorrows greeted her at the back door of the cottage with an indifferent shrug. He was the least animated dog she had ever known. His walk was slow, or if there was a need for speed, a little faster, but not much and he never ran and when his dinner was put in front of him, he would sigh as if he was being asked to martyr himself. His greetings also were a muted affair – a quick glance from under his eyebrows did the job just fine. When she had joked to Donnacha that he had gotten his dourness from his master, Donnacha had claimed that it was the other way around.

She took a beer from the fridge and some Nurofen from the cupboard and sat down at the kitchen table. Sorrows would be strolling from room to room pretending that his wandering was aimless, that he wasn't checking out where in the cottage Donnacha had last been. She, however, would not stoop to the same. And as much as she wanted to, she would not, like Sorrows, lay down in the spot where Donnacha's scent was the strongest and content herself with a fading trace of him until he reappeared.

The beer finished and the Nurofen having kicked in, she set off for the dorm house.

The only building on the acreage when it first was acquired by Lady Blythe, the old shearing shed, now clad with blue corrugated iron, had been made comfortable with a wide veranda and a roomy sitting room and eat-in kitchen. Either side of the added central hallway were eleven double and single bedrooms, some of which had originally been holding pens for the sheep waiting their turn with the shearer. His and her amenities blocks provided showers, toilets and washing machines. Compared to the backpacker hostels many of the staff had stayed at on their travels, herself included, the dorm was a luxury hotel.

Walking down the hallway, she smelt wood smoke and heard muffled taunts. The boys had lit a fire and dug in to watch a footy match.

She stopped at the very last room and holding her breath, tried the door handle. The door was still locked. She took the key out of her pocket and opened it.

Except for the fact that someone had been screwing in the bed, the room was just as she'd left it. Something at least had gone her way today. She went to the door that led onto the veranda. Sure enough, the latch was loose. If she begged, Beef might fix it this afternoon.

She pushed the soiled sheets onto the floor, sat on the bed and pulled out her phone. Half past three. No way would Donnacha make it down to the river by dark. He'd have to camp on the side of the gorge and if there was the slightest bit of wind, he wouldn't be able to light a fire.

I hope your balls freeze, you bastard.

Out the window, she glimpsed Lady Blythe's Rolls heading towards the homestead. If Janet Reedhead had seen her coming through the front gates, she might be unemployed sooner than later. Donnacha said it was rubbish and knowing Beef you'd never think it, but some thought Janet Reedhead was Lady Blythe's personal spy.

Suddenly the thought of being booted from Whistlejacket filled her with panic. Burragong was her home. What would she do? Where would she go? She had friends here. There were the yearlings she had been working so hard to civilize. And Mockingbird. She couldn't just leave her. Or BlueBuckle. She'd better get what she'd written about Lucien off the whiteboard in the stables. She might be able to talk her way out of using the front gates – she'd say one of the yearlings had caused her bruises and she'd felt too faint to make it to the other gate – but there'd be no explaining away the comment about Lucien.

Lady Blythe told Martin that Lucien would drive her home and popped out of the Rolls and up the steps to the front door, which Janet Reedhead was holding open for her. Inside, she paused, as she always did, to admire the life-size painting of the rearing stallion that dominated the entrance hall. Most people seeing it, assumed that it was the original, and she never bothered to correct them.

She greeted Janet Reedhead not quite but almost as though she were the lady of the house: in these times of eight-hour days and thirty-eight-hour weeks, a housekeeper that put the wants of her employer above her own was as rare as a faithful husband, and to be similarly appreciated.

'How was the hunt?' Janet returned, smoothing an imagined crease out of her donkey brown skirt.

Though there was ten years difference (in Janet's favour), and one was as thin as a piece of string and the other possessed of the physique of a shotput thrower, the two women appeared of similar vintage. Within a month of becoming Whistlejacket's housekeeper, Janet had had her wispy brown plait severed at her shoulders and was forcing what remained into her own version of a Maggie Thatcher comb-back. She had also swapped her usual kilt and puffy sleeved knits for skirts and cardigans of similar lines to those worn by Lady Blythe. And while her wage did not stretch to similarly fine fabrics, the silk scarf with which she artfully set off the day's outfit went some way to compensating for the manufactured fibres of her uniform.

'There was an accident. Not on the field, during the breakfast. Gill Findlay's got a broken leg.'

Janet's eyes shone with interest. 'What an awful thing. What will happen to the shop?'

'I suppose it depends how bad the leg is. Though whatever the case, she'll be off her feet for some weeks. A loose horse ran over her in the carpark. The paddock, rather. Lucien is going by the hospital with Simon then dropping him home. Simon's not fit to drive. He was knocking it back at the breakfast.'

'I suppose it's a strain being Master of Hounds,' Janet said in Simon's defence. 'Especially at the beginning of the season when you don't know how the hounds are going to go.' She liked Simon. He always made a point of asking her how she was when he visited Whistlejacket and one time when he'd gone to the Masters' Ball in New York with Lucien, he had brought her back a Hermes scarf, a genuine one.

'Lucien manages without writing himself off,' Lady Bligh said, then requested a tea tray in the office. 'No, make it coffee,' she decided. She wanted to have her mind absolutely clear when Lucien returned. 'And send Lucien straight over when he gets back. We're going to look at the new stallion.'

'Brian says he's very unsettled,' Janet said. (Never would anyone catch her calling her husband by his disgusting nickname. He was Brian, or when things got playful, Mr Reedhead.)

Lady Blythe turned on her. 'Unsettled? Lucien hasn't said anything about the stallion being unsettled.'

Seeing from Lady Blythe's expression that she was in a complicating mood, Janet backpedalled. 'Now I think about it, it wasn't the new stallion Brian was talking about, it was some other horse. I do get them all muddled.' She bore Lady Blythe's scrutiny without flinching, then, with a curtsey-like bob, said, 'Coffee in the office,' and quickly beat it for the kitchen.

The office, a rendered building that housed the stud records, its employees as well as the horses, was the weekday domain of Pauline Bowen, Whistlejacket's secretary, or Operations Manager as she preferred to be called. Known as Pinkie because her style echoed that of the famous rock singer – muscular body, short bleached hair, large green eyes and husky voice – Pinkie favoured groin high skirts and tank tops that allowed her to display her lush cleavage. Lady Blythe sat at the desk, switched on the computer and opened the email, noting the enquiries about stallion services, foaling down, accounts and requests for employment. She clicked on the bookings calendar and saw with satisfaction that Speed, Birdie and Stanislas each had a solid book of mares for the coming season. The new stallion, BlueBuckle, had bookings already too, even though his profile had not yet gone up on the website. She must remind Kevin to get onto it. As well as being hers and Whistlejacket's accountant, Kevin also managed the website.

The phone call register showed similar enquiries to the emails and if Pinkie's comment beside each was truthful, all appeared to have been satisfactorily answered. She extracted the bills to be paid and staff timesheets from the intray, flipped through both and put them aside for Kevin.

There was a tap at the door and Janet Reedhead followed with the coffee and some almond biscotti.

'All in order, no doubt,' she said, putting down the tray. Pinkie was her gossip partner and they reported to each other sometimes hourly, meeting up in the kitchen over something from the pantry or just from the oven.

Lady Blythe opened a drawer and pointed to the litter of chocolate wrappers threatening escape onto the floor.

'Except for this.'

'The clients send them to her,' Janet said, defending her young friend. 'It's a mystery how she keeps her figure.'

Lady Blythe sighed. 'Am I the only one who isn't a fan of Pinkie's?'

'I'll have a word,' Janet said.

'Sooner than later. Every single pen is sticky.'

'Sooner than later,' Janet repeated, making a mental note to give the office a good wipe over first thing in the morning. The pens as well.

Once more alone, Lady Blythe took a sip of the coffee and pushed it aside, it not being scalding as she liked. If Lucien wasn't back soon it would be too late to have BlueBuckle brought down from the yard. Perhaps she should ask Beef to fetch him? But that would annoy Lucien, who preferred his senior staff not to be called on Sundays unless it was for a scheduled event such as the Stallion Parade.

Oh well, the stallion was only one of the reasons she had come back to Whistlejacket. And definitely the lesser one. She looked at her watch. Lucien couldn't still be at the hospital! Perhaps he'd stopped at Simon's, maybe to put him to bed? Lord knows Eleanor wouldn't manage on her own.

She pressed his number on her phone and when he answered, asked him when he'd be home. 'Gill had just returned from xray and they were waiting to see her,' he said. Then he'd be on his way.

Too late to bring the stallion down but in plenty of time otherwise.

20

Gill watched groggily as the older of two nurses, a sharp faced woman with a long thin grey plait, started shooing everyone out of the room.

'You can come back in after we've got Mrs Findlay into bed and done her obs. We'll only be a few minutes.'

'I'm not going,' Olivia shrieked. 'You can't make me. She's my mother.'

Grey plait rolled her eyes. The younger nurse, who, in her navy-blue scrubs still managed to look like she'd stepped off a Milan catwalk, appealed for help.

India went to Olivia and gently turned her towards the door. 'Come on, the nurses just want to get your mother comfortable. They won't be long.'

Olivia let herself be led out of the room. The others followed. Outside, Olivia latched onto India's arm. 'I think I'm going to faint. I'm calling dad.'

'Mrs Findlay said not to,' Toby told her. 'Anyway, how can you call your father if you're in a faint?'

'I am going to faint,' Olivia insisted.

'You're probably hyperventilating,' Toby said. 'Breathe from below your navel. Slowly.'

India put her arm around Olivia's shoulders. 'Mum will be okay.'

Now there's a real duckling, Simon thought, staring at India.

I wonder if they'd let me see the xrays?' Toby said. 'At least then we'd know how bad the break is.'

'It wouldn't hurt to ask someone,' Vivienne said. 'You are a doctor.'

'I'll come with you,' Xavier volunteered.

'Could you get a drink for Olivia?' India asked. 'Something sweet. Chocolate milk, maybe.'

'Iced coffee?' Olivia said hopefully.

Toby shook his head. 'Coffee's the last thing you need.'

'And one for me, too,' said Hazel. 'I feel faint, too.

'Perhaps we should go,' Vivienne said. The last place she wanted to spend the afternoon was Burragong hospital, but Hazel and Toby had insisted they come.

'You see about the xrays,' Simon said to Toby, 'and I'll go to the café.' Maybe he could get a pie, something to soak up the champagne and wine sloshing nauseatingly about his stomach. But having thought that, he dropped onto a chair under the window.

At that moment the door of Gill's room opened and Grey plait appeared. They could go back in, for a minute only. Mrs Findlay was very tired and needed to rest.

Despite the nurse's caution, Olivia fell sobbing on her mother's pillow. 'Who'll look after the horses? How am I going to get to school? Where am I going to stay tonight?'

Vivienne stepped up to the bed. 'You can stay with us and go to school with Hazel until your mum gets home.' It was a sacrifice, but the circumstances considered, one that was needed.

Olivia lifted a tearstained face out of the pillow. 'What about the Cairns?'

'They can come too. We'll drop by your house and pick them up with your things.' Thinking that they could now leave, Vivienne looked around for Toby, but he wasn't in the room and nor was Xavier. They must have gone to see about the xrays after all.

'Thanks Vivienne,' Gill said. 'I'll be up and about soon, I'm sure.' She grimaced. The shot they had given her for pain in the ambulance was starting to wear off. The nurses had told her to ring if she needed something more, but she was reluctant while Olivia was there.

'I'll take the horses,' Simon offered.

He looks worse than I feel, Gill thought. Absolutely shattered. His face was puffy and his eyes were dazed and his shirt, which had come adrift from the waistband of his breeches, had a trail of wine stains down the front.

'Thanks, but Xavier's going to keep an eye on them,' she said. 'They're up the road from his parents' nursing home. I just hope I don't miss the whole season.' It was a truly depressing thought.

Simon dropped a kiss on her cheek. 'You'll be up and about soon.'

She turned away from his acidic breath and caught a glimpse of hurt in his eyes. She gave his hand a squeeze. 'The hounds were brilliant today,' she said weakly.

'Come on, Simon,' Lucien said, coming into the room – he'd been in the waiting room watching the races. 'Ma's waiting for me at Whistlejacket. She sends her love, Gill,' he fibbed. He smiled at India. 'Ah, the coat girl.'

Somehow Gill found the strength to introduce them.

Lucien nodded. 'Of course, Grace Levy's granddaughter. I thought you looked familiar. My mother was a great fan of your grandmother's.'

'Oh,' India said. In his breeches and long leather boots, gold buttoned yellow vest and white collarless shirt, Lucien made her think of one of those military patricians whose acts of killing and conquering appeared not to have touched their souls.

Simon and Lucien gone, Olivia slumped on the chair beside her mother's bed and took her hand. 'Please let me call dad. He might come and stay. Maybe he'll look after the shop.'

Gill almost laughed. Nicholas had been against the business from the beginning, saying she was wasting herself and money they didn't have buying it. In truth, she suspected he was against it because the idea of his wife having a shop déclassé.

'I'm afraid Blooming Beautiful will have to close for a while, angel.'

'But what about the rent?' Olivia cried. 'How can we pay the rent if the shop's closed?' She grabbed India's hand. 'AnnIndia'll look after it. She knows about the till and everything and Julie Rice will buy the flowers and do the arrangements. She won't mind. She still buys the flowers sometimes anyway. And I'll come every day after school and help. Hazel too …'

'Olivia your mother needs to rest,' Vivienne interrupted. Under no circumstances would Hazel be going to Blooming Beautiful after school.

'Good news, Mrs Findlay,' Toby said from the doorway. 'The break's clean so you won't need surgery. You'll be back on your legs in six weeks or so. You should have a scan for osteoporosis, though. And think about a vitamin D supplement.'

Gill's eyes flooded with tears. Things were awful, but not as awful as she had feared. 'Thank you. Thank you so much. How did you find out?'

Xavier was gazing at Toby admiringly. 'There was a white coat on the back of a chair in the nurse's station. He put it on and pretended to be the new Registrar and got the password for the computer.'

<h1 style="text-align:center">21</h1>

'Darling, you're home at last,' Lady Blythe said, uncrossing her eyes. With nothing left to do in the office, she had gone back to the house, settled in the library with a biography of Winx and fallen asleep.

While his mother pushed her hair into shape and discretely checked her chin for drool, Lucien picked up the book, fallen on the floor, and put it on top of the pile of *Bluebloods* on the games table next to the arm of the sofa. Next month the illustrious racing magazine would feature BlueBuckle as its star stallion. He grimaced, wondering if it was too late to get the story cancelled.

He forced a smile. 'Will I ask Janet to bring some tea? She's bound to be lurking.'

Lady Blythe shook her head and patted the cushion beside her. 'No, come and sit.'

He remained standing. Next to the *Bluebloods* was the jade bowl his father had used as an ashtray. He picked it up and carried it over to its pair on the table under the window.

'What are you doing with that bowl?' Lady Blythe demanded.

'Putting it out of the way. It stinks.'

'Your father did so enjoy playing the barbarian with beautiful things.'

Lucien looked at his mother, but her expression gave no clue as to how to interpret what she had said.

'Talking of stink,' he said. 'I need a bath. The hounds were all over me when I was putting them in the truck.' He had not been near the hounds during or after the hunt but was nervous that his mother might pick up the smell of sex lingering about his groin. (Lying in a hot tub with a large whisky and thinking about being up close with Eleanor would be almost as lush as the moment itself.)

Lady Blythe admired her son's legs; nothing showed off a man's figure, or lack of in Simon Sinclair's case, like a well-cut pair of breeches.

'Nonsense, you don't smell one bit. Must have been all that disinfectant at the hospital. Do come, come and sit. Though I wouldn't mind a G&T. I suppose it's too late now to go and see BlueBuckle.'

Lucien made a show of looking out window. 'It is, rather. It'll be dark soon. Sorry I was away so long, but I couldn't let Simon drive to the hospital. The last thing the hunt needs is for him to go DUI. It would be the end of the season for everyone, not just Gill.' Protecting the hunt had been the furthest thing from his mind when he'd offered to drive Simon. It had given him the perfect excuse to avoid showing BlueBuckle to his mother. And tomorrow, thank god, she was off to Sydney for the opera and her monthly tune-up, as she drolly called her visits to her plastic surgeon.

Feeling slightly more relaxed, he said, 'A gin and tonic sounds magic. I might go one myself. Where's the tray?'

'Janet must have taken it for polishing. She'll have everything in the pantry. But don't let her make the drinks,' Lady Blythe cautioned as Lucien headed out the door. 'She gets the mix wrong.'

When Lucien returned, Lady Blythe had drawn the curtains and turned on the lamps, making the room's blue grey walls glow softly. Of Whistlejacket's rooms this was her favourite, not in the least because of the Munnings. The stunning painting of a spent racehorse heading back to the paddock had come from a friend's estate in lieu of years of outstanding fees. Luckily for Jonno, the friend's family had had no interest in horses. But besides the Munnings, the library also contained every book ever written about the greats of the track: Crucifix, Grand Flaneur, Red Rum, Man O'War, Phar Lap, Cobweb... Many of the books she had read to Lucien at bedtime or in the air travelling from country to country and she liked to think that the weave of names and bloodlines of these greats was part of the fabric of their relationship.

Lucien returned with two long glasses, handed one to his mother and instead of joining her on the sofa, dropped into an armchair and crossed his legs to contain the scent rising from his groin.

'I've told Janet to shove off home to Beef,' he said. 'Which opera are you going to?' The question was asked coolly. No matter how much his mother blasted his ears with it, he had never yet discovered opera's attractions.

'La Traviata. Don't look so bored, darling, it adds years to your face.'

Lucien laughed and Lady Blythe joined in, saying, 'Don't you love it when we're alone together, when it's just you and me.'

Lucien sipped his drink. Arriving home from school on Friday nights and curling up with his mother on the sofa, often in this room, had been the best part of the week. When she had started to push him away, as mothers should, at first further down the sofa and then into an armchair, such as the one where he now sat, it had been unbearable. Unforgivable.

'Always. By the way, I'm selling that mare, Mockingbird. Leila's completely ruined her.'

Lady Blythe tucked up her legs and rested one arm along the back of the sofa. 'Donnacha said Leila has a very good seat, but I rather think it wasn't her seat on a horse he was referring to. I went to Dr Shepherd on Friday.'

'Everything okay?'

'Not exactly. She thinks I may have a fatty liver.'

'Sounds unpleasant. What's the deal?'

'I'm not sure,' Lady Blythe said vaguely. 'She wants me to have some more blood tests and some test under anaesthetic that sounds nasty. I told her I'd think about it when I get back from Sydney.'

'Perhaps you should see someone else while you're up there.'

Lady Blythe shook her head. 'No need, I have perfect confidence in Dr Shepherd.' Which she did have. She had not, however, thought the doctor at all serious when she had suggested she give up champagne and dining out and take up some form of exercise. She looked pensive. 'A fatty liver … It sounds sordid, doesn't it. Not at all what one would want attached to one's name for all eternity.' She gave a grim little smile. 'But it has made me think about certain things.'

'In particular?'

'Marriage.'

'Marriage! You've met someone?'

'Of course not. I meant it when I told your father I'd saved the best till last. One hundred percent.' Emphasizing the point, Lady Blythe fanned the air with her left hand, making the knuckle sized diamond with which Jonno had proposed shoot blue and yellow sparks about her ear. 'No. I was thinking about you, darling. I was thinking that it's time you were married.'

Feeling suddenly as though his balls were in a vice worse than that of Christie's fingers, Lucien uncrossed his legs. 'Me?'

'Yes, you. Lots of people get married, you know. At least once. Usually more than once.'

'You want me to get married?'

'Now you're sounding like you've got a speech impediment.'

Feeling paranoid, Lucien wondered if his mother had somehow seen the photos from Opal on his phone or knew about him slipping into the horse truck with Eleanor.

'Sit up darling,' she said. 'You look like a worm on a hook.'

'I am, aren't I?'

Lady Blythe smiled. 'I suppose you are in a way.' For all of Lucien's success in running Whistlejacket, she still controlled the finances. Lucien received a generous allowance from the stud but beyond this, he had no fortune of his own. That at least, Jonno had gotten right.

'And I'm ready for grandchildren. A doubleton at least.'

Lucien returned from dropping his mother at Le Manoir and seeing the glow of a cigarette in the shadowy depths of the pergola, got a couple of beers from the kitchen fridge.

'Thanks man,' Beef said as Lucien handed him one. 'Lady mother all tucked in?'

Lucien sat in the wicker chair out of the way of the smoke from Beef's cigarette and planted his heels on the edge of the table then dropped them again and crossed his feet under the chair. His mother had agreed to him having a quick shower before he drove her home, but thoroughly rattled, he had forgotten socks and his ankles were freezing. Beef on the other hand, as impervious to the weather as to Mrs R's nagging about his appearance, had on his usual outfit of a shapeless short sleeved shirt that covered his tummies, shorts, work boots and washed out Wallabies football socks. Comfort was his governing principle, as he said often. It was why he ate what he did, wore what he did, and kept the woman he did.

Lucien swallowed down half his beer. 'More likely she's roaming Le Manoir's hallways thinking about wedding invitations and babies' names. She wants me to get married. And she wants grandchildren.'

'Has she got someone in mind?'

'Not that she's said. But she'll have a list, I'd lay a grand on it.'

'You'll be like that bloke on *The Bachelor*, wining and dining all these glam birds so as to fillet out Miss Right.' Beef took a thoughtful pull on his cigarette. 'I'd like to see that list, so I would.'

'Jesus, Beef, you really know how to lift a bloke's spirits.'

Beef butted out the cigarette on the sole of his boot and slipped the end into a matchbox. 'There are worse things than being married.' What people didn't know about Mrs R was that under that pantomime outfit she insisted on wearing, was a body of milky white firmness, and stroked just the right way, she purred like a Persian cat. All that and she could cook a chop the way a man liked it.

He put the matchbox in his pocket. 'What I'm saying is that the wedded state's got its upsides if you're willing to take the bad with the good.' Something you've never had to do, boyo, he thought, yours having been the golden path. 'Littlies are fun. And it's all right when they grow up, too.' He and Mrs R had two girls, both now in good jobs.

Lucien stared into the dark. 'I can't get my head around it.'

'Kids make a man of you,' Beef said. 'Each in their own way,' he finished.

'You sound just like ma. Have you two had your heads together?'

'Nasty about Gill Findlay,' Beef said, his radar for changing the subject picking up a strong signal.

'That's it for her for the season. Send her across some hay for the horses. A couple of round bales.'

'I'll organise it in the morning.' For all his spoilt ways, Lucien did have a heart, Beef thought. Shame it was buried under a tonne of dross. He trickled the last of his beer down his throat.

'Leila's back in the dorm by the way. I fixed the door for her. She didn't know about Gill. She got all upset. But she wasn't looking too good herself. Nasty bruises on the side of her face. Must have taken a tumble somewhere.'

'She was fine last night. She waited on our table at the Bombay Duck. Do you think Donnacha hit her?'

'Never!'

'You know he's taken a couple of days off.'

Beef nodded. He had seen Donnacha when he was putting his backpack in his ute.

'They must be on the rocks,' Lucien continued. 'She might need a friendly shoulder.'

Beef shook his head. 'A good night's sleep's what she needs,' he said sternly. Good thing he'd fixed that door. Hopefully she'd thought to lock it.

'Mockingbird's totally screwed,' Lucien said.

Beef made no comment. He had seen the mare with Leila, floating with the lightness and turn of a swallow. He'd also seen her this afternoon, jittery and wounded not just in body but in spirit.

'You should be getting to bed,' he said after a while. 'There's a crowd coming at nine to look at the stallions and with Donnacha away it'll be you and me doing the lead up.'

Lucien took his phone out of his pocket; while he'd been sitting with Beef it had been vibrating almost nonstop. He scrolled through the call log. Christie, Christie, Christie, Christie, Opal, Isobel. Isobel? Ah yes, the Minister for Planning and Public Spaces' wife. Christ, that was going back. Xavier – what could he want? Christie, Christie ... Nothing from Eleanor.

He swallowed the last of the beer. Leila and Donnacha were never going to last. He might just take himself over to the dorm and tell her, give her a shoulder to cry on and offer a bit of distraction. He quickly changed his mind. Donnacha would be straight out the gate if he found out and with the serving season coming up he couldn't risk it. He shook his head. It had never mattered that the woman he desired was the girlfriend, wife, daughter or mother of a friend, but here he was turning off his manager's probably ex. He crushed the beer can. Christ, his mother must have really rattled him.

22

Donnacha made the last hour of the descent with only the moon and his torch to light the way. Luckily, the moon was almost full and the track had been used enough over summer to stop it becoming overgrown.

His campsite was an area of river beach that sat flat and smooth in the crook of the river and was bounded on one side by a cluster of massive rocks. Carved by water from the walls of the gorge, the rocks cast a shadow on the white sand that made him think of a gathering of giants. As he had done in his boyhood, he made a fence around his camp but instead of rocks and bracken, this enclosure was of driftwood from the riverbank: branches worn smooth and bleached by tumbling currents. He planted one of the larger branches at the base of the rocks and lay his swag there so that in the morning his head would be shaded and if he woke in the night he would not feel completely alone.

He sat and wrapped his arms around his knees, his back to the sentinel rocks. A star dropped down the sky, plummeting to extinction in an arc of white fire. He screwed the top off the bottle of Guinness and unwrapped one of the pies he'd filched from the hamper left on the tailgate of the truck parked next to Whistlejacket's. A stone's throw away the river sang its journeying songs in soft, low tones. His breath deepened and his eyelids began to droop as he drank, ate and listened to the river.

He woke with a start. The river had fallen silent, the stars shone so brightly in the black of infinity that it hurt his eyes to look at them. He rose stiffly, slid into the swag and closed his eyes.

But this time the longed-for oblivion did not come. The devils of jealousy rose up out of his heart and began their play. He seesawed between murderous rage and desolation. A vision of Leila and Pan Villon, naked and entwined blotted out the stars. He stood at their feet with a knife … He was draped with beautiful women, writhing women. Looking on, Leila was sobbing. An old man with his name, bent, bitter and alone, spat, and kept on spitting.

He started up out of the swag. He shouldn't have run. He had left the way clear for Villon. He should have stood his ground, he should have fought.

Maybe it was not too late.

But it was.

He was a fool, a fool, a fool. The word swirled in and about his head like confetti in a hurricane. His heart cracked and all the happiness he'd recently known leeched into the darkness.

Mid-afternoon the next day, having climbed back up the side of the great gash in whose depths he had spent the night, Donnacha decided to stop in at Simon's to see how the hounds had pulled up after the hunt.

With its neatly fenced paddocks, well-placed dams and preserved stands of bush Simon's property was orderly and pretty and somehow, he had managed to get planning permission for the stables to be attached to the house. The six stalls and a tack and feedroom formed the shorter arm of the L-shaped building and in front of this ran a low stone wall, perfect for sitting on and enjoying the view, which included a small lake surrounded by weeping Maples.

As he drove up towards the house, he could see the heads of Simon's and Eleanor's hunt horses hanging out over their stable doors. That was odd. Unless they were lame or injured in some other way, they were turned out early the morning after a hunt so they could move about and counter any stiffness from the meet.

He followed the driveway around the back of the house and pulled up beside the hunt truck.

'Where's the boss?' he asked the drum-tummied Jack Russell that sauntered up to sniff his ankles as he got out of his vehicle. Getting no answer, he headed for the house.

Simon was slumped at the kitchen table, a bottle of Stoli at his elbow. He raised his head and squinted at Donnacha.

'Ellie's gone.' Simon's reddened eyes filled with tears and he sloshed some vodka into the glass he was clutching. 'She's left me.'

Donnacha took the glass out of Simon's hand and deposited it with the bottle on the bench. 'Jesus, man, the hosses are still in the stable!'

Tears now flowing freely down his face, Simon shook his head. 'She's not coming back. I woke up and she was gone.' He looked around for his glass. 'Where's my drink? I need a drink. Ellie's gone.'

'Drink's the last thing you need.'

Simon dropped his head onto his folded arms. A series of soft snores followed.

Donnacha went to the living room and took out his phone. Beef answered after a couple of rings. All was quiet, he reported. The staff had all turned up for their shifts, and despite the instructions that Mockingbird was to stay on stable rest, he'd turned her out with Oyster. She was clearly feeling cooped up. He'd put white ointment over the lacerations on her flanks and more Vaseline on her poor lips and changed her stable rug to a cotton one to keep any insects off her wounds. Hopefully, seeing her out grazing Leila would think all was right with her.

'No,' said Beef. 'Eleanor Lonsdale was not at Whistlejacket as far as he knew. Blythe was alone in his office. He'd been there all morning. 'Why are you calling? You're meant to have gone bush.'

'Changed my mind,' Donnacha said, keeping the fact that he'd been unable to stand his own company to himself. The fact that he needed to be busy. That as far as Leila was concerned, it was Leila who? If she still had her things in the cottage, if she hadn't moved them to Villon's already, he'd bunk in the dorm until she did. It had been fun while it lasted but Whistlejacket was his patch.

'I'm at Gwynedd.'

'We need to think about that stallion.'

'Which stallion?'

'BlueBuckle,' Beef said impatiently.

Donnacha remembered that he had BlueBuckle's yard camera feed on his phone but had not checked it since just before the hunt, yesterday. Bloody women, they made you forget what was important.

'He's not gone down, has he?'

'No. Could any minute though.'

Well one thing was certain, Pan fecking Villon wouldn't be going anywhere near him. 'We'll go and see him when I get back. I shouldn't be more than a couple of hours. I have to see to the hunt horses.' Please God Simon hadn't forgotten the hounds as well.

He ended the call and stood looking at the portrait of Simon's wife, Rebecca on the wall next to the fireplace. She was wearing jodhpurs and a green rugby top and standing beside a bay horse. Her face was weathered, her hair, pulled back in a ponytail, grey. Her gaze held his unflinchingly, there were laughter lines at the corners of her lips. Standing eye to eye with her now, he felt sad that he had only known her as a ravaged, dying woman. A country girl, she had left the country for the city, wed a Pom with pockets full of dreams and little else, and returned with him to the country. She had lost their one and only child after forty-seven days, but neither that nor cancer had defiled her spirit or sullied her goodness. She would never have done what Eleanor had. Eleanor or Leila.

'He's out of bed, I see. It's a miracle he didn't break his neck on the stairs.'

Eleanor was standing in the doorway, leaning against the door-jamb. Her hair was buried under a beanie and her body lost in baggy grey overalls. From the dirt and her smell, she'd been down at the kennels. That was some small thing at least in her favour.

'He thinks you've left him.'

'Why would he think that?'

'You tell me.'

23

Olivia dropped to her knees and threw her arms around Jeffrey. She drew back, waving her hand in front of her nose. 'My god Jeffrey, your breath!' She turned to India. 'You're giving him dog biscuits. I told you, he's supposed to have chicken necks. That's what Grace always fed him. She swore by them.'

'There's no electricity at Mars House,' India reminded her. 'I can't keep anything that goes off.'

'But you're working now so you can get the electricity on. Jeffrey's got to have proper food and your hair needs a wash.'

India's hand went to her hair, brushed back off her face and braided to make her presentable.

'You could buy some chicken necks and keep them here,' Hazel said helpfully. 'In the back fridge. They shouldn't make the flowers smell. Jeffrey could have one before you open the shop and a couple before you go home.'

'Brilliant,' Olivia said. 'We'll go and get some.' She held out her hand to India. 'Give us ten dollars. And not out of the till. No, make it twenty. Jeffrey's probably feeling deprived.'

'We don't have time,' Hazel said. 'Mum's expecting us like about ten minutes ago. We've got to study for a maths test,' she explained to India. 'Mum says I have to get at least ninety-eight percent.'

Olivia gave a cynical laugh. 'No one ever gets ninety-eight in maths at our school. No one gets seventy-eight.'

Hazel undid the large safety pin that held the rolled-up waistband of her school uniform and held it out to Olivia, who had insisted they shorten their skirts for the walk down the high street.

'Come on,' she said as she tugged the hem of her skirt back down over her knees. 'We've got to go. Now.'

'She's getting scary, your mum,' Olivia grumbled, taking the pin and removing a similar one from her own waistband. 'She must be going through the change.'

'How's Gill today, Olivia?' India said. 'Sorry, I forgot to ask.' She stepped back in alarm as Olivia burst into tears. 'What's happened? Is she okay?'

Hazel pushed Olivia towards the door. 'Nothing's happened. Liv's just practicing the sympathy card so Mr Findlay'll come home. She's been doing it all day. Everyone at school's sick of it. We talked to Mrs Findlay at lunch time. She's much better. Toby says they'll let her out of hospital soon.' She pushed Olivia again, this time harder. 'Say goodbye to Jeffrey.'

Olivia's tears stopped as quickly as they had started. She blew Jeffrey a kiss and shrugged her schoolbag onto her shoulders. 'I told you, the best place to get chicken necks is from the butcher next to the Sourdough Bakery,' she said to India. 'They're organic. Grace only got organic.'

The doorbell tinkled and Blooming Beautiful was once again quiet. Jeffrey settled back on his bed and India opened her sketchbook and studied the drawing she'd been working on when there were no customers. She had Jeffrey right, and the man squatting with one arm around him and the other hooked through the reins tethering his horse. Of the horse, however, she could recall little beyond its size and haughty expression. She turned to a fresh page.

The doorbell jingled and she quickly closed the sketchbook.

It was Julie Rice, Grace's friend who had taken in Jeffrey. The small, stout, hurricane of a woman, had been Blooming Beautiful's original owner and had offered to do the flower arrangements, just as Olivia had said. She was also doing the banking and providing, as she scarily put it, a motherly eye.

Jeffrey rose and greeted her with a slight lift of his tail. She dropped a quick pat on his back.

'Place is quiet without you revving up the Maus, Jeff. I bet you're much happier being back in your own billet, though.'

India emptied the till. There had been a steady trade from regulars replacing spent flower and sales of bouquets for birthdays, anniversaries and 'Sorry I should not have said or done thats'. She put the cash bag on the counter along with a stack of Eftpos receipts.

'Great stuff,' Julie said, taking out three fifty-dollar notes and pushing them towards India. 'Not much I'm afraid, but it's something. I've just come from the hospital. Gill thanks you from the bottom of her sorry heart for helping out with the shop.'

'I always worked in London,' India said. She'd had to. Grace had paid her fees and given her a small allowance but with the expectation that beyond that, she would support herself, a more than reasonable deal. And as well as that, it was a relief to be doing something other than fretting about selling Mars House. Though she must get on with it. Perhaps Julie would watch the shop while she visited real estate agents? About to ask, she thought of Rob Marks' choking aftershave and comments about Grace's "stuff" and changed her mind.

'Your grandmother was always happy to lend a hand,' Julie said. She gazed frankly at India. 'You look like you need a steak. I suppose you're a vegan. Most of you creative types are aren't you? Making virtue out of necessity, I suppose. Meat's so poisonously dear these days. That coat looks like it could weigh down an elephant. A pashmina'd be just as warm. Much more the Highland's style. How do you survive in England with all that damp stone everywhere? Not to mention all that frigid-faced How do-ing?

'Yes, she was a friend indeed, our Grace, especially when one was in need. She used to serve tea and steer people towards the loo when I opened my garden for the Burragong Hospital Auxiliary. And we miss her greatly at the bridge club. She was the best no trump player in the Highlands. Absolutely tenacious in defence. Do you play?'

India shook her head.

'I'm surprised Grace never taught you. If you play bridge you'll have friends in every corner of the world. Would you like a coffee? What about a ham sandwich?'

India slid one of the fifties back across the counter. 'Just a coffee, thanks. But could you get Jeffrey some chicken necks?'

The door closed and the air became still. India opened her sketchbook and after making a few quick studies of Julie Rice, began again with Pan Villon's horse.

A short time later, Xavier came into the shop, looking sharp in a double-breasted black woollen coat and a tray with two coffees. He bustled over and kissed her on the cheek.

'Hmm, he said, wrinkling his nose. 'You're overdue for a bath.'

She stepped back and pulled the tweed coat tight around her. 'Am I that bad?'

'Not quite. But you will be by tomorrow.'

'Jeffrey sleeps right up against me.'

Xavier waved a finger at Jeffrey, who had opened one eye. 'You're a slut, Jeffrey.' He handed her a coffee. 'Small latte on full cream, no sugar.'

'Julie Rice is getting me one as well. I probably won't sleep tonight. 'I'd better get some more candles on the way home.'

Xavier looked smug. 'No need for candles. The power's on at Mars House. You'll be able to have a bath. And you,' he said to Jeffrey, 'can have one as well. Though not tonight. India and I have work to do.'

Before she had a chance to say anything, Julie Rice rolled in, coffee tray held out in front of her, eco shopping bags crowding the short lengths of her arms.

'Ah, Xavier,' she said. 'Just the person I wanted to see. We're running beginners' lessons at the bridge club. Get yourself signed up and bring India.'

Xavier relieved her of the bags. 'I wanted to see you too. I'm collecting for a painting for Gill, to cheer her up. India's doing it.'

Julie took the lid off her coffee and drank it half down. 'Who's we?'

'Vivienne, Simon and Eleanor. Lucien. Basically, the whole Hunt. You can put in for Lillian, as well.'

Julie's bosom grew even more shelf-like. 'Lucien? I doubt that very much. Lucien doesn't give a fig about anyone but himself. The mother's just as bloodless. She should have been sterilised at birth.'

Deciding not to point out the illogicality of this, Xavier said, 'Lucien's put in five hundred.'

Julie looked beadily at India. 'How much is this painting costing?'

'I don't know anything about it,' India said.

India had bathed and her hair, softly gleaming, was gathered in a loose chignon at the back of her head. Xavier smiled approvingly. Showering twice a day himself, he couldn't imagine how she had gone for so long without a soapy scrub.

The photos he'd been sorting were now in two piles. 'I've narrowed it down to these.' He pointed at the smaller pile, pushed the rejected one to the end of the table and laid out the chosen photos, four, in a line.

India bent over the photos. Standing behind her, Xavier stared at the feather, pinions dishevelled as if ruffled by a playful wind, that was inked in indigo on the nape of her neck. It was exquisite and erotic.

'Which do you like best?' he asked breathily.

India pushed the photos about, separating them, creating space around them, isolating them. In the first, Gill, elegant in her hunting kit and smiling broadly, stood next to an alert eyed and similarly elegant Hester. It was a classic pose, something you'd find in any horse magazine. In the next photo, Hester was galloping across bleached grass, Gill's gloved hands bunching the reins on her neck – they were flying. In the third photo, Hester was surrounded by hounds. Gill, feet out of the stirrups and legs hanging down Hester's sides, had taken her cap off and was cooling her face in the wind.

'Well?' Xavier repeated. 'Which one?'

'This one.' The fourth. They were on the top of a hill. The sky was the flat grey of slate. Hester was walking on a loose rein and Gill looked as though she had grown into, or out of the saddle. *Kentaurides*: half woman half horse.

Xavier drew the photo towards him. 'I love this one too. That's settled then.'

But it wasn't settled. 'What size?' India asked. 'Small, large, in between? And what medium? Watercolour, oil, ink? Watercolour and ink?'

'Isn't that your department?'

'What's Gill's house like?'

Beyond "old, modern country", Xavier couldn't say.

'It doesn't want to be too big then.' India held her hands apart at a distance just wider than her shoulders. 'About eighty by seventy. And oil, I think.' For its tonal depth, the luminosity, the mixing qualities that allowed for precise colour matching.

'Sounds perfect.' Xavier looked at his watch. 'I hope you don't mind, but I've got a dinner date.'

'Of course not,' India said, her eyes on the photo. She couldn't wait to start. She could do some sketches while the shop was quiet. She would set up her easel … where?

'You've got something for dinner?'

'Yes.'

'No you haven't,' Xavier said. 'Unless you're planning to cook up one of Jeffrey's chicken necks.'

India shrugged. Food was the furthest thing from her mind. Then she realised. Art materials. She had none. The sketchbook and some pencils, that was it. Everything was in London.

Xavier was on his phone, 'Are you sure eight's okay? Great, great. See you then.' He ended the call. 'I'm going to get you some food,' he told India.

'You don't have to. There's the wine you bought. Wine always fills me up. But I don't have any paint or brushes. No easel, canvases.'

Xavier opened his wallet and took out Lucien's five hundred dollars. 'You can get those yourself.' He waved a fifty. 'And you're paying for your dinner, as well.'

24

The pub was half an hour from Burragong, on the Sydney side. They had shared pleasantries, at first, bumping against the confines of manners as though blindfolded, while creating a space for intimacy.

Xavier leaned across the table and tucked Toby's fringe back behind his ear. 'It's sharp the way your hair does that.'

'Does what?'

'Falls down over your eye.'

'It's mum's cutting. She's magic with scissors and she's always studying fashion sites. That's what gives her her edge. She says the difference between a good haircut and a bad one can be as little as half a millimetre. Yah, she really understands hair.'

'Yah,' Xavier repeated. 'Is that what they say at your college?'

Toby looked at him through his dark eyelashes. 'No. It's what I say when I'm nervous. Anyway, I don't live at the college anymore. I'm in a unit in Camperdown, near RPAH. The hospital. Royal Prince Alfred Hospital.'

'Where does Vivienne think you are tonight?'

'Headed back to the flat. She'll be expecting a call in about an hour to say I've arrived home.'

'What would she say if she knew you were, we were …?' Xavier's voice trailed off. What were he and Toby doing, exactly? Having dinner? Yes, no? – a barely touched antipasto plate sat on the table between them. Toby was certainly flirting, and he was as turned on as hell, but really, they knew nothing about each other beyond the basics that everyone knew. Right up until the moment Toby had accepted his dinner invitation he'd not known if he'd been reading his signals right. And if he was reading them right now.

'Actually, she'd go off her head.' Toby ran his fingertips down the strand of hair Xavier's fingers had just touched. 'That's why we couldn't meet in Burragong. She has this idea that as soon as I've set up my own practice I'll marry a girl I met at uni, preferably from the North Shore and a doctor too, and we'll give her a salon full of grandchildren. It's something to do with the ancestors.'

'She's really got no clue that you're gay?'

'I'm sure she knows, but it's not up for discussion. Mum has total tunnel vision. It's how she's gotten where she is. But it makes it bloody difficult for Hazel and me.'

'So it's more than the gay thing?'

'She's absolutely okay about other people being gay. She loves you. It's just that she's had our lives mapped out for us since we were born. I was always going to do medicine at Sydney and Hazel law, and then our next duty is to make her a grandmother. I can live with the medicine bit, though I'd be just as happy as a GP. But the rest, well, as you can imagine, it's not so straight forward.'

Xavier had to ask. 'Is there anyone … special, in Sydney?'

Toby shook his head, his fringe again flopping over his eye. 'No. Lectures, study, work on the wards, squash and tennis – it doesn't leave much time for sleeping let alone anything else. Anyway, I wouldn't be here, would I?'

'I hope not. Squash, tennis?'

'If you want to get ahead at RPAH you have to stand out. Being sporty is one way to give yourself an edge. Self-discipline, competitiveness, the ability to lose without losing it are qualities needed in surgery. And it gives you something to talk about other than blood and guts and weird pathologies. And besides, I enjoy playing.'

'Hmm,' said Xavier, 'sweaty bodies.'

Toby laughed. 'There is that.' He turned the stem of his wine glass with his elegant fingers. 'I know mum sounds like one of those stereotypic tiger mums pushing her kids to get better grades, not letting them have a life of their own, but there's much more to her than that. She's funny and clever and her business mind is extra-ordinary. Really extraordinary. And because of what she's invested in us emotionally, she's also very vulnerable. And don't forget her feelings for her parents, my grandparents. To her, they are still alive. Them and their parents, my great grandparents.'

'Sounds like you should be doing psychiatry instead of surgery.'

Toby gave Xavier another disturbing glance from under his eye-lashes. 'I did think about it when I realised ...'

'It's not a weird pathology.'

'I know. It's just ...' Toby caught and held Xavier's gaze. 'Mum can never find out, that's the deal.'

Xavier pinched his thigh. This gorgeous, haughty, brainy boy was about to become his. Of all the magical things that had hap-pened to him, this was the best.

'Deal.'

Toby grinned. 'I've fancied you for years, you know. Yah, ab-solute years.'

25

Someone was in the room. Gill opened her eyes. A child-sized young woman in purple Mary Jane flats and a white coat that enveloped her body stood at the end of her bed. It was the Registrar.

'How are you today, Mrs Findlay? Any pain during the night? Headache, nausea, double vision?'

Gill shrugged her way up the pillows. 'No pain. No headaches. No double vision and no nausea. I'm ready to go home, thank you doctor.'

'Call me Siobhan, doctor sounds so old. I'm only wearing this coat because I spilt my lunch on my dress. We don't have to wear them unless we want to. They're practical though. Especially if you're a messy eater like me.'

'I shouldn't be worried,' Gill said. 'You look about twelve. Please call me Gill. And I am old.'

Siobhan took Gill's file out of the document holder at the end of the bed. 'Thirty-nine's oldish but not old, old. It's more auntyish.'

'Auntyish sounds older than old,' Gill said lightly – if she showed she was up to making jokes, this old child might discharge her.

Siobhan frowned over the chart. 'Well your obs are good, but your bloods show an iron deficiency. I've ordered a B12 injection. Have you been feeling tired?'

'No more than you'd expect running a business, running around after a teenager and riding at dawn every morning to get horses fit.'

'Well you won't have to concern yourself about the riding for a while.'

Blocking this out, Gill asked, 'So can I go home?' Between her lecturing tone and the black rimmed glasses perched on the end of her sharp little nose, Siobhan now seemed almost middle-aged.

Siobhan shook her head. 'I'm afraid not. I've booked a bone density scan and we need to xray the leg again to make sure everything is in place. The nurse noted some intermittent swelling below the cast. And I believe you've got steps at home, so we'd better get a physio assessment as well.'

'Great,' Gill muttered as, checking her pager and giving a brief wave, Siobhan headed for the door. 'Thanks for nothing.' She slid back down the pillows and stared into the gloom; Siobhan had not bothered to open the curtains.

A while later a nurse came in holding a kidney dish with a syringe. She had been on duty when Gill had come in. Her name was Trish and she and her boyfriend, also a nurse, were Canadians on a working holiday.

'Mrs Findlay, the doctor's ordered a B12. Your bloods show your iron is low. Have you been feeling tired lately?'

Not again. When did doctors and nurses start saying the exact same things? Gill tilted her head towards the bustle and clatter outside the door. 'Sounds busy.'

'Hospitals aren't very restful places, I'm afraid,' Trish said. 'We don't want patients to start feeling too at home. Is it okay if I give you the injection in your thigh? It's the best place for absorption because of the muscle and fat.'

Gill pushed back the sheet and exposed her thigh. 'No chance of me thinking this is home. I'm dying to get out.'

'Will your daughter be stopping by on her way to school?' Trish asked, deftly administering the injection so that Gill barely felt a thing. 'I'll put you first on the shower list if you don't mind waiting for your breakfast.'

'Thanks,' Gill said gratefully. 'Can you tell me why the bone scan?'

'Routine. Pre-osteoporosis, osteopenia, or osteoporosis is often a factor when someone in your age group has a fracture.'

'I was knocked down by five-hundred kilos of bolting horse.'

Trish made a note in Gill's file to say she'd given the B12 and put the file back in its holder. 'My nan says horses are more dangerous than black bears.'

Gill rolled her eyes and sank further down the bed. Black bears! what next.

The first visitor of the day was not Olivia, however, but Julie Rice. Olivia had rung to say that Vivienne had insisted on her and Hazel going straight to school because of a maths test.

'Phew I hate the smell of these places,' Julie said, handing Gill the coffee she'd brought from the high street. 'I don't know what they do to the air, but one scarcely dares to breathe. Am I taking you home?'

Gill groaned. 'I have to have a bone scan and an xray. And they want to check my blood again this afternoon. They've just given me an injection of something that's supposed to perk me up. I hope it works. I'm starting to feel quite desperate.' She sipped the coffee. 'This is the best thing I've had since I got here. Makes me wonder why I bother with private health insurance.'

'I expect because Nicholas pays for it.'

'There is that,' Gill conceded. 'Did you know horses are more dangerous than black bears?'

Julie snorted with laughter. 'Who said that?'

'One of the nurses.'

'Goodness, they are laying on the entertainment. India Levy seems to have things organised at the shop,' Julie said, changing the subject. 'Can't wait to see the painting. She's going to be a busy girl. I hope she'll still have time for bridge lessons.'

'What painting?'

Julie ran her finger across her lips in a zipping motion. 'Oops. Loose lips sink ships don't we know. Must be off. There'll be trouble at home if I tarry. Bath's full of rosebuds. Big christening to-morrow. One of the cricketer's first bubs. If you hear helicopters, do not be alarmed, thousands are descending. What was in that injection they gave you? See if you can find out. I could do with a little boost myself. Ta-ta.'

'They haven't combed your hair,' Vivienne said, brightening the room with her orange cardigan. 'And it doesn't look like it's been washed since Sunday.'

'Hello, Vivienne,' Gill said. 'The aide was in a rush and didn't have time for my hair. But at least I'm clean.'

'Shall I get a dry wash from the salon?'

'I couldn't possibly ask you to,' Gill said. But despite the effort at cheerfulness, her protest was half-hearted. She looked a mess and felt it.

'Of course, you can,' Vivienne said. 'I'm off right now. I'll only be a few minutes.'

True to her word, Vivienne was back in the time it had taken Gill to check *The Guardian* headlines on her iPad. (She had cancelled her subscription when *The Guardian* supported the hunting ban in England, but the reportage in other newspapers being shallower than an eyebath, she had taken it up again.)

Along with the dry shampoo and her combs and scissors Vivienne had brought a large leopard skin makeup case. 'I thought you might like your face and nails done.'

'Wonderful,' Gill said. She manipulated the recliner chair she was now in, pressing the control so that she was more upright. 'But don't you have a queue at the salon?'

'My first client's not until after lunch. Everyone else is booked though. I've had to put on another colourist.' Vivienne pointed at the maroon coloured cast enclosing Gill's lower leg, which was resting on a pillow on the foot of the recliner. 'I thought plaster was white. It was when Hazel broke her arm.'

Gill rapped the cast with her knuckles. 'Fiberglass. It's light and doesn't crumble. It's amazing what one learns in hospital. And it's harder for people to leave messages on. Which is not so silly when you think about it. If you only had one or two Get Wells, or whatever it is people write on casts, it'd be the same as not getting many Likes on Facebook. It's the sort of thing people can get really down about.'

'You could get India Levy to paint it,' Vivienne suggested, brushing powder through Gill's hair.

'Speaking of which,' said Gill, 'Do you know anything about a painting she's doing? Julie said something about it then ran away like someone had just let off a flea bomb.'

'Shhh,' Vivienne murmured. 'Relax.'

But Gill could only be still for a few moments. 'Thank you so much for taking Olivia. And the Cairns. I don't know what I would have done.'

'Oh, the Cairns are no bother,' Vivienne said, and because this made it sound as though Olivia was, she added, 'And neither is Olivia, of course.'

After the xray and bone scan, the nurses settled her back in the bed, opened the heavily packaged cheese sandwich waiting for her on the bedside table and left. She was staring uninterestedly at the sandwich when Eleanor Lonsdale poked her head around the door.

'Hi, are you up to visitors?' Seeing the sandwich, she said, 'Sorry, you're having lunch. I'll come back later.'

'No, no,' Gill said. 'Come in.' She dropped the sandwich onto the plate. 'It's supposed to be cheese, but I think it's some sort of recycled plastic.' She waved at the recliner. 'Have a seat. How did the hounds pull up after Sunday? You look gorgeous by the way.' She admired Eleanor's honey coloured cords and knit and knee-high leather boots. 'Everyone here dresses in pyjama suits or white coats. They look like they work in a cheese factory.'

Eleanor shifted the chair so that she was talking to Gill not the window. 'Does your leg hurt?'

'Surprisingly little,' Gill said.

'Well that's something. Have the doctors said when you can ride again? Will you be back before the end of the season?'

'Definitely,' Gill said. By her calculations and with the help of Dr Google, she would miss six or eight at the most of the season's fourteen weeks. 'Xavier's going to lunge Hester to keep her fit.'

'That's good of him.'

'Everyone's been great,' Gill said. The more reason to get herself up and back on her feet. All the attention, the kindness was making her feel guilty. 'Vivienne came in and did my hair and makeup. Now, tell me about the hounds. I want to hear about every single one.'

Eleanor went through the pack, giving an account of each: who had cut paws, who had scratches from wire, who wouldn't eat and who was stiff and where.

'You missed Blackberry,' Gill said when Eleanor drew breath. Blackberry, a sly hound given to hiding himself in blackberry patches while his colleagues worked, was irrationally one of her favourites.

'Simon thinks he's settling,' Eleanor said. 'Lucky for him.'

Picking up a note of weariness in her voice, Gill said, 'I can imagine there's not much conversation at home that's not to do with the hounds. It must get boring sometimes.'

'Simon's drinking again.' Eleanor put her hand over her mouth. 'Sorry, I didn't mean to say that.' She hung her head.

'I won't say anything.' Gill looked at Eleanor more closely and saw that unusually, she was wearing a lot of makeup. Had she been crying? Between the eyeshadow and layers of mascara it was hard to tell. But she was clearly down. Her heart went out to her. She liked her a lot. She had come on the scene at the beginning of last year and had taken the time to get to know Simon's friends and she had not, as another woman might have done, removed Rebecca's portrait from the living room. And she was as good for the Highlands Hunt as she was for Simon. And no doubt aware of the gossip that she was more interested in the lifestyle Simon provided than the man himself, she held her head high, kept her back straight and maintained her dignity.

She gave Eleanor a smile. 'Are you okay?'

Eleanor stared down at the floor. 'Probably not. But I'm not as bad as Simon. Hindsight's a wonderful thing isn't it. I shouldn't have moved in as quickly as I did. I've made a terrible mess of things.'

'It's never just one person's fault,' Gill said, thinking about her Nicholas and her marriage. 'Relationships work for a while and then they don't. It's just the way sometimes.'

Eleanor stood up. 'I'd better go. I really am sorry. I didn't mean to burden you. You've got enough worries of your own.'

'She looks terrible, dad.'

Gill opened her eyes as her husband bent to kiss her. 'Hi, Nicholas,' she said, giving him her cheek instead of her lips.

'You don't look as bad as I expected,' Nicholas said. 'From Olivia's accounts I thought you were at death's door.'

'She's been practising the hysterics just for you.'

Nicholas frowned. 'I doubt that. She's bound to be emotional. You are her mother, after all.'

The way he said "mother" it sounded like a curse.

'Dad came and got me from school,' Olivia said. 'He's come home to look after us. We're getting my things and the Cairns from Hazel's when we leave here. Mrs Teo'll be pleased. She doesn't think I care enough about schoolwork and the Cairns have been barking at the people coming to the salon. She's had to lock them upstairs.'

'The university has given me a couple of weeks off,' Nicholas said, sitting down on the bed. 'I can take longer if it's needed.'

Olivia rested her arm on her father's shoulder. 'It will be, dad.'

'You do look tired, though,' Nicholas said to Gill.

So much for Vivienne's hair and makeup job. 'My iron count's low,' Gill said, then cursed silently. The less Nicholas knew about her the less he had to screw with.

Olivia began to cry. 'Does that mean you've got cancer, mum?'

'Bloody hell,' Gill said. 'No it doesn't.'

But Olivia's tears had the desired effect on her father. He put his arms around her and patted her hair while she sniffled against his chest. He looked accusingly at Gill.

'It was only a matter of time before something like this happened. I've been saying for years that hunting's a dangerous sport. Not to mention utterly barbaric. I daren't tell Keith and Joy.' Keith and Joy, his parents, were violently opposed to anything that might injure any of their precious brood; growing up, Nicholas had only been allowed to ride his bicycle in the house.

'And if he ever bothered to get in touch, Oscar would say it was karma, no doubt.'

Gill gritted her teeth. There it was, regular as clockwork, the reminder of their son's flight. The reminder, as if she was ever able to forget, that Nicholas believed it to be her fault entirely.

'And I'm going to be reborn as a fox and have my throat ripped out by slavering hounds,' she said, unable to keep the bitterness out of her voice.

'You said it, not me.' Nicolas rubbed away Olivia's tears with his thumb. 'Are you okay, precious?'

'I think so,' Olivia hiccupped.

'Would a white chocolate chai latte cheer you up?'

Olivia nodded. 'I'm really thirsty, dad.'

'We'll be on our way, then,' Nicholas told Gill. 'No doubt the doctors have told you to rest.' He turned back to Olivia. 'I thought we might go out to dinner. Just you and me.'

Seeing the blazing love on Olivia's face, Gill felt as though a mouse was scratching in the pit of her stomach.

A few minutes after they had left, Xavier bounced in. 'What's that disgusting smell in the hallway?'

'Dinner, I expect.'

'Not this early, surely?'

'Sick people are like children you know. They have to be fed and tucked in by seven. How's Hester?'

'Typical. No "How are you today?", Xavier? "Sell any million-dollar houses today, Xav?" Nope, just "How's my horse?". Well she's fine. Not very pleased about having her feed cut down, though.'

'She probably can't understand why. She knows it's the hunting season. She loves it as much as I do.'

'No doubt,' Xavier said, dragging the recliner from under the window. 'Tell me how you're feeling. You don't look very sick.'

Gill ran her hand through her now silky hair. 'Vivienne gave me a makeover. It was wonderful. I had a mini facial as well.'

'Vivienne's been to visit?'

'And Julie, Eleanor and Nicholas and Olivia. But not all together, thank god.'

'The phantom husband's in Burragong?'

'He picked Olivia up from school. He's come to look after us.' Gill pulled a face. 'But I think his real agenda is to stop us hunting.

He'll be at me to sell the horses next. That was why I didn't want him to know I was in hospital. He's taking Olivia out to dinner. I can feel the pins going into my flesh.'

'So how is the phantom husband?'

'Handsome in that way of men who take no responsibility for their actions. You know, smooth browed from phantom worry. No lines around the mouth from sucking on hard truths.'

'You haven't had sex in a while then.'

Gill almost laughed.

'Better,' Xavier said. 'You've dropped ten years. Will I keep going? We might be able to push it to fifteen.' He stopped and stared as an alarmingly thin woman with jet black hair and snowy roots appeared in the room. She was dressed in the pink uniform of the hospitality department.

'Mrs Findlay your menu says you'll have a glass of red wine with tea,' she said. 'The doc's approved it so can I bring it now? Tea's on its way.'

'Yes please,' Xavier answered. 'And a glass for her visitor as well.'

The woman pursed her lips so they all but disappeared. 'We don't do visitors.'

Xavier took a twenty dollar note out of his wallet. 'Make it a bottle.'

The woman's lips returned. 'Have you got two tens? I'll have to split it with the cook.' She gestured at Gill. 'And mind the patient doesn't drink too much and overdose. If she does it'll be on your head.'

The bottle of red delivered and poured with the instruction that it was to be sipped not guzzled, Xavier settled back in the chair and Gill against the pillows.

'I was hoping to get out today,' Gill said. 'But now I have to have an infusion for my bones. I should be able to go home after that though.'

'When can you ride again?' Xavier asked. 'Have you Googled riding after a broken leg? I Google everything. It's fab. You just keep going until you get the answer you want.'

'I'll be back hunting in six weeks. Eight at the most.'

'Good.' Xavier refilled their glasses. 'This isn't bad.'

'Maybe there's a point to private health insurance after all.'

Xavier looked out the window and down at the doctors' carpark, two stories below. Though it was not yet completely dark, the concreted expanse was glaringly lit and mostly empty.

'It's certainly not the view.'

Gill sat up suddenly. 'Julie said something about India Levy and a painting. She wouldn't say anymore, but she looked bloody shifty and then took off. I asked Vivienne about it and she changed the subject.'

'Julie always looks shifty. It's all that time she spends on her knees ratting about for weeds. Bloody woman. She never could keep a secret.'

'So there is something she wasn't meant to tell. You might as well give it up. It's half out anyway.'

Xavier shook his head. 'Nope. Half a secret's better than no secret. He leaned close to Gill. 'Now, this is a proper secret. I spent last night with Toby Teo.'

'Vivienne's Toby? Hazel's brother? I didn't know …'

'Nor did I until that horse knocked you over. Every cloud has a silver lining.' Xavier grinned. 'God, that's the sort of awful platitudinous thing Julie would say.'

'Talking of Julie,' Gill said while she digested Xavier's revelation, 'she's chasing you to sign up for bridge lessons.'

'Well she won't catch me,' Xavier said. 'Grace tried to teach me, but I don't have the brain for it.' His face fell. 'You don't think I'm too stupid for Toby, do you? He's studying to be a surgeon.'

'You're going to see him again, then?'

'No question about that,' Xavier said. 'But Vivienne can't know.'

Gill had trouble digesting this. 'I'd have thought she'd be thrilled. She treats you like a second son. She cuts your hair herself.'

'Toby's destined for a smart marriage and lots of grandchildren for her to dote on. It's something to do with their ancestors.'

'I see,' Gill said, even though she didn't. 'Well I think it's wonderful.'

I'm Your Man – the ringtone he'd set for Toby – sounding on his phone, Xavier put down his glass. 'Grace would have known what to say to Vivienne,' he said as he headed for the door.

26

India waved at the departing Xavier and went up to Gill's bed and handed her a posy of yellow rose buds.

'From Julie. They're a bit past it but she thought you wouldn't mind. Her arrangements are intriguing. She's got such an eye for colour and form. It's like she's painting with the flowers.' India sat on the chair vacated by Xavier. 'You're looking much better.'

'Vivienne gave me a makeover. Hair, hands, nails. She even massaged my neck.' As she said this, Gill wondered if she should have offered Vivienne something. Even just for the dry shampoo. Not that she had any spare cash now the shop was paying India. Maybe she should ask Nicholas for a bit extra? Bad idea. That would really make him determined that she should sell the horses. Her stomach went tight.

'Your tea, Mrs Findlay. Tuna mornay.'

It was the pink uniform lady. She slammed a tray on the overbed table, picked the wine bottle up off the bedside locker and checked its contents. 'Your visitor's a thirsty fellow. He'll be blowing over the limit. The coppers sit right out the front of the hospital.'

Gill lifted the cover on the plate and dropped it. 'I ordered steak.'

'We always give breakages tuna. It builds the bones. Cheese too.'

And with that, the pink uniform lady was gone.

Gill nudged the plate away. 'I don't suppose you've got a plastic bag? Jeffrey's very fond of tuna mornay. God, I miss the Cairns.

Almost as much as I miss Hester. I can't wait to get home and see everyone. How's Jeffrey?'

'I think his breath's a bit better now he's getting the chicken necks,' India said.

'Glad to hear it,' Lucien said from the doorway. He strode to the bed, kissed Gill on the cheek, dousing her in Venetian bergamot. He plonked a bottle of Moët beside the dinner tray. 'Something to cheer you up. It smells like the floor of the fish market in here.'

'It's my dinner, I'm afraid,' Gill said.

Lucien grinned at India. 'Another reason to stay out of hospitals, don't you think, India?'

'You two have met?' Gill asked.

'In this very room,' Lucien said. 'You obviously don't remember much about Sunday afternoon.'

'I use my middle name, Ann,' India told him.

'India and Ann, an exotic and a safe bet. Knowing your grandmother, I'd have put money on you choosing the exotic. She certainly preferred it.'

India stood up. 'I'd better go. Jeffrey's in the car. He'll be getting cold.'

Gill pushed her dinner across the table. 'Take this. But don't let anyone see you with it. Especially anyone in a pink uniform.'

'I'll come tomorrow,' India said.

'Ring first,' Gill suggested. 'I'm hoping to be home.'

'Spikey, isn't she,' Lucien said after India had gone. 'And she certainly doesn't like to advertise. I bet she wears that coat in bed.' He picked up the wilting rosebuds, his expression thoughtful.

It must be quite a novelty meeting a woman that doesn't go to water when you look sideways at her, Gill thought, watching Lucien drop the posy in the glass on the bedside locker. Even though she thought him a shit, her own heart had started pounding when he'd kissed her.

Lucien backed the Audi out of the car space reserved for Burragong Hospital's Director of Nursing. Another bottle of Moët stood in a cooler bag on the passenger side floor between a pile of catalogues for a New Zealand bloodstock sale.

After a few turns and roundabouts, he was through the now quiet Burragong shopping and café precinct and headed out of the village. The road wound past clipped hedges and cavernous driveways shadowed by banks of rhododendron. He passed a black Golf with a girl in Garton's navy and jade striped blazer at the wheel, then the road was all his.

He drummed his fingers on the steering wheel and wondered what Christie had planned. Whatever it was, it would no doubt involve punishment. They had not been together since the cricketing museum, and up until this morning, he had not returned her calls or texts. Nor had he intended to. But after watching the auditions of two Victoria's Secret hopefuls, he had weakened. They were meeting at Jottings. Digger was out for the evening with some high-profile rugby players and she was being chauffeured down in the helicopter after the evening news.

The manicured outer suburbs gave way to larger acreages. His thoughts returned to his day's work. He had spent the morning going over Whistlejacket's accounts, not an area he usually concerned himself with. His job was publicizing the stallions, choosing the best matings for the broodmares and selling their offspring. And with his mother now less keen to travel, he was also spending more time promoting the Whistlejacket brand. Which was not to say that he took no interest in the stud's finances. His estimation of what a weanling or yearling might reach in the sale ring was consistently close to the mark and he could recite the sale and race earnings of Whistlejacket bred horses going back to grandfather Blythe's days. He could also recount the individual earnings, from their racing careers and foal sales combined, of Whistlejacket broodmares, that lengthy line of quiet stars as significant to the stud's success as the stallions that fronted it.

It was not these figures, however that had him opening the spreadsheets with the stud's operating expenses, its outgoings, against the incomings.

Stable bedding, feed, supplements, rugs, tack, farrier, veterinary, chiropractic. Wages, superannuation, accounting, insurance, internet.

Vehicle maintenance, fuel, fencing, building repairs, gas and electricity, garden supplies. Subscriptions, promotional material, stationery, flowers, groceries. The outgoings list was long and the figure beside each dizzying. But he was used to figures in the stratosphere. He liked them.

The morning passed quickly. After eating the baguette brought by Janet Reedhead while he watched the Victoria's Secret auditions, he opened the final file: last financial year's expenditure/profit reckoning. The stallions' service fees and weanling and yearling sales more than doubled the outgoings. Whistlejacket was not only solidly viable, it was making a healthy profit. He was elated. His detective work had paid off. His mother might threaten to sell Whistlejacket if he didn't marry, but he had every cause to call her bluff. She had given him control of the stud and it was running well. Better than well.

Then it hit him. There was no record of a payment to a Kentucky stud. The profit had been solid but nowhere near BlueBuckle's ten-million-dollar purchase price. How had he missed it? His mother must have paid for BlueBuckle herself, out of her own private money, and if she chose to call in the debt there would be no option but to sell up, and anyone would see that as a reasonable financial decision.

He had been so electrified by the chance to procure a stallion of BlueBuckle's calibre that he hadn't given a thought to where the needed millions would come from. He should have discussed it with Kevin instead of his mother. Kevin would have made him put the brakes on, helped him work out a longer-term solution for the stallion roster, one that the stud could afford. But now his balls were in a vice that made Christie's grip seem like a caress from a butterfly.

He turned his attention back to the road. More than ever now, he needed distraction.

Ten minutes later, Jottings' studded timber door creaked open and Christie beckoned him into an entrance hall the size of a tennis court. She was naked, her breasts quivering, her face lit up.

'Close your eyes and count to sixty,' she whispered.

Cocaine, he thought as he closed his eyes and began tapping his toe on the travertine. How much did she have? Hopefully a car boot full. He opened his eyes. He had a pretty good idea which way she had headed.

The door to the turret, off the hallway that led to the staff wing, was hidden by a rack of abandoned parkas and scarves. He began the climb up the spiral staircase. He was looking forward to seeing the turret room again, both the room and the glorious Aubusson carpet that had provided the silky surface for the imaginative sex he had enjoyed with Jotting's previous owner, Vicky Reach. But except for the Pomegranate Noir candle and Rockpool menu on the windowsill, the room at the top of the turret was empty. Possibly, Christie didn't know about it. Vicky's husband hadn't. He picked up the candle, the memory of Vicky's long black hair brushing his belly making his groin stir in a way that Christie's nakedness had not. She might not have been beautiful in the telling light of day, but in candlelight, Vicky had been breath-taking. No wonder Angus had chucked his first wife for her. He put the candle back and placed the bottle of Moët beside it.

Unoriginally, Christie was in the master bedroom, sprawled on a four-poster bed that he'd never seen before. She rose on all fours, a crazy-eyed fawn.

'Where's the coke?' he asked.

She gave a little giggle. 'Go find.'

'I've already played that game once.'

'Look, aren't I a naughty girl? I've wet the bed.'

'Yes you are. Now where's the coke?'

The sex was sexy enough, but the coke was spectacular.

Christie had told Digger she had decorators coming in the morning and the helicopter wouldn't be back to pick her up until mid-afternoon tomorrow. It would be their first ever night together. She had filled the fridge with fruit, eggs and bacon for the morning. She tossed her mane, cajoled and pleaded, yanked his penis then rubbed it with her breasts, but there was no way he was staying. Digger could be in the helicopter on his way to the Highlands at this very moment.

'He'll be legless by now and trying to pull girls off the street,' she wailed.

He rolled off the bed and reached for his jeans. 'The only girl he'll be thinking about pulling is right here. And come midnight, or whatever time he turns into a werewolf, he'll be calling his pilot and telling him to fire up the bird.' He ran a finger down her cheek. 'If this is to work, we have to be very careful.'

It was a line worn almost to transparency from centuries of use from New Guinea to New York, but Christie gulped it down.

'We will make it work, won't we?'

'Of course we will.'

27

Donnacha and Beef sat in the stable office, the air a rich mix of coffee, stable manure and the sweet, warm exhalations of the horses chewing their way through their breakfasts. The sky showing through the long, narrow window behind the office desk promised a fine day.

The news came on the radio and Beef cocked his head to catch the headlines. Stabbings, shootings, a house fire, bent politicians ... He sipped of his coffee and said, as he did every morning, 'Who'd live in the city?'

Donnacha studied the whiteboard. When the feed tubs were empty, he would set about dressing wounds and administering antibiotics and anti-inflammatories to the stabled horses. Each would be thoroughly examined so that he could decide if the recovery was proceeding as it should, or if the horse was ready to be turned out.

'That yearling with the cloudy eye,' he said. 'I might get Cherry to look at her.' Even in the low light it was apparent the eye was still far from right. 'You'd better make sure there's fuel in the truck. Cherry might want to send her to Sydney.' Horses with more complicated medical problems were seen at the Sydney University Veterinary Hospital, which, as well as its outstanding facilities, had several renowned specialist equine practitioners.

Beef scratched his stomach, this morning corseted in a pink tshirt promoting breast cancer research. 'Be a shame if she lost the eye. Blythe wouldn't be happy.'

'I imagine the filly wouldn't be either.'

Donnacha went to the coffee machine, put in another pod and steamed some milk. His gaze roamed the photos of Whistlejacket horses dancing about sale rings and whizzing past finishing posts. which covered the walls. No doubt the Blythes had bred some very good horses.

'I'll go another, comrade,' Beef said. Though he wouldn't wear anything with the stud's logo, the blue Whistlejacket mugs were his china of choice. They held just the right amount of liquid, hot or cold, as was a fellow's preference and the generous handle was a perfect fit for his fingers.

'Blythe got in late last night,' he said. 'Or rather, this morning. And he was still up at the crack of, looking like he'd had ten hours kip and an hour with his mother's stylist.' He gestured at Donnacha's bird's nest hair and crumpled shirt. 'Unlike some.'

Donnacha put Beef's freshly filled mug down on his thighs.

'That's not friendly, comrade,' Beef yelped, only just managing to lift the mug without spilling the coffee. 'Leila's still bunking in the dorm then?'

'It's a lesser man that asks questions to which he knows the answer,' Donnacha said sourly.

'You should get Pinkie to have a chat with her. She's got a counselling certificate, you know.'

'I wouldn't let Pinkie near Sorrows,' Donnacha growled. Sorrows, dozing on a saddle blanket under the desk near Donnacha's feet, raised his head and glared at Beef.

Beef rubbed his stomach with the flat of his hand as if the movement might release a genie, which was what it was going to take to get Donnacha down off his high horse: the misery was coming off him like burning dirt. Maybe it was him, not Leila, in need of Pinkie's counselling? That or a dose of Pinkie's pole dancer's breasts and thighs. Sighing equally over the thought of a naked Pinkie and Donnacha's mulishness, he changed the subject.

'Blythe said that mare's got to go.'

'Which mare? We've only got about a hundred.'

'The mare he took to the meet Sunday, Mockingbird. Do you know of anyone in the hunt that might want her? Though it might be better if she went out of the district. I get the feeling Blythe would rather not lay eyes on her again. There were ponies jumping better on Sunday apparently.'

'Might have helped if he weren't hanging off her mouth. Did he say what he wants for her?'

'Nothing crippling. A few thou. Any ideas?'

Donnacha shrugged. 'I'll let you know.' He swivelled his chair around and hit the return on the keyboard. The computer screen came to life. He tapped some keys and BlueBuckle's yard appeared.

'Take a look at this,' he said.

BlueBuckle was standing with his rump pushed into the corner of the yard. His head hung down near to his front fetlocks and his eyelids drooped over his sunken eyes. If it weren't for the occasional tightening of the skin around his nostrils, it would have been easy to think he was in a deep sleep. That or dead on his feet. Donnacha hit another key and the screen split, showing the corner of the yard closest to the laneway. The biscuit of lucerne tossed over the railing by Beef last night was strewn about and trampled into the ground.

Beef peered over Donnacha's shoulder. 'Blythe had a bit to say about him this morning as well.'

Donnacha hit another key and zoomed in on a pile of shredded plastic. 'Did you put the bucket in the yard?'

Beef took a step back. 'I did,' he lied. 'Last night when I left the hay.' He stared at the screen, thinking fast. Only one person at Whistlejacket would have been brave enough to go into Blue-Buckle's yard and he wasn't about to give her up. 'Doesn't look like he had any of it though. The bucket's done worse than the hay.'

'We'll have to get it out before Blythe sees it.' Donnacha returned the camera to BlueBuckle. 'Hoss must be a bit quieter if you got a bucket in. Cherry was asking about him. Still thinks he may have a brain tumour. I'll get him to see him after the filly.'

'I wouldn't,' Beef said. 'Not before you talk to Blythe.'

'Why's that?'

Beef pursed his lips: this one Donnacha could surely figure out. It didn't take long.

'He's thinking of getting rid of him?'

Donnacha turned to the computer and hit the zoom key. There was no comparison between the elegant speed machine that walked off the quarantine truck and the standing carcass now on the screen. They were two different animals.

'What's wrong with you, man?' he murmured. 'What's wrong with you?' He felt a stabbing in his chest and pressed his palm to the spot. His heart was thumping.

Beef stared at the screen and shook his head. 'And I get the impression that Blythe's looking to us to figure out how to send him on his way. To make his path a bit shorter.'

'You're joking, aren't you?'

'Wish I was.'

'I couldn't, man.'

'Me neither. Just the thought of it goes straight to my stomach.'

Donnacha switched off the screen. Surely Blythe wasn't that much of a bastard. In all the years he'd worked at Whistlejacket he'd never known him to stoop to something that low. But it was too easy to think that you knew someone when in fact they were as good as a stranger, as he'd just been reminded.

'Let's get that bucket out of the yard,' he said. 'Looks like we're in deep enough shite as it is.'

'How'll we do that?' Beef asked.

'Same way you got in there, man.'

A watery landscape painted on glass, a bowl of limes and oranges in the style of the Dutch Masters, a crying child and a medieval stone farmhouse. Lady Blythe looked thoughtfully at the images on her laptop. Though the subjects and styles were different, the deftness of the brushwork, the purity of colour and impeccable proportions in each were undeniable. Grace's granddaughter was a serious talent. And the Slade had certainly thought so. In her first year, she had been awarded the most promising new student for the crying child and in her third, a top of school for a painting of a pair of dead pheasants.

She clicked the thumbnail of this second work and an extraordinary image filled the screen. The detail was Durer-like and so electric was the combination of the birds' russet plumage, the emerald of their stretched necks and their insensible eyes, that the work could be taken either as a study of nature or as a protest against pheasant shooting. Whatever had been intended, it was a painting anyone would wish to own.

She returned the picture to a thumbnail and hoping to find that it was for sale, clicked on the link below it. "Purchased by the Tate Gallery". Goodness.

But not only did Grace's granddaughter possess exceptional talent, she had been near the top of her years in her academic studies. According to her CV, she had also taught drawing at Bedlington, the school favoured by the city's paleo bloggers, celebrity wedding planners and app designer parents. The couple that had bought Downton Abbey's Dowager House had sent their dreadlocked twins there.

Her nose picked up notes of birch and Moroccan jasmine. She pressed the ESC key and all trace of Grace's granddaughter disappeared.

'Hello darling,' she said as Lucien came in. 'You smell divine.' She gestured at the sofa. 'Sit, sit.'

Lucien fished Pavarotti, one of the dachshunds, out from under a cushion and plonked him on his lap. The nose of its pair, Caruso, peeked out from a cushion further down and disappeared with a tiny snort.

'I thought you might like to go out for breakfast,' he said. 'It's a stunning morning.'

Lady Blythe smiled fondly. 'That would be gorgeous, darling. And then I've an errand for you. Grace Levy's granddaughter is in Burragong. I want you to track her down. I thought I might get her to paint my portrait. No doubt she's looking for commissions now she's finished at the Slade. It's the least I can do for dear Grace.' She stopped and peered at the flaking patch on the back of her hand – hopefully it wasn't anything that needed attention.

'I know exactly where she is,' Lucien said. 'She's working at Blooming Beautiful until Gill gets back on her feet.'

Lady Blythe raised her eyebrows. 'Well, we'll definitely have to gather her up then. Imagine the fracas at the Bridge Club when I say that Grace's granddaughter is painting my portrait. They'll all be lining up to be next, Julie Rice with her elbows flapping so she can push her way to the front.'

'I'm afraid you're in the queue yourself, ma,' Lucien said. 'The Hunt's got India doing a painting of Gill and Hester. It's a sort of sympathy, get-well card.'

Lady Blythe sniffed. 'I'm sure the gal can work on two paintings at once.' Getting no reply, she saw that Lucien, absently pulling the sleeping Pavarotti's ears, was staring vacantly into the air. Jonno had used to come home after a weekend supposedly spent at his London club with that exact same look. And he too had smelt like he had emptied half a bottle of Aventus Creed over himself.

'Breakfast,' she said sharply.

Donnacha and Beef chose to walk to BlueBuckle's yard rather than ride the quadbikes parked outside the stables. The early morning air was as crisp as chilled champagne. Magpies carolled from the pin oaks that provided shade in the horse yards and the weanlings galloped about pigrooting and squealing as the men passed their paddocks.

Donnacha stopped at the top of the laneway and looked back. What did it matter that Whistlejacket didn't belong to him, if its pleasures were only borrowed? It was as good a place as any for a man without a berth of his own to call home. A movement in the distance caught his eye: Leila, leading one of the yearlings she was preparing for the Magic Millions sale. He signalled to Beef to walk on.

BlueBuckle had not stirred from the corner of the yard. He raised his head and fixed them with a brooding stare. The sweat that had dried in his coat made him look more black than grey and his ribs showed through his dull hide. His tail was a lank, dirty drape and there were golf ball sized hollows above his eyes.

Donnacha shook his head. 'Blythe might not be waiting long.'

'Can't come quick enough for him. I get the idea he's worried about being accused of neglect. It'll show on the autopsy if the horse has starved to death.'

'What's he expecting us to do?'

'Insulin, whack him on the head so it looks like he fractured his skull on the yard rails, break a cannon bone … I don't know, comrade.'

'Mill Reef broke a cannon bone and ended up serving mares for twenty years at the National Stud.' Donnacha looked at Beef to see if he knew the horse he was talking about. Kept on looking – anything to avoid looking at the horse dying in front of his eyes.

Beef was of the same mood. He hooked his thumbs over his waistband and leaned back on his heels. 'American bred but raced in England. Sire Never Bend, dam Milan Mill. Won the Coronation Cup, the King George, the Derby and the Arc de Triomphe in the one year. Sired Shirley Heights and Reference Point who also won the Derby. Some of Whistlejacket's mares are from his line. There's a statue …'

'Got the picture,' Donnacha interrupted. 'Thanks for the history lesson.'

'You asked.'

'I did, I did. Sounds like you and Blythe had quite a chat.'

'The Lady mother's got the thumb screws on him. If he doesn't take up the wedded state, the stud goes. I don't know exactly how, but the stallion here's somehow a part of it.'

Donnacha turned back to his contemplation of BlueBuckle. He scrutinised his eyes, his ears, his belly, his feet. What had he missed? There had to be something. But for all the world, he had no idea. He pulled a plastic bag out of his pocket and pointed at the shredded bucket.

In the time it took Beef to lift the gate chain, BlueBuckle was at the rails, rearing and striking at him in fury. Beef quickly dropped the chain back over the bolt and stepped back. BlueBuckle wheeled away and charged again.

'So how did you get the bucket in, man?' Donnacha asked.

'I didn't.'

'Who did, then?'

Beef started to walk away. Donnacha called after him. 'You might as well say. It'll be on the yard footage.'

Beef stopped. 'There's only one person with balls enough to go into that yard and it's not you me or Blythe.'

28

He had managed to stop himself opening a second bottle and later, in bed – she lay curled up like a grub-struck leaf – he made up his mind to tell her what he knew. He would tell her that the reason Lucien mostly slept with the girlfriends, fiancés or wives of his friends, with the daughters of possessive fathers, was as much to assert his superiority to other men as it was about pleasure. He would tell her that while Lucien might come back for seconds, he rarely came back for thirds.

He would tell her that while he had no proof she had slept with Lucien, if she hadn't, it was only a matter of time. The writing was on the wall. He had seen it many times before. One minute the boyfriend, fiancé, husband was orbiting the woman and in the next he was disappearing behind planet Blythe. Occasionally, boyfriend, fiancé, husband reappeared and was to be seen still in the orbit of their feckless partner but usually they did not and were not.

And perhaps because he knew he would be in this second group, after feeding the hounds and cleaning the kennels he had headed into Burragong rather than deliver his speech. And what would be the point anyway? His light had started to dim long before she'd started colouring up when Lucien looked her way.

The waiter brought his order: poached eggs on white toast and a pot of English Breakfast Tea, the same breakfast he had at home every morning. He ran the edge of the knife over the eggs and as the golden yolk flowed over the toast, added a splash of vinegar and sniffed the steam. Eleanor had stopped having breakfast with him because she couldn't stand the smell. He loaded his fork and, the napkin unused at his elbow, lowered his head and gulped and swallowed until the plate was empty. He sighed contentedly and poured out the tea, now the colour of terracotta. Eleanor drank only herbal.

When they'd first met, at a hunt ball in New Zealand, she was wearing a velvet sheath that showed off her creamy skin and wonderful arms and when they danced, he had felt as though he was in her arms, not she in his. On the next day's hunt, she had been at the front of the field, sailing the country and massive jumps with the same grace with which she'd danced. The lad who'd been helping with the hounds and hunt horses at Gwynedd about to leave, he'd offered her a job. He both needed her and desperately desired her.

She had been charmed by Gwynedd. She had observed that the kennels were laid out along the lines suggested by Lord Peter Beckford, who had first brought science to hound care and breeding, and she identified the features he was breeding into the hounds. And to his disbelief and joy, after a few weeks she had accepted his invitation to share his bed.

The days took on a natural flow. They tended to the property and the business of running the Highlands Hunt. He continued to pay her the weekly sum they had agreed on before becoming lovers, but as an allowance rather than a wage. He bought her diamonds and the chocolate coloured warmblood, Elvis. He paid for her visits to her family. He knew some of the Hunt said she was only with him for his money and hoped the talk didn't reach her ears.

And now he was facing the prospect of letting her go. But despite the carrion stench of Lucien's attention, despite her sometimes barely disguised distain for his ways, she was still an utterly lovely girl. Just not one for a man whose ways had been set by years with a woman for whom he could do no wrong. A woman who put vinegar on her eggs and left her napkin on the table instead of spreading it on her lap and who drank brick coloured tea.

But more than that, as he knew, in a deeper place in his heart, that Eleanor needed a bigger canvas than Gwynedd and the Highlands Hunt. She had wrested out of them all she could, and in truth it was this that was causing her to pull away. And who was he to begrudge her her freedom. Part of him had been waiting for this moment since that first night she had shared his bed.

These things too, he had planned to say to her.

He drank the last of the tea and signalled for the bill and bumbled towards the high street, tears stinging then flooding his eyes. He should be glad that a girl as lovely as Eleanor had chosen to spend the time with him that she had. And he was glad, but he was also angry – angry that Lucien Blythe was to be the means of her exit. She could have done better. He deserved better.

Making out Blooming Beautiful's sign, he decided to get Gill some flowers. She'd think him an idiot buying her flowers from her shop, but it would delay his return to Gwynedd a bit longer. He might even be able to string out the visit to the hospital long enough to justify staying in town for lunch. The Burragong Arms did a great bangers and mash and a schooner or three would wash them down just nicely. The tears stopped.

Grace Levy's granddaughter, India, appeared from the shop's back room; he remembered the overcoat. When she asked if he needed any help, he couldn't help staring. He'd seen photos of a much younger Grace and with her height, arrow-like eyebrows and sweet chin, India was her image.

'Oh,' was all he could say. Jeffrey, who had followed India to the front of the shop, tottered towards him. He squatted down to greet him and suddenly, the tears were back with a force that made it hard to breathe. Grace had been a cornerstone of the Highlands Hunt and a great friend, walking puppies, riding Field Master and whipping-in when needed, great at catching loose horses on the field and game no matter the weather or the country. They had been friends. He missed her. And now he would miss Eleanor. It was one grief too much. He pulled Jeffrey against his chest then sat back on his heels, the tears stopping as suddenly as they'd started.

'My god Jeffrey, your breath!'

'I'm feeding him chicken necks,' India said defensively.

'Must be his teeth then. He needs an examination under anaesthetic.' He heaved himself to his feet before Jeffrey could lick him again. 'You didn't notice his breath?'

'Everyone said it was because he wasn't getting chicken necks. Gill, Olivia, Julie Rice ...'

'I'd have thought Gill at least would have picked up that his teeth needed seeing to.' He held out his hand. 'Simon Sinclair. You were at the hospital after Gill broke her leg, but I don't think we were introduced. Everyone was in shock.' And as he now re-membered, he'd been dead drunk and the viper now in his nest had insisted on being his chauffeur. 'You're Grace's granddaughter. You're doing the painting. How's it coming along?'

'I'm working on the composition. On what goes in and what stays out.'

'I saw that sketch you did of Jeffrey for Julie. It's magic.' Hearing his name, Jeffrey smiled. 'What about I take you to the surgery?' he told him. He looked at India. 'Would that be all right? I'm almost a hundred percent sure there's something rot-ting in his mouth. Once it's gone, it'll be much better for Jeffrey, and the rest of us.'

'I'd be grateful,' India said. 'I don't know much about dogs. I'll get his lead.' She gave him a long look. 'Are you're okay now? You were upset when you came in.'

It was as though Grace was giving him the once over. He straightened his back. 'Sorry about that. Death in the family. It was expected, but you're never really prepared. I actually came in to get Gill some flowers.'

'You're going to the hospital?'

'I'll drop Jeffrey off on the way.' He took out a pen and finding an old betting slip in his pocket, wrote a number on it. 'Give the surgery a call in a few hours. You should be able to pick him up this evening. Don't worry about the bill. I'll have it charged to the Hunt.'

'You're up,' Simon said, having found Gill sitting in the visitor's chair. He kissed her cheek. 'Good to see.'

'I hope you didn't pay for those,' Gill said taking the posy of Forget-Me-Nots from him.

Simon shook his head. 'They're Julie's rejects. She brings them into the shop so India can give them to mugs like me that come in to buy you flowers.'

Simon's eyes were red and swollen, Gill saw, and he was unshaven and his curls looked like they'd been combed with a twig. His shirt, adrift from his trousers and unironed, was clean, however and she had not smelt alcohol when he'd kissed her. If he was drinking as badly as Eleanor had intimated, he'd be soaked by now. But it might be wise to keep him occupied, nevertheless.

'That'd be Julie. Guess what? I've been discharged.' She gathered up the crutches propped either side of the chair and wriggling them into her armpits, swung herself to her good leg. 'Is there any way you could drive me home? I called Nicholas, but it went straight to message. I know I look a fright, but I just can't wait to get out of here.' She was dressed in a white waffle weave cotton robe and her face was bare of makeup.

'I'll take you if you're wearing nothing under that robe,' Simon said. Their friendship had always been like that – flirty, fun.

She poked her plastered leg out from the hem of the robe. 'Nothing but this gorgeous piece of lingerie,' she said with her barking laugh, startling to people who did not know her and wince-making to Nicholas. Checking to see that Simon too was not offended – when Nicholas was home her paranoia was sky high – she saw a tear slip out of the corner of one of his eyes.

'Oh Simon, do you want to go somewhere for coffee?'

He brushed the tear away with the back of his hand. 'What, with you made up to the nines and in all your finery. Tongues would really start wagging, if they haven't already.'

'There's always the hospital café. The coffee's lethal but we could have a juice.'

Simon shook his head. 'Let's get you home.'

'Don't forget my flowers.' Gill glanced sideways at him. He looked so wretched her heart turned over. Eleanor had her life ahead of her, but Simon ... 'How are the hounds,' she said to distract him.

He was still talking about the hounds when they pulled up in front of her house. 'They're quick learners,' he said, wrapping up with Girl and Golden, who had had their first hunt on Sunday. 'Now, let's get you inside.' He got out of the Range Rover, opened her door and fetched the crutches. 'Here you go old girl, home sweet home.'

'Hey, hold it with the old,' Gill laughed. But the last thing she was feeling was happy. She stood swaying on the crutches, conscious of her injury in a way that she hadn't in the hospital. But at least now she would see the Cairns, she told herself. It had been agony without them. She hoisted herself onto the crutches and hopped up onto the nature strip in front of the house. As she did so, her Prado pulled up and Nicholas got out; in the Highlands he never drove the Honda CR-Z leased by Blooming Beautiful and upgraded every year.

'I've just come from the hospital,' he said. 'You could have told me you were being discharged. I'd have brought you home or you could have saved me a trip.'

Flustered, Gill said, 'I did ring. I left a message and then Simon arrived, and I thought … well, I didn't know where you were.'

Simon stepped forward. 'Simon, Simon Sinclair.'

Nicholas ignored his outstretched hand. 'We've met. I've been to dinner at your house.'

'Sorry, man, must have been a crowd there. Usually is at our dinners.'

Nicholas looked at Gill, his eyes resting on her robe. 'You'd better go in.'

Simon handed Gill's bag to Nicholas, along with the flowers. 'Look after her, man. We want her back before the end of the season.'

'Not sure that'll be happening,' Nicholas said. He took the bag and flowers and waved Gill towards the house.

'Your friend Simon's been hitting the bottle again by the look of him,' he said as he pushed open the front door. 'His memory is clearly screwed. We must have met at least a half dozen times. I wouldn't be getting in a car with him if I was you.'

Gill stared at the carpet runner, trying to think how she could get down the hall without tangling the crutches in it. Maybe she could clear a path by pushing the runner towards the opposite skirting with the crutch on her good side?

'Are you coming?' Nicholas called from the living room.

Her phone chimed, signalling a text. Thinking it might be Olivia, she fished it out of the pocket of the robe. It was Simon.

Remember your husband now. Thought he was a shit. Can't say he's improved. XO S.

She put the phone back in her pocket and teeth gritted, pushed herself off the wall with her elbows and balancing on her good leg and sweeping the crutch in front of her to push aside the runner, made her way slowly down the hall.

Halfway, she stopped to ger her breath and to ease the pain in her armpits. 'Where are the Cairns?' she called.

Nicholas had either not heard or chosen not to answer.

He was at the kitchen table, a newspaper spread out in front of him.

'Where are the Cairns?' she repeated, leaning against the bench and easing the crutches out of her armpits.

Nicholas waved at the back door. 'Outside. The last thing we need is for you to trip over them and break your other leg.'

Fitting the wretched crutches back into her armpits, she hopped to the door and made her way out onto the patio. 'Darlings,' she said delightedly as two bundles of white rushed at her. 'I've missed you so much.' As best she could, she bent and stretched her fingers towards their pansy shaped faces. 'They've got bark and leaves all through their coats and their chops are dirty,' she called back to Nicholas. '

'They're dogs,' came the reply. 'They've been sleeping outside where dogs are meant to sleep.'

It was an old argument, a tired argument. The allegation that she had turned the family home into a kennel was another of Nicholas's justifications for his infrequent trips home.

The chunkier of the Cairns, Fat Freddy, stood on his back legs and aimed a lick at her fingertips. She smiled at him. Why hadn't Olivia said something about the Cairns having to sleep outside? She turned on the crutches and headed inside, the Cairns pressed to her good heel.

Nicholas looked up from the paper. 'They're not coming in.'

Her eyes went to the top of his head, to the patch on the crown where his hair was thinning. When he had gotten his first lectureship, he had favoured dark trousers and ill-fitting suit jackets and black rimmed glasses, as if declaring to his peers and his students that intelligence was more important than youth. As he got older, however, his dress had begun pointing the other way. Now, his shirts were casual, worn over a statement tshirt, the frames of his glasses were a jazzed-up tortoiseshell and his hair was carefully cut. He also jogged before breakfast and there was the shiny red car. The thinning hair must really be bothering him.

He stood up. 'I'll put the fucking dogs out myself if you won't.'

'They're staying.'

'Then I'm not. If you can't see the dogs are a risk, I can't see the point. Although I'd strongly advise getting someone from the hospital to check on you.'

'I don't expect you to stay, and I don't need a nurse.'

'Your call. I'm sure Olivia won't mind leaving early. She's coming to live with me in Sydney.'

Gill shook her head. 'I don't believe you. She wouldn't leave Hazel or the Cairns, or Expresso and ...' The word "me" was on her lips but she couldn't get it out. 'And you can't just take her.'

'I'm not taking her. She wants to come. She wants to be with me. She's had a massive fight with Hazel, which of course you don't know about because the only thing you're interested in is how well she's riding and the dogs.'

'She and Hazel fight all the time. Girls that age do.'

Nicholas raised his eyebrows as if to say, "shows what you know". 'I've arranged for her to sit the entrance exam for Sydney Girls and I've no doubt she'll get in. They'll work out an academic pathway for her to ensure she gets into the university of her choice. Her principal's all for Sydney Girls. But school aside, I've told you over and over that I don't want my daughter participating in blood sports or living in a kennel. And even though you don't think it's true, I'm just as entitled to a say in her upbringing as you are. Probably more so, given your record.'

'She won't go with you. She won't leave Burragong.'

'You believe that, do you? Yes, of course you do. Well, it just shows how out of touch you really are. Olivia sees this as opportunity. An opportunity for us, as much as her. And for me, it's an opportunity to make sure that at least one of the children I've spent the better part of my life working to provide for actually sticks around.'

The look that Nicholas gave her made her feel as though a fist had been shoved in her mouth. The tiny flame of hope that he had any feelings for her at all, the flame she had kept feeding because they had once slept entwined, guttered and died.

Her voice cracked. 'She'll be freaking out in a few days. Sydney's fine for a visit, but the country's in her blood.'

Nicholas tucked the newspaper under his arm. 'That's the sort of rubbish you read in books. The books you read, anyway. She's leaving her clothes here. We'll get her some nice things in Sydney. Oh, and we're going to Italy in September. We booked the trip last night.'

29

Pan Villon ran his fingers along the length of timber clamped to the workbench to see if it needed a further go with the plane. He was making new yards with grey gum he'd had milled in Burragong. All the yards had been made this way, by his own hands from Big Hill's own timber.

His fingers found some unevenness at one end of the rail. He picked up the plane and cradled it for a minute, enjoying its weight, feeling the warmth of the other hands that had appreciated its humility and accuracy. Electric planes might get the job done faster, but he preferred hand planes, hand saws as well. Hand tools meant working at a pace that let you smell, feel and feel close to the timber. They also did not blot out the sounds of the wind, the birds, the animals; one summer's day he had heard the quiet passage of a black snake as it passed nearby.

Wondering why her master had stopped work, the Lab, Sadie, the self-appointed mistress of Big Hill and his life, raised her black head. The grey greyhound Benzo, so named because he always appeared half asleep, did the same. Beret the Jack Russell, however, was off somewhere with his true love, the dour border terrier, Ghillie.

He lowered the plane and Sadie and Benzo lowered their heads and returned to their slumbers.

The shed where he was working had been build facing north to avoid the ferocious winds that at times roared up the escarpment, and in winter turned the rain into needles of ice. It had been the first building to go up when he'd become Big Hill's owner and had also been his home for his first year in the Highlands. When he wasn't fencing and building yards or going to clearing sales, the source of the precious hand tools, he had walked over the property, learning the folds and hollows of its land, which grass, shrub and tree grew where and in what season and the languages of its many birds. He collected rocks and samples of dirt and had gotten to know the clouds and the moods of the big hill.

And always, always there were horses in his thoughts and dreams.

The property was just over four hundred acres, the front third flat and sparsely timbered. Beyond, a chain of spring-fed dams, the country rose in waves until it reached the slopes of the big hill, the brooding, timbered edifice whose back formed part of the Highland's escarpment and which had given the property its name. He had first seen the property in a real estate window en route from Sydney to Melbourne to catch the boat to Tasmania, where he planned to spend time in the island's wilderness. The two years past he had travelled the world to learn the language of horses. Now he was travelling to learn what the gods had next in store for him.

The photo in the real estate window having caught his attention, he had called his father's cousin to tell him about the property. He was advised to go to Tasmania as planned. If he was meant to have the property, it would still be on the market when he returned. If not, then the gods did not mean him to have it.

But he knew, he just knew that it was the place on which he would write his dreams. That would write its dreams on him for him to dream.

When he returned from the wilderness it was still on the market.

He went to Sydney and set about transferring the management of the trust left by his father to his father's cousin's accountant. Drinking ouzo and eating dolmathakia me kima and watching the harbour lights on his father's cousin's minute balcony, he at last felt some closeness to the father who had taken away with one hand and given with the other.

That was four years ago, and now Big Hill had not only a shed and yards, but stables and a house, chooks, dogs, goats and the pig. And horses.

His first dog, Ghillie, arrived via a clearing sale. She had trailed after him as he scratched about in dust coated boxes and when he bent down to give her a pat, he found that under her matted coat she was a bag of bones. 'Free to anyone who'll take it', the auctioneer said. The dog's owner, the owner of the property had died and he'd been wondering what to do with it.

His first Highlands friend, Grace Levy, had arrived via a poem. She was standing in the Burragong bookshop with tears running down her face. She waved the book she was holding. 'I can never resist a volume of Yeats. Have you ever read anything as moving as "The Ballad of the Foxhunter"?'

Though her voice was bright, her speech direct, he thought that she was crying about more than the poem. But yes, he did know it, knew it well. She returned the book to the shelf. She was tall – they stood eye to eye – the cut of her short, grey hair was classy, as were the circlets of jade that hung from her ears on pale gold hoops. He took her outstretched hand. Her grip was firm, her fine hands and wrists tanned. Despite the great gap in their ages, he was glad he had put on a clean pair of jeans and shirt and shaved for the trip to town.

'You're not from here,' she said.

'But I am,' he could say. 'I've a property on the Burragong Valley Road. There's a big hill.'

'You're the Englishman who's bought the McDonald place. I used to help them with mustering when they owned it.'

He had in fact bought only a portion of the property, the smaller portion, but he didn't say. He did say, however, that he wasn't English, but Greek. At that time, he was averse to anything connected with his birthplace.

'I suppose your eyes ...'

His wife had likened them to chunks of dead coal. Like his father, she gave with one hand and took with the other. But his father at least was becoming forgivable.

'And there's your name,' Grace said. 'Pan. God of the wild. Though his face was supposed to be unattractive. I imagine you're right at home on the Valley Road. Have you found the caves?'

'Caves?'

'There's a track up on the big hill that leads to some sandstone caves. The local Aboriginals wintered there. And maybe bushrangers.'

He said he had searched the summit of the big hill but hadn't found a track. She said she would show it to him.

They had stood toing and froing like old friends and suddenly they were old friends. The chance of two strangers from different hemispheres meeting because of a little-known poem was so remote that there had to be an unseen force at work. The hand of a god, perhaps.

A hand that gives and takes away.

His first horse arrived via an ex-lover of his father's cousin. Headed for the big purses of the Sydney Spring Carnival, the white-faced chestnut gelding had started dumping his track riders. One broke his collarbone and a more experienced rider was put on him. This lad fared no better and when a veteran race jockey with a steel lower jaw and similarly rigid hands was also dumped, the trainer called the horse's owner to come and collect it.

Frenchie, as FrenchTartin was affectionately called by his owner, had turned out to have a hairline fracture in one of his cannon bones. Not only would he have been frightened to gallop, but when made to do so, would have been in great pain. The fracture mended, he was more than happy to be ridden, but not wanting to risk him breaking down again, his owner left him at Big Hill after securing an agreement that Pan would spell and freshen up his other horses when they needed a break.

It was a brilliant offer and as a business it brought in a fair income. It was also the reason he was making more yards. Along with Frenchie, Chopper and the two other horses he was working with, there were also six spelling thoroughbreds and while he had set six as the limit, he had made an exception for a friend of Frenchie's owner and two more were arriving in a week.

Horses. Created by the gods to bridge man's nature and that of the wild.

30

Donnacha watched Leila slip the gate chain and step into Blue-Buckle's yard. BlueBuckle had raised his head and was observing her closely. She held onto the gate and bending her knees, reached behind her for the water bucket and dragged it into the yard. Blue-Buckle's eyes remained locked on her then, as if too heavy to hold his head drooped and his gaze returned to the muck in front of him.

He hit fast forward. Half an hour later. Leila, standing in front of the gate, beside the bucket. She gestured at BlueBuckle and at the water bucket. BlueBuckle did not move. Leila's hands dropped to her sides. It was like looking at a photograph. Everything was utterly still, even the shadows. Leila remained by the bucket, Blue-Buckle in his corner, both as inert as concrete. Then Leila began shifting the bucket closer to BlueBuckle. Closer. Closer. And then it happened, in such a rush that the first time he watched the footage he'd not been sure exactly what had happened.

Hearing the door open, he killed the screen.

It was Pinkie with a plate of sandwiches.

'Ha, caught you watching porn,' she said. 'I always knew that's what you got up to in here.' She was very tanned and her almost crewcut hair had been recently bleached Lady Gaga blonde.

'Hi Pinkie,' he said. 'How was Bali?'

Pinkie reached for the screen button. 'Come on, show us.'

He pushed away her hand. 'It's nothing you'd be interested in. It's got horses in it.'

Pinkie stepped back. 'That's disgusting. No wonder Leila's moved back into the dorm.' She sat down and pushed the sandwiches across the desk. 'Chicken and mayo. Lucien was supposed to be back from town but hasn't showed. Mrs R's in a ferment.'

He looked at the sandwiches hungrily. Now he was on his own again it was back to basics in the food department. A cup of tea and a couple of biscuits for breakfast and for dinner, grilled chops or a steak with mixed veg defrosted in the microwave. But despite his hunger, he could not bring himself to touch what Blythe had rejected.

'What's it to Mrs R whether Blythe's here for lunch or not?'

Pinkie crossed and uncrossed her legs, showing a length of bare thigh. Lady B's told him he has to get a wife and Mrs R's worried she'll be misplaced.'

'Displaced,' he corrected.

She picked up a sandwich. 'Whatever.' She nodded at the kettle. 'Tea'd be good.' She made a face and put down the sandwich. 'No salt.'

He made no effort to move. 'Beef says she's decided that salt's the cause of everything from curling fingernails to cancer. I thought you'd have known.' Pinkie spent as much time with Janet Reedhead in the kitchen as she did in her office. His thoughts returned to the vision from BlueBuckle's yard. Leila had been crazy. Crazy stupid. But you had to admire her guts.

Pinkie was talking at speed about her trip to Bali, about the cute Dutch boy she'd met at Kuta, sunsets on the beach and the designer knockoffs in the markets that were as good as the real thing. He got up and turned on the kettle – anything would be better than sitting listening to Pinkie's prattle. But he didn't mind her that much. She was harmless enough, despite all that makeup and bare skin. And the clients certainly loved her, the men at least. Blythe sometimes joked that if he'd been inclined, he could make more money out of pimping Pinkie than he did from the stallions.

She was still prattling when he put a mug of tea in front of her.

'Ta. I'll be peeing all day.' She giggled. 'Some guys are turned on by girls peeing.'

He sat back down with his own tea. 'Sounds like the company you were keeping in Bali wasn't that choice. A crapper doesn't have a door for nothing.'

'Oh, so that's the real reason Leila's back in the dorm? She didn't close the door when she was peeing so you kicked her out.'

He turned towards the computer. 'Nice to have you back, Pinkie, but I've got work to do. And no doubt you do as well.'

'She was crying the other night. The whole dorm heard.'

'God, girl, gossip sticks to you worse than fleas to a mangy dog,' he snapped.

Pinkie's cheeks flushed under her tan. 'Welcome home to you, too.' She started for the door. 'Mrs R thinks that Leila would make the perfect wife for Lucien. Right school, right sort of parents, knows all about horses. I think I'll go let her know before Lady B's likelies start queuing up at the gate.'

'I wouldn't bother,' he snapped. 'Pan Villon's is the only queue she's interested in and she's already made it to the front of that.'

'You're a sad shit, Donnacha Keough.'

Pinkie gone in a flurry of outrage and duty-free scent, he sat staring at the blank computer screen. Why would Leila be crying? Had things already gone bad with Villon? Maybe they hadn't gotten started. Maybe Villon had knocked her back. But it certainly hadn't looked like it from the clinch he'd seen at the meet.

He whistled for Sorrows, but the little dog was not in his usual spot under the desk. He left the office and headed towards the stallion yards, then changed direction.

The dorm kitchen and television room were empty. It looked like everyone was where they should be: two of the lads repairing a fence in the bottom paddock and the rest making up the afternoon's feeds, and there was no sign of Pinkie.

Leila's door was not locked. He peered cautiously into the room. Sorrows lay feigning sleep in the centre of the neatly made bed, his head on Leila's red hoodie, which he had scratched up into a pillow.

'So you think I'm a sorry sack of shite as well?' he said to him.

Sorrows' eyes remained firmly shut.

Fighting the urge to pick up both his dog and the hoodie and take them back to the cottage, he shut the door.

Oyster walked out briskly on a loose rein. Quivering with hormones, the Whistlejacket broodmares stood with their necks outstretched to catch his scent. In another paddock, Lucien's hunt horses loafed and scratched each other's withers with their teeth. Which did Lucien plan to take to next Sunday's meet, Donnacha wondered. He hadn't seen Leila exercising any of them, but she often rode at first light while the feeds were being made up.

He turned Oyster onto the gallop, the laneway that encircled the stud. Beef had recently mowed and the wide, grass track was inviting to speed. Oyster tossed his head, asking the question. 'Not today,' he told him. Sunday's meet had been tough and he wanted his legs to have another day or two's rest from galloping. As a concession, however, he let Oyster trot. They headed up the incline that followed the gentle slope of the property. The reins bunched in one hand he fell in with Oyster's bobbing stride. Somewhere near the halfway point of the gallop, Oyster's breathing became audible: the effort of the long trot was starting to tell. He dropped his weight into the stirrups and Oyster slowed to a walk and then a halt.

Oyster was content to stand. One ear turned towards his master, he arranged his weight on three of his legs and rested the fourth. Whistlejacket spread out below, the buildings toy-like, the fences dark lines the thickness of cotton, the horses, dots. High in the sky, huge, pillowy grey edged clouds cast moving shadows across the scene. Ahead, the gallop curved to the left, following the stud's boundary while to the right, the hill on whose slope they had been travelling continued to rise. Here, northwards, the bush became dense. Which was another reason for the gallop being laid out the way it was and Beef's scrupulous maintenance: with every laneway and every paddock connecting to it, the gallop could be used to evacuate the horses if a fire got into the hill.

Donnacha kicked his feet out of the stirrups, unzipped the pocket of his vest and took out his phone.

Stephan answered. Scott was giving a lesson and had another two after that, but if it was urgent, he'd find a moment to call.

'I've a hoss I'm wanting to agist. I need to move it as soon as possible. Like this afternoon.'

'You'll definitely have to talk to Scott, then.'

'Tell him it's the mare Blythe was riding at the opening meet. Mockingbird.'

Lucien watched India as she helped a customer having trouble deciding which bouquet they wanted. Instead of being hidden inside the overcoat, she was dressed today in a fine woollen jumper that brushed the tops of her thighs, jeans and a pair of worn but well cared for top boots, probably Grace's. Her hair, quietly gleaming, was pulled back in a loose ponytail. She was aware of him but after a quick glance did not look in his direction again.

The customer left. He went to the counter and found himself staring at the tattoo on the inside of India's wrist: a dandelion, the stem bent, the flowerhead broken, the seeds spreading in a line up the white skin of her inner arm.

She pulled her sleeve down over the inking.

'My mother would like to talk to you about you doing her portrait,' he told her. 'Her driver can call for you where and when it suits. She's here in Burragong.'

India frowned and he thought she was going to refuse. Perhaps she had heard something about his mother from Grace.

The doorbell jangled and a young woman with twins in a stroller came in. 'Sunday morning,' India said quickly. 'About ten. I'll be at my grandmother's. It's out of town a bit.'

'Mars House,' he said.

She nodded and turned to the customer.

Out on the high street, he headed for Pregos, where, ordering a double shot espresso and a bowl of butterscotch gelato, he took a seat outside. When his order came, he poured the espresso over the gelato, spooned it up greedily and ordered another. His phone rang. Christie. He answered on the second ring – here was the real antidote he needed to put his nerves back together, more of that fabulous coke. And with his mother banging on about marriage and grandchildren, he'd best enjoy himself while he could. Maybe he'd squeeze in a quick trip to Hong Kong after the Magic Millions. From the texts he'd been getting, Opal must be seriously thinking about a career in porn. What would old George say to that?

Donnacha arrived at Tarlo, Stephan's and Scott's property, in the late afternoon. He turned the float into the drive and following Scott's directions, continued past the house to the stables.

Scott came out to meet him. 'I've made up a stall,' he said as Donnacha backed Mockingbird down the tailgate. 'Poor girl. She certainly took a flogging.'

Head high and eyes dark with anxiety, Mockingbird swung around on the end of the lead rope and let out a pitiful whinny.

'So, what's the go?' Scott asked. He and Donnacha had only spoken briefly.

'She was for sale, so I bought her.'

Scott looked surprised. 'Not Leila? She raved about her movement to me. She thought the mare might have the makings of a dressage horse.'

'Let's just say the mare's my responsibility now,' Donnacha said.

Scott raised his eyebrows but said nothing to this. He pointed. 'The stall's that way.'

Donnacha led Mockingbird into the stable. After a quick waltz around her stall and a snort over the door at her neighbours, she dipped her head into the feed tub and began to eat.

'Well at least she's not off her feed,' Scott said. 'That's something. I'll turn her out in the morning and see how she goes. Hay morning and night, you said.'

Donnacha nodded. 'She drops weight pretty fast. Any chance you could work her a few times a week as well? Keep her muscled and continue her training? I'll leave adjusting her feed to you. Just put it all on the account. It'll be a few weeks before her flanks are healed, though,' he cautioned. 'Maybe just start with some gentle lunging.'

'For sure,' Scott said. 'Some horses can't bear even a soft brush on their sides after a bad spurring, let alone a girth or rider's leg.

It might be worth getting some myofascial work done. It'll lessen the scarring. I wish there was something for the emotional damage, though. But we'll take things slowly.'

With a last look at Mockingbird, Donnacha held out his hand to Scott. 'Thanks, I know the mare'll be right with you. But if you don't mind, I'd rather Leila not know she's here.'

Scott frowned. 'I'm not sure how I'll square that with Stephan.'

Donnacha shrugged. 'That's your business, man.'

31

Xavier greeted India with a kiss on the cheek and followed her into the living room. Jeffrey lay in front of the fire holding a stuffed rabbit between his paws.

'Oh good, you've found the toybox,' Xavier said. 'The rabbit's Jeffrey's favourite. It gets very smelly though. He licks its ears.'

'Simon Sinclair took him to the vet today. He had four rotten teeth.'

'That explains why he's drooling. You'll have to wash the rabbit sooner than later. There should be another he can have while it's drying. His breath'll smell better now, though and he'll feel a lot better.'

'Simon said it was rotten teeth all along. He told me to just give him mince for a while until his gums are better.'

'You'll have to look in his mouth every day to make sure everything's healing up properly. How's the painting?'

'I've done some sketches,' India said. 'They're in my workroom.' She had moved everything but a scratched-up chesterfield out of one of the bedrooms and with great difficulty, dragged in a table she'd found in the garden. Long, narrow and silvered by the weather, it was the perfect workbench. On it she placed the newly purchased paints and brushes and the leaves, seeds, feathers, stones and bones she had collected while walking with Jeffrey and some books from Grace's study.

Xavier bent over the sketches. 'Hester's fab.'

India picked up a book. 'I found this. It's helped. He was great with horses.'

Xavier looked at the cover. 'Sir Alfred Munnings.'

India pointed at the writing on the front page. *To India. Love always, Grace.* She flattened her hand over the inscription. 'Sometimes it's like she's here.' She closed the book and as Grace had bid her when talk became too personal, turned her attention to her work. And, as always happened when she did, that in her that would quiver and cry out became still and silent.

'I think Gill was being discharged today,' Xavier said. 'Her husband's come down from Sydney'. He gazed around the workbench, the sheeted floor, the prepped canvas leaning against the wall. 'It looks like a real studio, but it's bloody chilly. Let's go back to the fire. Unless you want me to piss off so you can get on with the painting?'

India shook her head. 'I need to put down some more sheets and set up the easel and get some better lighting.' She peered up at the frosted light shade in the centre of the ceiling, wondering how difficult it would be to remove.

'And a heater.'

India shrugged. She had her coat and Grace's woollies. Though Jeffrey might need some extra warmth.

Xavier put another log on the fire. They settled at opposite ends of the sofa and turned so that they were facing each other.

'I was always telling Grace that she should duct the heat from above the fireplace into the other rooms,' Xavier said. 'But she thought the idea of a properly heated house an extravagance.'

'Lucien Blythe came into the shop today,' India said. 'His mother wants me to paint her portrait. I'm going to her place on Sunday.'

'It's supposed to be utterly chic. You'll have to sneak some photos.'

'I don't know about starting another painting. I should be getting on with selling this place. Gill will be back in the shop by the time I've finished hers and I'd like to be ready to leave then.'

Xavier dismissed this. 'Aren't you happy here? What's so special about London, anyway? Is there someone you're pining for? A lover, friends from the art school?'

'No lover,' India said. And no friends she particularly missed. Her companions at the Slade had been paintings, sculptures, the work and written lives of artists she admired; a fellow student with whom she had had a relationship of a few weeks had accused her of living in a two-dimensional world. What about the sculptures? She had thought.

'I'm still paying rent on the flat in London,' she said. 'It's more than I'm getting from Blooming Beautiful.'

'Get someone to pack it up. If you give me your agent's details, I'll organise the refund of the bond once it's been cleared and cleaned. That'll easily pay for the storage and there should be something left over. At least you'll be square then.'

'I don't know ...'

'And don't forget you're doing my portrait as well. And Toby's.'

'Toby?'

'Toby Teo. Hazel's brother.' Seeing that India was staring into the fire with a distant expression, Xavier swung his legs up and nudged her with his feet. 'Hey, I'm telling you this major thing and you're not even listening.'

'Sorry,' 'India said. 'I am.' And she was, with one ear. She was also thinking. Perhaps she should let the flat go. She wouldn't be staying there after Mars House was sold, anyway. And if she could get a mechanic to get Grace's Land Cruiser going, she could get rid of the hire car as well. It would all help with the cash flow in the meantime.

'Toby's never been in love before,' Xavier was saying. 'He's going out of his brain. So am I. It's like being shoved out of a plane without a parachute. But Vivienne's determined that he's going to become the great Sydney specialist with the perfect harbourside house and wife and children. It's a nightmare.'

India reached under the sofa for her sketchbook and quickly drew an image of two naked boys tumbling through the air. She ripped out the page and passed it down the sofa.

Xavier pressed the drawing against his chest and burst into tears.

32

Gill felt around for the phone and not finding it, she opened her eyes and with a groan, propped herself up on her elbow and twisted so she could see the floor. The Cairns, a pillow of white fur at the other end of the sofa, gazed at her groggily.

There was the phone – on the floor in front of the sofa. She leaned over and stretched out her arm and managed to scrabble it into reach. She fell back on the cushions and panting from the effort, tapped in the password, Olivia's date of birth. The screen came to life, the screensaver a picture of three-year-old Olivia in a tshirt with a rainbow unicorn on the front. She was squatting in one of those horse feeders made from an old car tyre and her eyes were squeezed shut. They were playing hide-and-seek and she was hiding.

No messages. No missed calls. No emails, from Olivia, at least. Or even from bloody Nicholas.

She dropped the phone back onto the floor. She should be getting up and attempting a shower. She was still in the robe she'd left hospital in and no doubt smelled and was stiff and aching. The warm water would help that as well, as would some of the painkillers they'd given her at the hospital. But it was all too hard. Everything was too hard.

She closed her eyes and hoped against hope that she'd go back to sleep and that Olivia would text or call. She'd even welcome a call from bloody Nicholas.

Night was drawing in, the sounds of horses eating their evening feed came from the stalls.

'Where's Mockingbird?' Leila demanded.

Donnacha killed the computer screen. The bite from her eyes made him feel like acid had been poured over his skin. He brought his lips together and remained silent.

'Beef said she'd been sold. Who bought her? Someone in the hunt?'

Pride made him meet her gaze. She looked away. She was dressed in tight jeans, a cashmere version of her red hoodie and studded motorcycle boots. The look was sexy.

'Off into town, are we?' he said, or rather, rasped. 'Meeting someone special, are we?' Her hair, newly washed, shone with the same glow as the hollow of her throat.

She turned and was gone, leaving behind the scent of burnt vanilla.

'Stay away from Sorrows,' he yelled as the door closed.

Seconds later the door opened again. But instead of Leila returning, it was Beef.

'I just saw Leila running out of the stables and your sorry eyes look like they're bleeding. What's going on?'

'Nothing.'

'And my name's Lucien Blythe.'

'Leave it, man.'

'Well I can tell you one thing, Leila's meeting Eleanor Lonsdale at The Barmy for a drink and after what I've just seen, I wouldn't be surprised if she doesn't make a night of it. You'll be feeding the yearlings yourself in the morning and it'll serve you right.'

Donnacha rubbed his forehead to ease the throbbing between his eyes. Leila was meeting Eleanor, not Pan. The two girls often met for a drink and a natter. Well they'd certainly have a bit to talk about. He switched on the computer screen.

'This might interest you.' He ran the camera footage back and stopped it where it showed Leila entering BlueBuckle's yard. 'Pull up a chair.'

They leaned towards the screen.

'Look at that,' he said as BlueBuckle turned in the air over Leila's prone body. 'Why'd he do that? Why didn't he break her up when he could?'

'I said someone with balls put that bucket in the yard.' Beef shook his head. 'Bloody miracle she got out of there.'

'That's what I'm saying.'

'Show us again. Stop when he turns if you can.'

It took three more runs to get the freeze in exactly the right spot. Beef pointed. 'That might be your answer.'

'What?'

'Can you make his head larger? Just his head.'

Donnacha took a screen shot, opened it in a new window and enlarged BlueBuckle's head. 'What are you seeing, man?'

Beef gestured at BlueBuckle's eyes. 'Misery.' Beef leaned back and contemplated the image on the screen. 'He's not a murderer. His anger might be murderous, but his heart isn't.'

It fitted, Donnacha thought. And he certainly couldn't think of any other explanation as to why BlueBuckle had not run over Leila when he could. The turn that he'd made to avoid her would have caused his wasting muscles to almost flame.

'Let's take this to Pan Villon,' Beef said. 'And anything else you think. Blythe doesn't have to know. Pan might come up with something.'

Donnacha stared at the screen. Beef's eyes were on him, waiting for him to spit out the brick in his throat, but he couldn't. But by what right could he deny BlueBuckle this one chance? Horses had been his constant from the beginning of his memory. They had grown him up, taught him responsibility, unselfishness, courage, and tenderness. They had introduced him to other, equally grand creatures and features of the natural world and had given him a means of paying his way. They gave him wings.

If Pan could find a way to help BlueBuckle, BlueBuckle should have the chance. In the scheme of things, it was his right. And if Pan could make Leila happy, in the scheme of things, that was her right also.

He found a thumb drive. 'I'll put it all on this, but you'll have to take it to Villon.' And then it came out, like muck out of an abscess.

'He and Leila have a thing for each other. That's why Leila's back in the dorm.'

The main bar of the Burragong Arms Hotel, known by the locals as The Barmy, was panelled with blonde marine ply and the wall behind the wood heater, a popular spot on chilly nights, was covered with signed photos of the Highland's sporting famous. Leila and Eleanor bagged a table away from the bar and the knot around the heater. 'First's on me,' Eleanor said.

She returned a minute later with a bottle of Sauvignon Blanc. Leila checked the label. 'Nice. Are we celebrating?'

'Getting shit-faced more like it.' Eleanor said. 'Sorry, that sounded awful. Any fantastic yearlings coming along?'

Leila nodded. 'Some beauties. I'm taking five up to the Magic Millions sale next week …' She stopped. Eleanor wasn't listening. Perhaps the opening meet would be a better topic? But the thought of Mockingbird stopped her raising it.

'I love your outfit,' she said instead, even though Eleanor was not her usually impeccable self – her velvet jeans and cardigan were the same pretty tan as her knee-high boots, but she was wearing a lot of makeup and her hair was dull.

'I was just thinking the same about yours,' Eleanor said. She looked over at the bar at the tradies sneaking glances in their direction, smiled vaguely and turned her attention back to her drink.

Leila pushed her glass about the table. By now they would usually be deep into it, talking horses and trading gossip about Whistlejacket and the Highlands Hunt, but tonight, they sat stiffly, mostly in silence.

Eleanor emptied her glass and poured another. Leila put her hand over hers to say that she was taking it slowly.

Eleanor dumped the bottle back in the cooler. 'I screwed Lucien,' she blurted out.

'Lucien?'

Eleanor took a huge swallow of her drink. 'At the opening meet. It's over between me and Simon. It's been over for months, but I haven't had the guts to leave. Now there's no choice. Being unfaithful's a big deal for me. There's no way I could sleep with Simon again.'

No wonder you want to get shit-faced, Leila thought. 'Have you told Simon?'

'Not about Lucien, but he knows I'm leaving. It should only have ever been a fling. I knew it all along and what's sad is that I think he did too. The presents were all to make up for what wasn't in his heart. Or to make me nicer. He's the sweetest man and I've become a shrew. I don't know how he stood it.'

'Still, he must be shattered. Even if he doesn't know about Lucien.'

'I'm not sure he doesn't suspect. He's been drunk since the opening meet. I've been telling myself it's just the pressure of a new season and the fact that I've been such a bitch. But, well, he likes to play the fool but he's not stupid.'

'But you're not having an affair with Lucien?' Leila asked.

'No,' Eleanor said flatly. 'It was only ever going to be the once.' She turned her glass in her fingers. 'My mother says I deliberately choose men I'm never going to stay with because I'm too fundamentally selfish to love properly. Maybe it's true. Maybe I am just an opportunist as they say in the Hunt.'

'Crap,' Leila protested. 'Donnacha's always talking about the work you do for the Hunt and as for mothers ...' she rolled her eyes. 'Mine's always warning me off men altogether.' And maybe, her mother had a point.

Suddenly unable to bear the weight of her own aching heart, Leila rose and went to the bar to get some chips. She'd thought she might get Eleanor's take on Donnacha, but now it was out of the question. Not that she minded. There was little to say, really. And what was the use, anyway? Donnacha had not just slammed the door in her face, he had locked it and thrown away the key.

One of the tradies kept her with a bit of cheeky chat and when she returned, Eleanor was sitting staring zombie-like at the wine bottle.

She ripped open the chip bag and dropped it on the table. 'Here, get into these. So, what are you going to do now?'

Eleanor took a chip and held it. 'I've moved out of the house, but the problem's the Hunt. The state Simon's in, I'm not sure he'll be able to keep things going. Gill could have taken over as Field Master, but now she's got her leg and Grace is gone … It's all a mess, really.'

They sat in silence for a while, the buzzing around them intensifying their loss of words.

'I've had an idea,' Eleanor said suddenly. 'I've hardly spent any of the allowance Simon's been giving me. I'll use it to hire someone to help him with the hounds and the horses and you can take over as Field Master.'

'Isn't that a committee decision?' Leila asked. 'Anyway, I don't have a horse.' Her anger at Donnacha returned. She had asked Beef if he knew where Mockingbird had gone, but he'd said he didn't know. More likely he didn't want to say. Bloody men.

'The committee's me, Simon, Lucien, Gill and Lesley Bond, so there won't be a problem. You can ride Elvis. You'll love him. He's brilliant.'

Leila protested. Out of all the presents Simon had given Eleanor, Elvis was the one she had truly appreciated. 'I couldn't.'

'It's only right that Elvis stay with the Hunt,' Eleanor said firmly. 'What do you say? If everything is on track with the Hunt Simon will pull himself together in no time.'

'I don't know,' Leila said uncertainly. 'It sounds crazy.' It was crazy.

'You can work something out with Lucien so you can keep Elvis at Whistlejacket. You and Donnacha can go to the meets together.' Eleanor pulled a face. 'Just don't ask me to talk to Lucien.'

Leila broke a chip into tiny pieces. Elvis, the hunting – it would be a dream come true. She'd arrived at Whistlejacket mid last season and had had a few days out with the Hunt before the end of the season and the hunting had been fantastic. But keeping Elvis at Whistlejacket, travelling to the meets with Donnacha? No way. Maybe Elvis could stay at Gwynedd? But that wouldn't work either. He'd need regular riding to keep hunt fit and what time she had outside of work, especially during winter's shorter days, would be eaten up travelling between Whistlejacket and Gwynedd. There'd be virtually no time to ride. And that besides, she'd have to keep up the shifts at the Bombay Duck to pay for Elvis' feed and shoeing.

She crushed the broken chip with her forefinger. 'I don't think so.'

'Why?' Eleanor demanded. 'I can tell by your face that you want to.'

It was weak, but it was all she could think of. 'If Elvis is at Whistlejacket, Lucien will want to ride him. You know what he's like. If he wants something, he takes it.' Realising what she'd just said, she quickly apologised. 'Sorry, that came out badly.'

'It's okay,' Eleanor said. 'He did rather help himself. But remember, so did I. Come on, let's go to the Bombay Duck. We'll think better with food in us.'

33

Yolanda pointed Leila and Eleanor to a table near the fire. With its tapestries and thick curtains, the Bombay Duck was not particularly cold, but the fire gave the room a cosy ambience and the wood smoke added a pleasing note to the smell of spice.

Eleanor took a few steps towards their table and stopped.

'What?' Leila said.

Eleanor tilted her head towards a table on the other side of the fireplace. 'Lady Blythe,' she whispered. 'Let's go back to The Barmy.'

'No way,' Leila said in a normal voice.

Lady Blythe glanced briefly in their direction and after an even briefer smile, tuned her attention back to her friends.

Leila shoved Eleanor, propelling her forwards. At their table, Eleanor sat with her back to Lady Blythe.

'Do you seriously think she knows about you and Lucien?' Leila asked.

'I don't know what she knows,' Eleanor said. 'But I can imagine what she'd think, and that's terrifying enough.'

Leila laughed. 'I wish I had her memory. She knows the winner of every black type race in the world going back thirty years.'

'Take up bridge. It's supposed to help. You could get her to give you some pointers.'

'She's supposed to be rubbish at it.' Leila breathed in the scent of cardamom, cumin, turmeric and rosemary, and her favourite, chili.

Soothed, she allowed herself a moment to think about Mocking-bird. Hopefully, whoever had bought her would give her the life she deserved. And at least she'd never have to see Lucien again.

Yolanda came over with the wine list. 'Lenny's got a date tonight so I'm your wine waiter. Are we drinking red or white?'

Leila looked at Eleanor. 'Champagne?' What else did you drink when everything was crazy?

'Perfect,' Eleanor said.

'Let me choose for you.' Yolanda kept the wine list firmly under her elbow. She already had a bottle in mind that, unlike the Cristal tickling palates at Lady Blythe's table, would not cost the same as a pair of heels at Vittino's on the high street.

'Will you head back to New Zealand?' Leila asked after Yolanda had gone.

Eleanor shook her head. 'Washington. I was about to apply for a work visa for the States when it all happened with Simon. There's supposed to be great hunting in Virginia, which is not that far from the capital.'

For a moment Leila envied Eleanor the university degree that had gotten her a position high up in one of New Zealand's top banks, and that would now see her similarly employed in America. But then she thought about spending her days in an office. No thanks to that. And no matter how high your position, you couldn't keep a horse in an office. A dog, maybe, but not a horse.

She stood up suddenly. 'Back in a minute.'

Yolanda was in the kitchen with Stephan, tasting a sauce. 'Is everything all right?' she asked.

'I just wanted a quick word with Stephan.'

Stephan grinned. 'I'm all yours, as ever.'

'Um, Eleanor's asked me to ride Field Master and she's offered me her horse, Elvis, but I can't keep him at Whistlejacket. I was wondering if I could agist him with you? I'd need Scott to truck him to the hunts as well.'

Stephan shrugged. 'Not my area, but I'll call Scott as soon as this sauce has reduced.'

'Finger's crossed,' she said. 'I'd be very grateful.'

'It'll cost,' Stephan said.

A little discouraged, she said, 'I'll take any shifts that are going here.'

A while later, their table now loaded with copper bowls of Bombay duck, Tikka salmon, saffron dahl and fragrant butter rice, Stephan came over.

'Scott said okay.'

'Okay what?' Eleanor asked.

'Okay for me to agist Elvis at Tarlo,' Leila told her. She gave Stephan a grateful smile. 'Thanks so much.'

'Scott wants to know if Leila's taking over as Field Master because you're pregnant,' Stephan said to Eleanor.

'God, I hope not,' Eleanor said.

'I'd better go tell him then before he spreads it around the Hunt.'

'I can't thank you enough,' Eleanor said to Leila as Stephan loped off. 'You've no idea how relieved I am.'

They set to work filling their plates, soaking up the sauces with the naan bread, licking their fingers so as not to miss a morsel.

Picking over the last of the rice on her plate for any hidden scraps of salmon, Eleanor said, 'I'll take Elvis over to Tarlo Monday or Tuesday so he can get settled in before the next meet. Not that he's likely to be bothered by the move. He's so laidback. He should have been called Bentley instead of Elvis. No matter what's going down, he just purrs along. I'll pay for his agistment of course, for this season at least.'

'No you won't,' Leila protested.

'I'm only spending money that Simon gave me. It makes me feel better that it's going back to the Hunt. And you shouldn't have to be forking out when you're doing me such a great favour.' Eleanor pushed her plate away. 'I feel better about Simon now. He's a truly beautiful man. He deserves someone that will adore him like Rebecca did, and that he can similarly adore. I really hope he finds her. At least now he'll have the chance.'

Yolanda stopped at their table. 'Looks like you two were hungry.'

'It was gorgeous,' Eleanor said. 'Especially the extra chili in the salmon.'

Yolanda smiled. 'That was for Leila. Stephan knows she's a chili fiend.'

'We might get the bill,' Eleanor said, stifling a yawn. 'I'm ready for bed.'

Yolanda shook her head. 'Tonight's on the house. You've got us out of trouble a number of times,' she said to Leila. 'The least we can do is stand you the odd meal.'

'She's just got the Hunt out of trouble, too,' Eleanor said, looking at Leila gratefully.

They stepped out into the biting night air and started for The Barmy carpark where they'd left their cars.

Eleanor put her arm through Leila's. 'You don't think I'm terrible for screwing Lucien, do you? Ever been tempted yourself?'

Leila shook her head. All she cared about at that moment was going to sleep and waking up in the morning and hopefully discovering that the evening hadn't been a dream.

'I must admit he's pretty bloody yummy,' Eleanor said. 'I wonder if Gill would take over as Hunt Secretary? She's done it before. Simon said she was great. There's still all the ball stuff to sort out. I'm going to miss the Hunt. Some of the members I won't, but there's a lot I will. And it probably sounds strange, but I'm going to miss Simon horribly. I really wish it had worked out.'

'I know what you mean,' Leila said, thinking about Donnacha.

34

Stunned and bleary-eyed from lack of sleep and the morning's seemingly endless trail of customers at Blooming Beautiful, India squinted at the man standing at the front door.

'Hello, you,' he said as Jeffrey pushed past her and pressed his nose into his outstretched hand.

It was Pan Villon.

'Xavier told me you wanted to get Grace's Land Cruiser going,' he said.

She stepped back and opened the door for him. He was dressed in jeans and a faded rugby top with a once white collar and a pair of battered work boots. His cheeks and chin were darkened by a fine stubble and a pair of sunglasses held his hair back from his forehead. He looked and smelt of the outside and seemed to reach the living room in just a few strides.

He stood with his back to the empty fireplace.

'This is the first time I've been here since Grace died.' His mouth formed a resigned line.

'There's a box with your name on it,' she told him. 'It's full of horse things. You must take it with you.'

'Let's go and look at the vehicle,' he said to Jeffrey.

'Do you want –'

'I know where it is,' he said, cutting her off. 'And I've got a set of keys.'

He also knew the way out the back door and to the garage. He and Grace must have been very close. Lovers? If anyone knew it would be Xavier.

She put on the jug to boil and took the coffee tin out of the fridge. Should she make Pan a cup? Maybe not. It would mean going to the garage where she was clearly not wanted, and besides, she needed to get back to the painting. The mare's head was still not right. She'd spent most of the night going between the photo, the sketches she'd done for the painting and the painting itself. Wrapped in her coat just as dawn was beginning to lighten the sky – the fire long gone out – she had done a new sketch from the photo, to scale with the painting. Hopefully it would show where she was wrong on the canvas.

She poured the steaming water onto the coffee grounds and her stomach growled, reminding her that she'd had nothing to eat other than the chocolate croissant Julie had brought when she came to clear the till. But her hunger for the painting was far stronger.

'There's too much length between the nostril and the cheek.'

She'd forgotten about Pan but now he was at her side, in front of the painting.

'Sorry?'

He pointed. 'There. That nostril needs to come up about two millimetres. And the rim needs to be thicker. It's a serious bit of cartilage. And maybe you could widen the nostril a tiny bit. But otherwise it's not bad. You've got Hester's coat just right.'

Unable to see what he was seeing she went to the workbench and on the new drawing drew a circle around Hester's nose and marked the areas he had pointed to with small crosses, then beckoned him over.

'Here?'

He stared intently at the drawing. She smelt engine grease and spent leaves and saw that the line of his mouth was less severe than when he'd arrived.

He turned towards her. 'I'm sorry about earlier. I was rude. When I saw you in the doorway … It sounds insane, I could see Grace. I knew it wasn't her, but …' He picked up the pencil and altered the drawing and pushed it towards her.

She examined his marking and then went to the painting. She wanted him to go, but she remembered the Land Cruiser.

'Grace's car? Is it still okay?'

'I've taken out the battery. It should be right after a charge, it's only a year or so old. I'll drop it off at the garage on the way home. You'll have to get the registration transferred into your name. Have you driven a Land Cruiser before? They're brutes, especially to park.'

She shook her head. She was thinking about the registration. She had no idea how to transfer it. But Xavier would know.

'I'll take you for a drive when I put the battery back in and give you a few tips.'

The doorbell rang.

'Damn,' she said, without thinking.

'I'll get it,' Pan said. 'I'm going, anyway.'

He was gone, without taking the box from Grace. She put the lamp she used for extra light on the stool beside the easel and angled it towards Hester's head.

The sound of footsteps and sobbing came down the hallway. Pan reappeared with Hazel Teo.

'Hazel needs to see you.'

'What's happened?' she asked, reluctantly leaving the painting. 'Has your mum found out about the tattoo?'

Panting like an overheated pug, Hazel stared at the floor, tears dripping off her chin. Her eyes were so swollen they had almost disappeared in her face.

With a last glance at the painting, she went and put her arm around Hazel's shoulder and gently guided her out of the room. Pan and Jeffrey followed.

She led Hazel to the sofa and making a space for her among the cushions and books, told her to sit.

'I'll be off then,' Pan said.

'No, don't,' Hazel begged. 'Please don't.'

'Could you make some tea?' India asked.

'Brandy?' Hazel managed to squeak.

'Definitely not. But I do have fruitcake.'

'Did you make it?' Hazel asked. The tears had stopped and apart from the odd muffled sob she was starting to settle. She put out a hand to Jeffrey, who licked it consolingly. 'Did you use Grace's recipe?'

'No, I didn't. I bought it at the Burragong Hospital Auxiliary street stall.'

Hazel's mouth turned down. 'Jeffrey can have mine.'

India could hear the jug boiling. 'The tea's in the Twining's caddy and the cake's in the tin with a German Shepherd on it,' she called. Though if Pan had his own keys to Grace's vehicle, he'd likely know where everything was. She perched on the end of the sofa next to Hazel.

'How did you get here?'

Hazel pulled up her legs and arranged the tweed coat around herself so that only her head and hands were visible.

'Taxi. Mum gave me money for the movies. She thinks I'm with Alisha Haswell. As if! Alisha's a troll.'

Pan came in with a tea tray. He held out a plate with slices of the cake. 'Come on, it's almost as good as Grace's.'

Hazel shook her head. 'I'll vomit.'

'No you won't,' India said. 'It'll do you good. It'll help.'

Hazel's eyes again filled with tears. 'Nothing'll help. Mum's selling Dorothy and I'm starting at Garton House on Monday. Mum's told Scott Page about Dorothy in case any of his pupils want her and she's putting an ad in *Horse Deals* too.'

'Dorothy was supposed to come back to me when you grew out of her,' Pan said angrily. 'Your mum signed a contract.'

Hazel hung her head. 'She's asking twice what we gave you for her. Garton House's a prison. The girls are cyberstalkers and dipsos. They've all got vodka in their water bottles. They say it's to take away the pain of their braces but it's not. They're evil.'

She shuddered and went on. 'I just want to keep Dorothy and be a hairdresser and work with mum and maybe have my own salon one day. It doesn't matter that I'm getting too big for Dorothy. I don't have to ride her to love her. I'd work at the salon after school and on the weekends and pay for her keep myself if mum'd let me. Then I could save up for a new horse and do eventing. Dorothy would be its friend.' Her voice faded to a whisper. 'Toby says we have to do what mum wants because we're her world and why she works so hard, but I don't think it's fair.'

'Bloody parents,' Pan said, 'They're the last people that should ever have children.'

He knowns about mine, India thought as Pan's eyes met hers. She looked away. He couldn't. Grace never talked about them. She was being paranoid.

'I'll go and see Vivienne,' Pan said to Hazel. 'And I'll pick Dorothy up this afternoon if I have to. I'll say Scott told me she was for sale. He probably will anyway, but I'll call him just in case Vivienne checks.'

'That must make you feel a bit better,' India said to Hazel.

Hazel's voice quivered 'But what about Garton House and what about Olivia? She dropped her forehead onto her knees.

'What about Olivia?' India asked. 'You'll still be able to be friends.'

Hazel looked at her through her now slits of eyes. 'We won't. She's gone to live with Mr Findlay in Sydney. It's my fault. We had this massive fight. I … I said shit things about Oscar. She must have gotten a new phone because her number's dead. She's even gone off Facebook. It's like she's totally disappeared.'

Pan looked at his watch. 'What time's Vivienne expecting you home?'

'About four,' Hazel sniffed.

'Come on, I'll drive you. You don't want to make things any worse.'

India took Hazel to the bathroom, washed her face and re-plaited her hair and fetched one of Grace's knits, a bright red mohair jumper. Hazel looked at herself in the mirror. 'I look like a big pimple,' she said morosely.

35

'Who is it?'

Eleanor could just make out Gill's outline through the wavy glass. 'It's Eleanor.'

'I'm not feeling well enough to see anyone. I'm sorry.'

'Should I call your doctor?'

'I just need to rest.'

Gill's voice sounded wrong. Not like her at all. Perhaps she'd developed an infection. 'I really think I should come in.'

The door opened a little. Gill looked terrible. Her face was gaunt, her normally vivid blue eyes were dull and red rimmed and her hair as dirty as the robe she was holding closed with her free hand.

Trying not to show her shock, Eleanor gently pushed on the door, forcing Gill to hop backwards. 'I really think I should call your doctor. Or maybe we should go to the hospital.'

'I'm okay,' Gill said to the floor. 'Really, I am. I just need to rest.'

Eleanor stepped into the hallway. The Cairns' anxious white faces appeared around the door of the living room. She could smell the dead air from where she was standing.

'Is Nicholas here?' What was he doing letting Gill and the place get into such a state?

Gill swayed, looking for a moment like she was about to topple over. 'Nicholas has gone to Sydney.'

'When's he coming back?'

'He's not. And Olivia's gone with him.'

Eleanor put her hand on Gill's arm. 'Come on, I'll make us some tea.'

The kitchen benches were clear, the sink empty. The rubbish bin, when Eleanor peeked in the swing top, was half full of empty dog food tins. Typical of Gill that she could find the strength to care for her animals but not herself.

The milk was still in-date, just. While the tea was drawing, Eleanor set the tray she found leaning against the microwave and took the cellophane off some biscuits labelled JULIE'S GINGER CREAMS.

Gill was on the sofa, a little dog either side of her and her plastered leg resting on an ottoman. She had combed her hair into some kind of shape and retied the robe so that it didn't look so askew and the blanket that had been on the floor was folded and draped over the arm of the sofa.

Eleanor put the tray on the coffee table.

'When I heard your knock, I thought it might be Olivia coming home,' Gill said.

Eleanor handed her a mug of tea. 'I'm surprised she went.'

'Nicholas said she wanted to.' Gill's tone was despairing.

'I can't believe she'd leave Expresso. Or you. And what about Hazel? She and Olivia are like sisters.'

'Nicholas would have made Liv feel like she was doing the right thing. He can pass poison off as honey. Though I suppose she'd have called if she wasn't happy. I miss her so much.' Gill put down the tea and buried her fingers in the furry side of the little dog pressed against her left hip. 'Thank god for dogs.'

'He shouldn't have left you on your own.'

Gill took a biscuit. 'I'd dunk if you want to keep your teeth. Julie makes them in a cement mixer. They haven't even got any ginger in them.' She dipped the biscuit in her tea, broke it and gave half in turns to the Cairns.

Eleanor held out the plate. 'Take one for yourself. Or I could make you an omelette.' There had been eggs in the fridge when she looked.

Gill slumped back against the sofa. 'Thanks, but I'm really not hungry.'

This isn't the Gill I know, Eleanor thought. The Gill she knew never balked at anything. She had ridden for hours in freezing rain with a dead hound across the front of her saddle, jumped Hester over a cattle grid to catch a runaway horse and sat in a rising creek with Lillian Bickham's horse when it had slipped and gotten its leg trapped. She burned bright. She was an Amazon.

36

Pan rounded the last bend to the house. A dark blue Nissan ute, the door stencilled with Whistlejacket's rearing stallion, was parked in front of the garage. The pig, Pharlap, and Sadie, having planted their substantial bottoms next to it, were staring fixedly at the man in the driver's seat.

Sadie turned her head and gave a single sharp bark, the signal that his attention was needed. Pharlap shuffled her trotters but kept her gaze steady on the ute.

He pulled up and walked over to them, pondering the identity of the ute's driver. Donnacha would have gone inside or settled himself on the veranda and Lucien, who had once called on Hunt business, had driven his own vehicle, not a company one.

It was Beef Reedhead. He lowered his window. 'Is that pig all right man? I mean is it dangerous or anything? It's monstrous big.'

Pan gave Pharlap's back a scratch, causing her to show her terrifying teeth in a smile, snort and shudder all at the one time. Sadie pushed her black head into his other hand so she could get a scratch as well.

'Wouldn't hurt a fly. What brings you to Big Hill?'

Beef held up a thumb drive. He opened the ute door cautiously and stood gazing at Pharlap.

Pan glanced towards the stables with regret. The negotiation with Vivienne had been wearying – in the end she'd agreed to three-three-fifty, twice what she'd paid for Dorothy – and he'd been looking forward to getting out for a while on Chopper.

'Come inside.' Then seeing that Beef was reluctant to leave his vehicle, he told Pharlap and Sadie to bugger off. 'And you too,' he said to Frenchie, who was now ratting around in the back of the ute looking for food.

The shrubs lining the path to the house vibrated with tiny bush wrens feeding on the insects whose arrival heralded the coming dusk. The veranda was strewn with dog beds and water bowls and chewed bits of stick. Pan held open the screen door. 'Straight ahead and down the hall.'

The long room was minimally furnished with a scratched-up tobacco coloured leather sofa and armchairs, a coffee table, desk and an expensive looking telescope. A silk carpet, smudged by lolling dogs, ran the length of a floor to ceiling window that provided an uninterrupted view of the valleys leading to the big hill and the hill itself.

Beef stood captivated. 'You ever go up there?'

'All the time.' Pan went to the desk, turned on a laptop and invited Beef to sit. 'Set yourself up. Coffee or beer?'

'Beer thanks, comrade.' Beef placed the thumb drive on the desk. 'Hopefully I can get this jigger to work.'

When Pan returned, Beef had the yard footage up on the screen. 'This is confidential, you understand. Between you me and Donnacha. The stallion's name is BlueBuckle. Blythe bought him from a stud in Kentucky. Everything above board there and no dramas in quarantine we know of but now no bugger can get near him and, as you can see...' Beef shrugged at the screen.

Pan stared as BlueBuckle charged the yard rails.

'He came off the truck like a lamb and a day or so later, this started,' Beef said.

Another cut: BlueBuckle, nostrils pulsing red pools, bearing down on Leila, knocking her to the ground.

Beef took a sharp breath. 'Could've killed her.'

'But he didn't,' Pan said as BlueBuckle's hindquarters bunched and he pirouetted, his front hooves raking the air over the prone Leila.

'That's got me and Donnacha puzzled too.'

The footage switched to BlueBuckle pounding the bucket, his lips a snarl.

'Leila put the bucket in,' Beef said. 'Blythe stopped the stallion's water. Thought it might calm him.' It occurred to him that if Pan and Leila were having a thing, Pan would already know about the bucket. He'd likely know as much about BlueBuckle as any of them. But if he did, he was putting on a good show of not.

The screen filled with an image of BlueBuckle rock still in the corner of his yard, every rib visible, his hooves disappeared in his own muck.

Beef took a pull of the beer. 'Blythe's vet, Cherry, was at the stud the day he arrived, but we didn't think to get any blood taken. There was no reason to, anyway. Nothing stood out in quarantine. They take it every day there. The results came with him. Donnacha's spoken to Kentucky and by all accounts, the horse was a gent. Not just to handle, but around mares as well. Sweet as a peach.'

Pan hit replay and watched the footage again. When it came to the end, he shook his head. 'Something's happened to make death a better option.'

'Cherry said something about a brain tumour.'

Pan stared at the screen. 'I don't think a tumour's the problem.'

There was a racket of snorts and barks from outside and then a knock. Benzo and Ghillie, asleep together on a horse rug in the corner, raised their heads and briefly twitched their noses before returning to their dreams.

A call came from the front door. 'Hello. Hello.'

'Sounds like Leila,' Pan said. 'Keep coming down the hall,' he called.

So Donnacha had been right, Beef thought. But then changed his mind when Leila went straight to the window, saying, 'Wow, Donnacha said the view was incredible. He didn't say anything about the pig, though. It's a bloody security guard on steroids.'

'Pharlap? The only thing she's ever bitten is a pumpkin,' Pan said.

Beef looked from Pan to Leila. If they were having a thing, Leila would have known all about the pig as well. Either Donnacha was out of his tree or she and Pan were academy award winning actors.

'It is a particularly unsettling beast, Pan,' he said, the pig bothering him far more than what Pan and Leila were or weren't doing. It could stop an army in its tracks. Not to mention feed one. 'How'd it get the name Pharlap?'

'Because of her speed,' Pan said. 'If she charges you, don't bother running. She'll have you in seconds.'

Seeing Beef's look of horror, Pan grinned. 'I'm joking, man. I called her that because she's a chestnut. She was one of Lesley Bond's. She couldn't breed, but Lesley couldn't bring herself to give her the chop. Didn't you notice her human eyes?'

'I'd have given it the chop, no worries,' Beef muttered. Human eyes, what a shitload. The only thing he'd be running for was an axe.

Leila dragged herself away from the window and joined them at the computer. She gestured at the image of the wasted BlueBuckle. 'That's from the yard camera.' She held up her phone. 'I've got some film too, but this'll be much better. You and Donnacha will lose your jobs if Lucien finds out about this,' she said to Beef.

'You too if Blythe finds out you put water in the yard.'

Pan ran the footage again. Confronted with how close she'd come to being trampled Leila felt cold in the pit of her stomach.

'Any ideas?' Beef asked Pan.

'I really need to see him,' Pan said.

'Problem is, Blythe won't have you on the place,' Beef said. 'He's not your greatest fan, I believe. Something to do with a creek crossing.'

'Lucien's going up to the Gold Coast on Tuesday morning,' Leila said. 'We're selling yearlings at the Magic Millions.'

Pan pressed replay again, noticing for the first time that as Blue-Buckle bore down on Leila, his eyes were locked on the camera. 'What are you trying to tell us?' he murmured. BlueBuckle broke the contact, reared and wheeled away.

A shaft of light lit up the summit of the big hill. He stood up. 'Give him some water, a few times a day if you can. Add a little salt and molasses. Maybe a bit of kibble as well. Some mare's cubes. I'll hang on to the thumb drive, if you don't mind. I need to think. But I'll get back to you soon.'

He showed Leila and Beef out and returned to the computer and ran the footage again, and again, until he felt that his and

BlueBuckle's were the one flesh. Until he tasted the air as Blue-Buckle tasted it, felt with the same skin, heard with the same ears, drew in the same scents. But BlueBuckle's eyes remained closed to him. As much as he willed, he could not see what the stallion's gaze was fixed on.

37

Lady Blythe had Martin bring her a second coffee before he went to fetch India Levy. Yesterday's racing at Royal Randwick had not been the relaxed affair she'd been anticipating. She had planned for a pleasant afternoon in the suite of their host, a Turf Club executive and old friend of Jonno's, but Lucien had kept dragging her off to the parade ring. It had been exhausting, not to mention cruel, given the shoes she'd chosen in the expectation that much of the day would be spent lounging on the suite's suede sofas.

It wasn't as if there was any great reason to be in the parade ring. The Autumn Carnival was done and dusted and there were no Whistlejacket horses running. Just the odd youngster getting experience for the Spring Carnival and a few diehard favourites having a last fling before spelling, going to stud or into retirement. The top jockeys were either in Hong Kong for the weekend or in the air on their way to Dubai. As for the trainers, after the combat of the Autumn Carnival they looked plain and weary. Even the feathers on Gai Waterhouse's hat looked peaky.

But nevertheless, no matter with whom she was chatting, the ribbon of melting carpaccio or sliver of the smokiest smoked salmon she was about to drop into her mouth, at exactly a quarter of an hour before the runners were due to appear, Lucien muscled her away.

She could have accepted this attention had he then been content to watch the runners parade from a grandstand terrace. But no, they had to be viewed from the ring seats in the Theatre of the

Horse, where she was hustled and greeted by people she only vaguely knew or wished she didn't. More than once, her coatdress (Carol Middleton had worn the exact same one to her oldest daughter's wedding) was in danger of being doused with champagne and although the amphitheatre was sheltered by the back of the QEII Grandstand, there was enough of a breeze to fan her irritation.

And that had not been the sum of the day's annoyances. Digger Fahey's ghastly wife was partying in the adjoining suite with her celebrity girlfriends and a waiter left the adjoining door open. It was impossible to say which was more irritating: being jostled in the Theatre of the Horse or being surround by women loaded with diamonds to the point of vulgarity, breasts pumped up to near exploding. And to further refine her misery, Lucien had shown no interest in any of the gals she had brought into their conversations. If he'd looked twice at anybody or listened to a word they said, it was only to the drink waiters.

She put her hands either side of her mouth, pushed it into a smile and felt a little better. And then there was reason for a genuine smile. Grace Levy's granddaughter.

The gal's coat looked like it belonged to someone who slept on the streets. She told Martin to take it and examined what it revealed. An icy finger brushed her spine – it was almost as though Grace was in the room.

'Welcome, my dear. Welcome to Burragong and Le Manoir. Your grandmother is much missed by us all.'

'Thankyou.'

The gal's teeth were excellent and though her vowels were pleasantly clipped, her voice had none of the grandmother's military firmness.

'Please, please sit.' She waved at the sofa and herself sat on the ebonised, gilded chair that she favoured because it made her sit spar straight as a lady should. 'Martin has made Thai beef salad for our lunch.'

India remained standing. 'I didn't know I was staying for lunch.'

'We have so much to discuss about the portrait. What I should wear. Jewels or no jewels, and if jewels, which jewels? And there's the setting. You'll have to guide me.'

'I've always thought the wisteria loggia at Whistlejacket beyond pretty,' Martin said as he picked up the empty coffee cup.

She considered this, then shook her head. 'It's a chilly spot, don't you think? I'd come out looking shivery.'

'This is a beautiful room,' India said. Her eyes wandered the pair of Lady Blythe's chair and the mahogany writing table. 'Regency is one of my favourite periods.'

Lady Blythe raised an approving eyebrow. 'How clever of you.' Most of the room's furniture had come from the original Whistlejacket, and yes, were originals of the period. And, yes, it too was her favourite also.

'Perhaps a glass of champagne,' she said to Martin. 'And I'm sure the dachs would love to meet India.'

India sat down on the sofa. 'I prefer Ann. It's my middle name.'

'Ann is one of my favourite names. If Lucien had been a girl, or blessed with a sister, Ann would have been my top pick. I believe you were a pupil at the Slade. 'Can you tell me about my curtains?'

'William Morris,' India said. The gold lilies gleaming softly on the curtains' muted grey material, had been inspired by the Snakeshead meadow lily and the pattern first produced in Morris's London studio in 1876.

'Very good. You are clever.' And nothing at all like Grace, who put comfort above style. Though there was that coat the gal had been wearing.

Martin appeared with two flutes of champagne on a silver tray. India put up her hand as he offered the tray. 'Not for me.'

'Do,' Lady Blythe urged. 'Moët is so cheering.'

When Martin brought in the dachshunds, they were talking not about the portrait but about Versailles.

'Ann thinks that Versailles was the original Disneyland,' she told him. 'Isn't that precious?'

Martin let the dachshunds slide from his arms. 'It was known as the Pleasure Palace, after all.'

The little dogs went to their mistress and wove around her ankles in arcs that kept their sides brushing against her. She smiled tenderly and told them, 'Say hello, darlings. Ann's an artist. She might put you in my portrait. Or maybe you could have one all of your own.'

'Lunch is almost ready,' Martin said from the door.

Lady Blythe rose, brushing the creases out of her skirt, which clung to her narrow hips and thighs. She glanced at India. 'Thinking, thinking my dear. I can see the cogs turning. Come, you can tell me all your thoughts over lunch. I'm so enjoying getting to know you. I almost feel as though I finally have a daughter.'

Lucien had come straight from the hunt and was still dressed in his breeches and long black boots and blunt spurs. His jacket, however, had been swapped for a V-neck jumper of a similar navy to his mother's cardigan, but without the quirky cuffs. There were fine lines around his eyes from narrowing them against the wind. His colour was high, not from the outdoors but from a hit of coke.

He kissed his mother, who wrinkled her nose.

'You might have changed, darling. How was your hunt?'

'Fast. We covered a lot of country. Simon fell off. He was dead drunk. Couldn't get back on his horse. Donnacha Keough and Lesley bundled him into one of the follower's vehicles and got them to drive him back to the truck. Lord knows what they thought of it all.'

'I suppose you took over the hounds, then.'

'I got Donnacha to.'

'I'd have thought you'd have leapt at the opportunity.'

Lucien shook his head. 'Someone still had to ride Master. We had enough Whippers-in without Donnacha.' Feeling randy as a goat – Christie was certainly mixing crushed Viagra with the coke – he had in fact spent the rest of the hunt tailing Eleanor. For nothing, it had turned out.

He smiled at India. 'Afternoon India. Made a start on ma's portrait?'

'Heavens no,' Lady Blythe said. 'And please, she prefers to be called Ann.'

Lucien gave a "whatever" shrug and took up the chair next to the writing table. 'I thought you might at least have gotten to some sketches,' he said, leaning back in the fragile chair and stretching out his legs.

'We've been talking,' Lady Blythe said. 'I had no idea how many things portrait painters have to think about. Lighting, backgrounds, what to put in and what to not. It's fascinating, and Ann explains everything so well. I'm completely in her clever hands.'

Martin appeared with a coffee for Lucien. Lady Blythe's frown told him not to linger. As the door closed, she said to Lucien, 'I'm taking Ann to Royal Ascot. Ann thinks a visit to the London Portrait Gallery will help with my portrait, we'll fit that in as well. Kevin's making the bookings.'

Lucien sipped the coffee. Two business class flights with a stopover at The Palace in Dubai, a suite at the Lanesborough, a car and a driver, boutique shopping, hairdressers, manicures, massages, crates of Cristal – it would all easily eat up fifty thousand. Even for his mother it was extravagant. His head vibrated like an out of tune violin. Was India conning her? If the jaunt was a prelude to the portrait, how much was the bloody picture costing? Or was his mother sending him a message? Maybe she was dumping money so the need to call in what she was owed for BlueBuckle would become urgent. Or maybe she just wanted him to think that.

'What about Gill's shop?' he asked.

'Julie Rice won't mind looking after it,' Lady Blythe answered. 'Or Jeffrey. I'll call her myself.' She gave a happy sigh. 'I do love Royal Ascot and I'm so happy I'll have a companion this year.'

'You've always got companions at Ascot, ma,' he said. 'The Royal Enclosure's stuffed with your cronies.' He turned to India. 'Do you know what you're up for?' he asked, doubting that she'd ever been on a racecourse, let alone to one of the most prestigious meetings on the racing calendar.

India stood up. 'If you don't mind, Lady Blythe, I'd like to get back to Mars House. I've almost finished Gill's painting and there are some sketches I want to work on.'

Lady Blythe and Lucien also rose, Lucien offering, 'I'll drive you.'

'Martin is organised to take Ann home,' Lady Blythe said. She turned to India, 'He'll be in the downstairs sitting room if you wouldn't mind taking yourself down.'

When India had gone, Lucien dropped onto the sofa.

'I've asked you before not to wear your spurs in the house,' Lady Blythe said, not bothering to keep the irritation out of her voice. 'Aside from the fact it's not gentlemanly, you could catch one of the dachs in the stomach.'

He apologised. It was always better to play humble when his mother was on a burn, as she clearly was. He unbuckled the spurs and sliding them off his heels, rested them on his thigh. 'I thought India would have brought a portfolio with her.'

'She forgot it. She was up most of the night working on Gill Findlay's painting.'

'You don't think you're taking a risk pushing ahead without having seen her work?'

'I like her,' Lady Blythe said firmly. 'And I was very fond of her grandmother. She was a great friend.'

Lucien fingered the end of one of the spurs. His mother had loathed Grace Levy with a passion.

'I want to help her get established,' she continued. 'And to do that, she needs commissions. I'm going to get her to paint the stallions, too. I thought she might start with BlueBuckle.'

The vibrating in his head returned. He forced himself to sound enthusiastic. 'Fabulous idea. But she should do you first. Perhaps she should be aiming at the Archibald.' Seeing his mother was more than a little dazzled by the suggestion that her portrait be entered in Australia's most prestigious portrait competition, he ventured, 'I thought I might take Pinkie up to the Magic Millions. Digger's after a couple of horses and an extra pair of hands will be useful. I'm sure you can manage without her for a few days. Most of the clients will be up at the sale.'

Lady Blythe thought about this. 'I suppose it's sensible,' she agreed.

He rose. 'Good. I might head off then. I could use an early night.' He kissed his mother's cheek and once out of the room, he bounded down the stairs, jingling the spurs as though they were percussion instruments.

Kevin, who had brought takeaway for Martin's dinner, held open the front door. Lucien blew him a kiss and stepped out into the fading day. 'Slut,' he heard Kevin say. 'You'd better believe it,' he murmured.

Inside the Audi, he reached into the pocket of his hunting jacket and took out a rolled up fifty and the bag of coke Christie had given him at the races yesterday, along with the fastest blow job he'd ever had. Hoping Kevin was watching – he was in the mood for being watched – he raised one of his knees and tapped out a line. As stars exploded behind his eyes, he leaned back and imagined Pinkie licking champagne off Christie's thighs. The Gold Coast was going to be hot indeed. It was a good thing his mother would be taken up with her protégée. But then, it occurred to him as he started the engine, maybe her plans for India Levy went beyond helping her get established. Maybe she saw Grace Levy's granddaughter as the mother-to-be of her grandchildren. His heart started somersaulting like a gymnast on meth. Maybe his darling mother had hit on a way of wreaking revenge on her old foe and bringing him to heel in one fell swoop.

38

India left the spreadsheet Julie Rice had set up for Blooming Beautiful's orders and sales and went to the front of the shop. Pan Villon stood at the counter.

'I've got a new battery for the Land Cruiser,' he said. 'The old one wouldn't charge. I thought you might want to make a time to go for a drive.'

She couldn't think what he was talking about; Gill's painting was finished, but it had meant a full night without sleep. She gripped her plait and held onto it tightly as if it were the string of a balloon and she the ballon in danger of floating away.

A small knitted red and green Christmas stocking hung from the keyring he was waving. 'Grace's vehicle? The Land Cruiser?'

She yawned and apologised. 'Oh yes, sorry. Thanks, but I'm going to the UK tomorrow.'

The lines either side of his mouth deepened. 'You're leaving?'

'Only for a couple of weeks.'

'What about Jeffrey?'

Hearing his name, Jeffrey appeared from the back and slunk up to Pan, his tail flipping from side to side like a windscreen wiper.

'He's going to stay with Julie Rice.'

Pan squatted and wrapped his arms around Jeffrey, who laid his head on his shoulder and closed his eyes. 'Julie never lights the fire and her place is always freezing. And there's those bloody cats.'

As if he had understood what had just been said, Jeffrey began to shiver.

Pan held him tighter. 'He can come out to Big Hill. Grace usually left him with me when she visited you in London. I would have taken him after she died, but Julie sort of captured him. I'll pick him up this evening. I'll need his coat and his bowl.'

Xavier touched India's newly trimmed and artfully highlighted hair. 'You look like you've been to Vivienne.'

'Lady Blythe organised the appointment.'

'Lady Blythe!' Xavier held out a bottle of red. 'Let's get into this. I want to know every detail. Have you had dinner?'

'Hazel made me a toasted sandwich when I was at the salon.' India looked at the wine, thinking that it would instantly put her to sleep. She'd only been home long enough to light the fire – after Pan's criticism of Julie Rice she was nervous about him arriving and finding Mars House cold – feed Jeffrey and gather up his bowl and a few coats. She still had to dig out her passport and pack. But Xavier had already filled the glasses and when he handed her one, she sipped it anyway. There was always coffee if she was going to keel. And she could pack in the morning. She didn't have to be at Whistlejacket until eleven.

Xavier settled on the sofa beside Jeffrey, who was curled up on the tweed coat. 'Your hair does look very fab. Vivienne's a freak.'

'She certainly takes it seriously.' Vivienne had spent the first fifteen or so minutes picking up strands of her hair from different parts of her head and examining them. 'I was there most of the afternoon.' And when she left, her hair gleamed like washed sand and flowed over her shoulders and down her back with the naturalness of water finding its course.

She made a slippery coil of her hair and let it drop. 'And she's given me a bucket full of shampoos and conditioners and treatments. Apparently, my colour needs a lot of rare lipids to maintain it. Whatever rare lipids are.'

'Whatever they are, they're beyond the bank accounts of mere mortals. But you haven't told me how come Lady B's got Vivienne doing you favours. The rest of us have to book three months in advance.'

'I'm going to the UK with her tomorrow. To Royal Ascot.'

Xavier nearly spilled the wine on his white, white shirt. 'Royal Ascot. How did you get that gig?'

'She doesn't like travelling on her own these days, so she asked if I'd go with her. We're going to spend some time at the London Portrait Gallery as well to help with her portrait.' India gazed into the fire. Imagine if Lady Blythe had been her mother, not the fake hippy she'd been born to. Imagine growing up in a house like Le Manoir, a house full of beautiful things and genuine antiques and menservants.

'But what about the shop, what about Blooming Beautiful?' Xavier said.

'Julie Rice is looking after it. Lady Blythe called her.'

Xavier raised his eyebrows. 'Julie would have loved getting that call.'

Wondering about this but too tired to ask, India said, 'I'm meeting Lady Blythe at Whistlejacket tomorrow morning and we're going to Sydney airport from there.'

'You'll adore Whistlejacket. It's like a little village and the staff all look as though they've stepped out of a Netflix mini-series. Well, mostly, except for Donnacha, Beef and Janet Reedhead. I'm sure Lady B's hiring checklist has good looks at the top. The homestead is amazing. What are you charging for the portrait?'

India shrugged. 'I don't know. We haven't discussed it.' It was something she avoided thinking about. Putting a price on a painting was like putting a price on yourself, and how did you do that? And anyway, she might give Lady Blythe the portrait as payment for the trip to London. London. It seemed mad to be going there and coming back to Australia, but there was still Jeffrey and Mars House to sort out. And now Lady Blythe's painting and Xavier's, if he was serious. And Blooming Beautiful as well. While she had a job and could paint at night, the money issue was not so pressing.

Xavier clucked disapprovingly. 'How are you going make a living from painting if you don't know what to charge?'

'I've got to make a name for myself first. The thousand for Gill's painting was a bit generous.' Not feeling entitled to such a sum, she had put what she had not spent on art materials in a drawer in Grace's bedroom.

'Anything you do for Lady Blythe should be double that. Or triple. What are you going to charge me?'

'Nothing, of course.'

'That's ridiculous.' Xavier got up and poured himself another glass of wine. He held out the bottle to India, who put her hand over her still mostly full glass.

'I thought you artists were committed to drink,' Xavier said. 'And drugs.'

'Not me,' India said. Enough of the students at the Slade had thought vomiting the contents of their stomachs and minds onto paper and canvas was art, but to her, art was a journey of a different kind altogether. A drawing, a painting was its own escape and like the rabbit hole in *Alice in Wonderland*, it led to a world all of its own. Her job was to make this world real, not surreal and, as she had discovered as a small child, if she did the job well, her own world had some sense of meaning, of order, of peace.

'And anyway, I always had to work. There was no time for getting trashed. Grace paid my fees and an allowance, but I still had to pay my rent.'

'Working's good for the young,' Xavier said in a nannyish voice. 'Builds discipline. I had my first job at nine. I used to walk the dogs of some friends of my parents after school. I got ten dollars a week. My parents gave me two dollars and banked the rest.' He grinned. 'Maybe that's why I love spending now.' He pointed at his new Gucci loafers. 'I bought Toby a pair too. He's got these fabulous long feet. Wouldn't that make a great painting, me and Toby sitting together on a sofa wearing nothing but our Guccis?'

'Very Lucien Freud.'

Not knowing who Lucien Freud was, Xavier said, 'I expect I've gone down the line now Lady Blythe's taken you up.'

'Of course not,' she said. If it weren't for Xavier she'd be sitting in the dark alone. But she might also have sold Mars House and now be looking for a place to buy in London.

'I'll start your portrait the minute I'm back from London. And you're not paying me anything, you're going to sell Mars House. I'll expect to see a For Sale sign out the front when I return.'

Xavier protested. 'Now's not the time to be selling. Spring is when everyone starts looking.'

Ignoring this, India said, 'Gill's painting is finished. I'll have to leave the framing to you if you want her to have it straight away.' She went and fetched the painting from the workroom.

'Oh,' said Xavier, standing back as she propped the canvas against Grace's laptop. 'It's fabulous. The way you've done the sky is clever. It's so … airy. Gill's going to be thrilled. She and Hester look the perfect pair. She's always saying that hunting's better than sex. I'd curl up if Toby said that.'

'I wasn't sure about the size,' India said. After some deliberation and sketching on different sized pieces of paper she'd chosen fifty-five by seventy centimetres. Not too big and not too small.

'It's perfect. Gill's rooms aren't enormous, so it'll look great wherever she hangs it. My portrait's going to have to be life-sized so that Toby can kiss me on the lips when I'm not there. And in other …' He stopped as the doorbell rang.

It was Pan, the night's chill clinging to his oilskin jacket.

He went straight to the painting. 'Hester's head is just right now. I'll have to get you to paint Pharlap.'

'His pig,' Xavier explained. 'Bad luck,' he said to Pan. 'Pharlap will have to join the queue behind me and Lady Blythe.'

'Lady Blythe?'

'India's going to Royal Ascot with her.'

Pan turned to India. 'That's why you're going to London?'

India nodded.

'I'll leave you to it then,' he said brusquely.

'I've packed Jeffrey's things,' India said. 'And he's had his dinner.' Jeffrey had followed Pan and was gazing at him with loving eyes.

The garbage bag with Jeffrey's coats, lead and bowl and the last of the chicken necks was in the hall. She handed it to Pan along with the large envelope in which she'd put the drawing of him at the hunt with his horse and Jeffrey. She had inked the lines and added washes of colour and was almost pleased with it.

Pan looked at the envelope. 'What's this?'

'A thank you from Jeffrey.'

'Oh,' he said awkwardly. 'He's no trouble.'

Then Pan and Jeffrey were gone, without a backward glance. He was in a hurry, Pan said, because he had to find a runaway goat and still had horses in yards.

'He was in a bate,' Xavier said when India returned to the living room.

'Runaway goat and horses in the yard,' she said. 'Were he and my grandmother ever lovers?'

39

Janet Reedhead greeted India with the stiff back and composed face to be expected from the housekeeper of Whistlejacket Thoroughbreds.

'Glad to see you're on time. We can't abide lateness.' She ran her eyes over India, approving of her slightly downturned mouth and fine grey polo neck jumper. The black leather tote, too, passed muster, but the suitcase, a ratty fabric item as lumpy as a ruminant's stomach, absolutely did not. Nor the coat. She sniffed discretely. There definitely was an odour. Disappearing the coat as Lady Blythe had requested would not be so much a duty as a service to humanity.

She held the door open and stepped back. 'Lady Blythe said I was to give you lunch and let you have a wander. She and Martin will be here at two.' Martin was driving India and Lady Blythe to the airport then picking up Kevin, who was returning India's hire to the Sydney depot.

'Leave that,' she said as India went to pick up her suitcase. 'And your coat.'

India was staring at the painting of Whistlejacket that filled the alcove at the back of the entrance hall. The rearing stallion appeared poised to leap out of the gold frame and land at her feet. She had her phone ready for a photo.

'Come along,' she told her.

'Sorry. It's a superb reproduction. I thought I'd get a picture so I can compare it with the original when we're in London. The brushwork is beautiful.'

Appeased by the speed with which India had put away her phone, she said, 'Go on, then, take a picture.' And after all, the girl was Grace Levy's granddaughter and Grace had been the one person in Burragong that could make Lady Blythe froth at the mouth. 'But be quick. Lunch is ready.'

A refectory table and a sideboard that looked as though it had come out of a French farmhouse dominated the dining room, but India only had eyes for the bronze statue of a kneeling camel on the sideboard. That and the paintings.

'I hope you like potato and leek soup,' Janet Reedhead interrupted. 'The vegetables are from our garden. My husband Brian looks after it. It's much better to eat fresh I always say. Let me take your coat.'

'I'll keep it, thanks. My passport's in the pocket.' India dropped the coat over the back of a chair and to her surprise, Janet Reedhead swooped on it and filleting about the pockets, brought out her passport.

'You'll lose it in a minute if you keep it there,' she said. She put the passport on the table and left with the coat.

India went to the window. The garden was shrouded in the same fine mist she had woken up to at Mars House, and shivering despite the warmth of the room, she wished that Janet Reedhead had not taken her coat. She sat down at the single place setting at the end of the very long table; the centrepiece, a yellow pot, with a cloud of tiny white flowers, appeared miles away. Her eyes went to the paintings. One was a David Hockney – a figure reclining beside the dancing turquoise waters of a large swimming pool, the other, a bright, hard image of orange and red shipping containers by Jeffrey Smart. Their combined value would be more than that of Mars House.

Janet Reedhead appeared with a laden tray. A very large man in baggy shorts and a navy polo shirt carrying an ice bucket from which the neck of a half-bottle of Moët could just be seen followed on her heels.

'My husband, Brian,' she said.

India rose. 'The grower of leeks and potatoes. We met at Blooming Beautiful.'

Beef looked pleased. 'I told that to Janet. You know your grandmother grew a great cauli and could prune roses with her eyes closed.'

'The garden's gone a bit wild since she …' India stopped. "Died". It was such a small word, little and featureless like the eye of a crow. How had it come to stand for the immeasurable event that was the ending of a life? She gazed at the laden tray, food suddenly the last thing she wanted. 'Are you having lunch too?' she asked Mrs Reedhead's husband.

'I wish,' said Beef, loitering by the ice bucket.

'Sit,' Janet told India. 'And you should be down to the stables,' she told her husband. 'Lucien wants to see you before he goes.'

'He's off to a horse sale,' Beef told India. He pointed at the champagne. 'I'll open that.' The Moët bottle disappeared in his hands and a muffled pop followed. 'If you believe Lady Blythe, it's never too early for champagne. She buys it by the container load.'

'Get, you,' Janet told him.

Once more alone, India sipped the soup and gazed from the Hockney to the bronze camel to the Jeffrey Smart. If this room contained such riches, what did the others hold?

'Oh, I thought Lucien, I mean Mr Blythe, might be in here,' came a bright voice from the door. 'Don't get up,' the voice's owner said as India went to rise. 'I'm Pinkie, the office manager. Mrs R said to give you this.' She slipped a faun coloured trench coat over the back of a chair. Her eyes went to the Moët. 'I'll have that if you don't want it. Better than it being thrown out. Though Mrs R sometimes puts it in her scones.'

In her skin-tight jeans, thigh high black leather boots and clinging tshirt, Pinkie looked more like a hip-hop dancer than an office manager, but her face was friendly and her voice warm.

India pushed the ice bucket towards her. 'Help yourself.'

'Goodie, thanks.'

Pinkie downed half the Moët in one mouthful. 'You're off to Royal Ascot,' she said in a tone more suited to the announcement of a trip to a petrol station.

India nodded. 'Could you show me the library?'

Pinkie gulped down the rest of the Moët. 'Sure.' She pointed at the trench coat. 'Don't forget that. It's Burberry.'

The library shimmered like the treasure trove it was. Ming bowls, more museum bronzes, a rare jade bowl (used as an ashtray), silver snuff boxes … a Munnings. India stood transfixed.

'See you later alligator,' Pinkie said from the door. 'Have a happy time at Arsegot.'

The horse was so thin it could only be the fusing of hide to skeleton holding it up. The Spanish painter Goya came to India's mind: hating inks and paintings of horses reduced to caricature by their service in man's wars.

She took out her phone and leaning between yard rails, touched the camera icon. As she zoomed in on the horse's head, the phone rang and in a leap that covered almost the length of the yard, the horse was at the railing, lunging at her in a demented dance. She smelt rank water, funereal ground.

She ignored the ringing and continued taking photos.

Back at the house, standing on the front steps, she returned the call, hoping she had not blown the trip. Pinkie answered, telling her, between giggles, that Martin and Lady Blythe were on their way.

The front door opened. Janet Reedhead beckoned her up the steps and pointed at the travel bags at her feet – a rolling suitcase, garment bag, tote and briefcase – all Louis Vuitton.

'Your luggage.'

'That's not mine.'

'Yes, it is. Lady Blythe only travels Vuitton.' Janet Reedhead pointed to the roller case. 'I've repacked your things in there. And Lady Blythe will be very hurt if you're not wearing the trench coat.'

Lucien took the phone from Pinkie and tossed it onto a hay bale out of her reach. 'Turn around.'

Dressed now only in her long boots, Pinkie giggled as he bent her over.

He groaned. 'Now there's a sight.'

Still giggling, Pinkie rested on her elbows on the bale to steady herself. The hay made her itch and she hoped it wouldn't mark her skin. She'd have much preferred to be spread across Lucien's bed, but he never suggested they meet in his bedroom. It probably hadn't even occurred to him that she knew where it was. He certainly wouldn't know that when the mood took her and opportunity presented, she lay on it and breathed the citrusy scent of his hair and skin from his pillows.

'You're a goddess,' he gasped.

She wriggled her buttocks until he was out of her, turned and leaned against his chest. But then she started to giggle again and that set him off and they had to turn away from each other so that they could breathe.

'That coke's something else,' she said, her voice steadying as she concentrated on dressing. She'd have to shower and change her knickers and jeans before they left for the airport. But then, maybe she just wouldn't.

Lucien stood in the doorway, obviously high and recently laid from the look and smell of him. Donnacha turned back to the computer.

'Anything to report before I go?' Lucien said.

'BlueBuckle. Hoss is on its last legs.'

'Beef knows what's to be done.'

'Doesn't seem fair on the hoss,' he couldn't help saying. 'It just doesn't feel right. We should have been able to do better.' Like him and Leila. They should have tried harder. He should have tried harder. Done better.

'You're not to call Nelson Cherry.'

'But an autopsy might explain why the hoss turned like he did. Maybe there's a tumour like Cherry suspected.'

'Cherry was on the spot when he said that. He had to say something. If there is an autopsy and he finds nothing, he might feel obliged to contact the RSPCA. He can be tricky.'

'There'll be no insurance without an autopsy.'

Lucien ignored this. He looked at his watch and smiled. 'Best get on then, if there's nothing else. The girls'll be waiting. I'll give your regards to Leila, shall I?'

'Don't bother,' he said, and as Lucien's smile grew even broader, he regretted it. He had a vision of Leila drinking champagne with Lucien on a terrace overlooking lines of white capped waves. He knew who he'd choose out of Pan Villon and Lucien Blythe. Pan hands down. But then, he wasn't a woman. And who was to say Leila and Blythe wouldn't be a good thing? Leila's family would likely celebrate the match and moving into the homestead would be like returning home for her. And with Blythe's money at her disposal, she could hunt as much as she wanted. In Ireland and in England in the off season if she wanted. As for him, well, with Leila tucked up with Blythe, he'd have no choice but to move on. Perhaps to America. To anywhere that wasn't Ireland or Australia.

40

Dubai a fading sunset and London eight hours ahead, Lady Blythe raised the footrest and nestled under the exquisite blanket from the Emirates' cabin staff. A young woman with kohled eyes and the poise of a catwalk model asked softly if she wished for chamomile tea, warm milk and honey or some other nightcap of her choice?

She declined and gesturing for the curtain to be pulled across, switched off the light, settled a pair of earbuds in her ears and began checking her phone for calls or messages.

Ann India was asleep in the cubicle beside her. At least she assumed she was asleep. In contrast to her grandmother (even dead her presence was still that of the elephant in the room) her company was undemanding. True, she had no small talk, but that was better than her being a chatterer and when she did converse, she was mostly interesting, if a little learned. But more importantly, she looked stunning in the frocks, pencil skirts and silk shirts and linen trousers from Dubai's designer boutiques that now almost filled her luggage. Really, one might just as well shop in Dubai as London. The service was better and, more recently, the range. That charcoal and mist Armani suit, half boardroom and half schoolgirl, would make India a standout in the Royal Enclosure.

Ah, Lucien's number. Excellent. By the careful scheduling of shopping trips, lunches and salon treatments, she'd been able to catch the sale of most of the Whistlejacket yearlings. But she had missed the auction of the jewel, the Speed filly, Preenie, who not only had a trail of black type going back to foundation mares but also a knockout presence. And didn't she know it. She had gotten the stable name Preenie because of her habit of stopping to admire her reflection in the mirrors in the arena where Leila had taught her to lead, ready for her starring moment in the sale ring.

Enjoying the anticipation of hearing the filly had been one of the sale's top lots, she delayed listening to Lucien's message. Preenie's dam's next mating would be with the new stallion BlueBuckle, and hopefully that join too would result in a spectacular and highly commercial foal. Thinking about this, she realised she had not yet laid eyes on BlueBuckle. She would make a point of getting him led out the minute she got home. Perhaps his should be the first of the stallion portraits. If Pinkie's records were to be believed, he already had some very smart mares booked to him.

No matter that, it was time to get the good news about Preenie; she could wait no longer. Perhaps the filly had even set a new sale record? It was quite possible.

Lucien's message was some film, of the bidding, presumably. She touched the arrow on the screen.

No, no! She stared at the phone. Wasn't that Christie sprawled naked with her legs open and … and … Pinkie!

She thought she was going to faint and hearing Lucien's voice, she almost did. She jabbed a finger at the phone, but her nail stopped it from making contact and she watched with revulsion as Christie pushed Pinkie's head out from between her legs and said, 'Aren't you going to join us, Lucien?'

She ripped out the earbuds and covered the screen with her palm, her heart racing like that of a Tour De France cyclist halfway up the murderous Col Les Arcs. The film itself was revolting enough but if Lucien had sent it to her, who else had it gone to? People accidentally sent things somewhere other than where they were meant to go all the time. She broke out into a sweat. The film could have gone to Whistlejacket's clients. Many were her friends. Some would be at Ascot. How could she show her face in the Royal Enclosure knowing that they might have seen the disgusting footage? And if it had gone to Digger, the explosion would rock Sydney and Whistlejacket similarly. Digger would remove all his horses and have Lucien assassinated in the tabloids and on the networks by his media mates, not calling them off until Whistlejacket's reputation had been destroyed.

She thought about creating an emergency that would force the plane to return to Dubai so she could be at Whistlejacket when Lucien got back from the Gold Coast. But the last thing she needed was to add a lifetime ban from Emirates to her woes. She wilted into the seat and forced herself to breathe slowly, as she did on the doctor's bed at Bondi Junction. Her thoughts became less wild. A few discrete phone calls from the London hotel would reveal whether sickening footage had gone to anyone else. She'd say she thought Lucien might be planning a surprise visit and ask if they had heard from him. But no matter the answers, she would pass up Royal Ascot. How could she be even in the vicinity of HM after her eyes had been tainted with such sordidness. Pinkie would have to go of course. Janet would be devastated – she treated the silly girl like a daughter. And she wouldn't be the only one. As Janet was always saying, the clients adored her, the men and women both. Perhaps now she knew why.

She buzzed for the attendant and when she came, requested a single malt and took a sleeping tablet out of the pill box in her handbag. A while later, on the brink of merciful oblivion, she wondered if Lucien had unconsciously sent her the film, like a serial killer, wanting to be caught for whatever reason. But whatever that might be, BlueBuckle wouldn't be the only stallion being paraded for her when she got home. And one of the two would immediately be off Whistlejacket's sires list, and it wouldn't be BlueBuckle.

She told Ann India about the change of plan as the taxi took them from Heathrow to Belgravia. The Ascot crowd would be on edge hoping for a glimpse of or even an introduction to the Cambridges, she said by way of explanation, and she was suddenly not in the mood for slavish anticipation. She would enjoy London from the Lanesborough as one enjoys the company of a friend with whom the creation of new memories, the need for razzle dazzle, is unnecessary. Though Ann India, of course, could go anywhere she wished.

To garnish the charade, she leaned back into the seat of the taxi and sighed what she hoped was a wan sigh. 'And I'm not sure I don't have some jetlag coming on. I don't feel quite myself.' And indeed, the bitter fury was again rising. She began to feel nauseous. Had she eaten something tainted on the plane? No. The roiling in her stomach was the exact same black biliousness she had experienced in the later years of her marriage. The last time she'd felt it was just before Jonno died, and now Jonno's golden son had caused its return. She gave a defeated little grunt and turned her face toward the window.

41

Xavier pointed at the three-quarter empty bottle of Stoli. 'Jeez Simon, it's not even midday.'

Simon clasped his hands in front of him. 'Ellie's shoved off.'

Xavier picked up the bottle and turned it upside down over the restaurant sized pile of dirty dishes in the sink, pinching his nostrils shut against the smell of neat spirit and cold fat.

'Who'd blame her. Look at this shit here.'

'Nice,' Simon hiccupped. 'Thanks for the loving kindness, brother.'

'Any time. Whose is the blue ute?'

'A fellow called Garry Hume.'

'Garry Hume who's got the gardening business?'

Simon nodded. 'You know him?'

'He does some work for us. They call him Rowdy. He's a good worker but not much of a talker. You won't get much out of him.'

'Suits me,' said Simon. 'Eleanor fixed for him to do hounds in the mornings as a parting present. Bloody wasteful of you to toss that Stoli, man. It's been sitting there since Sunday.'

Xavier pulled out a chair and sat down at the table. 'Eleanor's really gone? Gone for good?'

Simon made a fist and blew *Gone Away*. 'Well and truly. She'll be in the next county by now.' Tears filled his eyes and he wiped them away with the back of his hand. 'I thought the hounds'd be all over Garry, but he's already got their ear. His father raced greyhounds. Might have something to do with it. He gets the job done in bluddy good time, too and he's interested in the horses. I'm keeping him on for the rest of the day to show him how to do boxes and clean tack. Don't really have the heart for it at the moment, myself.'

Xavier looked at the choked sink and filthy stove. 'Does he do housework as well?'

'Might do. He's keen enough.'

'I was joking'

Simon grimaced. 'Bit subtle for simple Simon.'

'Don't call yourself that. You're the best man with hounds in the country. Everyone says it.'

Simon shrugged. 'What brings you over this way anyway?'

'I've been looking at a property near here. Forty acres, mostly flat and cleared but there's a few good stands of trees. The fences are terrible and so's the house, it's fifties brick, but the dams are spring fed and it's not had stock on it for a while, so there's plenty of feed.'

Xavier gave the address and Simon nodded. 'I know it. That run-down place on the Reground Road. Been sitting empty for months. Rough bit of ground all round.'

Xavier rose and rolling up the sleeves of his shirt – he kept a spare in the car so wasn't worried about creases – went to the sink and moved some of the dishes so he could turn on the hot tap. Leila had told him about Eleanor and Simon's bust-up after the hunt on Sunday. The news had upset him. He liked Eleanor, she was hard-working and decent, but he loved Simon, and the hunt. Eleanor had obviously done what she could to get Simon some help before she left, but Simon clearly needed more than help with the hounds and the horses. And if he fell apart, the hunt would also.

'Leave those,' Simon said over the sound of the tap. 'It's embarrassing, man.'

'As embarrassing as not being able to stay on your horse on Sunday? Even Polar Bear was cringing.'

Simon rose and lumbered over to the sink. 'Yes, man, as embarrassing as that. As embarrassing as falling off in front of the whole fucking field.'

'You left out the drunk bit,' Xavier said, poking Simon's thick waist. 'Humpty Dumpty sat on his horse, Humpty and his horse got divorced …'

'That's bluddy harsh,' Simon said miserably. 'The last few weeks have been dirty. Very dirty.'

Xavier donned some yellow rubber gloves and squirted dish-washing liquid over the dishes.

'Well now it's time for the clean-up. I'll wash, you dry.'

'Eleanor never let me dry,' Simon protested. 'I break too much. Not my strong suite, the domestic arts.'

'Needs must,' Xavier came back. 'If you're going to be batching, you either have to get friendly with them or get a housekeeper. You really haven't had a drink today?'

Simon shook his head. 'Actually, I haven't had one since Sunday night.' The bottle had remained on the table to remind him of just how low he'd sunk. Coming off Polar Bear in front of the hunt had been bad enough, but his reaction to Eleanor when she'd told him she was going had been even more shameful. He'd spewed out the gossip about her as if he believed it. The memory made him cringe.

Xavier handed him a tea towel and a newly washed plate. 'If you drop it, I'll put the bits in your porridge. What about this weekend's meet? Are we still hunting?'

'Lord, yes,' Simon said. 'Leila's riding Field Master. Elvis has gone to Scott Page's. Ellie arranged that as well. She thought of everything. Always did. Even hounds' birthdays.' His eyes misted again.

Xavier felt a stab of pity. Eleanor must have been laying her exit trail for some time.

Simon stood holding the plate. 'We did have a few good months, though, you know. Bluddy good months. She just should never have moved in. That's why it's come to this. It's my fault. I gave her an ultimatum.'

'I never knew that,' Xavier said.

Simon put the wet plate gingerly on the bench. 'It wasn't your business to. I thought you knew about the dishwasher, though.' He pointed to the stainless-steel door under the bench, along from where they stood. 'Don't stop now, man,' he said as Xavier pulled off the yellow gloves. 'It's full anyway. But what movie's playing in your brain box? You've been in this kitchen a hundred times.'

Xavier put the gloves back on. He had, and on hunt trivia nights he had run the dishwasher himself. He looked out the window at the courtyard and kitchen garden, which appeared to be mostly bolted rocket and weeds. He'd get Garry onto that as well.

He handed Simon another plate. 'What about the ball?' Eleanor had turned the annual Highlands Hunt Ball into a very classy affair and in anticipation of this year's, he had dropped two grand on white tuxedos for himself and Toby.

Simon put the plate, which he had also neglected to dry, on top of the other one. 'It's probably half the reason Ellie shoved off. The committee's still bickering about the hors d'oeuvres.'

'Well they'd better shift it. The ball's in six weeks.'

Simon shrugged. 'Might call the bluddy thing off. Dancing's the last thing I feel like. Not that I was ever any good at it. Wooden top and wooden legs.'

'You can't call it off. Half the tickets are sold. You've got guests coming from America and England.'

'And Russia,' Simon said gloomily.

'Russia?'

'Hunted there last year. You should see the way they ride through those forests. No thought for life or limb. It was fucking mad. Nearly got staked on a branch but it ended up going into my horse's shoulder. Blood everywhere. Thought hounds might turn on us …'

'Maybe Eleanor's got someone to take over organising the ball as well,' Xavier interrupted – he'd already heard the Russian hunting story. 'She seems to have thought of everything else.'

Simon shook his head. 'She hasn't. The secretarial stuff, neither. She asked Gill but she didn't think she could.'

'I don't know why,' Xavier said. 'She'd be perfect.' He had an idea. If anyone could talk Gill around it'd be Simon. 'Are you sure you haven't had a drink? I need you to do something in Burragong.' If Simon went DUI, the ball would definitely be off the calendar, not to mention the rest of the hunt season.

Simon looked winded. 'What, I'm a liar now as well as an arsehole?'

'I never said you were an arsehole. Nobody did.'

'What do you want done?'

'Gill's painting. It's finished. I'm supposed to be dropping it around, but I've got another property to inspect. Could you deliver it? India's gone to Royal Ascot with Lady Blythe.'

'Has she now?' Simon cupped an ear with a hand. 'Is that Grace roaring on the wind I hear? I really bluddy miss Grace,' he continued, again morose. 'All these changes ... They started with her leaving us. Makes a fellow dizzy. No wonder I fell off Polar Bear.'

'You know Hazel Teo's not hunting anymore? Vivienne's sold Dorothy and put Hazel in Garton House. And Olivia's out for the rest of the season as well. Her father's taken her to Sydney.'

Simon looked even more upset. 'I didn't know. Been too wrapped up in the shit that's been going down here. Bloody Vivienne. Hazel's a grand little horsewoman. Olivia too. That father of hers is a piece of snot. Poor Gill.'

There was the sound of yapping and they both watched as Garry Hume crossed the courtyard, Simon's Jack Russell hard on his heels.

Simon pointed. 'He's even gotten in with Jack. Polar Bear'll be following him round next.' He tapped the window and getting Garry's attention, waved at him to come inside.

Xavier went to the dishwasher, open the door and quickly slammed it shut. 'Something's rotting in there.'

'Haven't seen the cat in a while,' Simon said blackly.

The kitchen filled with the rank scent of kennels as Garry came in with Jack the terrier, who rushed up to Simon and threw himself at his shins.

Simon bent down and rubbed his head. 'I thought you'd found yourself a new master. Any problems?' he asked Garry.

Garry shook his head and nodded a hello to Xavier.

Xavier nodded back. 'You don't know anyone that does house-work, do you? Simon needs a cleaner.'

'And someone to do the washing and ironing,' Simon added. 'Ellie always did it. And the horse rugs, bless her.'

'No wonder she left,' Xavier said under his breath.

'My mum does cleaning and ironing,' Garry volunteered. 'Her clients call her The Fairy because she works magic in their houses. I can give her a call. I think she had a cancellation today.'

'She'll need more than magic to transform this place,' said Xavier.

'She's quite used to celebrity tips,' Garry reassured him.

42

Not wanting to be in the house when Garry's mum arrived, Simon followed Xavier out. He might not be a celebrity, but the house certainly was a tip. Lord knew the last time his sheets had been changed or how many Stoli bottles and chip packets were under the bed, not to mention in the ensuite and his dressing room. While Xavier had been making a call, he'd asked Garry how much his mum charged and given him two hundred on top of that. He also promised that if she'd come to Gwynedd every week, she'd not have to face such a mucky bedlam ever again. The guest cottages could wait until she had time. At least the cottage Eleanor had now deserted would be clean. Immaculately so, no doubt. The bitchiness of this observation cheered him. Better that than all the self-pitying he'd been doing the last few weeks.

Gill's painting was wrapped in brown paper and tied with twine. 'Don't drop it,' Xavier said.

Simon took it with both hands. 'Is it any good?'

'Brilliant.'

'I'm not surprised. That India's stunning. Shame Lady B's got her claws into her. But if India's got any of her gran in her at all, she'll soon suss that when it comes to Blythes, all that glisters is not gold.'

Xavier got into his car and put down the window. 'Glisters? Is that a word?'

'Don't know your Shakespeare then. "Gilded tombs do worms enfold ..."'

'When did you start reading Shakespeare? You only read the *Telegraph*, Lord Beckford's "Thoughts on Hunting" and *Horse and Hound*.'

'Ellie thought a dose of Bard might make me less of a wooden top.' He pointed at the Silver RAV4 now turning into the gates down the hill. 'Think that's the Fairy? Bluddy efficient of her to get here so soon if it is. Best be making tracks myself then.'

Xavier started his engine. 'Let me know what Gill thinks of the painting.'

Simon hadn't minded Shakespeare; the stories were cracking. He had minded the opera, though and he'd especially minded the choral works Eleanor had also insisted on serving up. All that orchestral swelling made him think of a wave with no shore to break on, a doomed wave. Who needed to be on a boat to feel seasick? And as he tried to tell her, the horses, their stables bluetoothed off the house hifi, didn't think much of Hades, Moanzart, BroomHandle and FleaBritten either.

He lay the painting gently on the back seat and went and felt around under the driver's seat. 'Yes,' he said as his fingertips met hard plastic. He squatted and retrieved Kasey Chambers and Shane Nicholson's *Rattlin' Bones* and stood up with a satisfied grunt. It was his and Polar Bear's favourite. He might just buy Polar Bear Kasey's new CD while he was in Burragong. As he had to keep reminding himself, it wasn't just him that had been abandoned. Poor Polar Bear had lost the mate with whom he shared side-by-side digs in the hunting season.

Humming "No one Hurts Up Here" and wondering where Eleanor had hidden his collection of Marvin Gay and James Brown – "I Feel Like a Sex Machine" was the best song ever written – he got into the vehicle and snapped in the seatbelt. The RAV whizzed past and catching a glimpse of a woman with pumpkin coloured hair, he backed away quickly.

Gill must have gone out. Oh well, between the music shop, Pregos and Burragong Produce he could easily pass the hours the Fairy would need to shovel out the house. But what about the painting? Should he leave it on the doorstep? Perhaps not. He'd call back before heading home.

Turning away from the door, he glimpsed a shape in the glass oval. He pressed the bell again. 'Gill, it's me, Simon.'

'I'm not feeling great. Sorry. Come back another time.'

Her voice sounded gravelly, as if she had the flu. 'I've got something for you,' he persisted.

'Leave it on the doorstep. I think I might have a bug. I don't want you to catch it.'

'I don't care. I know about Olivia. Xavier told me.'

The shape in the glass grew larger and there was a shuffling and then the clicking of the latch.

He stared. Gill was wearing the same white towelling robe she had left the hospital in, but it was now grey, like her skin. Her eyes were swollen with crying and she stared at the floor as if they were too heavy to raise. It was only a week since he'd brought her home. Could a person make it to hell in such a small number of days? He didn't have to think about the answer.

Looking up and seeing his expression, Gill went to close the door.

He blocked it with his foot. 'You poor duck.'

Gill started to sob. 'Please go. Sorry, I really am a wreck.'

'I'm not in the best shape myself. Me or Polar Bear. We can be wrecks together.'

Though the tears continued to seep from her eyes, Gill's sobbing eased. She wobbled and steadied herself by leaning against the wall.

'What's wrong with Polar Bear?'

'Elvis's gone to Scott and Stephan's. Polar Bear's beside himself. Had to give him a shot of Ketamine last night so we could both get some sleep. I'm going to get him the new Kasey Chambers. Hopefully that'll settle him a bit.'

'Oh, poor Polar Bear. Eleanor's gone then.'

'You knew?'

'Only that she was planning to leave. How are you coping?'

Simon shifted the painting to the other arm. 'Better than you.' The great and the good certainly knew a thing or two when they said that if you want to feel better, think of someone worse off than yourself. Poor bloody Gill.

'Will we have a cup of tea?' he suggested.

Gill looked alarmed. 'The place is a mess. Even more than me.'

'Come on, as if I'd care? You've seen me after I've been cleaning the kennels often enough. Anyway, I can't leave without saying hello to the Cairns. They'll be mightily hurt if I do. And besides, you've got to look at this.' He held out the painting. Stepping past Gill, he headed down the hallway, leaving her no option but to follow.

The living room was not the expected disaster. He peeked into the kitchen. The benches were clear and the dining annex pin neat. Aside from the doona on the sofa, the house, at least what he'd seen of it, had an almost deserted feel. The Cairns, he assumed, were out in the yard. Then he saw the empty bottles of Stoli in the rubbish bin. He went and picked up the mug on the coffee table in front of the sofa. It was full of liquid the colour of water.

'Didn't have any Ketamine,' Gill said from the doorway.

Simon raised the mug as though toasting. 'I always knew you were a woman after my own heart. Let's get truly hammered and figure out what we're going to do with the rest of our lives.' He took a large mouthful of vodka. 'After we've thoroughly trashed El- lie and your snot of a husband that is.'

'Eleanor's a friend.'

'More of a friend than me?'

'Of course not. But it wasn't her fault you and she didn't work out, just as it wasn't yours.'

'Trust you to drag things out into the cold hard light of day. Perhaps you should do the same with your marriage. We might as well work on that before we become insensible. I'll lead the way.' His cheeks flushing, Simon took another gulp of Stoli. 'Man, this is good.'

'Hey, that's the last of the bottle.'

'I'll go get another,' Simon said. Thank god he hadn't had a drink last night – if he had, he wouldn't be driving anywhere.

But then, there was always a taxi. 'And I'll pick up some pizzas from Arthur's. You need a feed. I can hear your stomach growling from here.'

Gill crossed her arms over her stomach and jutting hipbones. 'Pizza and vodka for lunch!' she protested half-heartedly. Her mouth was watering – people came down from Sydney for Arthur's truffle margherita – and the Stoli was doing such an excellent job of numbing her pain.

Simon raised a silver eyebrow. 'Has to be healthier than Stoli and Stoli. Just don't tell Xavier. He thinks I'm off the drink. Will be tomorrow. We both will.'

Gill clumped over and took the mug and raised it. 'Here's to tomorrow. Now I think about it, Eleanor could be a tiny bit righteous.'

'A tiny bit!' Simon snorted. 'More like a bit twice the size of Burragong. The mere thought that somewhere on the planet someone might be thinking of pizza and vodka for lunch would have had her cranking up the Moanzart and working on a sermon. Her mother was the same. It's the reason she left home and hit the road.'

'Hopefully she'll find a sense of humour on her travels.' Gill giggled, despite herself.

Simon took back the mug. 'I'll drink to that, Now, give us your order. While I'm gone you can get into your party gear and open your present. Tell the Cairns I'll bring them back some garlic bread.'

Olivia's toiletries were everywhere – in the vanity cupboards, on the rim of the bath, on the vanity itself – and her Peter Alexander bathrobe, patterned with yellow ducks, still hung behind the door. She'd even left the terrifyingly expensive Lotus shampoo and conditioner, the only product that apparently didn't make her hair look synthetic.

Synthetic, what a good word for my life Gill thought. No daughter, no son, no hunting, no husband. At least Blooming Beautiful was still going. Without her, admittedly, but still going. That at least she still had. And the Cairns and Hester of course. And the house.

But for how long? Now that Olivia was living with him, Nicholas could insist on its sale and there was no way she could afford another place in Burragong. With careful accounting, Blooming Beautiful provided her with a small wage and paid the horses' upkeep as well as hers and Olivia's hunting subs, but after that there was not a lot left. Not enough to pay off a mortgage, even if she could get one.

She rested her forehead against the cold surface of the mirror. She'd given up checking her phone in case Olivia had called. She'd even given up listening for its ring. In the last couple of days, she'd done nothing but raise and lower the Stoli bottle. She'd told herself that when the last bottle was empty, she'd stop and pull herself together, but for what? So that she would be totally with it when the axe fell and severed from her what was left to give her life meaning?

The sound of scratching made her lift her head. The Cairns – had she fed them this morning? Shit! She couldn't remember. She tried to think back to before Simon had arrived. Sometime between then and when she had first woken, she had gotten up from the sofa and gone to the pantry, but beyond that she couldn't remember.

The scratching stopped. She must have fed the Cairns or whichever of the dogs that was scratching would have kept going. Anyway, they'd soon be enjoying garlic bread.

She really should make more of an effort with her appearance than splashing cold water on her face. She peered at her scalp. It looked scurfy.

She clumped to the bedroom and tottering on one crutch, slid open the wardrobe door, wondering what she could wear that would make her look halfway presentable. Clean underwear would be a start. As she fished a bra and some knickers from side by side cane baskets, she remembered the moss-coloured linen dress she sometimes wore on balmy evenings. Olivia hated it because of its shapelessness but being calf-length, it would at least cover most of the cast.

Her last shower had been when Eleanor had visited. How long ago was that? She shook her head, unable to remember. Maybe more Stoli was not such a good idea she thought for a fleeting second. The warm water pouring over her head and sluicing the stale bread smell off her skin felt good. She began to soap her body. She'd lost so much weight. Where there'd been muscle and springy flesh (a little too much springiness in places according to Liv), now her body had the life of a deflated beach ball. A fresh wave of tears cut her eyes. Nicholas was never coming back and nor were Olivia and Oscar. Not only the wife in her was now dead, but also the mother, the mother of a beautiful son and daughter. Her blood felt as though it was congealing in her veins. Time stopped and the animal howl that had been echoing in her heart forced its way up out past her lips.

A while later, clean, dressed and outwardly composed, she let the Cairns in. They came to her nervously, their little white faces a picture of worry, their coats bedraggled. She stretched out a hand towards them.

'It hasn't been fun for you, either, has it.'

Fat Freddy gave her hand a tentative lick. 'Dear thing,' she said, shaking her head as tears once again threatened to drown her. 'Simon's bringing you some garlic bread,' she said in a choked voice. 'We'd better try and look cheerful.' Perhaps she'd give them a brush after Simon had left. But she knew she wouldn't. She'd be stretched out on the couch oblivious.

She put some biscuits in the Cairns' bowls just in case they didn't want the garlic bread. Oh Lord, she thought as they fell on them, she mustn't have fed them after all. Thinking back, she couldn't remember the last time she had.

At the sound of Simon calling her name from the front door and a commotion of clinks and rustling and huffs and puffs she tried gulping away the tears. But they wouldn't stop.

A laden Simon appeared in the doorway. He dropped a stack of Arthur's boxes onto the table and let the bottle bag slide to the floor.

'I'm sorry,' she whispered. 'You really don't want to be here. I'll just drive you away like I did Oscar and Olivia. And Nicholas.'

'That sounds like dipstick Nic shit,' Simon said angrily. 'Anyone would want you for a mother. Or a wife. You're brilliant. Children never appreciate their parents. It's just a stage. Like it's something they need to do. But most come around. And as for Nicholas, why would you bluddy care? You don't, really, anyway. I've seen you two together. It's just pride that makes us chew on our hearts. And don't I know all about that.'

'Then why am I on my own?' she came back with just as much anger. 'Why is everyone gone?'

'That's good,' Simon said. 'Anger is good. You should be angry. You've got a lot to be angry about.'

And indeed, Gill could feel her blood starting to flow again. But still the empty rooms – Olivia's, Oscar's, Nicholas' office that he had not set foot in for months – still echoed her loneliness. Her shoulders slumped.

She heard Simon talking in the next room but couldn't bring herself to think or care who he might be speaking to.

'We're going back to Gwynedd,' he said when he returned. 'The Fairy's making you up a bed. Put some things in a bag. And the Cairns' coats.'

'I can't …'

'You bluddy can and you bluddy will. I'll carry you to the vehicle if I have to.'

'But what if Liv comes back?'

'I presume she's got a key. Get yourself going. I'll put the pizzas and stuff in the vehicle. You'll have to remind me to shower before I go down to the hounds this evening or they'll eat me alive. Pizza's their favourite. Look, the Cairns are drooling.' Simon bounced over to the bottle bag and then stopped. 'Maybe this should stay here. Though if Olivia comes back, it might not be such a good thing if it's laying around. I know what I was like with booze at fourteen. Come on,' he urged. 'Back in the saddle. I've got the new Kasey Chambers. There's this great song "Ain't No Little Girl". You'll love it, I promise. We can listen to it loud.'

43

India examined the little drawing of the whippet. Her thoughts went to Jeffrey. Grace wouldn't have left him with Pan if he were not in the best of hands, and Jeffrey would not have gone with Pan without a backwards glance had he not trusted him. But that lack of a backwards glance had stung. She had thought she meant more to him. Well, better that she didn't.

She tried and failed to turn her attention back to the exquisite drawing, gave up and walked on, past other just as captivating drawings, some with people gathered around them. London's National Portrait Gallery was almost a second home, but today, except for the whippet, nothing had held her attention for more than a few seconds. Perhaps she too had a touch of jetlag.

Time weighing on her in a way she was not used to, she set off for the Portrait Café. But her tote awash with the money Lady Blythe kept pressing on her, she changed direction for the restaurant.

The waiter, a boy with a ponytail and orange nail polish, asked if she had a reservation. She shook her head. He looked her over and pointed to a small table by the window. 'For you, ma'am,' he said in a hybrid accent.

She sat clumsily on the chair he pulled out, feeling like she'd been manoeuvred by a superior dancing partner. He waved at the view of the Houses of Parliament and Big Ben and the heavens scraping London Eye. 'Enjoy. Something to drink?'

She could just make out the position of Big Ben's hands. Two thirty. Well and truly lunch time. 'A glass of white wine.'

'Shall I bring the list? We have a number of Australian labels.'

'A glass of Bordeaux blanc, thank you,' she replied, wondering that her voice could have broadened enough in the brief time she'd been in Burragong for him to know she was Australian. She put her tote under her chair and after checking out the other diners – mostly men in jeans and blazers and women in understated outfits brightened with resin jewellery – gazed out at the vista.

The sky had gone from grey to a watery blue. A wind had come up and was disrupting the flight paths of the pigeons that had not sought the protection of the ledge perches. The wine arrived, along with a menu and a carafe of water and a glass, which the waiter half filled. She took a sip and held it in her mouth. When she had first arrived in London, it was the taste of the water that had brought home the fact that she was somewhere very different to where she had come from. It had a mouldering density, as if something of the centuries of dead that had liquefied under London's streets had seeped into its catchments and aquifers.

She picked up the menu, her eyes going first to the prices. Back in London only a couple of days, she had already reverted to her student habits of examining price tags and walking to save on fares.

Habits were meant to be broken. Fixing her eyes firmly on the descriptions of the dishes of offer, she chose the Burrata, braised artichokes, trevise and olives, which would go very well with the wine.

The food was excellent. She savoured every mouthful and choosing a double shot latté over dessert, watched the London Eye make a sludge-slow turn high in the sky. She had never ridden the famed structure. Grace had had no interest and there had always been more pressing calls for the twenty-five or so pounds it cost to ride. But perhaps today she would.

She pulled a pen out of her tote and began sketching the imagined faces of the Eye's passengers on her napkin. A not quite teenage boy, petrified gaze on the capsule floor, a small girl holding her doll up to the window, a couple filming themselves descending in the sky, a seagull riding the downdraft with them.

'That's French linen you know.'

She blinked, then recognised one of the drawing tutors from the Slade. He had begun each lesson with a mindfulness meditation and when her thoughts were threatening to dissipate like the dandelion seed heads inked on her wrist, she used the practice he had taught. She looked at the napkin. It was indeed linen, and starched. She had registered the resistance to the pen but ignored it.

He gestured at the chair opposite. 'May I?' Not waiting for an answer, he settled on the chair, unzipped his silk bomber jacket and pulled the napkin towards him.

'It's good, of course.' He pointed at the half drawn back of the boy. 'There, that line, it pulls everything together. Not something one can teach, fortunately. We thought you weren't coming back for a while. You've called Tim?'

It was Tim Keefe, another Slade lecturer, that had packed up her flat.

She shook her head. 'I'm not here for long. Only a week or so.'

'Tim calls you his unicorn. The beast of beauty and genius. The sublime and the infernal in one. He was delirious when you asked him about the flat. Don't expect a bill for the storage, he's probably made a shrine of your things.'

She shook her head, not understanding. 'He always said that if I needed help with anything to just ask.'

'Ah, the damnable unworldliness of genius. And of love. Don't fret my dear, Tim's a bright chappie. No doubt there's a method to his madness. Perhaps better the absent amour than one that might lead one to losing one's job. Still, it's hard on his wife. Where are you staying?'

'The Lanesborough.'

He raised his eyebrows and blew out his cheeks. 'My. The new fitout is supposed to be stunning. The gold leaf is all hand painted you know. We went to the auction of the old furnishings, but even the castoffs were beyond the purse. So, you've found yourself a patron. But of course you have. Who is he? Not an Australian, I hope.'

India felt her cheeks grow hot. 'She's not really a patron. She's a friend of my grandmother's. Was, I mean.' She looked at the Cartier watch Lady Blythe had insisted she wear so she wouldn't have to scratch in her tote for her phone when she needed to know the time. 'She'll be expecting me back. She's laid up with jetlag.'

He picked up the napkin. 'I'll keep this, if you don't mind. Make sure you guard your horn, lovely unicorn. And ware the silken hobbles.' And with that, like Jeffrey, he was gone without a backwards glance.

Even more unsettled, she signalled for the bill and wondered how she would pass the rest of the afternoon. She felt adrift, neither here nor there. She needed to be doing something, but what? Looking at London real estate, that was what. Getting some idea of where, of how the money from Mars House might be best spent.

She strode out of the restaurant, full of purpose, and regret that she had blown off the drawing teacher, who was no doubt a valuable contact. Out on the street, however, the feeling of purpose disappeared. The racket of traffic noise, the rivers of people, the static weight of the buildings and the spiralling pigeons overwhelmed her senses. She set off for the hotel, stopping only to blue a thousand pounds on the quilted leather biker jacket that caught her eye in Burberry's window. It was a screwed-up thing to do. But at least in the biker jacket she recognised herself in the mirror – Grace always said that if you don't know the person in the mirror, it's not you.

Nestled in the hotel sofa, Lady Blythe glowed like a Lalique figurine. She seemed pleased that she was back, so it was easy to confess the price of the biker jacket. She dismissed both the confession and the jacket. She had just ordered a bottle of Cristal and that was far more interesting.

India took off the Cartier watch and laid it on the writing desk, next to a vase of red roses and Lady Blythe's iPad. 'Thanks for this.'

Lady Blythe pulled her throw back up over her bare feet. 'Keep it. I've a drawer full of them. When Jonno was done with the girlfriend, he'd get his secretary, Fiona, to buy her a watch. Fiona would give it to me, and I'd write Miss, Ms or Mrs a card saying, "thanks for looking after my husband". Fiona was a gem. We called her Fiona the Formidable.'

Not knowing whether to laugh or say some word of condolence, India stared at a snippet of sun caught in the grey-blue curtains. The trapped light faded and disappeared. She went to the window and watched the lozenge shaped roofs of the red double-decker buses make their arc around Hyde Park. The champagne arrived with their butler, a young American interning at the Lanesborough to refine his service skills.

After he had gone, she put her untouched glass down next to the watch. 'I've never worn a watch before.'

'But you should always. Nothing makes a statement like a quality watch. It can finish off an outfit.' Lady Blythe glanced at the biker jacket. 'Well perhaps not all outfits. I've been watching the racing. I'm so glad we didn't go. The crowds, terrible! One wouldn't have been able to breathe.'

India opened the bottle of sparkling water the butler had also brought. 'There was an exhibition of Lucien Freud's drawings at the gallery. They were donated in lieu of death duties. He taught at the Slade in the fifties.'

'He sells for millions, so I expect they'd anything with a signature.'

Half listening to Lady Blythe's recital of names of her friends Lucien Freud had painted, India waited for a pause and then said, 'You're looking much better.'

Lady Blythe's face drooped. 'I'm still too wobbly to go out, I'm afraid. Jonno and I spent more time in planes than we did on the ground and I never got jetlag. I thought it was something people made up to get out of dinner parties.'

India twiddled the silky toggle on the sleeve zipper. 'Do you think you should see a doctor? Maybe it's not jetlag. Maybe you've picked up something.'

Lady Blythe held out her glass for a refill. 'It's definitely jetlag. One of my friends gets it so cruelly that she has to get a vitamin C shot the minute she lands. She's always telling me about it. I'm not sure that rest doesn't achieve the same thing as the injections, though. But you are a pet to worry. Poor you, I know I'm being a bore. Maybe you should trot out with some of your chums tonight. Have a catch up.'

India shook her head. There was no one to see, no one she wanted to see. She touched the centre of her forehead with her fingertips, remembering the creepy stuff the drawing tutor had said.

'But I thought I might go to the British Racing Museum, tomorrow,' she said. 'It's supposed to have the best collection of equestrian art in the world.'

'What a wonderful idea,' Lady Blythe enthused. 'We'll get our little butler to look up the trains.'

'I can do it,' India said. She had made the trip from Kings Cross to Newmarket, to the racing museum with Grace but decided not to say. Lady Blythe might mention her grandmother often, but when she did so, she changed the subject. 'I've got the BR timetable app on my phone.'

44

Lady Blythe left ten pounds on the pillow for the housemaid and set off for the spa. She had booked a deep tissue massage and a platinum extract facial. She might not be seeing anyone in London but in Paris at least, she would look her best, if only for the flight attendants, waiters, hotel staff and boutique assistants.

Ten minutes later, she was stretched out on a soft white towel and watching waves of turquoise light roll across the ceiling in a bergamot scented chamber.

The flames of the candles in the stone-lined niches barely trembled as the masseuse, a compact woman in fitted turquoise pants and a short-sleeved tunic, slipped into the room.

After greeting "mam", she helped Lady Blythe turn over onto her stomach and set to work.

'There,' Lady Blythe said as the masseuse rotated the pads of her fingers over the muscles between her spine and right shoulder blade. 'Right there.'

'There's a knart, I go in?'

'Yes, do. Please.'

Her fingers turning to steel, the masseuse began probing.

Lady Blythe groaned. She signalled for the torment to stop and raising her upper body on her elbows, drew her shoulder blades together and tilted her chin towards the ceiling.

'Magic.' The stiffness that had set in when she had opened Lucien's message, the literal pain in the neck, noticeably eased. Lucien was phoning every few hours, leaving messages which she deleted. *That* one, however, she had not.

The masseuse placed the flat of her hand on her back and pushed. 'If mam would lay down please.'

Lady Blythe surrendered as best she could.

'Mam,' the masseuse said, 'You're not relaxing.'

Nor would you be, Lady Blythe thought, but with a great effort she made her muscles slacken. Her mind, however, returned to the plan she'd been formulating since going into purdah at the Lanesborough.

First, she would fire Pinkie as she'd already decided. Next, Christie would be banished. If she didn't agree to have no further contact with Lucien, Digger would be told about her recreational activities and she'd be a divorcee in less time than it took her to put on her mascara. And knowing Digger, there'd be a prenup so tight she'd be lucky to come out of it with her wedding ring. Which left Lucien. Lucien would either marry Ann India or Whistlejacket would be sold, lock, stock and stallion with not a bean going to him.

It was a good plan, a neat plan. The only problem she could see was Ann India's unworldliness. It was difficult to imagine the gal organising a large, or even small dinner party, or seeing that the houseguests were properly looked after. And Janet Reedhead could become difficult without regular flattery. She could well take Ann India's lack of sophistication as wilful neglect and start up one of her dramas.

She kicked her feet, earning a soft smack from the masseuse. The smack jolted something in her. What would perfect the plan she realised, while obediently recomposing her limbs, was a Fiona the Formidable. A Fiona the Formidable would easily manage Whistlejacket's clients. She would keep its tricky housekeeper and master in good working order as well, leaving its mistress free to be its beautiful, artistic centrepiece and the darling daughter-in-law and mother she was also destined to become.

She grunted with pain as the masseuse, now kneading her calves, muttered under her breath, 'knarts, knarts, so many knarts.' The pain intensified and her mind went blank.

The masseuse moved onto her feet with merciful tenderness and Lady Blythe's mind returned to the plan. Yes, a Fiona the Formidable was the missing piece. As soon as she got back, she would contact some agencies. And Ann India would need a stylist, as well. It was too much to expect a Fiona to cover all the bases.

Knotless calves combined with the prospect of Lucien brought to heel and her very own grandchildren, filled her with the first happiness she had felt since that awful moment on the plane from Dubai. She'd give Lucien three months. No, two. Ann India would fall for him quickly, if she hadn't already. Every woman lost a crucial piece of her heart when she first met him. Like his father, he made sure of it. And Ann India had no attachments otherwise, as the occasional discrete question had revealed. That said, however, she had not lived a totally nunnish life.

She was almost floating. What had been a catastrophe had now, as catastrophes do when visited on those with fortitude, turned into a gift. It was even fortuitous that Ann India had gone to Newmarket. If the only thing she knew about horses was by whom they had been painted or sculpted, that would be enough to get her through lunches and dinners with owners and trainers. Another brilliant thought occurred to her. Ann India should move into Le Manoir when they got back. She'd suggest it this evening.

Able at last to totally surrender to the masseuse's machine-like hands, she let her mind drift to baby names and darling outfits and whether or not she might want to be called "Gan Gan" like HM was called by her little people.

45

The woman on the doorstep was dressed in skin-tight jeans, long black leather boots and a fitted cambric shirt. In her late twenties, she was neither short nor tall and had glowing olive skin, a gift from her Pakistani grandmother. Her long, brilliantly shiny and super-straight, black hair was pulled back in a tight ponytail, showing an angular face, not unlike that of a Siamese cat. And while her shoulders were narrow and her chest boyishly flat, the lush curves of her bottom and thighs were as attention grabbing as her amber eyes.

Pan stepped back into the hallway, sending Benzo, Sadie and the terriers, who'd followed him to the door but were now hiding behind his legs, into a growling tangle.

'Margot!'

Margot Apsley fixed her husband with a gaze that was half amused, half annoyed. 'You could be a tiny bit pleased to see me, darling. Just a tiny bit.' She lay a manicured hand with its familiar crested signet ring on his arm. 'Poor sweet. You look like you've seen a ghost.' Her fingers suddenly pinching, she continued, 'The drive here took an eternity. This place is the edge of civilisation.' She held up a silencing hand as Pan went to speak. 'Tell me later. Just get those animals out of the way so I can come in. I'm desperate for tea. My bags, first though, darling, if you wouldn't mind.'

The dogs sticking to his heels and peering warily out from behind his legs at the visitor, Pan stepped out onto the veranda and waved Margot into the house. Benzo, however, with an apologetic smile at his master, turned and slunk off after Margot.

He's just heading to his bed,' Pan said. 'It's his nap time. Kitchen's the second door on the right.'

A rental Camry was parked diagonally in front of the shed, Pharlap beadily licking its bumper bar. He pushed her away. 'Leave it, girl, it's not ours.'

Pharlap sighed heavily and sat down on her wrestler's haunches. Pan felt like joining her. The Camry's back seat was piled with expensive cases and bags, no doubt paid for from his father's estate. It looked like Margot was planning to stay for a year. Or, heaven help him and every animal at Big Hill, to move in. It certainly didn't look like she'd come about a divorce as he'd hoped after he'd gotten over the shock of seeing her on the doorstep.

He looked accusingly at the dogs, now sitting beside Pharlap. 'Why didn't you bark? We could have hidden until she went away.'

The dogs pretended to be interested in a line of white cockatoos screeching through the air towards the big hill.

Half an hour later, he was watching Margot finish the sandwich she had wheedled him into making along with the tea. It was almost three years since they'd been in the same room, but she was still as familiar and as alien to him as she had been at the end of their six-month marriage.

'Nice ham,' she said, looking down her short straight nose at the plate for a crumb she might have missed.

'It's from a friend's farm. Her pigs free-range and are slaughtered and hung on the property.'

Margot's eyebrows formed two perfect arches over her heavily mascara'd eyes. 'Oh, you've got friends, now.'

'Don't start,' he said wearily. 'We'll both go mad.'

'Not me, darling. I did so enjoy our fights.'

A major one being over his wish for solitude and hers to constantly stuff the London flat with her friends.

He pushed Sadie's head off his thigh. Her eyes fixed on the crust left on his own plate, she had begun to drool.

'Why are you here? You've always said Australia was the last place you'd ever be found.'

She smiled brightly. 'I'm your wife.' The smile turned to a giggle. 'You needn't look so terrified. I'm not planning to move back into your bed.' She threw him a coy look, 'Though if the gentleman were to ask …'

Pan rose and gave the crust to the slavering Sadie. 'I thought you might have come about a divorce,' he said hopefully, thinking about the indoor arena that would enable him to work the horses in all weather.

'What, you've met someone you want to marry?' Margot said. 'Is she here? Do bring her out. Show and tell was my favourite thing at school.'

'There's no girlfriend. I just thought … well, it has been years. A lot of time has gone by …'

Margot showed her perfect little teeth in a winsome smile. 'I know we probably should uncouple. But shop assistants and accountants are so much more respectful when one mentions a husband, and a ring on the finger comes in handy with pesky boyfriends. When I want to shunt someone, I tell them we're reconciling. Though it didn't make any difference with the last one. He turned out to be a bit of a stalker. It was quite thrilling.'

She stopped and looked disapprovingly at Sadie. 'You know there are dating sites for pet-friendly partners in the UK. There's bound to be something similar here. There's probably even one for Labrador owners.' She pointed at the teapot. 'Let's have another. It's so nice to be able to talk with someone who's not forever taking selfies or wanting a selfie with One. You wouldn't believe how sick of London I am. The cars are multiplying as fast as the pigeons and everyone is getting about in hi viz running shoes. I'm starting to think I might be a country girl after all. So, here I am. Just think of all the money you're saving not paying for the flat.'

'I thought your father was paying for it.'

'Not anymore. I've let the lease go. Everything's in my brother's barn. I'm homeless and footloose.' Margot raised her empty cup. 'And still parched, darling.' She looked around the room. 'There's nothing like drinking tea in a country kitchen for picking one up. Even if it is in the middle of nowhere.'

Pan got up and filled the kettle. Out of the corner of his eye, he saw Benzo delivering a precisely aimed stream of urine on the bags he'd dumped in the hallway. 'You'll certainly get a good dose of country here,' he said.

'Shame you're so far from that nice little village Kookaburra, or whatever it's called in English. The shopping looked almost decent. I thought ...' Margot stopped as Pan's mobile began to ring. 'So you really do have friends,' she said as he checked the number and picked up the call.

Pan waved at her to be quiet. 'Get a yard and a stall ready,' Donnacha was saying. 'We're on our way. I've given him some subcutaneous fluids. Hopefully that'll keep him going until we can get some IV in. I've got the stuff. We should be there in about three quarters of an hour. We'll need the tractor and a sling to get him off the truck.'

'I'm onto it.' Pan ended the call. 'I've got an emergency with a horse,' he said to Margot. 'I'll be down at the stables. You can see them from the path next to the garage.'

Margot went to the pantry and finding a bottle of Tanqueray and a row of tonic bottles in the fridge door, made herself a large G&T and set about exploring.

Three bedrooms, the long sitting room with a startling view of – a volcano? – kitchen/dining room, library/office, laundry and mud room and two bathrooms, that was it. All of it. And it all smelt of wood smoke and dog. She scuffed the floor with a toe of the boots she'd bought at the surprisingly swanky shop in Kookagong. There was grit under her foot. And no cleaner, either.

In the larger of the bedrooms, Pan's she assumed from the clothes on the stool at the end of the bed, a second greyhound, this one in its dotage, nestled in the duvet. Christ, how many dogs did Pan have? And what was the point of a mud room if it wasn't used by the animals!

The room she chose for her own had not been slept in for a long time, if ever – the dust on the cane bedhead was thick and similarly so on the glass top of the bedside table. The built-in robe was completely empty and the air chill and almost spookily still. But for that, it was an elegant room. The walls were umber and the white stripes in the yellow curtains echoed the woodwork. Pan hadn't gone totally feral.

She dragged an armchair to the window and dusting it with a sweep of her hand, settled down with the remains of her drink. Not far beyond the veranda, a stand of silver-trunked trees huddled together, the branches and leaves forming a shifting drift of grey green that all but blotted out the sky. She shivered. How typical of Pan to bury himself somewhere like this. Just so long as she didn't end up buried here as well. But it was unlikely. As a reward for this outback sojourn, however long it was to be, the next stop was New York.

She had been telling the truth when she said she had a stalker. But it was not, as she had joked, at all thrilling. His name was Felix Haylock and he worked for a shipping firm. They had met at Annabel's and though older than the men she was usually attracted to, he worked out and knew how to show himself off with bespoke shirts and the right watch and haircut.

After they had been dating for a couple of months, he had started talking about getting a flat together, about marriage. Already restless – a shared interest in *Game of Thrones* and oral sex was not enough to sustain any relationship – she had given him the sack.

At first there'd been the occasional evening when his car was parked in the street outside the flat. Then he began to follow her, just occasionally. To burn off the nervous energy this caused, she increased her visits to the gym from twice weekly to daily. Until she saw him on a treadmill up from hers.

Unnerved, she went to stay at the family home in Berkshire. But returning from picking up a hamper from the Royal Farms Windsor Farm Shop, she found him having drinks with her parents and discussing their engagement. Her parents thought him charming and were thrilled she was planning to remarry, even if she'd seen fit to keep the fact a secret from her nearest and dearest. But they too could now share their own secret: the farm was on the market and they planned to divide the sale proceeds between their offspring. Their beloved daughter and new son-in-law would be starting married life cashed up. Wasn't that just perfect timing?

No, it was not.

A friend of her brother's, a detective at Scotland Yard, advised her to take herself away, somewhere far away. It was obvious where that somewhere might be. With the looming prospect of a decent nest egg it was time to let Pan go. But first, he could do her this last favour.

Her eyes rested on the horses grazing the nearby paddock. Maybe she should take up riding again while she was here. She had been an excellent little horsewoman in her childhood, picking up ribbons in local shows and going out with the local hunt when her brothers deigned to have her along. She squeezed the minuscule roll of fat at her waist that had appeared since she'd stopped going to the gym. A few good canters and that at least would be gone. All was not total gloom and doom.

46

Pan backed the tractor round Margot's car and down to the stables. Leaving the keys in it, he went and laid down a deep bed of straw in one of the double stalls and turned on the solar powered system that provided water to the drinking wells in the stalls and yard. It was hard to concentrate. Every few minutes he stepped outside and holding his breath, listened for the Whistlejacket truck.

The sound of yapping and growling came from the feedroom. Pharlap had bailed up the terriers again. He must have left the door open. He ran towards the racket.

'Go,' he told Pharlap, giving her rump a firm slap. With the expression of one much misunderstood, Pharlap backed out the door and he lifted Ghillie and Beret down off the bales of hay where they'd gone to escape her snapping jaws. 'And you two, clear off,' he told them. 'This isn't the time for games.' The last thing he needed was the dogs under his feet, but he couldn't shut them in the house as he usually did when he wanted them out of the way. Margot would let them out immediately. He could imagine the time she was having going through his house. Hopefully she wasn't gathering up the dog beds for a bonfire. It was the sort of creative thing she did when she was bored or felt she was being ignored.

Back in the stall, he found Frenchie eating the straw he'd just laid. 'You can piss off too,' he said. Frenchie kept chewing, a thoughtful expression on his long white face. Though if BlueBuckle arrived alive, he reflected, Frenchie would be a good companion.

He loved being stabled and when his feed bin was empty, called for room service with dainty taps of his hoof on the door.

He shut Frenchie in the stall, laid a bed in the smaller next-door stall and hung up a Himalayan salt lick, Frenchie's absolute passion.

Tap, tap, tap. Frenchie was bored with the straw and ready for another course.

And there was the sound of a truck.

He grabbed Frenchie's forelock and led him into his stall and his heart in his mouth, went to meet the truck.

'Is he still alive?' he asked as Donnacha leapt out.

'Was when we left. Joost.'

He climbed into the truck and knelt beside BlueBuckle's head. The stallion's eyelids were slits and his breath came in shallow snorts. He placed two fingertips over the artery under his jaw, feeling for a pulse. Donnacha knelt beside and checked that the cannula he'd put in for the IV was still in place under the piece of tape on the side of his neck.

'Pulse is very thready,' Pan said. 'How long has he been down?'

A couple of hours at the most.' Donnacha pinched up a fold of BlueBuckle's skin and watched it slowly flatten out. 'We need to get more fluid into him pronto.'

'We'll have to take the front off the stall,' Beef said, appearing out of the stables. 'The door's not wide enough to get him through.'

Donnacha took a toolbox out of the truck storage hold. 'Let's get on with it.'

'There's a ladder in the feedroom,' Pan said.

Watched by a fascinated Frenchie, they worked swiftly and soon had the stall door off. Disassembling the wall took longer. Every so often their eyes would meet as each wondered if the gut-busting work was in vain. But almost as if any hesitation would be BlueBuckle's deathblow, they did not stop to check if he was still breathing.

He was, mouth now gaping, tongue flaccid and grey.

'How'd you get him into the truck?' Pan asked from the tractor seat as Beef and Donnacha attached the sling bar onto the chain of the pallet fork stabiliser and the sling straps to the sling bar.

'Hobbled him front and back, put a lanyard through and rolled him onto it with the bobcat,' Donnacha said. It had been some operation and a few times he had thought that the bobcat would soon be digging BlueBuckle's grave instead of trying to save his life.

'Right to go, comrade,' Beef told Pan. 'When he's up, start backing until I tell you to stop.'

Beef and Donnacha walked either side of the precariously suspended BlueBuckle and after a few agonisingly long minutes of cautious manoeuvring, he was gently lowered onto the straw. While Pan and Beef started reassembling the wall, Donnacha hung a bag of saline solution for the IV from a beam. He knelt by BlueBuckle and attached the fluid line to the cannula in his neck. 'It's up to you now fella.'

Pan pressed his shoulder against the wall panel, holding it in place so Beef could start putting the bolts back in. 'Good thing Blythe's off to Hong Kong,' Beef said.

Donnacha put his shoulder beside Pan's. 'A trainer mate bought a couple of the yearlings at the Magic Millions and he wanted to be there to settle them, so he said. Pinkie and ...' he stopped, unable to get Leila's name past his lips. 'Pinkie's coming back on the truck.' But Pan would likely already know Leila and Pinkie's movements. Unless he'd been passed over for Blythe. But then wouldn't Leila be going to Hong Kong instead of coming home? He shook his head. There were better things to think about.

'Did the yearlings sell well?' Pan asked, keeping the conversation going in an effort to relieve Donnacha's sudden bleakness.

Donnacha shifted along so Beef could position the ladder. 'One of the fillies was just off the top price.' But this Pan might also already know.

Beef rattled the ladder. He was huffing and there were rings of sweat around the armpits of his shirt. 'How about you go up, comrade?' he said to Donnacha.

Donnacha scaled the ladder, the bucket of bolts and electric drill in his spare hand. Beef leaned next to Pan. 'Blythe bought a horse at the sales,' he said when he had caught his breath. 'A grey colt. Pinkie told Mrs R.' He nodded in the direction of the lifeless Blue-Buckle. 'Donnacha thinks he's planning to do a swap with our friend here.'

'What about the brands?' Pan said. 'They'll be completely different.'

Donnacha came back down the ladder. 'He'll have something worked out so that the brand won't be an issue at the autopsy.'

Pan shook his head. 'He'll lose more than the insurance if he's caught.'

'We're talking ten million,' Donnacha said tersely. 'People risk a lot more for a lot less.'

Pan gazed at BlueBuckle. 'Why wouldn't Blythe just get the same dodgy vet to do an autopsy on him?'

'Because he thinks he's already dead,' Beef said.

'Who's dead?'

'Shit!' Pan said as Margot came walking towards them. She was freshly made up and reeking of scent and wearing the jumper Grace had knitted him.

'Darling,' she said as she joined them. 'I thought I saw a pig looking in through the window. And it's freezing. I thought it was always beach weather downunder.'

'Is that pig about?' Beef said, trying and failing to drag his eyes away from Margot.

Margot's gaze lingered on Donnacha. 'Aren't you going to introduce us?'

'Donnacha Keough, Beef Reedhead, Margot Apsley,' Pan said.

'You left out "the meet my wife bit", darling.'

'Wife?' Beef said.

Margot smiled at Pan. 'His very own.'

Beef shook his head. 'You're a dark one, Pan.'

'They say it's the dark ones you have to watch.' Margot gave Donnacha a long look and scrunched the baggy woollen around her hips, showing that inside there was a very female form.

Donnacha stared at Pan. What a player! He'd lay money on the fact that Leila knew nothing about this living, breathing, knockout wife.

Pan took Margot's arm and guided her away from BlueBuckle's stall. After a cursory glance she had shown no further interest, thank god.

'We're almost finished here,' he told her. 'Head back to the house. I'll be up soon to light the fire.'

Margot turned towards Donnacha. 'Come for a drink when you've finished.'

'I'm in,' Beef said.

'The door.' Donnacha pointed. 'Let's get the fecking thing back up.'

He and Pan got either side and with Beef's muscle, manipulated the door back onto its tracks. 'Any more secrets you've been keeping?' he said under his breath to Pan as Beef got to work on the bolts.

'Margot's no secret,' Pan said. 'We were married for six months. It's been years since I've seen her.'

Donnacha shrugged. 'Whatever. Just get the stallion back on his feet and don't let anyone know he's here. Come on man,' he said to Beef, who was sweating over the last of the bolts. 'It's nearly feedup time.'

'What about that drink?' Beef said. He'd twigged to the reason for Donnacha's downwards mood shift and wasn't buying in.

Donnacha went to the stall door and stood gazing at BlueBuckle. Only the faint fluttering of the straw near his nostrils told that that there was still any life left in his body. 'Some other time.'

Margot stood in the doorway, defending herself as Pan pointed angrily at the tangle of clothes she'd dragged out of his wardrobe and dumped on the bed.

'I told you, I was perishing.'

'But all those bags. Surely there's something in there you could have put on?'

Margot began fussing with the sleeves of the jumper. 'Most of my bags are still in Bali.'

'Most? Bali?'

'You couldn't expect me to make the flight in one trip. All that negative gravity pulling down on the face. The last thing one would want in one's wife is flight attendants' jowls. Though ...' Margot made a sucking movement with her lips and smiled.

Pan looked away. 'How long were you in Bali?'

'A while,' Margo said vaguely.

He picked up an armful of the strewn clothes and shoved them back onto one of the empty shelves. Another bloody bill he would no doubt be expected to pay.

There was a sneeze and Jeffrey poked his nose out from under a tshirt.

'That dog needs to be put down,' Margot said. 'I could smell it from the front door. It's obviously got something rotting in its gut. It's older than my grandfather. I thought it was a good idea to cover him. At least the smell's not so bad.'

'Margot …' Pan stopped. He gathered up the rest of the clothes and ran a soothing hand over Jeffrey's flanks. He needed to get back to BlueBuckle and for that he needed Margot out from under his feet. There was no point appealing to her better nature – he'd given that up long ago – and coming on strong was equally useless.

'Margot, I've got to get back to that horse,' he said, trying the truth. 'Sorry, I know it's boring for you.'

'Off you go, then,' she said, her voice steely. 'I'll sit here and freeze.'

'There's a heater in the office and a TV. There's Netflix and a DVD player. You'll find some Australian series in the bookcase.' He looked at his watch. Four o'clock. If Margot got engrossed in a series or a film, there'd be time to sit with BlueBuckle for a while and settle the other horses before she started baying for something to eat. 'I'll be back up at six to make us dinner.'

Margot looked a little brighter. 'You'll have to get everything going for me first.'

47

'BlueBuckle's gone.'

Donnacha kept walking.

Leila followed him into the office. 'Where is he?'

Donnacha sat down at the desk and turned on the computer.

'What, you can't even speak to me now?' Leila said.

Donnacha gazed at her, thinking how beautiful she looked. A week of Gold Coast sun had turned her skin rose gold and, as the close fit of her brown jodhs and green shell jacket with its Magic Millions logo clearly showed, she had not overindulged in the gourmet offerings that were a feature of the sales and the racing that followed.

He pushed back the chair and got to his feet. 'Best don't mention the stallion. Now, if you don't mind, I've got to sort out stalls for the horses arriving tomorrow.'

Legs braced and arms folded across her chest, she blocked his way. 'Is BlueBuckle at Big Hill?'

Donnacha met her gaze. 'He's married, you know.'

'Who?'

'Villon.'

'Everyone knows. What's that got to do with anything?'

His anger suddenly feeling like foolishness, Donnacha wondered the same thing. But like a rat in a wheel cage, he couldn't help but continue on his futile path.

'She's turned up, the wife, at Big Hill. She's quite a stunner.'

'You should make a play for her, then.'

'That'd suit you, wouldn't it? Clear the way.' The words were out with lightning speed.

'So BlueBuckle is at Big Hill,' she said wearily. 'I was scared he was dead.' Her shoulders drooped.

There were tears in her eyes, Donnacha saw, and under the tan, the tightness of exhaustion. He wanted to kiss away the tears, hold her against him and breathe the vanilla fragrance of her hair. He had read about a hospital using the scent of vanilla to sooth its patients having chemotherapy ...

Their eyes met and with a pitying stare, she was gone.

He sat back down, pulled out his mobile, found Pan in the contacts and pressed "Call".

'How's the hoss?'

'Hasn't roused. I'm with him now. I'm going to sleep here. I've put a swag outside the stall.'

'I suppose the fact that he's still with us is something. The drip should run through in about three hours. Put up another bag when it's finished and call me if anything changes, no matter the time. What about the wife? She'll not be so pleased about being left alone.'

'I've given Pharlap the job of keeping her in the house.'

'Give her a bone from me. The pig, I mean.'

Pan laughed. 'She'd rather a Guinness.'

'I'll bring her one tomorrow. Leila's twigged. She might show up.'

'Tell her not to.'

'She might be a help,' Donnacha said, then growled softly as an image of Leila on the swag next to Pan came into his mind, 'Fuck off, would you!'

'What's that?' Pan said.

'Mosquito.'

'Bit cold for mosquitos, isn't it?'

'Anything you need, then?'

'You don't want to come and entertain Margot, do you? I've a feeling Pharlap's going to lose interest pretty quickly.'

'Thanks for the offer, man, but no thanks. She looks like trouble.'

'You'd better believe it.'

Donnacha placed his finger over "End Call" but found himself reluctant to push it. Beyond seeing Leila and Pan together at the opening meet, what evidence did he have that there was anything between them? If he were man enough, he'd ask Pan about the scene. If he were man enough …

'Are you there?' Pan said.

'Yup,' he answered.

'Everything okay?'

'Thanks for what you're doing for the hoss, man. You're a top fella. A top fella with the hosses and a top fella.'

'Let's not get ahead of ourselves.'

'Sure.'

'If Leila shows, I'll send her straight home.'

'Do that.'

Leila propped the pillows up against the bedhead and dropped onto the bed, too tired, even, to take off her boots. How had BlueBuckle gotten to Big Hill? Donnacha couldn't have done it on his own, even with Pan's help. She sipped her coffee. There was a poker game going on in the kitchen, but nobody had asked her to join in. They'd toned it down, though.

She sunk back against the pillows and stretched out her legs. The noise in the kitchen returned to its previous level. The wind rattled a piece of loose iron with terrier-like persistence. She didn't mind wind. Rootless, wayward, possessed of as many moods as there were colours, it was a reminder of life's capriciousness.

As if she needed reminding.

The Magic Millions had been hell. With Pinkie mostly AWOL, it had been her and Jack, the truck driver, caring for the Whistlejacket yearlings. In an unfamiliar environment, constantly abuzz with the clatter and calling of strange horses and humans, the yearlings had been alternatively petulant and hyper. When she wasn't making up feeds, checking Jack had cleaned the stalls properly or walking the yearlings out for prospective buyers, she had been busy soothing the young horses so that they didn't burn off their condition before they got to the sale ring. And as if the days hadn't been full enough, after a yearling from another stud was found dead, she'd camped in the stall allotted Whistlejacket for a feedroom and set her mobile to alarm every two hours so she could keep an even closer eye on her charges.

She didn't go to the sale ring herself. Over the months spent teaching the young horses to lead, grooming them and pulling their manes and tails so they looked like little show horses, they became dear to her. It was almost unbearable seeing them go, even though their departure from Whistlejacket was the very reason for the care lavished on them. As Pinkie led them away, the more sensitive and less secure of them, sensing her distress, would turn and call to her.

And god only knew what Pinkie was off doing, and with whom. Half an hour before a yearling was due in the sale ring, she'd stroll up, take the horse and head off with barely a word. Lucien was just as elusive. Sometimes he'd return with the yearling after it had been sold, other times not. Like Pinkie, he seemed to barely register she was there.

Yes, it had been an all-round shitty week. So shitty she had spent the flight home debating whether or not it was time to move on from Whistlejacket. Debating yet again.

She switched off the light and pulled a pillow to her chest for comfort. She woke some hours later, half frozen. The dorm was graveyard quiet and the wind gone elsewhere. She kicked off her boots, crawled under the doona and pulling the pillow back against her chest, kissed it and fell into a deep sleep.

Donnacha was curled around her, knees fitted behind hers, his chin resting on the top of her head. BlueBuckle stood at their feet, head drooping, eyes half closed, his breath rising and falling in time to the rise and fall of the faraway ocean.

The dream fractured into tiny pieces and vanished, leaving a wash of anger in its wake. Grey light came through the window and the clatter of crockery and smell of bacon came from the kitchen. She checked her phone. Six thirty. She should have been up an hour ago. The truck with the horses Lucien had bought at the Magic Millions would be arriving any time now and she also needed to get over to Stephan and Scott's to exercise Elvis. It was going to be a full day. But first, she'd call Pan. She pushed off the doona and braced as the chill morning air hit her.

48

Pan stepped back in disbelief and nearly came down as his foot caught the swag strap. He grabbed the door to steady himself and, heart pounding, peered back into the stall. It was definitely empty. The bag of saline he'd put up around four was dripping into the straw through the cannula which, when he'd last checked, had been seated in BlueBuckle's jugular, and the back door of the stall was open, its leaves swinging separately in the morning breeze.

His phone rang. He let it ring. The message service kicked in. It was Donnacha.

'Hey man, call as soon as you can. Haven't slept much.'

He opened the stall door and in a few quick strides was at the yard.

'Bloody hell!' BlueBuckle and Pharlap, side by side and shivering together in the brisk air, turned and looked at him briefly and then back at the goats lining up on the dam wall to catch the first rays of the sun. Blue Buckle was not quite steady on his feet, but his eye had a definite glint.

Pan examined the stall doors. There were scuff and what looked to be teeth marks around the slide bolt of the bottom one. 'Did you do that?' he said to Pharlap.

Pharlap eyes stayed fixed on the goats.

'Ruddy bugger,' he told her. BlueBuckle swung his head around and gave him a nasty stare. 'And you're no better,' he told him, but more gently.

He returned to his study of the door. The slide bolt that held the top leaf was also out of its keep, but unless Pharlap had access to a ladder and could climb it, there was no way she could have reached it. It must have been left undone and he'd not noticed.

The patch of sunlight on the dam wall was spreading up the paddock and lines of birds ribboned the sky. Rubbing his hands together to warm them he watched a magpie pick through the clover under the bottom rail of the yard and drag out a worm.

His phone rang again, earning him a withering glance from Pharlap.

It was Leila. 'He's okay,' he said over her stuttered 'Is he, he's …?' 'He's up and on his feet.' It sounded like she was crying. 'Are you all right?' There was silence, then her reply. 'Yes, yes.' 'You realise that no one can know he's here, don't you?' he said. 'Donnacha and Beef will lose their jobs. They might lose them anyway. I don't know how they're planning to explain his disappearance.' Another call was coming in – Donnacha. 'I'd better go.'

'He's gone,' Donnacha said straight off without any greeting. 'He's gone, man, isn't he? I'm still glad we did it. We did what was right. At least we can say that. But tanks, man, Beef and me'll come over and bury him when feedup's done.'

'He's here in the yard with Pharlap.'

Donnacha couldn't grasp it. 'In the yard? How the fock did he get into the yard? I spose he wanted to die out in the open. I've heard of that. But what's with the pig?'

'He's not dead. He's in the yard with Pharlap. She undid the bottom bolt. She's a bugger for getting in and out of places.'

'The pig.' Donnacha repeated. 'The pig let the hoss out.'

Pan smiled – it felt good. 'I'm having trouble believing it myself. Hang on, I'll put the phone on video call.'

Seeing BlueBuckle standing with Pharlap in the yard, Donnacha exclaimed, 'It's a fecking miracle. I was sure the hoss was dead.'

'I was thinking I might try him with a small feed,' Pan said.

'Make the pig one too,' Donnacha said. 'And put a can of Guinness in it from me. I'll be over as soon as I can. Send a photo to Beef. No, best not. Best there aren't photos.'

'It's early days,' Pan cautioned, as much for his own benefit as Donnacha's. 'Don't be cracking a bottle yet. He's so weak that if the wind gets up, he'll blow into the fence.'

Donnacha grunted, then asked casually, 'Leila show last night?'

'No. She rang just before.'

'Okay man better go. A truck's arriving.'

With a last look at BlueBuckle and Pharlap, Pan headed back through the stall to the feedroom. He filled the kettle and dropped four teaspoons of coffee into the plunger pot and a dollop of molasses into a bucket.

There was a scuffle outside, and the expectant faces of Sadie and the terriers appeared at the door. At some stage during the night they'd left the stable and disappeared into the dark. Hunting, as their dirty muzzles and chests now told.

He filled the water bowl by the door and watched them lap thirstily. From the state of them, it looked as though they had covered some ground. He hated them going off at night in case they roamed too far and got lost, or stuck down a wombat or fox burrow, or, his worst fear of all, picked up a bait. Usually, he made sure they were secured in the mud room before he went to bed or if he was going out, but Margot had insisted they stay in the stable with him. And of course, hunters that they were, stay they had not.

He poured boiling water over the coffee grounds and watched by the hungry dogs, added the rest of it to BlueBuckle's bucket along with some lucerne cubes.

'I suppose you want breakfast, too,' he said to them. Benzo and Jeffrey would be wanting theirs as well. Christ! Benzo and Jeffrey. He'd shut them in his bedroom and if they hadn't already, they'd be desperate to relieve themselves. BlueBuckle would have to wait for a feed. He poured the coffee into a cup, added three spoons of sugar and taking a scalding sip, headed for the house. But for all his tiredness, the complication of Margot, he was profoundly happy. A new teacher had arrived at Big Hill.

49

'Is Beef about?' said a sulky looking Pinkie. 'I need him to drive me home.' She gestured at Jack, who was now also out of the horse truck. 'This arsehole wouldn't drop me off.'

'Haven't seen him,' Donnacha said. He pulled his mobile out of his pocket. 'I'll give him a call.'

Pinkie began walking off. 'Tell him I'm with Mrs R and that my bag's in the truck.'

Donnacha put his phone back in his pocket. 'Good trip, then?' he said to Jack.

'Bitch needs her claws cut,' Jack said. 'Thought all my Christmases had come at once when the boss said she was to come back with me, but except for when she needed a pee, she slept the whole way.'

'Let's get these hosses off,' Donnacha said, opening the truck door and reaching for the ramp switch. The cabin floor was a mess of chip packets, empty water bottles and Red Bull cans. He thought about taking Jack to task, but the lad looked so tired he didn't have the heart.

'She's too old for you anyway, man,' he said as the ramp eased towards the ground.

The smell of ammonia and manure was overpowering and desperate to be free from their confinement, the four horses onboard the truck were beating the floor with their hooves. Ears pricked and nostrils flaring, they swung their heads towards the fresh air and returned the calls of the nosier Whistlejacket horses, for whom every truck and float that arrived or left was of great personal concern.

'What have we got?' Donnacha asked Jack.

'The two fillies at the front were bought for the stud. And the grey colt. The other filly belongs to Mr Fahey.'

Donnacha caught a glimpse of a Whistlejacket SUV heading up the drive towards the big gates. Probably Beef taking Pinkie home – he must have been up at the homestead with Mrs R. He turned his attention to the filly straining against her headcollar so she could see past him.

'Easy girl,' he said as he unlatched the partition. The filly shook her head and high stepping in her float boots, let herself be backed a few steps and then turned and led down the ramp.

He handed her to Jack and bent to undo the float boots, moving with her as she sidestepped and sidled. The boots off, he stood back and ran an appraising eye over her. Straight legs, good angle on the pasterns, strong rear end and muscled stifle – on these points alone, she looked a winner. No doubt Blythe had an eye for class. He might not have a brain for pedigrees like his mother, but when it came to young horses, he could read bone and tendon like no one else.

The next two fillies also earned an approving nod as Jack led them away.

He was untying the colt when Jack called up from the bottom of the ramp. 'The boss said you'd know where to put this one.'

Donnacha nodded. He did indeed. 'Oh aye. Now, off you go and get a proper feed and some sleep.'

'What about the truck?'

'I'll get one of the others to clean it.'

Jack looked almost cheerful. 'The logbook and fuel card are in the glovebox.'

'I'll see that Pinkie gets them,' Donnacha said. Pinkie put the kilometres and petrol usage of the Whistlejacket vehicles on a spreadsheet that went to Kevin. 'Do you know this fella's catalogue number?'

'Didn't see any of the bidding. Me and Leila were too busy in the stables because a certain person who was also supposed to be working was only working on her tan. There's a catalogue in one of the gear bags, I think.'

'What day did he come up for sale?'

'Don't know. First time I saw him was when we were loading. Oh, the boss said he was to be rugged. Feels the cold, apparently. I kept the rug on him for the trip even though he sweated up.'

Unloaded and standing on even ground, the colt easily made sixteen three hands. He was short backed and steep shouldered, and while his neck was patterned with dark grey dapples, his face and mane and tail were a distinctive steel grey.

The grey colt stood chewing on a biscuit of lucerne in BlueBuckle's old yard.

Beef put his foot on the bottom rail next to Donnacha's. 'Pretty near the original, I'd say.'

'If you don't look too hard,' Donnacha said.

'And if you've never seen the original, which most haven't. Do you think Blythe's planning to parade him?'

Donnacha shrugged. 'Who knows. He didn't buy him through the sales though. I went right through the catalogue. Then I realised that he wouldn't have made it in anyway because of his age.'

'Where's he from?'

'A stud in Scone. Small operation. Breed a few for the track but mostly showjumpers. The brand's even similar. Come and see.' Donnacha undid the chain and swung open the gate.

The colt looked up from his hay then returned to his munching.

'True, comrade,' Beef said after examining the marking on the colt's shoulder, which, as well as the breeder's initials, showed that he was not quite three. 'The dapples help, though. It's harder to read the brand on a grey.'

'He's to be kept rugged. I presume that's in case he stands in front of the yard camera for too long.'

'You haven't turned it on yet, then?'

Donnacha rubbed the colt's neck. 'I will when I get back to the office. He's quite a nice fella. Good stride on him, too. Would make a decent hunter.'

Beef's attention returned to the brand. 'Jack obviously didn't notice his age, then.'

'I don't think he was noticing much at all. Pinkie was in a foul mood. I'd say she'd been giving him a hard time.'

'From the way she was walking, she's the one that's been getting a hard time. She looked like she'd been very busy.'

'Well she'd better get her mind back on the job. The stallion parade's coming up fast.' Donnacha held out the headcollar and the colt obligingly dropped his head into it. Getting Beef to hold him, he got his rug off the fence.

'Do you think Blythe expects us to call him BlueBuckle?' Beef said.

'Probably. But I won't be.'

'Me neither.'

Their eyes met. Donnacha grinned. 'Fecking amazing, isn't it. A pig. That pig! Who'd have thought.'

Beef looked nervously at the yard camera, positioned atop a high post in what looked like a wooden bird house. 'You sure that thing's not on, comrade? Don't want to lose my job just yet.'

'We're done here anyway,' Donnacha said.

'I was thinking,' Beef said as they headed down the lane back towards the stables. 'We should phone Kentucky and find out if our friend had a special mate. That's one thing we never asked. It best be you, though. If Mrs R sees the number on the bill, she'll ask questions. And if the name of the place comes up beside it, she could say something to Lucien. The Lady mother called from Paris this morning, by the way. We didn't go to Ascot. Struck down by jetlag, apparently. We'll be back Thursday. Wanted to make sure Pinkie was about Friday morning. We're getting worked up about the stallion parade, I suppose.'

Donnacha stopped suddenly. 'Shit. I need her to tell me where to put the new yearlings. They're in stalls. They'll be breaking their legs for a bit of a gallop.'

Beef looked in the direction of Donnacha's gaze and seeing Leila's Forrester turning out of the gates said, 'She might be heading to Big Hill. Taking one of the hundred or so days off she's owed. But I tell you now, miracle or no miracle, you won't be seeing this black duck anywhere near the stallion if that pig's within cooee. It's a nasty, nasty animal.'

50

Leila turned off the engine and walked back to the sign on the fence flanking the cattle grid.

HIGHLY DESIRABLE FORTY- FOUR ACRES
THREE BEDROOM HOUSE
SPRING FED DAMS
Agent Xavier Swift 0417058007

The unfenced drive wound through a large, empty paddock, leeched of colour by the dry summer and autumn. The pasture was a mixture of phalaris, cocksfoot and fescue with scatterings of wallaby grass, all reasonable grazing grasses. More importantly, however, there was no serrated tussock or thistle, both of which could swallow up viable pasture in no time. At the end of the drive a cluster of gums hid, presumably, the house and whatever infrastructure there was. She crossed to the other side of the cattle grid, hoping to see more, but whatever was behind the trees remained hidden.

She got back in the car. She could always call Xavier and ask him to show her the place properly. No, it'd be insane. The property was bound to be far beyond what she could afford and only yesterday she had been ready to leave Burragong and not look back. Nevertheless, as she steered the Forrester back onto the road, she

"

glanced in the rear-view mirror just in case the new vantage point gave a glimpse of the house. It didn't.

Ten minutes later she turned through Gwynedd's gates, crossing her fingers that Simon was home. She should have called, but if he'd responded with any coolness, or been drunk, and there was a chance of both, she'd have lost her nerve.

The stables were empty, the hunt horses either out for exercise or enjoying a midweek spell in their paddock. Three vehicles were parked at the back of the house alongside Simon's Range Rover, one of them Gill Findlay's Prado, which she recognised from the Blooming Beautiful sticker on the back window. Surely Gill wasn't driving yet?

It was Gill that opened the door, however, a little gaunt but cheerful.

'Leila, what a nice surprise. Simon's taken the hounds out, but he should be back soon. Have you got time to wait? I'm hiding out in the study. The cleaner's here. I'm sure she'll make us some tea.' Without waiting for an answer, Gill swivelled on her good leg with the help of the crutches and led the way across the short entrance hall to the living room.

'June, this is our friend, Leila,' she said. 'Leila, June. Any chance of some tea?'

The trim little woman with pumpkin coloured hair stopped dusting the hound figurines on the mantlepiece and smiled. Her apron was embroidered at the top with "Loved by a Persian" and the image of a round faced grey furball formed the pocket below.

Relieved that Gill had introduced her as a friend, Leila returned June's smile. Gill had not taken sides in Eleanor and Simon's split, it appeared.

'June's sorting the house,' Gill said as she lowered herself onto the study sofa. 'Her clients call her the Fairy and it's easy to see why. Nothing's too much trouble.' She waved at an armchair and as she lifted her plastered leg onto an ottoman covered in faded blue velvet, said, 'Phew. That's better.'

'Does it hurt?' Leila asked.

'Not at all. It's the crutches that are murder. Simon cut up a numnah and wrapped it around the arm rests, but everything fell off.' Gill gave a snort of laughter. 'Simon's not what you'd call a handy man.'

'I saw your car. You didn't drive here, did you?'

'Lord no. June's son, Garry brought it over. He runs it every few days so that the battery doesn't get flat. But I'm looking forward to being able to drive almost as much as getting back on Hester. It's awful being dependent on others.'

'You certainly look better than when I saw you last.' Leila said. A touch of mascara and silvery blue eyeshadow deepened the almost navy blue of Gill's eyes, and her tousled grey blonde hair had Vivienne Teo's signature class.

'It's probably the chicken soup June's pumping into me. She and Garry have been a godsend. Garry's helping Simon with the hounds and doing the stables and cleaning the tack. There's no way Simon could have managed on his own. How's Eleanor, do you know?'

'Sorry. Guilty. Hurting for Simon. She's taken off for the States. For Washington.'

'Give her my love, won't you? I hope she keeps in touch. Simon does as well.'

Tears pricked Leila's eyes. There was still reasonableness in the world – sometimes it was too easy to forget. 'She'll be grateful for that. How about Simon? How's he?'

'Starting to breathe freely again, I think. He knew he and Eleanor were finished months back but kept shoving his head further and further into the sand.'

June came in with a rattling tea tray and the Cairns, who greeted Leila briefly then jumped up next to Gill.

'Little devils,' June said. 'They heard the biscuit tin. Want me to pour?'

'If you don't mind,' Gill said. 'Where's your cup?'

'I'm having mine outside with a ciggy,' June answered.

'Don't let Simon see you,' Gill said. 'He might want to start again.'

June gave a throaty laugh and putting a plate of buttered oat biscuits on the desk out of reach of the Cairns, headed off for her cigarette.

Leila held out the biscuits to Gill, who took one and broke it up for the Cairns, who were watching intently with their bright black eyes.

'Any idea when you'll be back riding?' Leila asked.

Gill looked down at her cast. 'Hopefully this'll be off in another couple of weeks, then I guess I'll see.'

'I'm just on my way to Scott's and Stephan's to work Elvis,' Leila ventured.

'Simon's so pleased Elvis is staying with the Hunt. He was going to call you. He's hoping you'll ride Field Master this weekend. I've organised a committee meeting so it can be ratified. Lucien's the only one who might object, but he'll be outnumbered.'

'That was why I came over. I wanted to make sure Simon's okay with everything. Eleanor said he would be, but, you know, I wanted to do the right thing.'

The Cairns stopped trying to hypnotise another biscuit out of their mistress and turned their little faces towards the door and yipped. A minute later Simon came in.

Despite his dishevelled hair and day's worth of white stubble, there was nothing defeated about him. And he certainly wasn't drunk. His step was firm and his voice its usual jolly croon.

'Leila. Fantastic! Can you start as Field Master Sunday? We had some person from Sydney last week and they were hopeless. And Gill needs some help with the bluddy ball as well. It's all rather fallen in her lap. The ball stuff I mean.' He turned to Gill. 'Garry found the golf buggy under a pile of rugs. He's killed the redback spiders and put the battery on the charger. You should be right to go in a few hours. Any tea left? I'm parched.'

'It'll need a top up,' Gill said. 'And you'll need a cup.'

Simon picked up the pot. 'I'll be back. Don't let the dogs eat all the biscuits.'

As he left the room, Leila raised her eyebrows questioningly at Gill. 'Golf buggy?'

'So I can get down to the kennels and to the horses. I'm staying here for the moment. I wasn't really managing on my own. Nor was Simon. Things pretty much went to shit for us at the same time. Hester and Dorothy are here too.' She stopped, waiting for

Leila to comment. It was well known that Simon preferred not to have mares at Gwynedd. The hunt horses were all geldings and they fought one another for the mares' attention.

When Leila made no comment, Gill added, 'Olivia's in Sydney with her father.'

Simon came back holding the teapot aloft.

'You'll scald your scalp and won't be able to get your cap on on Sunday,' Gill told him.

Simon put the teapot on the desk, poured himself a mug and drank it off. 'Phew I was dry,' he said, pouring another, which he also gulped down before reaching for a biscuit.

'Has Gill showed you her painting, Leila?'

She shook her head. Simon beckoned her to follow.

Gill and Hester's portrait had been hung on the living room wall opposite Rebecca's. Leila studied it, standing first close and then further way. 'It's stunning.'

'I know,' said Simon. 'I sit and look at it when there's nothing on tele.'

'You can see every hair of Hester's plaits. Isn't she gorgeous!'

'I was rather thinking that of the rider,' Simon said.

Leila looked at him, not sure she'd heard right. 'You're okay, then?'

'I am now. Thank you for being Ellie's friend. The messy stuff all got left to her. I was too useless to face it. She could have just walked, but right to the last she was thinking of me and the Hunt. She's a top girl. Tell her I said that, won't you? She deserves a proper fellow, not a curmudgeon like this old self.' Simon shook himself like a hound shaking off water. 'But enough of that. You're onboard for Sunday? I know you'll do us proud.'

Leila nodded. 'I can't wait.'

Leila increased the pressure on the left rein and slid her right leg back behind the girth. The big gelding began tracking diagonally away from the arena wall. She counted half a dozen strides, moved her leg forward and turned him along the short side of the arena and put him on a twenty-meter circle. Elvis again obliged. She brought him to a halt, rubbed his shoulder and thanked him for his good work then walked him on a long rein so he could stretch.

The only problem she'd found was his tendency to lean on the bit. He didn't pull, but the pressure on her hands was always there, unless, like now, his head was perfectly free. But overall, he was a lovely boy. Willing, solid not only in his nearly seventeen hand high body but also in his character. Clearly he had known only fairness and consideration in his relationships with humans.

'He's working well,' came Scott's voice from the entrance to the arena. 'Ready for the jumps?'

Leila rode over to him. 'He's a perfect gentleman. Eleanor must have hated leaving him. Maybe he's the reason she stayed as long as she did.'

Scott rubbed Elvis's dark brown face. 'It wouldn't surprise me. I've set the jumps at a metre. Do you want them down or up?'

Leila kicked her legs out of the stirrups so she could shorten the leathers. 'A metre's fine as long as they're not too close together. He'll struggle with tight turns.'

She followed Scott out of the arena and down a wide path to the jumping paddock. Scott's and Stephan's was one of her favourite properties, more so even than Whistlejacket. Though far more modest, the layout was intuitive and felt spacious and the crushed granite paths, photinia hedges and enormous urns of sculpted box gave it an Italian feel. She thought about the property for sale near Gwynedd. If she owned it, she would ... She pushed the thought out of her mind.

Scott opened the gate and she walked Elvis around the jumps, a combination of uprights and oxers, and let him have a good look.

'Nothing too scary?' Scott called from the milk crate on which he'd parked himself.

Leila gave Elvis' neck a rub. 'All good.' Some horses got hot and bothered at the sight of jumps, but Elvis hadn't even quickened his pace. She picked out three jumps and drew a mental line across to the oxer. The oxer's spread was about a metre and a half and to face it squarely, Elvis would have to lengthen his stride immediately after the turn. It would test him, but not too much.

'Okay buddy.' She shortened the reins and asked the big horse for a canter and as he fell into a roll, she pointed him at the first of the jumps. His stride was slightly jarring but again he went so kindly that other than keeping him collected, she had to do little more than maintain her own balance.

A few strides after the oxer, she brought him back to a trot and then asking for a canter on the other lead, took him around the jumps in the opposite direction.

'You two are made for each other,' Scott said as she rode back.

She swung down from the saddle, ran up the stirrups and loosened Elvis' girth, still not quite able to believe he was hers to hunt. She untacked him at the wash bay and decided to sponge him rather than hose him down. He had hardly sweated and according to the weather app on her phone, it was going to be a cool night. He stood quietly for his rubdown, turning his big face towards her and blowing down his nose and occasionally exploring the rubber sides of the wash bay with his whiskery lips.

'You're very good fella,' she told him, rubbing his saddle and girth area with a towel. She would take his saddle and bridle back to Whistlejacket. It would be less for Scott to pack and she wanted to maintain their perfect gleam. Like everything of Eleanor's, they were top quality, the saddle a gorgeous County.

She untied Elvis and led him to the small yard next to the stables where he spent his nights. Spying the hay Scott had put out for him, he trotted off and attacked it with more animation than he'd shown since she'd arrived. Mockingbird would have stayed for a pat and chat, she thought. If she had her own place, Donnacha might say where she'd gone.

It was crazy thinking. Mockingbird never would be hers. Same with the property. A distant neigh caught her attention. Mockingbird? It couldn't be. She was well and truly losing the plot.

51

Its colours the drab greens of stagnant water, the dull char of bush-fire, the hues of a moonless night, the big hill's mood had infected the country from which it had been forced up millions of years before the memory of man. The birds, the hidden creatures that churned the detritus of the bush floor, the tunnellers and pollinators were all quiet and still, as if they had quit their work and gone elsewhere. The feeling in the air was that of a brewing storm yet no clouds broke the flat grey of the sky.

Pan felt a dolefulness settle over his shoulders like a wet woollen coat. He looked down and saw that Jeffrey had somehow made his way down to the yards.

'What are you doing here?'

Jeffrey trembled violently, he too, it appeared, infected by the grim mood of the big hill. He squatted and put his arms around him and he collapsed against his chest with a sigh of sorrow.

They stayed like that for a few minutes, then he said, 'Let's get you back to the house.'

He rose and put his hand on Jeffrey's collar. Jeffrey went rigid.

'Come on, man, you can't stay down here. Let's get you somewhere warm.

Jeffrey turned his head in the direction of the house, his trembling shaking his whole body.

'Margot turfed you out, didn't she?'

Jeffrey dipped his head, grateful that he had been understood.

The silence of the countryside, the lethargic sky, the big hill's sullenness suddenly made sense. An intruder had come among them.

He had married Margot because she was the first woman he had truly enjoyed sex with. She had chattered and laughed her smooth laugh and wriggled and jiggled so much that he didn't have a chance to be shy or self-conscious. And he found in their intimacy – the incredible closeness of skin on skin, the way she hid nothing from his gaze – the love that he'd dreamed about. So he had thought, had thought for a time. She had wanted marriage as much as him. It seemed a properly adult thing to do.

Managing investment portfolios for self-funded retirees, he was insanely bored, but having embraced city life, he rejected as too simple his instincts. His yearning for untramped earth, unbridled sky, the breath of animals. And Margot and London's ceaseless clamour kept him apart from himself in other ways. He hadn't worked out that his shyness was a natural reserve. That he was selective about what he wished to share and his craving for time alone was not loneliness.

In other words, in the deeper reaches of his and Margot's characters there were no matches. Theirs was a marriage of opposites and their attraction, though not without moments of loveliness, a brief spark, which by the end of their Barbados honeymoon, was already spluttering.

Allergic to responsibility, Margot lay the blame squarely at his feet. Why have friends if he never saw them? What was the point of living in London if he didn't ever want to go out? How could social media possibly be an intrusion? Why did he want to sit alone and read when he could snuggle up with her on the sofa and watch a film? Didn't he want to snuggle up with her? Was he bored with her already? Were her friends boring? Her Instagram posts, her breasts?

Forced to defend himself, he journeyed deeper and deeper into the features of his person that so irritated her. One night, in a ferment after a row that had come about because he wanted to get a dog, he had gotten in the car and driven to Scotland, not stopping until he was in the Highlands. Finding a brochure for a coast to coast horse trek in the B&B in the village where he'd sought refuge, he booked the trek, resigned his job and told Margot he was taking time out from their marriage.

Margot, of course, told him he could spend the rest of his life in Scotland. Their marriage was over. It had lasted six months and had delivered him back to himself. It had affirmed his appreciation of silence, of birdsong, of distant thunder and the meditations of cloud and stars. It had returned him to horses and horses to him. He was once more, as he'd been during his best moments, in a dance with nature and in a way, he owed it to Margot, which was why he did not seek a formal end to their marriage. Though she had demanded an eye watering allowance, as he saw it, his debt to her went beyond money. Besides that, the marriage was an insurance policy of sorts. A ready handbrake. If he were ever to find himself on a similar road again, the fact that he was still married would be enough of an impediment to buy him the time he needed to come to his senses and not return the way he'd come.

After the dust settled, they had formed a friendship of habit, calling every few months and ending the sparse conversation with the promise they would always be there for each other but with neither believing that the promise would ever be taken up.

But now Margot had. She was at Big Hill, in his house and her timing was atrocious, her presence the same.

He let go of Jeffrey's collar and gave his head a reassuring rub. 'It's all right, man. We're okay here for the moment.'

He pushed all thought of Margot out of his mind. He needed to concentrate on BlueBuckle, who, though still skeletal, was now sharing a small tub of lucerne cubes and molasses with Pharlap, the second tub for the day.

He clucked his tongue and BlueBuckle and Pharlap glanced in his direction then, exchanging a look – the stallion arching his neck towards the pig and she, smiling her leering smile – returned to the feed. Clearly, they had something going on and had apportioned him a very minor role. Which was fine for the moment. Until Blue-Buckle got more strength back, at least.

'Looks like love, to me,' came Donnacha's voice from behind him. He dropped a pat on Jeffrey's head. 'Hello old fella.' His gaze returned to BlueBuckle. 'Had to see it with my own eyes and now

I'm seeing it I still can't believe it.' He shook his head. 'I thought the hoss was gone for sure.'

'You and me both.'

'Wait till Beef sees it. He wants me to ring Kentucky and find out if the hoss had a stable friend. A pig, like.'

'Is that wise? It might get back to Blythe.'

'It crossed my mind. I'll use my own phone. No problem getting the feed in the yard? You're obviously still in one piece.'

'Pharlap's the problem. She's turned into a bloody guard dog. Points with her trotter where the bucket's to go and then gives me an eye that says "right, now piss off".'

Donnacha laughed then shut up as Pharlap gave him the death stare.

'Blythe has bought a grey colt,' he said. 'It came on the truck from the Gold Coast this morning with some fillies. He didn't buy it at the Gold Coast, though. Beef thinks he is planning to pass it off as this fella here.'

'Can he get away with it?'

'We'll see, I suppose. If that's what the plan is.'

They stopped as BlueBuckle strolled over to the water tub and took a drink.

Donnacha returned to the subject of the grey colt. 'He's a nice hoss. Nothing of the class of this bugger, though.' He whistled at Blue-Buckle, who lifted his head, the water dripping from his muzzle.

With a nasty look at Donnacha, Pharlap bustled BlueBuckle back to the feed.

'Looks like she's got the hoss well and truly under the trotter,' Donnacha said, shaking his head. 'Life's a queer thing isn't it! You know, Beef's more frightened of the pig than he is of the stallion.'

Margot was wrapped in a blanket and watching an episode of the ABC drama *Janet King*.

'This isn't bad for an Australian production,' she said, without looking up. 'Any chance of a drink? Maybe a glass of that white you opened last night.'

'What'll you have Donnacha?' Pan asked

Margot hit the mute button, 'Oh, company, darling. You didn't say.' She jumped up and the blanket slid to the floor, revealing violet lace bra and knickers worthy of the Victoria's Secret catalogue.

Donnacha took a step back and bumped into Pan, who said sternly to Margot, 'You can't complain about the cold if you get about like that. Go and put something on.' Indeed, an intruder had come among them.

Margot shivered, just enough to make the tops of her breasts tremble. 'All my clothes are dirty and the washing machine's full of dog hair.'

Pan's cheeks flamed. 'I use the washing machine in the stables for the dog coats. Anyway, when did you ever do any of your own washing?'

Margo pouted. 'Most of my luggage got lost somewhere between here and Bali,' she said to Donnacha. 'Pan won't do anything about it. I don't suppose you have a contact at the international airport?'

'Let me help with the drinks, man,' Donnacha muttered to Pan.

'And something to snack on, darlings,' Margot said. 'I'm famished.'

Donnacha leaned against the kitchen bench and watched Pan put olives and a wedge of cheddar onto a plate. 'I'd say that pig's the least of your problems, man.'

'You've got that right.'

Pan sloshed some wine into a glass and took a few quick sips. It would soon be getting dark and there were animals to bring in and feed and of course he had to organise the dogs so that they stayed out of Margot's way. Last night she'd accused Benzo of hogging the fire and thrown a book at him, which had ended up with Benzo in a sulk and the book in the fire.

He poured some wine for Donnacha and held out the glass. 'There's beer if you'd rather. I don't usually drink this myself either, but any old port in a storm. You couldn't stay and entertain Margot while I sort the horses, could you?'

'Sorry man, I'd be more help with the horses,' Donnacha replied. 'She's lovely, Margot, very attractive, but ...' Unable to think of anything that would not get him into further trouble, if it was trouble that he was in, he gulped the wine.

Pan's expression lightened. Margot's game was to turn men into slaves or sneaky pervs and Donnacha was showing signs of neither. He picked up the bottle and another glass and pointed to the cheese.

'I'll light the fire and you keep her glass filled. Then I will get your help with the horses. It's the dogs that are the problem, though. Margot doesn't like them in the house.' He had bundled Jeffrey into his bedroom via the veranda door.

Donnacha shook his head. 'Can't help you there, either, man. Sorry.'

Behind the big hill, the sky was the colour of a bruise. Torn between the view and the horsemanship books on the sofa, Donnacha chose the view. Pan got the fire going and, still kneeling on the hearth, was suddenly surrounded by dogs.

'Dogs out,' Margot ordered from the doorway. She was dressed now in skin-tight jeans and a clinging fuchsia pink V-neck. Her hair was freed from its earlier ponytail and she had elongated her eyes with khol and drenched herself in *Black Jade*.

Donnacha held out a glass of wine and waved at the sofa. Glaring at Pan, who was kissing Ghillie's whiskery face, she sat and after arranging her legs, looked over the cheese platter with a disgruntled expression.

'Your scent's upsetting the dogs, Margot,' Pan said testily as Ghillie began to sneeze. 'You'll have to go and wash it off. It's awful anyway. I don't know why you wear it.'

'Because you bought it for me, darling,' she answered. She pointed to the drifts of dust around the base of the coffee table. 'It's not my scent, it's that. You live like an animal. And that window makes me dizzy. Think of all the heat you're losing through the glass.'

'It's triple-glazed.'

Margot ignored this and turned towards Donnacha. 'How long have you been in Australia?'

'Six years, give or take,' Donnacha answered.

'And what do people do for excitement in Kookaburra?'

'There's the hunting,' Donnacha said, rubbing his nose, which, like Ghillie's, was starting to itch.

Margot sat up. 'You've got a Hunt Club?'

Donnacha looked at Pan. Had he said the wrong thing? Apparently – Pan's expression was thunderous.

Margo clapped her hands. 'When's the next meet? I'll take that little liver chestnut in the paddock near the house. We'll have to go to Sydney, Pan. I'll need a kit and I can't imagine there's anything in Kookaburra. We can drop in at the airport and see about my luggage while we're there.'

'You haven't ridden for years, Margot,' Pan said tersely.

Margot stretched out a leg and pointed her toe towards the ceiling. 'I'd say I'm supple enough, wouldn't you Donnacha?' Having stopped going to the gym, she'd taken up yoga, learning from a DVD series endorsed by Gwyneth Paltrow.

Donnacha stared. 'You wouldn't want to be doing that on a horse.'

Margot brought her leg down and smiled at him. 'You'll look after me, won't you? Catch me if I fall?'

'He's a Whipper-in,' said Pan. 'He'll be busy with the hounds.'

Margot smiled. 'A Whip. How exciting. You'll definitely have to be my chaperone.'

'What's the story with the liver chestnut?' Donnacha asked Pan, trying to stop the landslide he'd triggered.

'It's Hazel Teo's mare, Dorothy. Or rather was. I bought her back off Vivienne. She thought Dorothy was distracting Hazel from her schoolwork. She's moved her to Garton House.'

'The poor kid. The place is supposed to be hellish.'

'Is Leila coming out on Sunday?' Pan asked.

Donnacha shrugged. 'I couldn't say. She might well have made some arrangement with Blythe while they were away but if she has, I don't know about it. I thought she might have been here,' he said, thinking about the Forrester leaving Whistlejacket earlier.

'Hazel, Vivienne, Leila, Blythe,' Margot interrupted. 'Are they in the Hunt Club, darlings? I can't wait to meet them all.'

<h1 style="text-align:center">52</h1>

Lucien sprawled on the ginormous bed on the forty-fourth floor of the Mandarin Oriental suite where he and Opal Manning had spent the better part of last night and the morning. Seated in front of the mirror, Opal combed her very short hair back from her short forehead and smiled into the reflection of her eyes as though sharing a joke with herself.

'Will you marry me?'

Opal stared at him through the mirror. 'Of course not.'

'Why not? By the way, you don't look a bit flattered.'

Opal swung her legs around so that she faced Lucien and the view of Victoria Harbour beyond the bed. 'Ten reasons. And that's without having to think.'

Lucien ruched the sheet around his groin – if he was going to be subjected to an assault on his person, he'd best defend his assets. 'Off you go then.'

Opal made a fist then stuck up her thumb as if signalling approval. Which she definitely was not. 'One, you're not husband material. Sooner or later you'll sleep with all of my girlfriends.' Her index finger came up next to the thumb. 'Two, you're not father material. You're too much of a child yourself. The only time you concentrate is during sex or when a Whistlejacket horse is running in a race. Three, you live in the wrong country. Hong Kong is my home and I won't live anywhere else. Four, my father would see me dead rather than married to you. Five, my father would see you dead for even considering the idea. Six, you're not rich enough. Seven, you're too old. Eight, your mother is the number one woman in your life. Nine, you eat too much meat and ...'

Opal turned to the mirror and busied herself putting in the diamond earrings that had been part of last night's turnout: clinging white silk shift that showed off her spectacular legs, crystal encrusted high heel sandals that made her legs look even longer, flesh coloured underwear that turned her sleek body into that of a goddess.

Lucien grinned. 'That's more compliments than I've had all year. But I resent number seven. I'm not even thirty. Keep going. What's ten?'

'Why the marriage talk, anyway?'

'Ma's got the screws on me. She's suddenly panting for grandchildren. I thought it'd be the last thing she'd want. They'll make the dachshunds' lives hell and wreck the garden. But she's adamant.'

'Yes, well, when your mother wants something ...' Opal laughed her smoky laugh.

'Come on, what's ten?'

'I'm already engaged.'

Lucien sat up. 'Who to?'

Opal checked her Chanel bag to make sure she had her phone and lip gloss. 'Got to go. I'm meeting some friends for lunch.'

Lucien got up off the bed. 'Tell me who's the rich old culture buff you've chosen to sire your children. Or rather, George has chosen to sire his grandchildren.'

Opal smiled smugly. 'I chose him. And he's not old and nor is he particularly rich. Well, he might be a little bit.'

Lucien went to put his arms around her, and she pushed him away. 'You need a shower and I have to go.'

'Do I know him? You're not wearing a ring. When's the wedding?'

'He's a jockey, but I'm not telling you his name. The ring's being resized. We're getting married in three months. So be a good boy, no more texts or calls. And if you wouldn't mind, give the lobby staff and the doormen something so that they won't tell dad I was here. Something decent. I'll take care of the taxi driver.'

At the door, she turned. 'When you get the wedding invitation, it might be better if you find an excuse to refuse.'

And with that, she was gone.

Lucien flopped back on the bed. Who was the jockey? Was he local, an English, American or Australian that had made Hong Kong his base? Someone from Japan, or France? He had no idea. But whoever it was, Opal wouldn't stay faithful to him he thought snakily. Opal Manning or whoever she'd be calling herself in three months had more than a good share of her father's genes.

The skyscrapers lining the Kowloon shore shimmered like a mirage and a cruise liner nosed its way across the ink coloured harbour towards Tsim Sha Tsui, barques and sampans bobbing in its wake. He always enjoyed visiting Hong Kong, but would he enjoy it as much without hook-ups with Opal? He doubted it.

He checked his phone to see how long before his plane left. It was just past nine. The airport ran like clockwork but the traffic on the Ting Kau bridge could be unpredictable, and unless he wanted to call a helicopter, he needed to shift it.

He lay back down on the bed and gazed out into the hazy sky. Opal had been right to a point about her girlfriends. He'd already slept with some of them. He couldn't say the exact number, but she would know. It was stretching things to say he'd sleep with all of them, though. Number two, well that was a fizzer as well. But three, four and five were on the money. Over the years, he and Opal's father, celebrating big race wins, had partied with some of Hong Kong's most beautiful and talented call girls. And then there were the parties in Dubai, London, Sydney … Opal probably knew about those as well. The subject of his wealth had been mentioned only to pad out the list, and as for his age, that was also just for effect – her first lover, a Hong Kong Jockey Club steward, had been a contemporary of her grandfather's. But it was true that he preferred meat above other foods. And he couldn't argue with her statement that his mother was the number one woman in his life. Aside from George not wanting him as a son-in-law, it was the most accurate of all her objections. Bloody accurate. Bloody like his balls.

He buried his face into the pillow where Opal's head had lain. He hadn't been altogether joking when he'd asked her to marry him. If she'd said "yes", he'd have gone out and bought a ring straight away. The sex was fantastic and for her nineteen years, she had the worldliness of a woman who had lived several lifetimes. Added to that, she was Hong Kong rich and together they'd have been able to free Whistlejacket from his mother's grasp. George would have come around, he was sure.

Perhaps he should stay and ask her again. He rose from the bed. No. With his mother still not taking his calls and the grey colt to sort out, he needed to be at Whistlejacket. He could always come back in a week or so.

<h1 style="text-align:center">53</h1>

India shivered and pulled her coat closer around her. But instead of tweed, her fingers gathered the buttery slick of fine leather. The biker jacket. She'd hardly had it off, but it was not warm like the old coat. She must get that back, and her suitcase.

She nudged the Louis Vuitton tote on the floor with her foot. Hopefully her toiletries were in it. Kevin had unloaded the rest of her acquired luggage at Le Manoir while Lady Blythe was attempting to talk her out of returning to Mars House. She had insisted, however, saying she needed to pack up her paints and easel. It was partly true. The greater truth was that she had wanted to be alone, and Mars House was the perfect place for that.

So here she was, in the icy hallway, woozy from crossing time zones, wondering if she would have been better off stopping at Le Manoir. She blew on her fingers. She would have been warm there at least. They had left the Highlands in the Autumn and now it was winter and the plane had descended out of a grey sky into a chilly wind and equally grey day. On the drive from Sydney to the Highlands it had started to rain, the rain stopping only just long enough to allow Lady Blythe a dry passage from the Rolls to the front door of Le Manoir.

An hour later, cocooned in a mohair from Grace's wardrobe and parked on the sofa in front of a crackling fire, she sipped a coffee and let her mind drift. The wind strengthened and the rain wrote undecipherable letters and lines on the French doors. The garden was an amorphous grey mass of shifting, sometimes crazy shapes. She reached for her sketchbook and rested it on her knee, where it remained.

Night came, absorbing the garden. The rain continued, muted but unrelenting. She rose stiffly, dropped a log onto the fire, pulled the curtains and turned on the lamps. In the fridge were the remains of a brie and a few olives. She fetched a bottle of wine from the pantry and carried the scant meal back to the fire.

The mohair gave off the smell of dog, reminding her that Lady Blythe had said that Jeffrey was in terrible pain with arthritis and ought to be put out of his misery. She turned the pages of the sketchbook until she came to a drawing of him. He was old, but in pain? She couldn't see it. His expression, as he slept on the hearth, was tranquil. But what did she know about dogs? Nothing really, unlike Lady Blythe, who had talked constantly about her dachshunds and called Kevin every day to check on them.

How did you go about getting a dog put down? And what did you do with their body?

She closed her eyes and slept and when she woke, sick and sweating, her heart pounding, the fire had burned down and the rain, she realised as the racket from her heart faded, had stopped. She'd been dreaming. A clearing in the bush. A knot of people whose faces she could not make out but who were somehow familiar. The pounding started again. It was not her heart, someone was at the door. She couldn't think what to do. Her mobile started ringing. She dug in her bag and saw that it was Xavier.

'Let me in,' he said. 'It's bloody freezing.'

'Oh,' she answered groggily. 'I'm coming.'

Pale-faced and looking like a forty's gangster in a sharp black overcoat, Xavier was hopping from foot to foot.

'The lights were on, so I assumed you were still up. I hope you've got a fire.'

She closed the door behind him. 'What time is it?' Remembering the watch Lady Blythe had given her, she peered at it. It was just past two.

Xavier caught her wrist. 'Cartier. You must have picked up some bloody good commissions while you were away.'

She pulled her arm out of his grasp. 'It was a present,' she said, setting off down the hall.

'I needn't ask from whom,' Xavier said. 'Lady Blythe must really have plans for you.'

She took a couple of small logs from the wood basket and scrunched them down into the embers. 'What are you doing out this time of night? Not putting a For Sale sign on the front of the house, I imagine.'

Xavier dropped onto the sofa. 'I told you, winter's not the time to be selling. Toby and I had a rendezvous at Berrima. He's in the operating theatre at six so hopefully he won't have to do anything more than hold a retractor. I'd murder a coffee.' He picked up the drawing of Jeffrey. 'You are clever, it's exactly him. I saw Pan in Burragong yesterday.'

India poked at the logs so the flames from the one that had caught touched the other. 'Lady Blythe says Jeffrey's full of arthritis and in constant pain. She thinks it would be kinder to have him put down.'

'Rubbish,' Xavier protested. 'There are excellent veterinary drugs for arthritis.'

'She knows a lot about dogs. She said Grace wouldn't let him suffer.'

'Lady Blythe has small dogs, there's a difference. She's right about Grace though. If Grace thought Jeffrey was in pain, she'd have him at the vet in a flash. But I don't think he's got arthritis at all.'

The logs now well and truly burning, India added a larger one and took the sketchbook from Xavier and put it under a cushion.

'I've got no milk.'

'Black's okay but make it strong.' Xavier's mouth turned down. 'Toby's still refusing to tell Vivienne about us. To tell anyone. It's killing me. I don't think he's even coming to the Hunt Ball. He's worried someone will put two and two together.' He attempted a smile. 'Sorry, there's nothing worse than being dumped on in the middle of the night. 'I want to hear all about London, about the Lanesborough and about Paris. And why you didn't go to Ascot. I've been getting updates from Kev and Martin. They're looking to upsize their cottage for something with a bit more garden.'

'So that's how you knew I was back?' India said.

'I'm in real estate, I know everything.' Xavier looked gloomy again. 'Except what to do about Toby. It's a shame there's no brandy. Grace always gave us brandy when we were upset.'

India went to the pantry and felt about. Her fingers closed on a bottle. Brandy. It had been there all the time.

54

Donnacha looked up from the computer. 'Morning to you, sir.'

'And to you comrade.' Beef let his bulk down into one of the office chairs and doffed his cap at Sorrows, who having risen from his spot by Donnacha's feet, was now sniffing his shins.

Even though the day was cold and the air damp from yesterday's rain, Beef was still dressed in shorts and a tshirt. 'Lady B's arrived,' he said.

Donnacha marked his place on the list of the remaining bales of lucerne and bags of chaff and oats and supplement mixes he'd been contemplating and from which he would calculate next month's feed order.

'I know, saw the Roller.'

'And Blythe phoned Mrs R to say his plane had landed and he'll be home for lunch. Sounds like he's ready to get into it. Lady B as well. She's booked Pinkie for a meeting at eleven.' Beef regarded his stomach regretfully, thinking of the extra tucker he would now be denied with Lady Blythe and Lucien back from their travels.

Donnacha rubbed his hand over the beginnings of the beard he'd let grow while Blythe and his mother were away. He supposed he'd better shave and put on a clean shirt and a better pair of boots than those he'd been wearing because they, Sorrows and Oyster were his comfort.

Beef's eyes went to the computer. 'That thing doesn't record, does it?'

Donnacha gave up on the stocktake. 'Of course it doesn't man. Paranoid or what!' As if in agreement, Sorrows rolled his eyes and returned to his resting place at his master's feet.

Beef took off his cap and scratched the thin frizzle of his remaining hair. 'No harm in taking precautions as the vicar said to the barmaid.' He leaned close to Donnacha. 'I went over there this morning. Got the new Pom to help with the feedup. He needs the experience anyway. I don't think he'd ever laid eyes on a horse before fetching up here. Must have lied on his application. Anyway, you wouldn't believe it. It was like the other day never happened. Like he hadn't been a whisker from death. I've seen horses come off the racetrack looking worse.'

'Pan said you'd been out.' After Leila and Sorrows and Oyster, BlueBuckle was next on Donnacha's mind when he first opened his eyes in the morning.

'He's eating his head off. Hay, pellets, anything that goes in the trough. Trouble is, Pan still can't get near him. He stands in the corner while Pan's putting out the feed and then he and the pig start moving in on him, driving him out of the yard, like. I saw it with my own eyes. It's horrific. It's like they're planning a massacre. I was thinking though, it might be a good thing if Pan doesn't get our friend cosying up to him. Buggered if I know what we'll do with him if he does.' Beef swung his cap around on his index finger. 'You or Pan might have yourself a new hunter. Wouldn't that have Blythe turning himself inside out.'

'More likely he'd be going after our heads with a posse of his barrister pals.'

'True enough. Mrs Villon wasn't up and about this morning. Probably waiting for Pan to bring her breakfast in bed.'

Seeing he had lost Donnacha's attention, Beef got to his feet. 'I might go and see how Pom Pom got on with the feedup.'

Donnacha frowned. 'What'll we tell Blythe if he asks about the body?'

'He's not likely to, do you think?'

'He might. We are talking about a ten-million-dollar hoss. He'll probably assume the carcass has gone into the trench, but he might want to be sure, and it's plain that nothing's gone in there for a while, not even a cat.' The trench was the long wide ditch where dead horses, those that didn't go to autopsy, were buried.

'I'll take the tractor and rough up a bit of ground,' Beef said. 'I'll do it now before I run down the Pom.'

'Best do.' Donnacha looked out the window behind the desk. From the look of the sky more rain was not far away. Hopefully it would clear for Sunday's hunt but no matter if it didn't. Rain would keep the dainty at home by the fire, making for a better day's sport.

Lady Blythe and Janet Reedhead sat at the table in the kitchen where Beef came for his meals and Pinkie to gossip.

Janet patted the L'Occitaine gift box Lady Blythe had brought her. 'I do love L'Occitaine. Everything smells so … fresh.' In truth, she would have preferred something from Hermes or Chanel, but experience told her that gratitude was the better option.

Lady Blythe beamed. 'The glorious scents of Provence. I should take you to Provence one day. Or send you and Brian.' After this recent trip, she had enough frequent flyer points to send the entire Whistlejacket staff flying about the world.

That would be something, Janet Reedhead thought. 'It'd be lovely, but I can't even get Brian on the train to Sydney.' She laughed her version of a fluty laugh. 'He's a homebody, I'm afraid.'

Lady Blythe nudged her cup. 'Then it will have to be you and me. I will have another coffee, thank you.'

Thinking about fields of lavender and standing with Lady Blythe and admiring the Palais des Papes frescoes, Janet swooped on the priceless cup and sprung to her feet.

'Will you be staying for lunch with Lucien?' she asked as she put down the freshly filled cup. 'It'll just be pumpkin soup. He wanted something vegetable. He's still over the moon about the Speed filly selling so well. Very good for the stud. You must be pleased too. Brian says the filly's half-sister is even better. I suppose that's why she didn't go to the sale.'

'Lucien is back today?'

'His plane landed half an hour ago. I thought he would have let you know.'

Lady Blythe gave a dismissive wave. 'I'm sure he's called. My phone's probably still set to flight mode. I'll get Kevin to reset it. I'll see Lucien later. I'm lunching at the Bombay Duck.' She followed an age line in the table's timber with the edge of a resined fingernail. 'But I've something very awful to do first, I'm afraid.'

As if protecting it from the fall of an axe, Janet's hand went to her throat. 'Oh? A slice of cake? Some biscotti? It sounds like you're going to need your strength. I made almond bread yesterday.'

Lady Blythe leaned back and flattened her hands over her miniscule waist. 'No, no. We gorged in Paris, absolutely gorged. But you go on and have something. It's your morning teatime after all.'

Janet shook her head and sat down. 'Something awful?' she repeated.

Lady Blythe took a sip of coffee and then placed the cup back on the saucer with a precise click. 'I have to let Pauline go.'

'Pinkie? But she's the best office manager you've ever had.' The words flew out of Janet's mouth, but she didn't care. How would she get through the day at Whistlejacket without Pinkie? How would she know what was going on in the stables and in the dorm? Going on anywhere?

'She's been extremely indiscrete,' Lady Blythe said in a tight voice. 'Actually, extremely doesn't come close. But that's as much as I'll say, and hopefully Pauline will have the decency herself to keep her ... exploits to herself. Though you never do know with girls like that.' She pushed the still almost full cup of coffee away and rose. 'No doubt she'll be in soon. I'd rather you didn't say anything. In fact, I'm asking you not to.' She pulled her cardigan tightly around her. 'I'm truly sorry. I know we're like a little family here, but we're also a business with a reputation to maintain and believe me, if you knew what Pauline has been up to, you'd be locking the kitchen door.'

She looked at her watch. 'Maybe it's better if you send her straight in when she arrives.' If she got rid of Pinkie early, there'd be time to call Christie. Now Lucien was back, she was probably already thinking about or planning a rendezvous. She gave a grim little smile. Two birds with one stone – a truly bloody morning's work. Hopefully she'd still have an appetite for lunch.

'I'll be in the blue room,' she told Janet. She had given herself half an hour in the office she kept at Whistlejacket to go over Pinkie's severance papers.

Janet dumped the coffee cup on the bench, ducked into the pantry and extracted her mobile from its place among the pasta jars and pressed her husband's number. The call went to voicemail.

'Pinkie's about to be shunted,' she breathed. 'Ring me.'

'Mrs R?' came the cheery call. 'Are you there? Is the kettle on?'

Janet stepped out of the pantry and trying to keep her voice normal, greeted Pinkie. 'You look nice. You've got a tan.'

Pinkie plonked herself down in the chair vacated by Lady Blythe and stretched out her legs so that the crutch of her jeans would not pull so tightly. She touched her newly platinumed hair, now not quite, but almost prison cut.

'The Gold Coast is gorgeous. I could have stayed forever. This cold's shitty. I've got the heater cranked up, but the office is still freezing. I might have to get some of those gloves that make you look like a safe cracker or a pickpocket. You know, the ones with the fingertips cut off. Oh, I almost forgot. I brought you a present.' She tossed a bright pink cap with the Magic Millions logo onto the table.

Janet stared at the cap. 'Lady Blythe's waiting for you in the blue room.'

'I've still got twenty minutes. Our meeting's not until eleven. Can I have a hot chocolate?' Pinkie picked up the L'Occitaine gift pack. Is this what she brought you from OS? They're on special on the David Jones website. I bet she bought a truckload of them.'

'She's expecting you.'

Pinkie made a harrumphing sound and pushed back her chair. 'In a twist about the stallion parade, I expect.' She picked up the briefcase she'd brought with her. 'Means we'll be hours. What's for lunch?'

Janet Reedhead shook her head slowly. 'Dear girl,' she said under her breath. 'Dear, silly girl.'

Lady Blythe pushed the "Stop" icon on he screen of her phone.

Pinkie's face had paled to the colour of her hair. 'How did you get that?'

'It doesn't matter. It's what's on it that matters. So you can understand why it's impossible for you to continue working here.' She pushed the envelope Kevin had prepared across the desk.

'Your owed wages and leave have been deposited in your bank along with two months' severance pay, which I think is ridiculously generous, but Kevin says is correct according to some industrial award. Your service record is also there. You're to leave straight away, without speaking to anyone. I realise you need to collect your bag from the office, but just in case you're tempted to make a call to any of the other staff, remind yourself that I have this recording.'

Pinkie shook her head. 'This is the best job I've ever had. What about the stallion parade?' She was crying now, gasping between her tears. 'I'm sorry. Lucien wanted it. He...'

Lady Blythe rose from the chair. 'Please don't make this more unpleasant than it already is, Pauline. What has been done cannot be undone. I suggest you focus on moving forward, not looking back.'

'What'll I tell mum and dad?' Pinkie sobbed.

'I've no idea. But be assured that unless you continue with any further recklessness, they'll not hear about, or see, this recording. Now if you wouldn't mind, it's time for you to go.'

Lady Blythe stood at the window and watched Pinkie stumble along the path to the office. She was tempted to feel sorry for her, she was young and a good worker. But years of being bailed up by sobbing innocents who believed Jonno's claims of love were real had quite worn out her heart.

Pinkie was leaving the office. She had covered her head with a beanie and was visibly shaking. She paused for a moment at the path to the stables, then continued towards the staff carpark and the back gate.

Lady Blythe turned away from the window. If there was anyone to be pitied, she thought, it was herself. She might have been freed by

Jonno's death, but her stomach was once again churning bitter curd because of his golden son. Never had she dreamed it would be so.

She took the piece of paper with Christie's number out of her phone case and picked up the landline handset.

Christie answered after the third ring. 'Hello darling, you're back. So naughty of you to piss off like that without saying goodbye. I've been ringing your mobile in case you haven't noticed. When can we meet?'

'Christine, it's Lady Blythe. I have something I want you to hear.' Lady Blythe touched the "Play" icon on her phone and held it up to the handset mouthpiece. A minute later, she touched "Stop" and put the handset to her ear. As she expected, the line had gone dead. She hit "Redial" and when Christie's voicemail came on, said, 'If I find out you have either called or made any attempt to see my son, I will send this recording to Digger. And I shall do the same if Lucien makes any attempt to contact you. Goodbye. It's definitely not been nice knowing you.'

55

BlueBuckle pinned his ears and stamped his foot warningly. Pan rose quickly, and slipped back through the rails and out of the yard to safety.

'That horse is nutso,' came Margot's pronouncement. 'And the pig. You should be getting them put down. They're obviously dangerous.'

'According to you, all my animals should be put down,' Pan said, noticing that the dogs, earlier sleeping in a patch of sun by the stables, had disappeared.

'Only the horse and its nasty friend and the stinky greyhound.' Margot pouted. 'At least then you might have some time for me. We've spent, what, an hour together since I arrived?'

'That's not true,' Pan said, watching BlueBuckle examine the mounting block he'd been sitting on when Margot appeared. If she hadn't turned up, BlueBuckle might have been nosing him instead he thought with frustration.

'I want you to take me to Kookaburra,' Margot said. 'I need some warm clothes.' She shivered theatrically, even though she was wearing his best cashmere over his next best lambswool and a puffer vest, his also. 'This place is colder than London.'

He eyed the puffer, which had his old school logo on the shoulder and had been missing since he moved to Big Hill. 'Go inside if you're cold. Or put on a beanie. I'm sure you'll know where to find one.'

307

Margot tucked her hair behind her ears. 'I don't suppose Kookaburra's got a decent hairdresser? I expect not. We'll have to go to Sydney for that as well as my hunting kit. Looks like it's going to be an overnighter, at least. You'll have to find us somewhere decent to stay. Which reminds me, sunscreen. We must absolutely get some. Nicole Kidman's always talking about how damaging the sun is here. She won't go outside without it.'

'I'm not taking you to Sydney and you're not coming hunting. You haven't ridden for years. And anyway, I don't have a horse for you.'

Margot gave him her best smile. 'The little mare will do just fine. For this meet, anyway. She went quite nicely for me earlier. Her coat's a bit rough, but she'll polish up. Fancy, me on a one-eyed horse! I must love you after all.'

Pan looked across to the paddock where Dorothy was grazing. The dark patch on her back could well be from a saddle blanket. He shouldn't have left her where Margot could see her. But then stopping Margot when she was set on something was as likely as him biting off one of his testicles.

'You were taking a risk riding a horse you don't know,' he said.

Margot narrowed her eyes at BlueBuckle. 'Far less than you're taking going into that loony horse's yard. What's with him, anyway? Is he worth millions? He looked dead when he arrived. Millions or no millions, I'd have let nature take its course. Though he's not looking so bad now, I have to say.'

Pan started walking away and as he'd hoped, Margot followed. 'He's an eventer,' he fibbed. 'Loads of potential, but also some tics his owner wants ironed out. If he has a few good seasons she'll consider breeding from him. His jumping bloodlines are strong, apparently. When Donnacha and Beef were bringing him over, he colicked, unfortunately.' Hopefully it was a story that Margot could swallow.

'It didn't look like any colic I've ever seen,' she said.

He walked faster. 'And you've seen a lot.'

'Hey,' she said sharply. 'What's the hurry?'

'Do you want to go to Burragong or not?'

Now he had her attention.

'You'll have to change,' she said, catching up. 'I'm not going anywhere with you looking like that. And I wasn't joking about that horse. Anyone can see it's dangerous. I'm only thinking about you.'

Well that would be a first, Pan thought. He sighed. It looked like he'd have to put BlueBuckle out in one of the paddocks away from the house, well out of sight of Margot. But that was if he could catch him. And what if he couldn't catch him again? He'd be feral in no time and a feral stallion was the last thing he needed.

'Did you hear me?' Margot said. 'Of course you did. Don't forget I know you. I know when you're trying to run away.'

He stopped. His eyes went to Dorothy. Ah! 'The mother of the girl that owned the little mare has a hairdressing salon in Burragong. She's always booked out weeks in advance, but if I call her, she might find an appointment for you.'

'Brilliant, darling,' Margot said, speeding ahead.

Dazed from the ferocity with which Margot had been spending, Pan didn't argue when, seeing a smartly suited couple heading into the Bombay Duck, she announced that they'd also lunch there. With her hair appointment still not for an hour, at least his cards would have a chance to cool down a little.

Leila showed them to their table. He could tell that she wanted to ask about BlueBuckle, but he inclined his head towards Margot. She got the message.

'Not at Whistlejacket today?' he asked her.

'I've got a long weekend, time in lieu for the Magic Millions. But just my luck, look who's here.' She nodded discretely at the table where Lady Blythe was lunching with her friends. 'Thank god there's another waitress.'

Pan's breath caught in his throat. The sight of Lady Blythe reminded him of the magnitude of the risk Donnacha and Beef had taken bringing BlueBuckle to Big Hill. What they'd done was insane. What he was doing was insane.

'Aren't you going to introduce us, darling?' Margot said, interrupting his thoughts.

For a terrible moment he thought she meant introduce her to Lady Blythe. He reached for the water jug.

Margot's eyes ran over Leila and as if what they had seen was not worth a second look, came to rest in the air next to her right ear. 'Perhaps the other waitress …?'

'Shut up,' Pan told her. 'Margot, Leila Caffrey. Leila, Margot Apsley.'

'Pan's wife,' Margot said sweetly. 'Though he seems to enjoy pretending otherwise.'

Leila held out the menus. 'I remember, Grace mentioned you. Welcome to Burragong. I heard that you're staying at Big Hill. Are you here for long?'

'Oh, so I'm not totally persona non-gratis.' Margot turned towards Pan. 'How long am I staying, darling?'

Pan began studying the menu.

'The specials are on the board,' Leila said to cover the silence. A stunner, Donnacha had said. More like stun gun from the look of Pan. 'Something to drink?'

Margot gestured at the ice bucket on Lady Blythe's table. 'A bottle of the same, thanks.'

Pan looked out from behind the menu.

'Hello, darling,' Margot smirked. 'We thought you'd disappeared on us.'

'What's Lady Blythe drinking?' Pan asked Leila.

'Vintage Mumm,' Leila said.

Margot's eyes lit up. 'A woman after my own heart.'

Pan shook his head. 'No way.'

Margot put a hand on his arm. 'Don't be so stiff, darling.'

'Something local for Margot and a sparkling water for me,' Pan said to Leila.

'Your waitress friend is the rudest thing I've ever encountered,' Margot said as Leila retreated. 'No people skills whatsoever. I can't imagine how she's gotten herself employed at such a nice little eatery. They must be desperate for staff.' She wrinkled her nose. 'It is a bit pongy here, though.'

'It's the spices,' Pan said, thinking that he'd rather be lunching with Pharlap.

Margot inclined her head towards Lady Blythe's table. 'Is she a real lady or an Australian one?'

'I didn't know there was a difference,' Pan snapped. 'Keep your voice down. And you'd better be bloody nice to Leila. She's Donnacha's girlfriend.'

'Well that would explain his moody look. Though I do love a brooding brow.' Margot stared frankly at Pan. 'Yours is way too high. Perhaps that's why we never lasted.'

'We never lasted because you slept with my groomsman at our wedding.'

'Is that why you were so snippy at the reception. I thought it was because you didn't like my dress.' Margot shook open her napkin and dropped it over her lap. 'I don't know how you could possibly be cross. It was your fault for having such dishy groomsmen.'

'Grooms*men*?'

Margot smiled prettily. 'I did so enjoy our wedding.' Her expression became less smug as Leila came to the table.

'I'm starting as Field Master on Sunday,' she told Pan as she put down an ice bucket.

'Donnacha said Eleanor had taken off, but he didn't say anything about you taking over from her,' Pan said. 'Congratulations. You'll be great.'

'I'm a bit nervous,' Leila confessed. 'Eleanor …'

'There's nothing to it,' Margot interrupted. 'I was the Field Master with our local hunt when I was a child.'

'That's a complete lie, Margot,' Pan said.

Margot pinched the back of his hand. 'You've become such a wet blanket, darling. Or is that what Australians call charm?' She turned to Leila. 'My tip is to leave your knickers at home and ride short so that your bottom's pointed at the field. No one will want to pass you, I can assure you. It'll be hell for a few days after, but totally worth it.'

Pan grabbed Margot's menu and thrust it at Leila, who had flushed bright red. 'We'll have the Bombay duck, thanks. And two servings of mixed naan. No entrée.'

'Definitely not one for the earthly delights, is she?' Margot said as Leila took off. 'Poor Donnacha.'

'Not everyone constantly thinks about sex,' Pan said, thinking that Pharlap would definitely have been a better lunch companion.

Margot sighed. 'Well that's certainly true in your case. Maybe you and your waitress friend should get together and let me look after the boyfriend.' She narrowed her eyes at Leila, who was now showing two television exec types to a table. 'She does have legs, I suppose. And some men like that beaky look. They think it means intelligence. If I was her, though, I'd get the nose trimmed.' She looked around the restaurant, which was now quite full. 'I do like your little Kookaburra, darling. I could quite settle here.'

Please gods, no, Pan thought tiredly.

Their first stop had been the equestrian outfitters and saddlery in the neighbouring village of Mossvale. Margot had gathered up three pairs of cream breeches, a black jacket, a vest, four white shirts, gloves, boots, a helmet and a hunting tie with the efficiency of the serial shopper that she was. When he had scorned the solid gold tie pin that she had also insisted she needed, she had stalked out, leaving him not only with the bill, but lugging the whole lot to the vehicle. Her excellence at adding insult to injury had not waned in their years apart.

The next stop had been Burragong, where after again demanding his credit card, she had set off alone along the high street, leaving him distracting himself as best he could in the bookshop while she briskly accumulated alpaca and cashmere jumpers and RM Williams shirts and jackets.

Remembering his card, he realised that she hadn't returned it. He sighed, wondering what further damage a haircut at A Cut Above was likely to inflict.

The food arrived and after hoovering up most of it, Margot pronounced it "almost edible". Now on her third glass of champagne, she was deep into the tale of Felix the stalker.

Nodding at what he hoped were suitable intervals and making the odd sympathetic grunt, he risked a glance at Lady Blythe's table. If she was back, India would be as well. He'd already put the new battery in the Land Cruiser, but he'd have to find a moment to drop

Jeffery back at Mars House. No doubt the poor fellow would be greatly relieved to be out of Margot's sights.

Lady Blythe caught his glance and gave a little wave.

'You know her?' Margot asked.

'She lives in Burragong.' He rattled off the type of precis that was Margot's second language. 'She and her son Lucien own a boutique thoroughbred stud not far out of town. Lucien's father was Jonno Blythe. He had a stud in Kent. Your father might have known him.'

'I doubt it. Papa says racehorse people aren't proper county.'

'I presume that goes for the Royal Family as well,' Pan said dryly.

'They're different, of course. They're everything. City, county, country, town, highlands ...' Margot suddenly sat up straight. 'She's going to stop by our table.'

Lady Blythe was indeed approaching. Pan went to rise, but she waved at him to stay seated. 'Afternoon, Pan,' she said, looking at Margot enquiringly.

'Lady Blythe, Margot Apsley. Margot, Lady Blythe.'

'Pan's wife,' Margot said, the sweet smile back on her face.

'We're separated,' Pan said quickly.

Lady Blythe's shrug showed this was of little interest. 'I wanted a word about Grace Levy's old hound. I believe he's with you at Big Hill.'

'I'm planning to drop him back to India when I get a moment.'

'That's the thing. It's impossible for the dog to return to her. She's moving into Le Manoir. But in any case, the animal's riddled with arthritis. It would be much kinder if it was put down. Ann quite understands this. It's how her grandmother would look at it. If you'd rather not do it yourself, I'd suggest Nelson Cherry. He'll euthanise the animal very humanely. He'll do it at Big Hill if you prefer. You just have to ask.'

With a smile aimed at the top of Margot's head, Lady Blythe glided off to her waiting friends.

'I told you that dog needs putting down,' Margot said. 'She looked speculatively at Lady Blythe's departing back. 'Perhaps papa did mention something about a Lord and Lady Blythe.'

'No surprise there,' Pan muttered.

'Darling, you sound as though you've got tetanus,' Margot said, turning towards him. 'What's gone wrong with your jaw? You can't be upset about the dog. You know it's cruel to let animals suffer when it's in our power to do something about it.'

56

The slate and steel facade of A Cut Above made Pan think of a private bank rather than a hairdressing salon. And given Vivienne's determination to get as much out of him as she could for Hazel's little mare, perhaps it was.

'Smart, darling,' Margot, said approvingly, wobbling slightly from four fifths of a bottle of champagne.

Vivienne met them at the door and they paused for introductions in the atrium, a generous room painted in different shades of grey like the building's exterior and containing only a solitary black leather bench. She pushed Pan's fringe off his forehead with her brown fingers. 'We'll have to get you booked in as well. And this is your friend, Margot.'

Letting herself be examined head to toe as if she were a lesser mortal, Margot put on her sweet smile. 'His wife, actually.'

'I remember Grace saying there was a wife,' Vivienne said, as if the matter was one of regret.

Margot tapped Pan's chest. 'Who is this ghostly Grace? You've not mentioned her, but she seems to know all about me. Is she a girlfriend?'

Vivienne put her hand on Margot's arm. 'I've a chair ready.'

Margot went limp. 'You don't have a masseuse, do you? The flight from Bali was murder. You can't swing a cat in business class these days.'

'We do indeed have a masseuse,' Vivienne said, waving to Pan as he backed out the door. Two hours, she mouthed, raising a wrist with an enamel Aquaracer in case he hadn't got the message.

Pan strode angrily along the high street. It wasn't worth returning to Big Hill. In less than an hour he'd be heading back to Burragong again. Bloody Margot. She still had the knack of wasting great wads of not just his money, but his equally precious time. He passed Blooming Beautiful and stopped, wondering if India might be there. He could let her know that the Land Cruiser was ready to roll and talk to her about Jeffrey.

Janet Rice popped up from behind the counter.

'Hello Pan. Looking for Gill?' she said in her furious way. 'She's at Gwynedd. Staying with Simon Sinclair. Her and the Cairns. The horses as well. The whole lot of them. Can you believe it? Don't know what she's thinking. What either of them are. Though I'm only assuming …'

'Hello Janet,' he said. 'Is India here?'

Janet flapped her apron. 'She's not. And I doubt we'll be seeing her again. The girl's gone over to the dark side. Drawn a Yarborough and thinks she's in slam. Grace'd be turning in her grave if she had one.'

"Dark side", "yarborough", "slam" … Pan had no idea what Janet was saying. Then he remembered a conversation with Grace. Yarborough and slam were bridge terms, one meaning a hand with no points and the other a contract worth a huge amount of points.

'Something has to be done,' Janet said, almost pawing the ground. 'Lord knows what though.'

He backed out of the shop. Ten minutes later, headed for Pregos with a copy of *The Goldfinch*, which he had started reading in the bookshop while waiting for Margot to finish raiding the high street, he saw India coming out of the Sourdough Bakery. It was impossible not to. Head and shoulders above everyone around her, she was wearing a very slick biker jacket and a red beanie that sat pixie-like on her head. Baguettes protruded from the bag she was carrying.

He strode after her and catching her up, stepped in front of her, forcing her to stop.

She smiled, 'Hello. I was going to call you.' She pointed at the book. 'That's one of my favourite novels.'

Her eyes were guileless, the arrows of her brows drawn almost together as she studied the novel's cover. His anger exploded. 'I'm not having him put down.'

'Sorry?'

'Putting him down would be criminal. It'd be murder. It's bullshit about the arthritis.'

A tinge of pink coloured India's cheeks. 'Oh, Jeffrey. I was going to call you about that.'

'No doubt hoping the deed was already done,' he said coldly. 'And he's a "he", not a "that".'

India held the baguettes against her chest as if shielding herself from him. 'Lady Blythe believes he's in terrible pain. She said Grace wouldn't let him suffer.'

People were staring, but he couldn't help raising his voice. 'Grace would be sick at the thought of you having anything to do with Lady Blythe let alone listening to her opinion about her dog. About any dog.'

'She and Lady Blythe were friends.'

'Friends? I think not.' He lobbed *The Goldfinch* into the nearby rubbish bin and turned on his heel, leaving India standing rigid on the footpath.

A few minutes later, he sat in his vehicle and leaned his brow on the steering wheel. 'You're a shit, Villon,' he told himself. 'A total shit.' He fished the keys out of his pocket and started the engine.

Progress along the high street was slow, the traffic hindered by the idling cars of shoppers and coffee seekers looking for car spaces. Once off the high street, he drove over the railway bridge, past the tractor yard and the Co-Op where he bought his stock feed. The road widened, the traffic thinned and all but disappeared. He put down the window. The vehicle filled with cold, sharp air and the heat went out of his eyes.

At a corner marked by the skeleton of an ancient harrow, he slowed and turned. The road wound towards home. The big hill came into view, disappeared, reappeared and then disappeared again. A few kilometres on he pulled off the road and turned off the engine.

A mob of cockatoos crossed the sky, their screeching like a fork scraping a blackboard. Then there was silence. His anger returned, a fury that reached into his every corner. Its blacklist was swiftly compiled. Margot's name was at the top. For using him as she always had, for appearing at the same time as BlueBuckle and then again at the very moment he had become curious enough to tolerate his presence in the yard. For her distain for his dogs and Pharlap. For siding with Lady Blythe about Jeffrey.

And he was next on the list: for having lost it with India on the high street. For desiring her like he did. Though Margot's infidelities had doused his libido, it had not been extinguished and in the past weeks, like an animal coming out of hibernation, it had attached itself to India with a hunger he had not felt before. And now she would have nothing to do with him. He would not be able to warn her that Lady Blythe would paralyse her with honey-coated venom and after she had eaten her soul, hand her shell over to her vile son.

He fished his phone out of his pocket and called Vivienne's and told the girl that answered to order a taxi for Margot Apsley when she was ready to leave. Then he rang his father's cousin.

'I want to divorce from Margot. Immediately. I don't care what it costs.'

There was silence at the end of the phone. His father's cousin always thought before he spoke.

'Well,' came his voice at last. 'It shouldn't cost you everything. You sound upset.'

Unable to bear this concern – sometimes it is the gentle touch that brings the strong undone – Pan deepened his voice so it wouldn't waver.

'She's here, at Big Hill. She just turned up. She had some trouble with a stalker in London. It's unbearable. She's unbearable. She's doing my head in.' And my heart, he thought.

'I need to check a few things. I'll get back to you. Remember, you can always come to us if you need to get away.'

Back at Big Hill, he found BlueBuckle stretched out asleep with Pharlap in the fresh bed of straw he'd laid in the double stall at first light.

'I'll have all the time in the world for you soon,' he told the stallion.

Back in the house, he made a cup of tea, black – while they were in Burragong Margot had not thought to mention that she had used the last of the milk – and after loading the wood heater, settled on the living room sofa. Sadie and Benzo climbed up either side of him and Jeffrey and the terriers stretched out in front of the roaring fire.

He was halfway through the tea when his phone rang.

'Is Margot with you?'

'She's in Burragong. I'm at home.'

'Good, I can speak freely then. It looks like escaping a stalker is not the only thing that's brought Margot to Big Hill. She's had divorce papers prepared herself. Her fellow in London was reluctant to send them but I said you needed me to go through them immediately. I've had a brief look. The terms are short and sweet. She's not taking the matter to court so obviously she wants things over and done quickly with as well. But the settlement she's wanting is outrageous, of course.'

'What do you advise?'

'I'll get to work on a settlement that will leave you with at least one of your testicles. Maybe one and half. In the meantime, I'd suggest you find her copy of the papers. I'll email you the copy I've got, of course, but it might be to your advantage if she knows you've seen hers. It's all tactical from here on in. If things get nasty, tell her you're happy to go to court. Tell her it's your preference. That will calm her down. She's already had far more than a fair share of the estate and a court hearing will mean costs. I'll make sure the London lapdog knows it as well. She's been quite circumspect about what she's revealed to him.'

Such was Margot's arrogance that she hadn't bothered to make the divorce papers difficult to find. They were in a parchment envelope at the bottom of a yet to be unpacked bag. He added ice to a generous fifth of Laphroiag – Margot had also neglected to say that she had finished the gin as well – and after hiding the bottle in the linen cupboard behind the dog coats, took the drink and the envelope back to the sofa.

The big hill's summit was now veiled with rain, which was rolling towards the farm. Tomorrow, he promised himself, he would ride up the hill and breathe the newly washed air of rock and eucalypt and unmeasurable time. He could already feel its bite in his lungs.

But for now … He opened the envelope, took out four pages of paper similarly heavy to that of the envelope and began to read.

Outrageous didn't come close to it. Margot was letting him keep Big Hill, but that was pretty much all.

He finished the whiskey and went to the computer. No email from his uncle. He gazed out the window. The rain was now falling over the paddocks and dams, slicking the horses, blackening the fences and weighing the limbs of the gums so their leaves pointed at the ground. He checked the email again. Nothing. Four o'clock. Margot would be a while yet, especially if she had a massage, and the rain would add ten minutes at least to the trip from Burragong. He rose and returning the divorce papers to the envelope, headed for Margot's bedroom.

On the way back to the living room, he stopped in front of the drawing India had done of Grace when they were in Greece. Grace was stretched out on a cane lounge, her long legs and feet bare, her hands, still. She looked calm content, beautiful. But now, a yellow sticky note with "Levy? known artist" in Margot's handwriting, was attached to a corner. He pulled it off. Margot had obviously been making an inventory for the settlement. He lifted the drawing off the wall and took it to his bedroom.

'What else has she logged?' he asked Jeffrey, who raised a sleepy head briefly from the end of the bed. The landscapes and portraits that had been his father's, the ceramics he had allowed himself to purchase over the years? The Sidney Nolan?

Back in the living room, he tossed the sticky note into the fire and sat down in front of the computer. Still nothing. He tapped his fingers on the edge of the desk and then, calling the Burragong bookshop, ordered another copy of *The Goldfinch*. He ended the call and rechecked his email.

There were two attachments, one labelled "Pan" and the other "Margot". He opened the attachment with his name on it and sent it to the printer.

57

Lucien took a table at the back of Pregos and sat with his back to the door. The last of Christie's coke was glowing in its foil, but he resisted its call. How he'd managed to stop himself stuffing it all up his nose after yesterday's blood and guts in the blue room though, he had no idea. When his mother had showed him the bit of film on her phone, it had gotten so hot in the room he'd thought the curtains might burst into flames. But then, after she'd proposed his marriage to India Levy, he'd felt a chill that would have put out the fires of hell. But the more he thought about it, the more it stacked up. India's sleeping beauty aura didn't do a thing for him, but as his mother had pointed out, Mars House would bring millions if it was subdivided. And, though this he didn't say to his mother, of course, when his ownership of Whistlejacket was beyond any legal challenge, he could divorce the sleeping beauty. Maybe after she'd produced a child or two to keep his mother off his back.

Pregos was full of breakfasters eating Bircher muesli and poached eggs with smashed avocado and reading their devices. His attention returning to his surrounds, he checked out the younger of the female clientele. Perhaps he should ditch hunting and take up polo. It did look like serious fun and the groupies were getting more spectacular every year. The class players like Aldofo Cambiaso, were riding ponies cloned from their best mares and if he could get his hands on one of them, better still a string, he'd be playing in the most glamorous tournaments around the world in no time.

He might even use the money from Mars House to set up a cloning operation at Whistlejacket. With one of the ponies recently selling for two million and an American top goal player ordering a hundred, it was potentially far more lucrative than playing the genetic lottery with thoroughbreds. And think of the ponies he'd have to ride. It would be a whole new chapter for both Whistlejacket and for himself.

Thank you, ma. Or rather, thank you Pinkie and Christie. He'd better drop a thou or two in poor Pinkie's letterbox.

Unable to sleep she had risen in the middle of the night and now, with midday approaching, two small paintings were drying on the workbench. One, a small oil of Jeffrey, curled up asleep, the other a knot of faceless figures, leaning in towards one another and encircled by bushland.

Her aching eyes locked on the canvas now on the easel, the much larger square of white onto which she'd outlined the furious Pan tossing *The Goldfinch* at the rubbish bin. Anger, it terrified her. It made her feel as though she was blindfolded in the middle of a storm. Blindfolded, gagged and bound.

Her phone was ringing. She dragged herself away from the canvas, went to the bench and picked it up. It was Xavier.

'Toby's not answering my calls or returning my messages.'

'He's probably taking out an appendix.'

'It's the weekend.'

'Oh yes, it's Saturday. I forgot. What's up? Besides Toby troubles, I mean.'

'I'm returning your call. What are you doing?'

'Working.'

'On my portrait, I hope. Though maybe I should get you to do Toby first. Looking at his picture's as close as I'll get to him now he's pulled the pin.'

Remembering why she'd rung, she said, 'Do you know the name of the vet Jeffrey went to for his teeth? I thought I'd talk to him about his arthritis.'

'I don't, but I can find out. I'll get it off Simon and text it to you.'

She put down the phone and it rang again.

'India Levy,' she said automatically.

There was a pause, then Lady Blythe's voice, sounding slightly puzzled, said, 'Good morning, Ann. Kevin will be in Burragong in an hour or so. Should he swirl by and collect you? Your rooms are all ready and I'm lunching late.'

She looked at the bedlam around her, trying and failing to imagine it in one or more of Le Manoir's rooms.

'I'm working on some drawings.'

'For my portrait?'

Her gaze slid past the easel to the two small paintings. 'Well ...'

'How thrilling,' Lady Blythe interrupted. 'I suppose we mustn't disturb the artist then. Just quickly though, I told Lucien we'd join him at the breakfast tomorrow. The Hunt's meeting at Colo in Sutton Forest. It belongs to some very dear friends, the Vilanders. The property is divine, and so are they. I can't wait for you to meet them. He's my age and still hauling himself up on his horse.' Lady Blythe paused, then said, a thoughtful note in her voice, 'I know you're keen to get my portrait underway, my dear, and I can't wait to see the sketches, but we haven't really talked about it and you sound jetlagged. Irrespective of where one sits in the plane it can still bring one to one's knees. Look at me in London. Promise you'll give yourself time to rest before meeting the Vilanders. They may well become clients. And think about putting your drawings in a folio and bringing them back here with the rest of your things after the breakfast.'

The call ended, India scrolled through the phone until she found the photos that she had taken of Lady Blythe on the powder blue sofa in the Lanesborough. The composition was conventional but pretty, Lady Blythe, that day, having something of an art deco figuring about her.

<h1 style="text-align:center">58</h1>

Donnacha hit the snooze button and rested his hand on Sorrows' side and listened for the sounds of wind or rain. All was quiet and still. He gave a little nod. Rough weather didn't bother him, but the horses were less fractious when it was calm, the hounds easier to keep packed up and it was handy being able to see the country instead of galloping and jumping on the wings of a prayer. But for that, however, nothing cleansed a man's soul better than going full tilt in scouring rain and a decent bluster.

The tip of his nose was icy. Maybe there was a frost. If Leila had been still in the cottage, he'd have kept the fire going through the night but now she was gone, he didn't bother. In the mornings, he put the radiator on in the kitchen and ate his breakfast in front of it.

The alarm chirruped again. He turned it off and slid out of bed. The freezing air woke him smartly. It was a hunting morn. He was almost happy.

Dressed in his work clothes and with a beanie pulled down to his eyes, he followed the path to the stables by instinct. There was no frost, but an icy chill rose from the ground. Far into its journey toward the northwest horizon, the waxing moon was a hazy crescent in an otherwise starless sky. Good. Haze meant cloud, which, if it didn't dissipate too early, would keep the sun from burning off the scent.

He turned on the stable lights and collected the buckets he'd made up last night – a mix of oats, lucerne chaff and soaked beet pulp. Oyster came to his stall door and whinnied. In the next stall, Hugo, the horse Lucien was hunting, also called impatiently. Unlike Oyster, Hugo, also a Percheron cross thoroughbred but standing at seventeen one, was rugged head to toe. He was a bugger for laying in his manure and staining his white coat and messing his tail. In fact, with his pushy nature, boneshaking stride and thick neck he was a bugger all round. But he was the one horse at Whistlejacket Lucien had never managed to intimidate.

The moon, what there was of it, had disappeared and there was a pearling in the eastern sky. A pair of headlights bobbed along the drive towards the front gates. It had to be Leila – she must still have the remote control for the gates. She'd stayed in the dorm because of Pan's wife, he supposed. But as he thought this, the suspicion that he was wrong about her and Pan returned. Beef swore that he was, that it was all in his mind. But whether he was or wasn't wrong, whether it was or wasn't all in his mind, the wall that had gone up between him and Leila still seemed to be getting higher every day. He hadn't even known she was the new Field Master.

He thought about sending her a text, it was a big day for her and alone or not, he'd wager she hadn't slept much, but his phone remained where it was, in his pocket.

The gear stowed in the truck, the horses ready to be loaded and the sky now the colour of Oyster's belly, he headed back to the cottage.

His phone rang as he was putting his breakfast on the table and his heart leapt. Leila had been reading his mind. But it was Blythe wanting to know what bit he'd put on Hugo's bridle, and what noseband.

'A plain jointed snaffle and a cavesson,' he told him.

'He needs something stronger. A Dutch gag and a drop noseband. Are you still there?'

'I'll put them in the truck.'

'See you at Colo. Eight sharp.'

He dropped the phone on the table and gave Sorrows some bacon, then some more. The Dutch gag had four rings, the top for fastening the bit to the cheek straps and the three below. Blythe would of course put the reins on the lowest, creating maximum pull in Hugo's mouth through the increased lever action on Hugo's poll, the top of his neck behind his ears. And done up to its tightest, the noseband would mean Hugo would be unable to open his mouth to get away from the pressure. It would also push on the nerves of his face.

He shook his head. Despite what many believed, bits and nosebands were not the only way to control a horse's direction and speed. Pan often hunted in a bitless bridle and Grace always had. And sometimes, the more gear you put on a horse, the harsher the gear, the less control you had. The horse's mind became hazed by pain and fear and it could become dangerous. Or just as bad, its mind and spirit went elsewhere, out of reach.

But there was no point trying to explain this to Blythe. He turned off his phone. It was his day off. Lucien could load his own bloody gear.

Kitted out in the new breeches, shirt and jacket and boots, Margot twirled in front of Pan. 'What do you think?'

Pan glanced up then returned to the eggs he was pushing around the pan. 'You'll get dirty loading and tacking up.'

Margot blew him a kiss. 'You can do that. I'll accessorise.'

'I bloody well won't,' Pan said. Along with Chopper, he'd already caught and groomed Dorothy while Margot, after snapping 'piss off it's too ridiculously early' when he'd gone to wake her, had stayed in bed.

'I can't understand why you don't have some help around here. It's not like you can't afford to employ anyone.' Margot tapped the floor with her toe. 'These boots aren't nearly as comfortable as the others. Or as smart. You were mean not to let me get them. I shouldn't have let you stop me.' The boots she had wanted had had oxblood leather tops and another three hundred dollars on the price tag.

'You know you can't just go out in top boots. They're accorded to longstanding members, like club collars and buttons and cuffs. It's the same in every Hunt. It would have been the same when you were a child.'

Margot sat down at the table. 'All that club stuff's rubbish. Everyone knows that to get a collar or buttons, or even a pink coat, you just have to bung the Master a few thousand. I bet you've got the lot.'

Pan glanced over his shoulder, checking that the divorce papers were still on top of the pile of books on the table. They were. He hadn't decided when he'd give them to Margot, but assumed he'd know when the right moment arrived. He turned off the heat from under the eggs. Margot had her ponytail in her hand and was inspecting it, a satisfied look on her very madeup face. She'd spent yesterday with her hair piled on the top of her head while it soaked in some no doubt savagely expensive concoction from Vivienne's, and she was clearly pleased with the result.

'We didn't get you a hairnet,' he said. 'You'll have to borrow one.'

'No one wears a hairnet these days. They went out with Queen Victoria.'

Pan took two warmed plates and a third piled with buttered toast from the oven and put them on the bench.

'You'll be sent off if you don't.'

'Oh, I forgot, we're in the colonies. You're fifty years behind the rest of civilization.'

He kept his silence and begun loading the plates. She was wanting him to bite so they would row, and she could claim injury and thus, reparation. Something she wanted, like the top boots.

'I presume there's no salt in that,' she said waspishly as he lifted a saucepan of bacon, onion and tomatoes off the stove. 'And if you don't get rid of those dogs, I will.'

Knowing who he'd rather get rid of, Pan looked down at the five pairs of eyes following his every move; the smell of bacon had even gotten Jeffrey up. It was hard to look at him without remembering the scene with India on the high street. India Levy and Lady Blythe – how the hell had that come about?

But now wasn't the time to be thinking about it. Breakfast should have been done half an hour ago and there was still Blue-Buckle's breakfast to get. When he'd called for an update last night, Donnacha had said that Blythe would be at the meet. 'You'll be all right with that, man?' he'd asked. 'Won't be spooked?' Not in the least would he be spooked. In the part of his heart in which he heard the crying of horses made wretched by humanity's ignorance and the belief that the earth existed only to meet the wishes and whims of its desires, BlueBuckle no longer belonged to Lucien Blythe.

From the look on her face, Margot was readying to hustle the dogs out of the kitchen. He took out the wax paper wrapping with the rest of the bacon and calling them, headed for the door.

When he returned, Margot was holding up the divorce papers. 'Well, aren't you a sneaky shit!'

Pan raised his eyes to the gods in thanks. 'I suppose you won't want to come to the meet now. There's a bit to read.'

Margot tossed the papers on the table. 'Unlike you, I get others to do my menial work.' She made a little moue with her lips. 'It leaves more time for fun.'

In the past that smile had made his blood run cold, but not today. Not anymore. 'Best get stuck into your breakfast, then,' he said. 'Sounds like you'll be needing all your energy.'

'She will ring, love,' Simon insisted.

Gill put the phone back down on top of *The Fox-Hunter's Bedside Book*, which she'd been reading last night when Simon had talked her into letting him into her bed.

She slipped her arm back under the duvet and speaking softly, as people do in the dark, said, 'I'm frightened I'll never see her again.' It had been three weeks since Olivia had gone to Sydney, three weeks without a word. She didn't know if she was happy or sad, liking or hating her new school or if she missed Expresso or the Cairns. If she missed her mother. There'd been no word from Nicholas, either. She'd rung and rung his mobile but he never picked up and she was reluctant to ring the university in case he claimed harassment.

Simon brushed the hair back from her forehead. 'What if I went to the police and said that Nicholas has abducted her?'

'He said Olivia wanted to go.'

Simon kissed her gently on the lips. 'Then I'll go to Sydney and find her and get her to ring you.'

'I wonder what Nicholas would make of that?'

'I'll take Polar Bear in case he wants a fight.'

Gill traced the words on the tshirt he had on with his pyjama bottoms. "Child at heart". 'My knight on his white steed.'

'Polar Bear's been to the university before. To the vet hospital. He didn't mind it at all. The nurses fussed over him and gave him bits of apple.'

'The vet hospital's in Camden. Nicholas is at the main campus, in Glebe.'

'Glebe's only half an hour on from Camden. Polar Bear'd find it interesting. All those earnest young minds and learned older ones. He could graze on the quadrangle lawn while I sought out Mr gruesome Findlay.'

'You're not even allowed to sit on that lawn. He'd get shot.'

'He wouldn't. Universities are full of vegans. They breed them there.' Simon moved his hand down to her breasts. 'Talking of knights, what does milady think of her knight's sword?'

The duvet released a waft of sex as Gill awkwardly shifted her plastered leg so she could press against him. 'Milady likes her knight's sword mightily,' she laughed. Then said, as she had dared not earlier, 'Milady's not too baggy for the knight?' Rather than her plastered leg or the fact that it had been years since she'd had sex, it had been the thought of Simon comparing her body to Eleanor's that had caused her to initially refuse him.

'I think that's for the sword to answer.' Simon leaned back a little so he could rub against the soft skin between her hips. 'What say you, sword?' He grinned. 'Sword says he's always thought milady stunningly attractive and Polar Bear will testify under oath that he's had a major crush on you since the first day you rode with the hunt.'

They made love, as they had earlier, with as much laughter as lust as they negotiated around the cast. And suddenly the sky was lightening and it was time to get up and ready for the meet.

Naked after her shower and propped on the crutch, Gill used her free hand to wipe the mirror to check if Simon's stubble had rubbed her face. Would people know, she wondered? But what matter if they did? Even if the joys of last night and this morning had been a one-off, she was still desirable, and she had not forgotten how to laugh at herself and the world.

Her cheeks were definitely chafed. Like other parts of her. She unscrewed the top of the moisturiser.

59

'Get off my pony!' Hazel Teo flung herself at Dorothy and grabbed hold of Margot's leg. 'What are you doing on my pony? Get off her!'

Margot swung at Hazel with her whip and Pan jumped off Chopper and ran towards them. Xavier got there first. He grabbed Hazel's arms and pulled her away.

Hazel wrenched free. 'You've sold her,' she shrieked at Pan. 'You've sold Dorothy to that fffucking bitch.'

'Stop it, Hazel,' Xavier told her. 'You're upsetting Dorothy.'

Hazel dropped to the ground. Pan knelt beside her. 'I haven't sold her. She's got a lovely big paddock at Big Hill. That's a friend of mine riding her.'

Hazel turned her swollen face towards Margot, who was watching the scene with an amused smile. 'She's a bitch, I can tell. And you can absolutely fuck off,' she screamed at Daisy and Matilde Hart, who had stopped their horses nearby.

Thank you, darling.' Margot saluted Pan with the handle of her whip and rode off towards the Harts.

Lucien gave the restless Hugo a sharp pull in the mouth to make him stand. 'Who's the girl on Hazel Teo's old pony?' he asked Donnacha. 'She hasn't been out with us before.'

'Pan Villon's wife,' Donnacha said reluctantly. He pointed his whip at a hound that was sneaking off, no doubt intending to wrap its jaws around one of the Vilanders' rare white peacocks. 'Pack up there, you,' he growled. 'Look to Master.' The hound slunk back to its fellows and fixed his gaze on Simon, who was waiting for the fracas with Hazel to be sorted so he could open the meet.

Lucien turned in his saddle to get a better look at Margot. 'I'd heard something about a wife. She looks a bit classy for Villon. Where's she been hiding?'

Shit, Donnacha thought. The last thing they needed was Blythe cosying up to Margot. Who knew what she might say about the unconscious grey horse that had arrived at Big Hill?

'She's been living in London,' he said hastily. 'She and Villon were separated but they're back together. Very committed,' he added.

'You've met her?' Lucien said.

Unable to think of a reply that would not expose the fact that he'd recently been at Big Hill, Donnacha ignored this. 'Good, Gill's gone to Hazel. The poor kid. It must be doing for her seeing someone else on her pony.'

His eyes still on Margot, who, reins so short Dorothy's chin was against her chest, was threading her way to the front of the field, Lucien said, 'Gill's here? She's out of the cast already?'

'No, she's still in it. She's living at Gwynedd.'

'Is she!' Lucien looked across at Simon, now raising his hunting whip to summon the field's attention. 'Who'd have thought.'

'We're getting ready to move off,' Donnacha said. And indeed, looking almost overmounted on the very large and darkly gleaming Elvis, Leila was staring with fixed attention at Simon. He made a quick count of the hounds. Lesley too was ticking off each with the hook of her hunting whip. He caught her eye. 'Twenty-one,' she mouthed. He nodded. Ten couple plus one. 'All on board Master,' Lesley then called.

Gill draped Simon's down jacket around the shivering Hazel's shoulders and poured her a cup of tea from the thermos. Hazel had grown taller and lost weight and the bumpy patches of acne on her brow and cheeks were new. Had Olivia also gotten taller and developed spots?

She held out the tea. 'Drink this, you're freezing.'

'Has it got brandy in it?'

'No brandy. I've got fruitcake though.'

Hazel's eyes filled with tears. 'No thank you,' she whispered.

Gill poured a cup of tea for herself and sat down on the camp chair next to Hazel. 'How did you get here?'

'Taxi. I took some money out of mum's bag.'

Gill had seen the taxi and assumed it was a Hunt member that had missed their ride with their horse.

'Where does mum think you are?'

'At a friend's.'

'So you're making friends at Garton House,' Gill said brightly, attempting to lift Hazel's spirits. 'That's great.'

Hazel stared into the tea. 'They're all bulimics and anorexics and Daisy and Matilde are total trolls. They only come hunting to get pictures of Lucien Blythe. They sell to the other girls and they sell them to their mothers.' She put the untouched tea on the ground. 'Garton's a hhhhellhole, Mrs Findlay. I can't bear it. And I can't bear it that mum sold Dorothy, And I just can't fffucking bear it that Liv's gone too.'

'Have you heard from her?' Gill asked, trying but failing to sound casual.

'She's not allowed to talk to any of us. Especially you.'

'How do you know?'

'A girl at Garton's got a cousin at her school. She said Liv's scared that if she doesn't do what Mr Findlay says, he'll sell your house and you'll have nowhere to live and won't be able to keep the Cairns and the horses. Mr Findlay checks her phone all the time and he's put lockouts on her laptop. Liv's utterly fucked up. Mr Findlay's girlfriend is pregnant and keeps telling Liv how excited she must be about getting a new baby brother or sister.'

Hazel wiped her dripping nose with the back of her hand. 'The girls at Garton think it's hysterical. Like something out of *The Bold and The Beautiful*. They are so totally shitful, Mrs Findlay, you wouldn't believe it.' She looked at Gill pleadingly. 'I know your leg's broken, but you have to help. We're all so dddesperately fuckedup.

And Toby too. He won't come home anymore because he's gay and mum wants him to be married but not to a man.'

Because she couldn't think of anything to say, Gill covered Hazel's freezing hands with her own. Of course, Nicholas would have a girlfriend. When had he not? But a girlfriend that was pregnant? The broken leg began throbbing unpleasantly. Had she done something to it during last night's gymnastics, or was it telling her that she was a useless cripple that had let her daughter slip into a stinking swamp? Both, likely.

She rearranged the open front of the down jacket so that it covered Hazel's chest. 'You and Olivia had a fight,' she said, remembering the last conversation she'd had with Nicholas. 'What was it about?'

Hazel shrugged. 'Nothing really.'

Gill could see that she was not telling the truth, but what did it matter? She was a failure as a mother, a failure all round. And no doubt Simon thought so as well. He'd obviously been desperate for sex and was probably now wondering how to tell her he wanted her gone. She flushed at the memory of her carryings on during the earlier foolery in bed.

The sound of the horn broke the silence, clear at first then growing fainter as the minutes passed. Gill heard her name. Garry was walking towards them.

'The Hunt's gone over the hill,' Garry said. 'The other vehicles are leaving. We should be getting after them.' This was his first hunt and he was keen to see all he could.

Gill reached for her crutch and hauled herself onto her good leg. 'Hazel this is Garry who works with Simon. Do you want to come in the vehicle with us?' She should really call Vivienne and let her know where Hazel was, but Hazel would be safe enough and Garry could drop her home after the meet.

Hazel was on her feet. 'Can I sit in the front? Have you got a spare helmet? When Dorothy sees me, she'll dump that bitch on her and I can ride her home.'

'Easy with the swearing,' Gill said. 'You never used to swear. It's not you.'

'It's Garton House, that's what it is,' Hazel muttered. 'Every second word's fuck or shitter. Matilda and Daisy…'

'Enough,' Gill told her, looking apologetically at Garry and mouthing "teenager". She turned back to Hazel. 'Put that jacket on properly and do it up. There's a spare beanie in the vehicle.' The windows of the Range Rover would be down and once they got up on the hills, the air would be even colder. Hopefully they'd get a glimpse of Simon working the hounds – she might as well get used to seeing him from a distance.

Donnacha freed the hound's paw from the wire and after checking the skin wasn't broken, sent it off after the rest of the pack. Back along the top of the hill, Leila rode towards the panel he'd jumped to reach the trapped hound. The wooden fence was dauntingly wide at its base and had a steep downhill landing. Elvis was galloping hard, but Leila was doing nothing to check him. Glimpsing her smile as Elvis rose up over the panel, landed on the other side and bounded down the hill in a single seamless movement, he couldn't help his admiration. She and Elvis were a perfect fit. It was time to think about moving Mockingbird on. The mare would now be nothing more to Leila than an unwelcome reminder of a failed relationship. He picked up Oyster's reins and swung up into the saddle.

Halfway down the hill, Leila and those riders that had followed her over the panel, rested their horses and waited for the rest of the field. The panel was not proving straightforward for the others that had chosen to jump it rather than go through the gate in the top corner of the paddock. A good number of the horses were refusing, their riders not bold enough to throw their hearts over the panel or skilled enough to provide the support needed to successfully negotiate it.

The sound of Simon's horn came from the hill over, the short, low, almost keening notes telling that the fox had gone to ground. Donnacha scanned the fences in case the hound he'd released had gotten caught up again. He was a clumsy fellow, forever getting himself where he shouldn't. There was no sign of him and happy to give Oyster a rest, he slouched in the saddle and enjoyed the feel of the almost warm sun on his shoulders. The rain had brought a tinge of green to the sand-coloured hills and darkened the neat rows of trees that marked the fence lines. It was pretty country, much of it left fallow, though the Vilanders did run a small herd of Murray Grey cattle in the paddocks closer to the house.

He yawned, almost dozing. Another rider having at last scrambled his horse over the panel, found their way down to Leila. Silhouetted against the sky, a line of horses was now trotting along the fence towards the gate. Behind, keeping their distance, were half a dozen vehicles, Simon's among them.

Oyster threw up his head suddenly. A horse was hurtling down the hill. He recognised the horse before the rider. It was the little one-eyed mare, Dorothy, clearly in a bolt. Or was she? Margot Villon appeared to be doing nothing to slow her or change her line, which would take her straight into the group with Leila.

He set off down the hill. Leila and the field scattered as Dorothy galloped through the middle of them and kept on going.

There was a horse hard on Oyster's heels. Hugo, Blythe spurring him on. 'I'll catch them,' he yelled as he galloped past.

They had pulled up in the dry creek bed at the bottom of the hill. Lucien, still holding onto Dorothy's reins, was saying, 'How did you get her over the panel? She never jumped more than a few centimetres for Hazel.'

Dorothy's flanks were heaving as she fought for breath. Sweat ran down her face and dripped off her stomach and her single eye was white rimmed with fear and distress. Neither Margot nor Lucien were paying her any attention. Margot's hair was loose round her shoulders.

'Hello Donnacha,' she said, smiling. She gave Dorothy's neck a cursory pat. 'We were having a bit of a gallop.' She pushed back the brim of her cap, showing off her flushed cheeks and dimpled chin. 'I wanted to see who might come to my rescue if I was in trouble.' Her eyes rested on Lucien's Rolex. So far so good. A Whipper-in and …?'

Lucien let go of Dorothy's reins. 'Lucien Blythe. Joint Master.'

Margot's eyebrows rose. 'I really have done well.'

Lucien laughed. 'I hope you'll remember which of us got here first.'

'And I hope you'll tell your darling mother that her son is not only totally dishy but a hero as well.' Margot turned to Donnacha. 'And you can tell yours the same.'

Lucien's eyes narrowed. 'Do you two know each other?'

'Donnacha brought a very sick horse to the property.'

Donnacha thought his heart was going to stop. 'One of Pan's rescues,' he said quickly. 'I was helping him out.'

'What happened?' Leila said, riding up. Her gaze took in the trembling Dorothy and then went to Margot. 'Mrs Villon. Leila Caffrey, if you remember, from the Bombay Duck. Are you all right?'

Margot looked at Lucien, who said, 'Everything's fine, Leila. Drama's over.'

Donnacha scratched at one of Oyster's plaits. Leila had her eyes on him. If he said that Margot had galloped through the field for the fun of it, he would become the enemy and Margot and Lucien would get even cosier. And who knew then what more she'd say about BlueBuckle's arrival at Big Hill. She'd already said too much.

Most definitely, it was not the time for the truth.

The silence lengthened. He returned Leila's gaze and shrugged. 'As Lucien said, everything's fine.'

'Truly, I am fine, Linda,' Margot said to Leila. 'Though I must say, only thanks to my rescuers. Donnacha especially.'

Leila reached into the pocket of her jacket and brought out a hairnet. 'I'll get you to put this on,' she said, holding it out. 'Take Dorothy's reins, Donnacha,' she said. 'We wouldn't want her taking off while Mrs Apsley hasn't got her helmet on, would we.'

Seeing that Hazel was about to jump out of the vehicle, Gill told Garry to hit the child locks. They had a clear view of Donnacha, Lucien, Leila and Dorothy's rider but couldn't hear what they were saying.

Hazel thumped the armrest. 'Let me out. Dorothy needs me. I have to get to her. I'm going to report that bitch to the RSPCA.'

'Dorothy is okay,' Gill said. 'She wouldn't have galloped down the hill if she wasn't.' Thank God that Hazel, thinking Dorothy wouldn't be asked to jump the panel and thus busy unwrapping a Mars Bar, hadn't seen her being galloped at the panel and then, as she was about to stop, hit with such force on her shoulder that she jumped out of pain and fright.

Hazel slumped back and crossed her arms over her chest. 'I could report you for keeping me prisoner.'

For a moment, Gill was tempted to tell Garry to release the locks; things could hardly get any worse.

Garry's eyes met hers in the mirror. 'Don't worry, Mrs Findlay, you'll be back in the saddle soon,' he said, misreading her wretchedness. 'In a few weeks, Simon reckons.'

60

'We're going home,' Pan said.

Margot put her hands on her hips. 'We're not. I'm starving.'

Pan clipped up the leg straps on Chopper's travelling sheet. 'The horses are tired and need to be turned out. Anyway, we didn't bring any food. Unless you packed something?' Fat chance of that, he thought.

'Someone will share,' Margot said. 'One of those friends that ring you all the time. I want to stay.'

'No.' Pan rubbed Chopper's broad brown face gently. The gelding had not put a foot wrong the whole hunt. He had even galloped with the rest of the field without panicking. 'You did well,' he murmured. Chopper nudged his hand then licked it.

'Disgusting animal,' Margot said.

Pan went to Dorothy and began unsaddling her. He stopped and pointed at a welt on her shoulder. 'What's this?'

Margot shrugged. 'I had to get her over the panel somehow. She was about to stop.' She pulled a face at Chopper, who, now without the protection of Pan's presence, was eyeing her nervously. 'I could have been killed. Not that you'd have cared.'

'Well you won't be riding her again, so there's no chance of that.' Pan squeezed out the sponge and lifted it to Dorothy's shoulder, his heart aching as the little mare cringed. 'You're all right,' he said softly. 'You're okay.'

Margot snorted. 'God, Pan, it's only a horse.'

Pan bit his lip – if he started, who knew where he'd stop. But he could not help saying, 'They're flesh and blood, Margot, like us. They feel pain just the same as we do. If I hit you like that, you'd be screaming. And then you'd be screaming down the phone to your snotty lawyer.'

Margot tossed her head. 'I'm screaming now. With hunger and boredom.' Her face lit up as Donnacha appeared from around the side of the float. 'Ah, one of my brave knights. Can we breakfast with you? My darling husband didn't think to pack any food.'

'I'm heading off,' Donnacha said. He had come to tell Pan about Lucien Blythe and Margot meeting up on the field, but now was clearly not the moment. He made an I'll phone gesture and when Pan nodded to show he'd got the message, he headed back the way he had come.

Pan gave Dorothy a carrot and watched her chew it. 'Help us load the gear,' he told Margot.

'No way,' Margot said. She wandered away and a minute later returned waving a boldly printed flyer. 'Look,' she said dreamily. 'A hunt ball. I adore hunt balls.'

The tack at last packed into the back of the Land Cruiser and Dorothy and Chopper secured in the float, Pan shut his door and put the key in the ignition.

Margot climbed in next to him and stowed the flyer in the glove compartment. 'What's this?' She picked up a carry bag from the seat, peered into it and brought out a small canvas and passed it to Pan. 'It's a painting. Must be from another of your friends. It's signed "lovey".'

'Levy,' Pan muttered. The signature in the bottom right hand corner was easily recognisable. 'It's Lady Blythe. You met her at the Bombay Duck. That was her son on the big grey, the Joint Master.'

Margot grabbed the painting. 'Of course. Lucien. He's just as glam as his darling mother. He'll definitely give us breakfast.'

Pan started the Land Cruiser and let off the handbrake. 'Close your door, I want to get the horses home.'

Margot slammed her door. 'I'm glad we're getting a divorce. I never thought it possible, but you've become even more of a bore.' Leaving her seatbelt unbuckled, she studied the painting. 'It really is very good. Such a pretty room, too. I love that blue. Levy ... Isn't that sketch in your office by the same artist? That's excellent as well. Levy. I feel I should know the name.' She held the little painting at arm's length. 'Yes, I like this a lot.'

And you're welcome to it, Pan thought. But no way was Margot getting the drawing of Grace. She could take the Nolan, but not Grace.

'But you haven't said why it's in your car, darling. Are you two lovers? Is that why she was so frosty at the restaurant? Is that why you want a divorce? She's a bit old for you, don't you think?'

Gill sighed with relief as she watched Pan's float head towards Colo's gates. She'd sent Hazel with Garry to help with the hounds, but she'd returned soon after, claiming Garry said she was in the way. Which was probably a fib, as she'd then said, 'I've got just enough time to see Dorothy before he comes to take me home.'

She pointed at the vehicle and float now turning out the gates. 'Pan's already leaving.'

'Shit and fuck!' Hazel said, her expression black.

Gill didn't have it in her to pull her up again. Hopefully Garry would be here soon – hopefully Hazel hadn't fibbed about that too. She slumped in the chair. Garry might as well take her home, too, home to Burragong. Better that than Simon having to pull the pin. Although with Eleanor having so recently pulled the pin on him, it might give him some satisfaction. That's unfair, she told herself. Simon didn't have a mean bone in his body.

Hazel took another Mars Bar out of the pocket of Simon's jacket and unwrapped it, demanding at the same time, 'Are you going to speak to mum? And what about Liv? It'll be totally your fault if she gets bulimia and ruins her teeth and her chances of having children.' She broke off, seeing India and Lady Blythe walking up the Vilanders' lawn together.

'What's AnnIndia doing with Lady Blythe? Grace couldn't stand Lady Blythe. AnnIndia's fucked up too. Everything's gone to shit since Grace died,' she moaned, stuffing the Mars Bar into her mouth.

It certainly has, Gill thought. A trickle of chocolate had run down Hazel's chin. Maybe she was bulimic? She'd have to follow her to the toilet. But what on earth did you say to a vomiting teenager?

'Morn' Gill, morn' Hazel.'

This brisk greeting left her no time to think about it. That or the sight of India with Lady Blythe.

'Morning Lillian,' she said to the small weathered woman with a barrel chest, grey crewcut and youthful large brown eyes that had pulled up beside Hazel. Though it was already past midday, Lillian Bickham was not someone you contradicted. In her late sixties, she had retired early from the diplomatic service in Canberra so that she could spend more time in the Happy Hunting grounds, as she called the Highlands. She rode her two virtually identical buckskins, both called Passionfruit, at alternate meets and was hashtagged by her partner, Julie Rice, as "Ms Undiplomatic".

'Leg coming along all right?' Lillian barked, pointing at Gill's cast. Without waiting for a reply, she turned to Hazel, 'Who was that jezebel on Dorothy? She was absolutely swimming in scent. It's a wonder Dorothy wasn't asphyxiated. I nearly was. Hounds had to stay upwind the whole meet. Quite ruined the day. I'm going to see she's permanently barred.'

Hazel's voice wavered. 'Dorothy's been sold. I'm not allowed to hunt anymore. I'm supposed to be concentrating on my schoolwork.'

'Ridiculous,' Lillian said. 'On all counts. Tell Vivienne she won't see me or Julie at the salon until she gets you another horse.' She turned to Gill. 'Where's Olivia? I haven't seen her since the opening meet, either.'

'Nicholas has got her into a selective school in Sydney,' Gill answered, her brisk tone, hopefully that of a proud mother, intended to discourage further comment.

Lillian sniffed, 'What, our schools aren't selective enough? But never mind that, surely Olivia can get herself down for the weekends. There's the train if her father's too busy.' She pushed her hands into the pockets of the lilac parka that had replaced her black jacket. 'Looks like I'll be boycotting Blooming Beautiful as well.'

She stopped as Simon rode up on Polar Bear. 'Morn Master,' she said, crisply. 'Not a bad day's sport. Despite the harlot on Hazel's horse.'

Gill stood tall with the help of the crutch and put on an indifferent face as Simon slid off Polar Bear. If she was going to take a fall, she was ready for it.

'Thank you, Lil,' Simon said. 'Didn't notice any harlots myself, but you know I'm short-sighted.'

'You'll be happy to go a few rounds with me at the ball then,' Lillian beamed.

'It'll be my pleasure.'

Simon glanced at Gill and Lillian took the hint. She made a point of ignoring hunt gossip but had pricked up her ears when she heard Gill was staying at Gwynedd.

'I'll leave you and pegleg here to get on with whatever it is you have to get on with,' she said. 'Don't forget to give your mother my message, Hazel.'

She strode off. Simon nudged Polar Bear so that he was standing between Hazel and Gill.

'Garry said you looked upset,' he murmured to Gill. 'You're not sorry ... you know, are you? Because I'm bluddy not.'

'What are you whispering about?' Hazel demanded, ducking under Polar Bear's neck.

'Not you,' Simon told her. He held out Polar Bear's reins. 'Take Polar Bear back to the truck and give him some hay. If you stop whingeing and help Garry with the hamper you can stay for breakfast. Garry said you hardly stopped carrying on the whole of the hunt.'

'Good old Garry,' Hazel said bitterly. She stomped off, towing the obliging Polar Bear behind her.

Good old Garry, indeed, Gill thought, not sure whether she should be pleased or displeased that he had told Simon about her misery.

'Gill?' Simon touched her arm.

She turned towards him, breathing in the mix of Acqua Di Gio and horse sweat. 'You smell wonderful,' she managed to rasp out.

They stared at the ground like a pair of teenagers, knocked sideways by their brand-new happiness.

'Well that has to be a good thing, pegleg,' Simon said, breaking the silence.

The hounds were resting in the truck, the hunt horses picking at stuffed hay nets. The Vilanders' trellised courtyard was filling with foldout tables and camp chairs as everyone settled in to enjoy their breakfast. Two long wooden tables had been placed at the top of the courtyard, one for the hunt staff and the other for the Vilanders and their guests, who included Lady Blythe, India, and Lucien.

Leila, Garry and Hazel, Scott and Lesley and her husband were already settled in. The table was strewn with plates of food and open bottles. Simon stood by as Gill eased her plastered leg along the wooden bench and then squeezed in beside her. Lesley held up a half empty bottle of champagne. Simon shook his head and pointed to the sparkling mineral water Garry had taken out of the Gwynedd hamper.

'That'll do for us. Where's Donnacha?'

'I saw him driving out,' Lesley told him.

'He never said anything,' Simon said. It was a usual courtesy for the hunt staff to inform the Master when they were leaving the field or the meet.

'Maybe he told Lucien,' Gill said.

Or maybe he was meeting up with Margot Villon, Leila thought, having scanned the courtyard and established that Margot was also not there. But determined not to spoil what had been otherwise a fabulous morning, she sipped her champagne and helped herself to a slice of Scott's, or rather Stephan's salmon quiche. Donnacha had moved on and it was time she did the same. More than time.

Her eyes drifted to the Vilanders' table. Perhaps Eleanor had been smart. Perhaps the cure was right under her nose. She unwrapped the black forest cake she'd picked up from the Burragong Bakehouse and watched Simon casually drape his arm over Gill's shoulders. It certainly was a day of firsts.

'You did excellently today Leila.'

Simon had raised his glass to her she realised with embarrassment.

'Excellent,' he repeated. 'Here's to the Highlands Hunt's new Field Master.'

'Elvis made it easy,' she said over the rumble of 'hear hears' and 'well done Leilas'. 'He knows the job inside out.' She looked at Simon. He had every right to ask for Elvis' return, and what would she do then?

But Simon was busy piling food on Gill's plate, and she wondered if he'd even heard her. Her hips starting to ache, she stretched out her legs under the crowded table as best she could. She was used to narrow thoroughbreds, but she had meant what she'd said: Elvis was the perfect Field Master's horse. Calm when other horses were hard on his heels, gentlemanly when asked to slow or turn and a fearless jumper. Typical of Eleanor that she had left him for the Hunt rather than claim the thousands selling him would have added to her bank balance.

She glanced again at the Vilanders' table. Lucien was talking to a scruffy blonde who looked like she'd escaped some rock star's groupie entourage. Lucien's eyes, however, were darting everywhere. Bad luck if it was Margot Apsley he was looking for. He'd been beaten to the jump.

She took one of Gill's chicken and mayo sandwiches and as she chewed, remembered the name of the blonde. It was India Levy, Grace's granddaughter. She'd been at the Bombay Duck with Gill and Olivia. Thank god Grace wasn't here. If she had been, whatever mischief Lucien was up to would have been very smartly halted.

Thirst slaked and stomachs full, a steady stream of hunt followers came to the table to congratulate her, say hello to Gill and to meet Garry, who Simon was introducing as the new hound man. Gill, eating little despite Simon's insistence, offered them sandwiches and her Vietnamese spring rolls. There was still plenty of Scott's quiche left as well and Lesley's egg and bacon pie. Hazel Teo had demolished the black forest cake, however.

The buzz at the table grew louder as more people settled into the chairs they'd brought from their vehicles and others squashed onto the benches. Simon headed over to the Vilanders' table, etiquette requiring him to spend some time with the day's hosts. Gill caught Leila's eye and raised a thermos, asking if she wanted coffee. Leila nodded.

Gill handed her a steaming mug and speaking quietly so the others couldn't hear, said, 'I hope you don't think I've taken advantage … That it's too soon after Eleanor.'

'No,' she said, and meant it. A muffled ringing sounded from the pocket of the yellow woollen vest Eleanor had also given her. 'Excuse me,' she said, fishing out her phone. It was Xavier. The auction that had kept him from the meet was over and he could be at the property near Gwynedd in three quarters of an hour if she wanted.

'See you there,' she said without hesitation.

Strips of blue now ribboned the sky and there was enough warmth for the tough to discard their puffer vests and jackets. At the Vilanders' table, however, despite the warmth and the warmth of the Vilanders' delightful friends, who they had met on a trip to the Galapagos, Lady Blythe was still cold. The sight of Lucien and Ann India with their heads together over Lucien's phone didn't come close to warming her. Ann India had made no effort whatsoever with her appearance. She looked as though she hadn't changed since they'd gotten back from London, nor, possibly even, bathed. It was very unsatisfactory. All praise to Lucien for making an effort. But then, she had left him with little choice.

The gal's manners, too, had gone missing. She'd hardly spoken a word to Maddie and Charles, or their friends. Then there was the painting of Grace's wretched dog. All very well and good that Ann India had been quick to mutter (what had happened to her beautiful voice?) some excuse about it being the wrong painting, but it was just too aggravating. Especially when Maddie offered to buy the work. And as if that wasn't chilling enough, Charlie had asked Ann India if she'd paint Maddie, and in the photo he'd taken out of his wallet and handed around Maddie was completely starkers. Obviously, it had been taken years and years ago, but that was hardly the point.

She shook her head. Mars House was definitely not the proper environment for Ann India. She should be at Le Manoir. But when she had again suggested that they go straight back there after the breakfast, Ann India had said in an unaccommodating way that she was working on a painting and wished to stay at Mars House.

She raised her glass at Lucien, who lifted the Mumm out of the ice bucket and filled it, saying, 'Having a happy time, ma?'

'What are you two looking at?' she said, ignoring the question, which was no doubt a taunt.

Lucien slid his phone across the table.

It was a photo of an elegant looking Grace smiling from the back of a similarly elegant bay horse. Ann India's eyes were glued to it.

'We were hunting at Yass,' Lucien said. 'She'd just ridden me off at a panel. That's why she's looking so smug.'

'I thought you weren't supposed to carry your phone on the field,' Lady Blythe said snippily. Hopefully Lucien and Ann would find more in common than looking at pictures of Grace.

Maddie Vilanders, obviously flirting – Lucien had looked at her photo far too long – reached across the table for the phone. 'Show.'

But at that moment Simon appeared and there was a shuffling as the men went to stand and Simon waved at them to stay seated.

'Master,' he said to Lucien, who replied with a similar greeting and then held up the Mumm. Simon refused, saying he'd have coffee if any was available.

After everyone was introduced, Maddie asked if anyone else wanted coffee and rang the housekeeper with the order.

'Excellent sport today, Simon,' said Charlie, whose face still had a purple tinge from his ride.

Simon nodded. 'It's been a good season so far.'

'Wish I wasn't so tied up in the city and could get more of it,' Charlie huffed.

They talked about a horse Charlie had heard was for sale and that he thought might suit him, then, as the coffee came, Simon said to India, 'How's Jeffrey?'

'The darling greyhound in the painting?' Maddie said, stirring sugar into Charles' cup.

'Simon, where's Eleanor today?' Lady Blythe said to create a diversion; she knew that Eleanor had moved out of Gwynedd but could not bear the talk returning to Grace's dreadful hound.

'She's left me,' Simon said brightly. And as all eyes turned to him, he continued, 'But Gill's moved in and she's much better at looking after me. I'm probably going to have to shoot her husband, though.'

'Oh,' Maddie said over the silence. She shoved a piece of banana cake at Simon. 'You'll be needing this then.'

Everyone laughed too loudly. Lady Blythe turned to India to see if she too was laughing, but the seat next to Lucien was empty. She looked around and saw India heading towards the back of the courtyard, towards the paddock where the trucks and floats were parked. She was carrying the bag with the little painting.

61

'Will I leave you to think about it?'

Mucky from four hours in the saddle and a good measure of Elvis's sweat, and Xavier immaculate as usual in Armani trousers and a blinding white shirt, Leila kept her distance.

'Yes. I mean no. I mean no I don't want to think about it and yes, I want to put in an offer. I think.'

'Fab,' Xavier said. 'That's the best news I've had all week. It almost makes up for missing the hunt.' Despite the run-down 1950s brick house and the rusted iron sheds and raddled fences, he thought the property had potential and had fantasised about turning it into his and Toby's country retreat. But the likelihood of him having a future with Toby, let alone a country retreat, was now looking as remote as snow in the Sahara.

'You'd better get your offer in soon, though,' he said. 'Small acreages are being snapped up. People ring about them all the time.'

'Is that Xavier Leila's friend talking, or Xavier the real estate agent?'

'Leila's friend the real estate agent.'

'What's the asking price?'

Xavier named a figure.

Leila gasped. 'That much?'

'It's not outrageous given the market. And I wouldn't think about doing much bargaining, either.'

The figure was at least a hundred thousand more than Leila had expected. She'd already accepted she'd have a big mortgage, but not one that big. And, she had to consider, the banks might not even lend her the money. The Blythes paid well, but many in the horse industry did not and she wasn't trained for any other work. But even as her spirits were sinking, she was thinking about the Brisbane flat. It had to have increased in value since she'd bought it. She'd email the agent that managed it first thing in the morning.

'I have to do a bit of leg work, but it might be okay.'

'Great,' Xavier said. 'Actually, your real estate agent friend has been a bit naughty. We haven't done any advertising yet because the owner's been sick, so the only enquiries we've had are from people who take this road. Which aren't many.' He smiled. 'If I wasn't your friend, I'd be adding that to the selling points.'

'It's a selling point in my book,' Leila said, releasing the breath she hadn't known she'd been holding. 'Definitely.'

Xavier inclined his cheek for a kiss. 'You may thank me now. But,' he cautioned as Leila leaned forward and landed a brief peck, 'don't set your heart on the place. Much can go wrong before the deal's sealed. I'm starting to believe one shouldn't set one's heart on anything.'

Leila nodded. But she had set her heart on the property. In her mind it was already home.

After Xavier had gone, having told her to lock the house and shut the gate when she was leaving, she sat down on a large, turtle shaped rock next to the old clothesline.

The house was ugly, no doubt about it, and there was no garden to speak of, only a sparse square of lawn fenced with sagging wire netting and weathered sapling posts. But the quiet, the prettiness of the surrounding country, the lines of gumtrees that drew the eyes upwards to the sky! Her gaze returned to the immediate surrounds and a lush vegetable garden and an orchard with chickens and geese sprung up before her eyes, and beyond the sagging fence, yards and stables and a covered arena appeared. The unloved house acquired new window frames, gravel paths and a veranda with climbing roses.

But all these things took time and would have to be paid for, and between Whistlejacket and doing extra shifts at the Bombay Duck and hunting, she'd have little time to do much for a while, let alone spend on big, or even little ticket items. But no matter.

The house was liveable, and the hunting season only went for just four months. Elvis could stay with Scott and Stephan for the season then come home for the summer and by the time the next season came, she might have a float. The first thing she'd do was work out a spending priority list.

Home. Her own patch of dirt.

She could billet hound puppies until they were ready to learn the business of the hunt. She might even build the kennels herself – the Burragong TAFE was always advertising woodworking and other practical courses like home plumbing and welding. But first she'd need to get a garden established, some shade trees at least. The paddock beyond the yard had shade and shelter from the stand of gum trees, but the house and yard were very exposed. And maybe she'd even find Mockingbird, she thought again.

Stop. Xavier had cautioned her not to set her heart on the property and he was right, absolutely. The last time she'd fallen this hard was for Donnacha and look how that had turned out. Though ... though it had led here, to this perfect property, so perhaps the pain had been worth it.

No, that was magical thinking. She needed to keep tight rein on both her heart and her head. She'd had her few minutes happy dreaming and it was time to get real.

She followed the concrete path to the house and stepped through the back door into a narrow, enclosed porch. The black and white lino showed streaks of what looked like rust and many of the panes in the louvre windows were either cracked or missing. The flooring was the same in the kitchen. However, here were faded green Formica bench tops, a yellowing pine breakfast nook and a view of one of the dams from the window over the sink.

The carpet in the living room, hallway and bedrooms was the same colour as the dam water. The rooms were bare of any furnishings and the bathroom's green and pink fitout was almost fashionably retro. Almost. Phew, it was all pretty awful, really. But with the carpet pulled up, a coat of paint ...

Stop. It was way past time to get real. Way past.

But on the drive to Scott's and Stephan's her mind continued to race. How much was the Brisbane flat worth? It brought good rent.

Maybe the tenants would be interested in buying it? They were always saying how much they liked the flat and how convenient it was to their work and if they did want to buy it, she wouldn't have to go through the estate agent and that would be a huge saving. Enough to put in a new kitchen or re-do the fences. Though the fences might be something she could do herself as well.

Stop. She was getting ahead of herself again. Again. Her phone rang. She slowed and picked it up off the seat.

'Where are you?' Xavier asked.

'On my way to Scott's and Stephan's.'

'Still thinking about putting in an offer on Yarra?'

'Yes,' she said trying to sound casual. 'Yarra. That's pretty. I was wondering if the property had a name. Do you know any solicitors that aren't ruinous? I've got a flat in Brisbane I need to sell.'

'Send me the details. I'll do it.'

'It's with an agent. It's tenanted. Though the tenants may be interested in buying it.'

'I'll do the negotiating then. For a fee.'

'What would that be?'

'The person I was taking to the ball has bailed. I was wondering if you'd come with me instead?'

She swerved to miss a hawk as it swooped to pick up a scrap of roadkill. 'Sure,' she said as she righted the car.

'We'll have to coordinate outfits.'

'Of course.'

'It's a deal. Send me the details of the flat and the tenants' number.'

'Will do. Better go, I'm coming into Burragong.' She dropped the phone on the seat. The Hunt Ball – she'd completely forgotten about it. Who had Xavier been taking? She hadn't known he was seeing anyone. But then he wouldn't know about Donnacha, either, that they had gotten and ungotten together. How would she cope if Donnacha turned up at the ball with Margot Villon or whatever her name was? Probably by getting disgustingly drunk. One thing was certain though, she couldn't now be thinking about dulling her pain with tincture of Lucien Blythe. Xavier said that Lady Blythe had given Pinkie the shove because she'd slept with Lucien at the Magic

Millions. Given Pinkie's no shows at the stables, it was very likely. But still, it was ruthless of Lady Blythe to sack her, and equally so of Lucien to let her do it.

She shivered. In any case, if Lucien found out about BlueBuckle she'd be facing the same fate. It would not only be goodbye to any chance of owning Yarra, but to working in the thoroughbred industry in Australia. She might even end up with a criminal charge. She pulled off the road. What had she been thinking! It was ridiculous to be considering taking on a big mortgage when she might be out of a job sooner than later.

Xavier's phone went straight to voicemail. 'Call me,' she said.

62

Lucien scrutinised the grey colt. 'He's put on condition. He even looks like he's matured a bit.'

Donnacha hunched his shoulders and pressed his arms to his sides to make himself less of a target for the biting wind. 'He certainly likes the good tucker. And he's friendly as a cat.'

'Unlike the other bastard.'

This was the first mention of BlueBuckle since the phone conversation after he had collapsed. Donnacha waited to see if Lucien would say more. He did.

'You're sure that only you and Beef know what happened?'

'None of the others have any cause to come up here.' Donnacha pointed at the camera in the corner of the yard. 'And I go through the footage every morning,' he continued, hoping Lucien would assume he was saying that he hadn't seen anything untoward.

'And Leila? Mrs R? No one's said anything to them?'

'Beef never talks hoss with Mrs R and Leila was at the Magic Millions.' Donnacha changed the subject. 'What's the story with this fella, anyways? What's the plan?'

'Couldn't jump a chalk line on the ground or win a race if he started at the finishing post. Thought the barrier stall was a good place for a nap. Though to look at him, conformation wise, he should be able to jump and run.' Lucien caught and held Donnacha's gaze. 'This is between you and me. You're not even to tell Beef. If a single word of it gets about you'll be no longer employed or employable. The doors of every stud and racing stable in the world will be nailed shut on you.'

Donnacha nodded to show he'd gotten the message.

The plan for the colt, however, was only partially what he and Beef had speculated.

'You're going to go on as if BlueBuckle's still alive?' he said after listening for a while.

Lucien looked pained. He hated having to explain himself but, in this case, he needed an ally. 'BlueBuckle's already got mares booked and other owners will be considering him. Half the people at the stallion parade will have come just to see him, maybe more, but he won't be able to parade because he'll be lame. People will be able to see him in his stall, of course, but only very briefly.'

Donnacha nodded again. 'But the horse they'll be seeing is this fellow, rugged to his ears. And the bandaged leg will be a hind, of course.'

'Correct.'

'Which is not going to recover enough to allow him to serve any mares because he won't be able to carry his weight on just the one leg.'

'Correct. But when he does, the season being over, he'll serve a few Whistlejacket mares, which ...'

'Won't get in foal, and it will turn out he's infertile. What about Cherry?'

'Nelson Cherry is no longer Whistlejacket's vet.'

Donnacha raised his eyebrows. 'That so?'

'We'll screen a promo of BlueBuckle at the stallion parade,' Lucien said. 'We've got all those photos and footage from Kentucky. Brilliant stuff. Same as we used on the website and for *Bluebloods*. But as soon as the season starts, we'll refund the fees we've taken for BlueBuckle and close his book. You're okay with all of that?'

Donnacha shrugged. 'Sure.' Did he have a choice? And for the time being at least, both the grey stallions had a chance at life.

Lucien checked his watch. 'I've got an appointment so I'd better head. Don't forget to put the rug back on.' And with this, he started back down the laneway to where he'd left the Audi.

Donnacha pulled the colt's halter and rug off the rail and went into the yard. 'You're a big dope,' he told him, rubbing his head after he had done up the halter. 'Nothing like the others.' The stallion Birdie could turn fractious without notice and Speed's special charm was using his head as a club. Stanislaus' thing on the other hand was taking out small dogs.

He slid the rug over the colt's shoulder and murmuring nonsense to keep his attention, secured the neck and leg straps and unbuckled the halter.

A short while later, settled in front of the office computer with a mug of tea, he began copying all the footage of BlueBuckle, from his arrival to his collapse, onto a thumb drive. He then ran the recent footage of himself and Lucien with the new colt. With the volume turned up full, every word of their conversation could be heard. Every word of Lucien's plan. He grunted with satisfaction as he copied this also onto the thumb drive, which he then ejected and sat in front of him on the desk.

If Blythe did find out BlueBuckle was alive, his deceit was on file and there was little, if anything he could do to them, to him, Leila, Beef or Pan, to BlueBuckle and his dozy stand-in. He leaned back in the chair, cheerful for the first time since he and Beef had driven the near lifeless BlueBuckle to Big Hill. The cold tea even tasted good.

Vivienne had not long returned from Le Manoir where, declaring herself *burdened*, Lady Blythe had had much to say about her son.

'Mama is not very happy,' she said.

Lucien brushed his fingertips across her belly. 'What's today's drama?'

Vivienne caught his hand and moved it down. 'I'm sure you know.'

'I'm not making fast enough progress with India Levy?'

'She's upset with the girl as well because she's still at Mars House and because she went to the hunt breakfast with dirty hair.' She gasped as Lucien's fingers found their mark. 'Now that's dirty,' she said, grabbing his hand.

'What about this then?' He pinned her hand to the pillow next to her head and climbed on top of her.

A while later they lay side by side, sated and relaxed.

Knowing that she'd have to now wash it, and enjoying the fact that she didn't stop him, Lucien combed Vivienne's hair back from her face with the fingers he'd just had inside her.

'I'd much rather marry you than India.'

She raked his nipples with her fingernails, like her toenails, painted black to match her hair. 'That doesn't say much for the future Mrs Lucien Blythe.'

Lucien entwined his fingers in hers. 'I won't be giving you up, be certain of that.' They had been lovers for over five years, their meetings arranged on the phones kept solely for that purpose. Sometimes they would have no need of each other for weeks. Other times, calls were made several days in a row. In bed she closed her eyes so he had no idea what she was thinking, or for that matter, who she was fucking. Out of bed she was an ageless, desirable stranger. Other than sexually, she made no demands on him and had little interest in what he did when he was not with her. On the other hand, he enjoyed listening to her talk about business and hair, which aside from her children, were her passions. If he was asked his idea of a perfect marriage, it would be this relationship he would describe.

'But I might give you up,' Vivienne teased, thinking about the triangle of Prince Charles, Lady Diana Spencer and Camilla Parker-Bowles. A marriage to India Levy would not last. Denied the unique comforts that she, his mistress provided, as his marriage crumbled Lucien would beg to return. And when she did allow it, it would be such a homecoming that she would become princess to the prince of Burragong. She had been in London when Diana's life was taken but had been far more interested in the woman waiting in the wings for the world's tears to dry.

'It might well be for the best.'

'I doubt that,' Lucien said, cupping the heavy, sculpted breast laying artfully against his bicep.

'So, you really are going to go through with this marriage?'

'It's either that or lose Whistlejacket.' Lucien swung his legs off the bed. 'Anyway, don't arranged marriages have the best chance of lasting? I'm taking India out to dinner tonight.'

Vivienne sat up and began coiling her hair into a knot at the nape of her neck. 'Mama said you disgraced yourself with Pinkie at the horse sale.'

'Now that really was dirty sex. It's a shit of a time to have lost Pinkie, though,' Lucien grumbled. 'Ma should have waited until after the stallion parade. Pinkie's a bigger drawcard than the stallions. Half the clients only come to perv at her. There'll be a very bloody riot when they find out she's not there. Charlie Vilanders will be heading it.'

They went to the ensuite, which, along with the grey-walled and carpeted bedroom and sitting room, he assumed was kept solely for their liaisons.

Standing next to him in the room-sized marble shower, Vivienne said, talking to herself, 'So I won't be seeing Pinkie at the salon anymore.' Whistlejacket's prettier female staff usually found their way to A Cut Above.

Lucien turned off the hot water and increased the pressure of the cold, gritting his teeth as the icy water sluiced his skin and caused Vivienne to jump out of the cubicle.

They dressed, readying to go separate ways – Vivienne to the salon via the door off the sitting room to which only she had the keypad combination and Lucien to the lift, which would take him down to Vivienne's garage. Standing in front of her, Lucien put his fingers under Vivienne's chin and tilted her head back a little so that she was looking directly up at him.

'I wouldn't let Hazel come to the meets,' he said. 'Pan Villon's wife, Margot, is back, and she had Dorothy out on Sunday. Hazel went for her. It was nasty for everyone, particularly Margot.'

63

The Highlands Hunt Ball was to be held at Tulameen Berry Farm, a wedding venue about five kilometres out of Burragong. The farm owner's son, Ben, was a member of the Hunt and wedding bookings being sparse because of the arrival of winter, he had talked his parents into hosting the ball. Tulameen's high beamed hall would easily fit the expected two hundred and fifty ball-goers and the attached industrial kitchen meant the food could be cooked onsite. The Bombay Duck, which would be closed for the evening, would provide the food and the bar and wait staff.

All was set for a glam and riotous gala. A string quartet would greet the guests and alternate sets with a DJ friend of Ben's. As in other years, the auction would be a brawl, with tables egging each other to cough up for the sealed envelopes that might contain anything from a receipt for a load of firewood to a Highlands Hunt saddle cloth or a night for two at a five-star hotel. The horn blowing competition also always got ball-goers on their feet. This year the entries included the Huntsmen and Masters of the Sydney and Hunter Valley Hunts, who, with their partners and a fair number of their members and their horses, would be billeted about Burragong and would hunt with the Highlands the day after the ball. A book had been opened and was already taking bets on who would blow the best horn.

Gill entered the ticket sales from the morning mail in the spreadsheet and clicked the $total column. Great. The amount was now more than that of the venue hire and the catering, which, as well as an entrée, main and dessert, included two bottles of champagne and a red and white wine plus bottles of non-alcoholic cider and sparkling mineral water for each table. And with more promised ticket sales and the auction and the profit from the bar, the ball would be a significant contribution to the hounds' upkeep for the following year.

Using both hands, she shifted her cast leg a bit to the left, taking care not to disturb the Cairns and the startlingly long-nosed Jack, who were dozing on the floor under the table. Her leg once more comfortable, she began ordering the ticket requests so that they could be easily referenced should someone not receive their tickets or claim to have requested tickets when no request had been received.

She'd had no idea how much time the ball's organisation took. It was something Eleanor had taken over. Thank god she had booked the venue, gotten the tickets printed and already secured a few donations for the auction before she left. If only she had started the seating plan as well. Then she'd have been in line for sainthood.

Gill pushed her hair back from her face and tried to picture the names on the spreadsheet in front of her arranged into groupings that would not result in bloodshed. Having pretty much missed the beginning of the hunt season, she had no idea who was currently hating or loving whom. She was bound to cockup and put lovers on opposite sides of the room and sworn enemies next to one another. And the bloody Harts had three tables of their, if Hazel was right, vommity Garton House mates who of course couldn't be sat within cooee of the Burragong High School table or else there'd be more sniping than in a jungle war.

Then there was the plague of Lucien. With a hefty serving of the ball-goers, men and women, dressed (or undressed) to attract his attention and whatever else might hopefully follow, wherever his table was, trouble would visit. And on top of this, with India's name among his party, (accompanied by a note from Lucien that she be seated between him and his mother), Julie Rice would have both guns out and blazing. Perhaps, though, with the Blythe party including a table of Whistlejacket staff, no one would hear the shots. But there was another minefield. A table of farmstay workers. What was Lucien thinking! They'd be ducking out for joints and whatever and getting lost and fetching up among the berry canes and the committee would have to shell out for a year's lost berry crop. And probably unblocking the lavs as well.

Her groan startled the terriers, who raised their heads and looked at her blearily. She had another awful thought. Why was Vivienne letting Hazel come? It was almost sadistic. At least the poor child would have her brother for company and Toby might ask the right kind of questions if Hazel kept disappearing after every mouthful of food. But with Toby entombed in the bosom of his family, where should she put Xavier? And Donnacha and Leila, who were well and truly dead in the water according to Simon, what should she do with them?

She groaned again, more softly so as not to disturb the dogs. And as for the complete unknowns that had bought tickets, if they found themselves at a table with one of Burragong's legendary bores or a troupe of Cruiser stoned schoolgirls with no conversation and even less manners, there could be more trouble.

Simon found it all hysterical. His suggestion that, except for the hunt staff, the ball-goers draw their seats out of a hat when they arrived, would most certainly ensure that the night descended into a bloodbath. She'd be checking the underneath of the Range Rover for bombs for months.

She closed the spreadsheet. At least the tickets were ready for Garry to drop at the Burragong Post Office on his way home. She might have failed, yet again, to start on a seating plan, but she'd achieved that at least.

'Come on,' she told the terriers. 'Time to go out.' She fitted the crutches under her arms and swung herself across the limestone tiles and over to the door that led from the kitchen to the laundry and mudroom. Using the tip of a crutch to push aside the dog beds and blankets strewn about in an earlier game, she made it safely to the back door. Hopefully Simon and Garry had shut the yard gate. If they'd forgotten, the terriers would make a beeline for the kennels and march up and down the fence tormenting the hounds.

The dogs out, she put on the kettle and got out the date loaf the Fairy had baked. And there was another potential seating disaster she realised as she cut a thick slab of the molasses smelling cake. Simon had given Garry a couple of ball tickets and he wanted him at one of the hunt staff tables. Initially, Garry had said he'd bring his mother, who could talk to anyone about anything, but now his date was a girl he'd met at The Barmy. Garry at least could converse a bit about hounds and the hunt, but what if the girl knew nobody but Garry and nothing about hunting or horses? It would mean an awkward night for Garry and a dull one for whoever was seated the other side of her. Grrr.

She poured boiling water over a teabag, added drops of milk until the tea was the desired redbrick colour and settled back at the table.

Despite the trials of organising the ball, not to mention racking her brain about how she could make herself look half decent with a leg in a cast, she was glad to be busy. Simon had found her a family law solicitor in Burragong. The solicitor, Maria, whose hair and skin were the same gingery red as the Highland cattle she bred, was frogmarching her scarily fast towards a proposal for Nicholas that included divorce and joint custody of Olivia.

She picked up the tea and pressed her other hand hard over her aching heart. The misery she had felt when Nicholas first started staying away had been unbearable, but it was nothing compared to the pain of being parted from Olivia. She missed the smell of her hair and her growly 'thank you mum' when she gave her her wake-up cup of tea in the mornings. She missed ironing her school uniform and making her lunches after they'd returned from doing the horses, and arguing about homework and the wisdom of going to bed early before exams.

She missed her daughter as much as she missed her son. And Simon got it all.

Her eyes rested on the photo on the bench of a beaming Simon, sitting proudly on Polar Bear. What a joyful man. What bliss to be able to talk horses and dogs and weather and country without guilt. How wonderful not to have to go over the house with a magnifying glass for any trace of mud or any animal hair that might have escaped the vacuum. Being with Simon was like emerging out of a cave into the sun and try as she might to keep the brakes on, she was falling in love. But she had to stay realistic. Simon was on the rebound. When he was over Eleanor, a frumpy florist with mothering and financial issues would be the last person he'd want around. And besides, if Olivia ever did come back to Burragong, she would be expecting to return to her home.

The terriers were scratching at the back door. The gate must have been shut. She let them in and they sat as one and gazed at her plate with its crumbs of date loaf. The railway clock between the cupboards and the wall oven showed it was just past four. Outside, the afternoon sky was already lowering. She decided to take the ball tickets to Garry rather than wait for him to come to the house. She'd been sitting at the computer most of the day – not her style at all. She put the envelopes in a bag and added a couple of apples for Hester and Expresso.

Closing the back door, she braced herself with a few deep breaths of the freezing air, rolled her cramped shoulders and set off for the garage. Simon had taken out the passenger seat of the golf buggy so it could accommodate her cast and sweetly attached a large silver G to the keys.

Her fingers closed over the keyring. Eleanor had been mad to let him go.

64

Margot narrowed her eyes. 'What do you mean, you won't?'

'Precisely that,' Pan said. 'I won't ring her.'

'But you have to. She said she has no more appointments before the ball.'

'Then what difference will me ringing make? No appointments means no appointments.'

'You got me one before.'

'That was a cancellation.'

'There might be another.'

'Before the ball? I think not. Anyway, you've just had an appointment. Why do you need another?'

Pan got up from the table and went to the sink to rinse his coffee cup.

'Where are you going?' Margot demanded

He put the cup on the bench. 'Down to the yards.'

'What about my hair? What about getting me something to wear for the ball? I need you to take me to Sydney.' Margot nudged Sadie with her foot. 'This dog is too fat. You should be feeding her less.'

Sadie rose and with a brown stare at Pan, stalked out of the kitchen.

'She's not fat,' Pan said crisply. 'She's actually a perfect weight. I've got to go. There's a horse coming this afternoon.'

'Another lame duck, I suppose.'

'It's what I do, Margot. I work with horses with problems.' Which ninety-nine times are their owners, Pan thought, but didn't say. He looked at the clock. Two already. The new horse, a dressage horse that had started refusing to go into the competition arena and was now rearing in the warmup area, would be arriving in less than an hour and he wanted to spend some time with BlueBuckle.

'There's no reason you can't take yourself into Burragong,' he said, starting for the door. 'If you call at A Cut Above and do that sob thing you're so good at, Vivienne might take pity. And you can also find out the times the Sydney trains run. There's a carpark at the station. You can go up tomorrow morning and come back in the evening. Or stay the night if you run out of time.'

Margot looked stony. 'You know I don't do sobbing. Or trains. And what about getting me a decent horse? You can't expect me to keep hunting on a one-eyed pony.'

No way you'll be riding Dorothy again, Pan thought.

Sadie was waiting for him at the back door and after checking that Margot was not behind him, greeted him with a sweep of her tail and attached herself to his calf. He pulled the door shut behind them. Normally he would have left it open, but Margot's constant complaining about the cold meant it had to stay closed and he was now forever opening and closing it for one or other of the dogs, except for Benzo, who this morning, rather than ask to be let out, had peed against Margot's door.

Pharlap and BlueBuckle were working on a biscuit of lucerne, with Frenchie watching enviously through the rails. He whickered and pointed with his hoof in the direction of the hay.

'Come on big fella,' Pan told him, running his hand over Frenchie's icy wither. 'We'll make you up a net.' The day was cold – up on the big hill the trees had merged their canopies to form a blanket over its slopes – but vain Frenchie preferred not to hide his splendour under a rug.

Frenchie on one heel and Sadie on the other, he headed for the feedroom. Where should he hang Frenchie's hay? The last thing he needed was Frenchie hanging around assisting when the new horse arrived.

He slid the haynet over two biscuits of lucerne and said to Frenchie, who was watching approvingly from the door, 'I'm afraid it's jail for you for a while.' They set off with the net for the small paddock behind the yards. Frenchie nudged his shoulder to make him walk faster. 'Keep that up and I'll let Margot ride you,' he told him. Bloody Margot. It was like Big Hill had been taken over by soldier ants. He was constantly on the defensive, trying to shake off her tormenting grip or wondering into which part of him the pincers would sink next. He struggled to give anything his proper attention. If Margot's plan was to wear him down so he'd agree to the demands of her divorce, she was making a good fist of it.

He closed the gate on Frenchie and his feast and called to Sadie, who was rolling, hopefully just in the grass and not in something revolting he couldn't see. She bounded back, her pitch-black flanks showing only a few droplets of dew that had survived the weak sun. He squatted and put his arms around her, grounding himself in her solid flesh and slightly rank smell.

A short while later they stood together at BlueBuckle's yard. Though still rake-thin, BlueBuckle was picking up condition. His coat had the quiet gleam of riverbed stones and proportionally perfect like a catwalk model, he now looked elegant rather than starved, and like the model's drapery, his mane and tail hid his sharper angles. His anger, however, had returned. It shimmered in his eyes like simmering oil, ready to boil over into murderous rage. There was no going into the yard with him now.

Pan turned his back on the yard and leaning against the rails, closed his eyes and raised his face to the sky. In, out, in, out – his mind followed his breath and they became one. In, out. His breathing slowed, his mind emptied and filled with stillness. The part of him that was free left him to travel the air on the wings of the birds, the soft breath of the wind. He felt the beating heart of the big hill, that ancient heart to whose rhythm he slept and woke.

He felt words on his skin.

When he turned back to the yard, BlueBuckle appeared to be dozing. Then his eyes opened and rolled back in his head as though he was having some kind of seizure. The moment passed. His eyes returned to normal, he yawned, chewed the air and shook himself as though sloughing off an old skin.

He took out his phone and rang Donnacha's number. 'You didn't manage to find out if our friend had a special companion, did you?' he said when Donnacha answered.

'I did, man. I've been wanting to call but it's fecking crazy here. Lady Blythe's got us rehearsing the stallion lead-out for the parade and Speed's got a fat leg. Bitten by a spider the vet thinks. Anyway, Blythe had me call Kentucky to get another copy of BlueBuckle's last sperm count. He's claiming it wasn't with the documents that came from quarantine with him.' Donnacha's pause told that the claim was fabricated. 'I spoke to the foreman,' he continued. 'And you'd never guess.'

'I think I might.'

'It was the foreman's daughter's pet. Well, it started out that way. Our friend got so obsessed with it that the grooms had to take it to the races with him. They had a pretty good feeling that it wouldn't go down so well with the boss, so they kept it under wraps. The critter was a miniature, though. Nothing like that brute of yours.'

'I don't know, in Pharlap's mind, she's a dainty little thing.'

'In her dreams you mean,' Donnacha laughed. His tone changed abruptly. 'Got to go, vet's just back. The new chappie, Costello. Blythe's shunted Cherry.' Again, he paused, cueing that this was also something to note. 'What about a beer at The Barmy tonight? We can start planning the wedding.'

About to accept, Pan remembered Margot. There was no way he could go out without her and there was no way he was going out with her. 'Another time, man.'

He ended the call. Horses in the racing world often had animal companions, but they were usually other horses, like the Triple Crown winner American Pharaoh's gelding friend, Smokey. Several big racing stables, though, had resident goats, which slept in the horses' stalls and in some cases, bonded strongly with their stablemate. Horses and pigs were a less common pairing, however, pigs being generally less placid and more emotionally complex than goats. But it was not unheard of. An American racehorse,

Strong Impact, had had a pig friend called Charlie, who had lived with him the whole of his career.

So, it looked like it really was wedding bells for Pharlap and BlueBuckle. And perhaps now that Pharlap had her own special somebody, she might stop stalking the goats and the female visitors to Big Hill.

He sat down on the grass. Soon enough the new client would be arriving, but until then he would do nothing. If feeling happy was doing nothing.

A while later, hearing a vehicle on the drive, he went out to meet it.

The sweet-faced warmblood mare unloaded without any trouble. In the stable, she seemed concerned only with the haynet. Her owner, a vet student with an authoritative voice and anxious eyes, sighed with relief. They went to the tack room and reviewed the profile of the mare he had put together; usually, he took clients up to the house, but with Margot there he daren't. The mare's file included the results of the tests he had requested to help rule out any physical cause for her behaviour – shoulder and hoof xrays, blood work and a saddle fit – but he still had some questions.

The interview didn't take long and the client was soon leaving for the return trip to Sydney. He checked the mare again and let out Frenchie, who went straight away to introduce himself to the mare. Stretched out together in the yard, BlueBuckle and Pharlap appeared oblivious to the comings and goings around them.

It was getting dark and the temperature had dropped another few degrees. Even Sadie, who loved the cold, broke into a trot on the way back to the house.

They climbed the steps onto the veranda and found Jeffrey shivering by the door.

'What are you doing outside?' Pan said to him. 'Come on, let's get you in. I'll find your coat and make you some warm milk.'

Jeffrey stayed glued to the spot, his paws seemingly nailed to the boards.

Maybe he'd hurt his back or done something else equally awful.

'Close that door if you're not coming in,' came Margot's howl. 'It's bloody arctic.'

Jeffrey let out a moan and collapsed. Pan got his arms under him and carried him through the door and down the hall to his bedroom. The front door slammed and Jeffrey retched as though he was going to vomit. Pan lowered him gently onto the bed and tucked the doona around him.

'It's all right old fella,' he said softy, stroking his head. But his mouth was a grim line.

The mattress shook as Sadie bounded onto the bed and settled next to Jeffrey, who gave a deep sigh and pressed against her. Pan drew the curtains and turned on the panel heater and went to find Margot.

She was in his office, curled up in the armchair she'd had him move from the living room, watching *House of Cards*. The heater was on full and the room stifling.

'You left the door open,' she grumbled.

He picked up the remote and switched off the television. 'Why was Jeffrey out on the veranda?'

She held out a hand for the remote. 'Bad timing, darling. We're about to find out about the Tibetan sand paintings.'

'What did you do to Jeffrey?'

Margot shrugged. 'Nothing.'

'He was in a state. He was inside when I went down to the stables and he can't get out by himself. What did you do to him?'

'We are in a paddy, aren't we, darling. How exciting. But not as exciting as the Tibetan sand paintings, I'm afraid. Now give me the remote.'

'You'd better believe I'm in a paddy. What did you do to Jeffrey?'

'Nothing he didn't deserve.'

Pan's anger boiled over. 'He's old. He deserves respect and warmth and kindness and ...'

'And I'm young,' Margot interrupted. 'And I deserve parties and shopping and fun.'

'Well go find them, then,' Pan said, tossing the remote up onto one of the shelves. 'Because you won't get them here.'

Margot leapt out of the chair, amber eyes yellow with fury. 'Exactly! Because the only conversations you have are with bloody animals.' She threw up her hands dismissively. 'It was bad enough in London, but now ... now you're surrounded by them.'

They stood facing each other, fury facing fury.

Pan broke the silence. 'You still haven't said what you did to Jeffrey.'

Margot shook her head as if she couldn't believe what she was hearing. 'He's an animal, Pan, an ANIMAL. Animals are meant to serve humans, not the other way around.'

'So Jeffrey asked you to make him a G&T then?'

'That's almost funny.'

Taken aback by the bitterness in Margot's voice, Pan felt his anger start to recede. 'Mags,' he said, using the name he'd called her in those few weeks they had been happy together, before they'd made the mistake of marrying.

'Mags,' he repeated. 'The sooner we call it quits the better. We're never going to see things the same way. There's no crime in that and nor should there be but hanging about together is turning it into one.'

She looked at him almost sadly. 'Fabulous education, gorgeous looks, fantastic cock, money and you're wanting to waste it all on a pig, broken down horses and useless dogs.' She smiled mirthlessly. 'Not the cock of course. We hope not, anyway.' She spread her arms. 'I can't believe that this is what you want. That you gave up London for this. You could have done, been, had anything. Everything.'

Pan said nothing. His aunt's farm, the Institut Le Rosey, the extraordinary horsemen and women he'd worked with around the world, the horses themselves – they had all been steps in the path laid for him by the gods to Big Hill. Now he needed them to lay a path for Margot, one that led out of his life. He was waiting, he told them.

She tucked her hair behind her ears and assumed an imposing stance. 'There is one thing at least we agree on, we're never going to see things the same way. My lawyer said I should sign your divorce. Go and get the frigging thing. Your cousin, or whatever relation he is, should have an office in LA. If I were a man, my balls would be well and truly busted. I'm keeping the painting of Lady Blythe, though. A little something to forget you by.' The anger went out of her and she smiled. 'By the way, I always hated being called Mags.'

65

Lucien peered through the leadlight panel in the door. There was a light on at the end of the hall but no sign of any movement. He stepped off the veranda and walked back down the path to see if there were any other lights on in the house. There appeared not to be. He turned on the light on his phone and tried the path that led around the back, but finding it overgrown, decided not to bother.

He called India's number again, and again got the message service. She must have already taken herself off to Burragong. They'd obviously got their wires crossed. He went back to the Audi.

A while later he pulled into the carpark at the back of The Barmy. He was hungry and needed a drink. Several drinks. He was about to seduce someone he wasn't attracted to and he had to get that thought out of his mind. If only he'd saved some of Christie's coke.

One glance around the restaurant told him that India was not there. She must be in the bar. But she was not there either. He looked at his watch. Seven exactly. Where was she, he wondered irritably? He hated lateness. He ordered a double scotch and propped on a stool. A familiar figure came in through the door. Now here was someone he most definitely wanted to seduce. Him and every other man in the bar.

He raised his hand to attract her attention and studied her as she came towards him. She was just as breedy-looking on her feet as she had been on Hazel Teo's pony, and those amber eyes! He'd teethed on beads the exact same colour.

'Thank god,' she said. 'Someone I know.'

'No husband?'

'Ex,' she said. 'We've just signed divorce papers. I'm celebrating.'

'On your own?'

Margot's shrug covered up how shattered she felt. Despite having not driven Pan's terrifying road in the dark, she had gotten in the Camry and headed for Burragong: the company of strangers had to be better than that of an ex-husband and hoard of smelly and similarly sullen dogs. And besides, she needed to think. Should she head for New York or return to London? The idea of Felix turning up on her doorstep again made London unappealing, but for some reason, the big apple was also, suddenly. Perhaps she should head back to Bali and think about it all there.

'I thought I could get a meal at the Bombay Duck.'

'It only opens Thursday to Sunday.'

'So I found out. A bit backward, isn't it?'

'Discourages city types from moving to Burragong. But the chef here can cook. Shall we have champagne? We can toast Mr Villon's receding back.'

'You're not meeting anyone?'

'It appears I've been stood up.'

'Lucky me.'

Lucien leant forward and discretely sniffed the air in front of Margot's left ear. She was wearing scent. And even better, Black Jade.

'Lucky me,' he echoed.

The sky was still dark. India checked the little clock on the bedside table. She'd slept for fourteen hours and felt as though she could sleep for fourteen more. She snuggled into the blankets and closed her eyes.

When she next woke the sky was newly light. She got up and went to the painting and put her fingertips on the goldfinch's tarnished breast. Like the eternal flame, such a pool of light found its way into all her paintings. But other than this and the scrawled title, no other detail marked the book's flight through the air. The crowd on the high street were smears of grey and she, amidst this blur, outlined in thick grey strokes, like the edges of a rain cloud. Pan however, was photoreal. His eyes were as black as the back of a mountain cave and having unleashed the book, he too, like the book, whirled in the air. Pan, the woodland god who dispersed his enemies with a terrible cry, who the Romantic poets had made their wildwood god.

The painting had exercised her technically. But more importantly, it had exorcised the feelings of blindness and being bound, and she had a voice again. She lifted it off the easel, put it on the floor and turned it to the wall.

In the kitchen, she put on the kettle and turned on her phone. It rang immediately.

'I'm after India Levy,' came a male voice.

'Speaking.'

'Burragong vet here. You called yesterday, about Jeffrey, your grandmother's dog.'

'Yes, about his arthritis. How bad, exactly, is it?'

'Considering his age, I'd say not bad at all. Why, do you think he's struggling? I didn't notice anything in particular when Simon bought him in for his teeth. Has there been any change since? Something sudden?'

'No. I was just ...'

'He's a very nice dog. Should go for a few years yet now he's had his teeth done. He was a great companion to your grandmother and I'm sure he's the same to you.'

'Thank you,' she said. But the vet had already ended the call.

She collected her tote and got the Land Cruiser keys out of the fruit bowl. Pan had left a note, while she was away, saying that he had put the new battery in the vehicle.

It started first turn of the key. What now? Where was reverse? There were faint lines on the top of the gear shift, but anything else was long worn away. She pushed in the clutch and started feeling her way through the gears. If Grace could handle the vehicle, so could she.

Three quarters of an hour later, more than twice the time it would normally have taken to drive from Mars House to Burragong, she pulled into a parking spot on the high street and turned off the engine. Checking her phone, she saw that Lady Blythe had called three times and Xavier, the last caller, once. She pressed Xavier's number – she had been planning to ring him to get directions to Pan's.

'I've got a commission for you,' Xavier said, without bothering with a greeting. 'Charlie Vilanders really does want you to paint his squishy wife in the nude and he'll pay squillions. He said you'd seen a photo. No matter that though. Can I come over? I want to know every detail.'

'I'm in Burragong.' Every detail? What was Xavier talking about?

'Fab. I'll meet you at Pregos in twenty minutes.'

'Okay,' she said. He could draw her a map of how to get to Pan's. Or even better, show her how to set the Google app. She climbed out of the Land Cruiser and, in desperate need of something in her stomach, set off for the Sourdough Bakery.

As she passed the Op Shop, she stopped. Was that ...? She peered through the window at the trace of tweed showing between a bottle green cape and some check curtains. She went into the shop. It was. She took the coat off the hanger and looking around, spied the suitcase among a stack of smart travel bags. She hauled it out and took it and the coat to the counter.

After handing over twenty dollars, she slipped her arms into the coat and felt a welcome flush of warmth; she was dressed in the same jeans and thin cardigan she had put on two days ago when the sun had been almost shining and she had started the goldfinch painting.

The woman behind the counter peered at the suitcase. 'Oh yes, that, we almost threw it out.'

Outside the bakery, she gulped down a coffee scroll and then went in and bought another and eating this more slowly, headed for Pregos. At Blooming Beautiful, however, she stopped and pushed open the door.

Julie Rice greeted her coolly. 'Lady Blythe's let you out for the day has she?'

'Let me out?'

'From Le Manoir. Haven't you moved in?'

India shook her head. 'I'm at Mars House.'

Julie's voice softened a touch. 'Glad to hear it. Fabulous place. I'd have thought it would do you nicely. The garden's got away a bit but there's nothing a good go with a pruning saw can't sort. Tell you what, you look after the shop a couple of afternoons and I'll tackle the garden. I don't mind a good wrestle with a delinquent camellia or seven.'

India bit the edge of the coffee scroll. She liked the chaos around Mars House but didn't want to appear ungrateful. 'Thank you. But it's not asking too much? It's a real tangle in places.'

'Now's the best time to do it,' Julie said firmly. 'Before it gets a new start on in spring and the snakes come out of hibernation. They never bothered your grandmother, but slithery things give me the heebies.' She shuddered. 'Still, I'd rather be tramping a snaky garden than stuck in here all day. I'm panting for Gill to get back into harness.' She fixed her little eyes on India. 'I doubt she'll be up to being on her pins for shop hours straight off. She'll still need some help.'

'I could do it,' India said.

'I'll tell her,' Julie said. 'Though you could tell her yourself. I hear you're coming to the Hunt Ball. I'll be there with Lillian. You know Lillian still wears the vest Grace knitted her. Worships it, more like. It's covered in cats, of course. Like Lillian when she's home. Grace couldn't take to the cats herself, but it didn't stop her knitting something kitty for Lillian. She could be like that your grandmother – beyond thoughtful. I'll introduce you to Lillian at the ball. She's a great girl, if I say so myself.' She stopped and peered up at India through her snowy fringe, her eyes suddenly piercing. 'Though if you're on Lady Blythe's table, you might not care to mingle with the hoi polloi.'

India took a step back. 'Lady Blythe has been very kind to me.'

Julie opened her mouth then shut it as the doorbell jangled and a young girl in shorts and gumboots came into the shop and started looking at the buckets on the floor.

'I'd better go,' India said, thinking that she was now probably late for her meeting with Xavier.

And either she was, or he was early.

Dressed in his usual black trousers and white white shirt, a yellow V-neck vest his only concession to the plummeting temperature and gathering clouds, Xavier had a cappuccino and a half-eaten ham and cheese croissant in front of him. But despite his immaculate appearance, the apparent care he had taken with his shave and the light sheen of moisturiser giving his cheeks and forehead a dewy gleam, there was something lifeless about him. It was almost as if his impeccable exterior was just that – a shell.

'Sorry,' she said, sliding into the seat opposite him. 'I stopped at Blooming Beautiful.'

'So how was it?'

'Julie Rice was there, but Gill should be back soon.'

'I mean how was last night? Pretty wild from the look of you.'

India put her hand to her hair. She must look like she'd emerged from the bush. What had the Op Shop lady thought? And Julie? She couldn't remember brushing her teeth either.

'Your phone was turned off,' Xavier said. 'Things got cosy pretty quickly?'

'Cosy? I've been painting. I turned off my phone so I could sleep.' Then she realised. She'd completely forgotten about dinner with Lucien Blythe.

66

The hammering in his head was so loud he was surprised the bed wasn't shaking. Then he realised it was coming from outside. He slid out of bed cautiously – there was still a nasty thumping inside his skull – and eyes narrowed against the pierce of the light, pushed aside the curtains.

Frenchie's rump filled his vision. 'Piss off,' he said, tapping the glass to get his attention. 'You know you're not meant to come onto the veranda.'

Frenchie swung his head around and his face only centimetres from Pan's, widened his eyes in a masterful imitation of innocence.

'Get off the veranda you bugger,' Pan repeated.

Frenchie sighed and once again tapped the boards with a hoof.

'Right. You're going into the big paddock with the goats.'

He struggled into his jeans. There was the hollow sound of clopping and then the thud of hooves on stone as Frenchie went down the steps. The threat of being put out in the big paddock had obviously found its mark. Frenchie hated being deprived of the comings and goings at the stables almost more than he hated missing a feed.

His stomach threatened to heave as he buttoned his jeans. He looked longingly at the bed. Another hour or so wouldn't bring the sky down. But despite feeling like he was suffering from some hideous tropical disease, he decided to push on. First, he needed water, litres of it, and then litres also of tea and a fryup of eggs, bacon, tomatoes. But everything but the water would have to wait until he'd checked the new horse and fed BlueBuckle and Pharlap, and bloody Frenchie and the dogs. Though the terriers had probably taken advantage of his unscheduled lie-in and gone hunting.

He downed two glasses of water and screwed the lid back on the few remaining fingers of Laphroaig left in the bottle he'd opened last night after Margot had taken off. He stashed the bottle behind the bag of potatoes in the pantry where Margo was unlikely to find it. Presumably she was still asleep. He downed another two glasses of water and picked his sunglasses up off the sideboard. He hadn't heard her come in, but then he hadn't heard much of anything after the sixth shot of the glorious firewater.

Outside, he quickly put on the sunglasses. Benzo was raising his leg against something propped beside the door. 'Hey,' he said. 'Not there.' Benzo dropped his leg, and clearly in a mood, tippy toed aloofly down the steps.

Frenchie tapdancing on the veranda, Benzo peeing where he shouldn't – what other punishments did the animals have in store for him? He picked up the object Benzo had been about to relieve himself on. It was another small canvas, a painting by India of Jeffrey curled up on a yellow cushion, his outline indistinct until the eye found the curve of his back, the half-buried nose, the bird-fine bones pressing outward on the skin from within. It was a lovely work.

He held it gently, wondering how it had fetched up on his doorstep. He looked around. There was no sign of India or a strange vehicle. Perhaps the painting had somehow come into Margot's hands and she had left it outside as a further statement of her feelings towards his animals. He set off for the stables. The painting could go with the other things he'd secreted away from her.

The new mare seemed pleased to see him. He took off her rug and dropping it noisily over the stall door, watched to see how she'd react. The mild look in her eye did not change.

'Good girl,' he said, rubbing her face. He fetched a rope halter and going back into the stall, slid it over her nose and with a hand on her poll, asked her to drop her head. She immediately obliged. Again, he rubbed her face. When she was not under any pressure, her emotional control was good, and she didn't appear to be shut down, driven almost to catatonia by harsh and confusing treatment as Frenchie had been when he arrived at Big Hill.

He led the mare out of the stable. It was a day of fast-moving clouds and though it looked like rain, there was no reason the mare shouldn't go into the paddock next to Chopper and his mates. Having little turnout opportunity in her Sydney digs, she would enjoy the open air and a muddy roll when the rain did come.

Free, the mare took off at a trot to the fence where Chopper and his paddock mates, Dorothy and two spelling racehorses were gathered. Her movement was springy, her stride lovely, her head carriage neither high nor low. He could see why her owner wanted to persist with her. Hopefully he would get to the root of her problem, but there were no guarantees. Sometimes the right course of action was to accept that the horse was not suited to its owner's ambitions, or to its owner. He made it clear that this might be his finding before he took on a new horse.

His heart lightened. Just in case Margot changed her mind, he had scanned the signed divorce papers to his father's cousin last night before he became insensible. An email had come back straight away saying that the papers would be at the Family Court the minute it opened. He rolled his shoulders, enjoying the feeling of having shed the weight of a piece of bridge timber. His future was his own. No, check that. Like the past and the present, the future was the property of the gods and it was folly to think otherwise. To repay them for freeing him from Margot, however, he would work harder helping the creatures that more than any other were the embodiment of godliness.

He left the mare, now alternating between picking at the grass and staring towards the big hill, seeing, hearing and tasting on the air things he never would.

Jeffrey was sitting by BlueBuckle's yard, an unusual place for him. He patted the old dog's head. 'What are you up to?' Following the direction of his gaze, he froze. India was in BlueBuckle's yard, drawing, it appeared. How long had she been there? Maybe for some time. He could have passed by and not seen her; her coat was a similar colour to the yard's grey dirt, making her not immediately obvious, especially to hungover eyes. Not knowing whether to shout or whisper to her to get out of the yard or to throw himself between her and BlueBuckle, he stood unmoving by the gate.

Pharlap looked at him and gave him her best oily smile.

'You're lovely', he heard India murmur to her, and as BlueBuckle dropped his head so that his lips rested on Pharlap's back she murmured again. 'And you too.' She tucked the sketchbook under her arm, raised her hand and brushed BlueBuckle's nose and cheek with her fingertips. 'Thank you.' She turned towards the gate.

Barely daring to breathe, Pan lifted the gate chain and eyes fixed on BlueBuckle, held the gate open for India. BlueBuckle's eyes, now pools of calm - the storm in them spent - met his.

India pulled her coat around her and looked at him nervously. There was an awkward silence, then she said, 'I'm sorry, I didn't mean to trespass. I went to the house but I thought no one was home. I did knock.' She dropped her hand to Jeffrey's head. He was now at her side and pressing against her legs. 'I thought you might only be gone a little while and I didn't want to take Jeffrey without seeing you. You might have thought something had happened to him.'

The iron hand that had gripped his heart when he saw her in the yard loosened its grip, but still he couldn't quite catch his breath.

'I hope it is all right to take him,' India said. 'I talked to the vet. I was wrong about the arthritis. He said he's good for his age. But if he does show any sign of pain, there are tablets. He told me what to look for.'

'You mean Lady Blythe was wrong?'

India looked at the ground. 'She's been very kind.'

The words sounded rehearsed rather than felt. Another silence followed.

'She wanted Jeffrey destroyed,' Pan said, after a time. 'That's not in any way kind.'

'I understand why you were angry.'

Pan took a step away. He wanted to touch her so badly that he didn't trust his hands. 'I was over the top. I bought another copy of *The Goldfinch*,' he finished lamely. He felt a nudge on his shoulder and Frenchie pushed past and thrust his face at India.

India ran her fingers along Frenchie's not quite donkey length ears. 'Your animals are so friendly.' Frenchie purred and almost fainted with delight.

'They are with you.' He glanced into the yard. BlueBuckle was lying down in what appeared to be a deep sleep, his eyelids fluttering and his body twitching dramatically as the pain he'd been holding made its way out of him. Standing over him, Pharlap was keeping guard.

It was starting to rain, a light smattering of drops, but the sky was getting lower by the minute.

'But aren't you staying at Le Manoir?' he said, and as India shook her head, continued, 'How did you get here?'

'The Land Cruiser.' India waved in the direction of the garage. 'It's around the side there.'

He hadn't seen the Camry on his way down to the stables either, Pan realised. It must be on other side of the garage as well.

The raindrops were getting bigger. He gave Frenchie a shove and pointed in the direction of the house. 'Let's go in. I'll get Jeffrey's things.'

'You found the painting?' India asked when they reached the veranda.

'It's lovely. I've hidden it in case my ex-wife sees it. She's already appropriated the one of Lady Blythe.' Hopefully, Pan thought, Margot was still in bed. But so what if she wasn't? "Ex-wife". Just saying it felt good. He stepped aside to let India and Jeffrey in the door and left it open for the still absent terriers.

'I put the one of Lady Blythe in your vehicle by mistake,' India said. 'You were supposed to get Jeffrey. Lady Blythe was not amused. It did get me a commission though. Charlie Vilanders wants me to paint his wife.'

'In the nude, I expect.'

'You must know the Vilanders very well.'

'Not that well,' he said, following her and Jeffrey down the hall. He stopped as his phone rang. It was Donnacha. 'I'll take this, if you don't mind,' he said, pointing the way to the kitchen. 'Donnacha,' he said, stepping back out onto the veranda.

'How's the hoss?'

'The most unbelievable thing happened.' He started telling Donnacha about India. 'Then she just walked out of the yard and he didn't move a hair. But then, this is the most amazing thing, he went to sleep. I was talking to India but I could see he was releasing a lot of bad stuff.'

'Sounds like she's got her grandmother's touch,' Donnacha said. 'And a bit more. You'd better keep her there.'

'If only.' If only indeed.

'So, what's next?' Donnacha asked.

'We start behaving around him as though everything's normal. In a quiet sort of way. There's no rush. But we'll have to think about gelding him.'

'You really believe what happened with India's made that much of a change?'

Pan had a vision of BlueBuckle bearing down on Leila and quickly replaced it with the picture of India stroking his nose. 'Yes, yes I do. I've seen it before. But I'll leave him for the moment. The rain's setting in here.'

'Here too,' Donnacha said. 'It looks widespread on the radar.'

Pan put the phone back in his pocket and rubbed his forehead to ease the thudding that had started up again behind his eyes. He really did need that cup of tea, not to mention something to eat. His stomach felt like a sandpit.

'Sorry about the mess,' he apologised, finding India picking packets of spaghetti up off the floor and putting them back in the pantry. The damp had turned her hair into an ivory rope, which, slipping over her shoulder as she bent to retrieve a packet of chocolate biscuits from under the table, almost brushed the floor.

'Looks a bit like Mars House at the moment,' she said.

'The rain's getting heavy. Do you want to stay for a cuppa? I'll light a fire.' He looked at the biscuits in India's hand. 'We can have those.' Hopefully some had survived his juggling efforts during last night's solitary celebration.

A while later, India stood at the living room window and watched the rain sweep the country while Pan studied a page in her sketchbook.

'Are you sure no one else has seen this?' Pan asked. It was BlueBuckle, in his yard at Whistlejacket, skeletal, emotionally and spiritually wasted. A few days from death.

'No one,' India said. 'Why?'

Pan closed the sketchbook and gazed at her; he could pass hours looking at her face alone.

'Why?' she repeated.

'He's supposed to be dead. Only a few people know he's here. The people who brought him, and one other. They work at Whistlejacket. They'll lose their jobs.'

'How did he get into such a state?'

'He was pining for a friend he'd left behind in America. A pig. He thought he couldn't live without her.'

India nodded. 'But now he's got your pig. Grace talked about that sort of thing. She said people don't realise that animals can get just as attached as humans.' Her mouth turned down. 'I wish I'd spent more time here with her. In her world.' Her gaze returned to the window, to the rain veiled valley, the cloud-wreathed big hill.

'It's your world too,' Pan said, then cursed as Sadie's tail swept the biscuits onto the floor.

'You've left the front door open again,' came Margot's voice from the door. 'The wind's howling through the place and it's bloody well freezing.'

Sadie backed away from the biscuits and Jeffrey hid behind India's legs.

Margot was looking at India. 'Nice to see you didn't waste any time pining for me, darling. Do introduce us.'

'Margot, this is India Levy,' Pan said curtly. 'India, Margot.'

'Pan's ex-wife,' Margot said. 'But don't let that put you off. That road of yours is a nightmare, darling. My nerves are shot.' She looked at the tea tray. 'Tea would be divine.'

'You've just got in?' Pan asked.

Margot ran her fingers dreamily through her hair. 'Vivienne's been giving me a treatment.'

Meaning, Pan thought, that she had not come home last night – no way would she have gotten up early to drive into

Burragong. Whose bed had she slept in? If India hadn't been there, he would have asked. But then maybe he wouldn't. He cared as much about where she had spent the night as about how she had gotten the appointment at A Cut Above.

67

Seeing his mother's name on the call screen, Lucien felt a stab of anxiety. Had she discovered that he hadn't dined with India? Or worse, that he'd dined with another woman? He'd never quite worked out the extent of her network.

'Hi ma,' he said, keeping his voice light.

'Hello darling. How was your evening?'

She sounded relaxed, a little girlish, as was usual when she wanted information.

Thinking about Margot Apsley's round brown bottom, (it was impossible not to), he said, 'Great fun.' There was silence at the other end of the phone. Damn. Fun was not a word that might easily be associated with India. 'She's very interesting when you sit down with her,' he added hastily. Which was certainly true of Margot.

Lady Blythe 'hmmed' as if she were deciding whether to pursue the first or the second half of this. Then she said, 'She called just before.'

Shit, now he really was gone. India had probably rung to say she'd missed the dinner because ... Because of some stupid reason that would in no way save his balls from being separated from his body in the next few minutes. His balls or his head.

'It was a strange call. She's staying on at Mars House. Something to do with that dreadful dog.'

She couldn't have mentioned the missed dinner, then, he thought. She must have totally forgotten about it. He cupped his neck with his free hand. For the moment he was keeping both his balls and his head. But as soon as his mother was off the phone, he'd ring India and work out a story. Or maybe it would be better to go and see her. They could work out a story together.

'She's animal mad like her grandmother,' he said to steer the conversation into safer waters. 'Like Grace.'

'I hope not. Grace smelt like she'd bathed in a horse trough. And washed her clothes in one. I'm wondering if the dog is just an excuse, though. You didn't rush things, did you? You didn't spend the night at Mars House?'

It was so far from the truth he almost laughed. 'No, ma, I did not.' At least on that count, he didn't have to pretend to sound sincere.

'It would have been very foolish. Those that try don't always buy.'

Unsure how to respond, he said nothing.

'Keep that in mind,' his mother continued. 'Have you made another date? What about the theatre or ballet in Sydney? I have my season's tickets, don't forget.'

A sigh followed this, and he could hear her flicking her thumb nail with her index finger as she did when she was perturbed.

She was, in fact, greatly perturbed, she explained almost immediately. She had been looking forward to Ann coming to stay at Le Manoir. The stallion parade was in hand and her bridge partner, Maddie Vilanders was down with the flu, or, more likely, unable to face her after Charlie had brought out that disgusting photo at the hunt breakfast. And with no Ann and no bridge, the week ahead now seemed drearily empty. Perhaps a holiday from her cares was needed? London had hardly been the jolly jaunt she'd anticipated.

'I might go up to Noosa,' she said. 'I can get some sun before the ball and Martin can get the paths pressure-cleaned.'

'Good idea,' Lucien said. He had promised Margot he would take her to Sydney so she could get something for the ball, and with his mother out of the way they could stay at the Darling Point flat. 'When do you think you'll head off?' he added, careful not to sound too interested. 'Would you like lunch before you go? We seem to have been like ships in the night lately.'

'No, darling, but thank you. Kevin will find me a flight and he can take me up to Sydney. I'll get him to drop Ann's things at Mars House as well. I daren't ask what she wore to dinner. At least we got rid of that awful coat. Janet took it to the Op Shop. The gown we bought her in Paris is utterly divine. You'll be the best-looking couple at the ball. I'll expect a full report when I get back. Oh, and Jottings is on the market by the way.' And with this, the call ended.

What had Christie said, he wondered? He and Digger had spoken a few times since the Magic Millions and Digger's talk had been about winning the two plus million-dollar Sydney Cup with his gelding BayTree. He leaned back in the chair and gazed out the window at the rain sheeting the garden.

Catching the train to Sydney. Staying O/N. Don't drink all the gin, XXXX M.

Pan tossed the note at the recycling bin. Margot catching a train? Not in a trillion years. But at least he wouldn't be paying for her jaunt. After India had left yesterday, he'd gone into Burragong and put a freeze on the accounts she usually drew from. No doubt there'd be squawking when she found out, but not for very long. Whoever it was that she had in tow had money her smugness had suggested.

The rain had cleared, revealing a metropolis of spiderwebs in the long grass, mathematically precise structures that looked like they had been crocheted out of diamonds. The tang of eucalyptus rolled off the big hill's flanks and across the valley, sharpening the air.

He filled the hay tubs and leaving them outside the feedroom, headed for BlueBuckle and Pharlap's yard. From their bedraggled look, they had spent the night out in the rain, probably at Pharlap's insistence; she had been ploughing, as the furrows of oily, mucky mud told. Disturbed by the sight and the obvious smell, he left their hay outside the gate and returned to the stables for a halter.

As he stepped into their yard, he slowed his breathing and emptied his mind. When the memory of BlueBuckle charging Leila flashed up, he overlaid it with the image of India stroking his nose and cheek.

A few arms lengths from the pair, he stopped. 'It's time you two went into a paddock,' he said, his eyes averted so that BlueBuckle would not feel he was being challenged. 'Pharlap, you know the one I'm thinking of. It looks out over the big dam. It's got a good view of the goats.'

The magpies that had been carolling the end of the rain fell silent, as if they too were waiting for Pharlap and BlueBuckle's reply. He heard a squelching and felt a nudge on his thigh. It was Pharlap, her cheeks as round as golf balls, her black little eyes star bright. She smiled and looked back over her shoulder at Blue-Buckle, who walked up as if obeying an order.

He held the halter open under BlueBuckle's nose and waited. Minutes passed. Minutes in which he maintained the rhythm of his breathing and focused not on BlueBuckle, but on the picture of him dropping his head into the halter he held in his mind.

Then it happened: BlueBuckle dropped his head into the halter. Tears of happiness stung his eyes as he knotted the halter and with a gentle movement of the loosely held lead rope, invited him to walk with him to the gate. He took a step forward. BlueBuckle followed.

Outside the yard, he picked up the tub of hay and, Blue Buckle walking calmly beside him, headed for the paddock. Inside the paddock, waiting for Pharlap, who had stopped to plough a puddle, he laid out the hay and then put up a hand to rub BlueBuckle's face. As his fingers brushed the stallion's cheek, a warmth spread through him, a subtly aromatic warmth, as though his body had become imbued with the scents of distant forests and seas.

Pharlap came into the paddock at last. He undid BlueBuckle's halter and stood while the stallion began nosing apart the hay so that it could be better shared with Pharlap.

'Thank you,' he told him as he brushed his shoulder with the back of his hand. 'Thank you.' BlueBuckle lifted his head and met his gaze with a dark, pensive stare and again he was almost overwhelmed by tears. BlueBuckle would not forget what had happened to him – for its own reasons, nature did not intend him to – but his wounds could now be borne.

The magpies resumed their song. Sadie, panting from the trapped ray of sun in which she'd been lying, was waiting for him at the gate. He looked back at BlueBuckle, seeing for the first time his nobility. His head was fine, his neck long, his chest deep and his legs straight and clean and when he got some flesh on him, when muscle had returned to his chest and haunches, he would be godly.

After a last, lingering look, he headed back to the stables to find the hay tubs upended and Frenchie chomping away with the singlemindedness of a termite. He pretended to be angry, but Frenchie knew he was laughing inside and let himself be marched out of the stables.

The grey mare greeted him with a friendly whinny and seemed almost as interested in him as she was her breakfast. He stood with her a while, letting her nudge his pockets, drop lucerne into his hair and move about him so his fingers could find her itchy spots. She followed him to the gate, making him think that instead of leaving her to settle in for a few days, he should perhaps lunge her this afternoon.

Chopper too was glad to see him, along with his paddock mates. He spread out the hay and when the horses had settled to their in-dividual biscuits, he returned to Chopper and knelt to check the bandage on his near fetlock, which had blown up after the hunt. Though muddied and wet, the bandage was still in place. He rose and giving Chopper a rub on his shoulder, told him he'd be back to liniment and rebandage him after he'd had his own breakfast. Chopper should have been in a stall, but he preferred to be out.

Back at the stables, he made himself a coffee and dragging a chair out into the sun, sat down amongst the scatter of dogs. He took out his phone and pressed Donnacha's number.

'How's our friend?' Donnacha said, this now his usual greeting.

'In the paddock eating breakfast with his true love.'

'In a paddock?'

Pan couldn't keep the triumph out of his voice. 'He caught me man. I stood in the yard and he came up and put his head into the halter.' What he didn't say was that as he'd stood in front of BlueBuckle with the halter, he had felt more vulnerable than he had hanging off the face of the Eiger's Murder Wall, the so named Swiss peak that had claimed over sixty lives.

'Amazing,' Donnacha said.

'Amazing,' Pan repeated, recalling the rush of emotion caused by the touch of BlueBuckle's lips brushing his hand as he dropped his nose into the halter.

'It's a pity,' Donnacha said, 'but I think we should geld the hoss sooner than later. The longer it's left, the greater the risks. He's lucky to be getting a second chance. What about I come over after lunch? I'll bring the gear and we'll decide if he's up to it. He might need a bit more condition.'

'Fits with me, man,' Pan said. He stood up and stretched his warmed limbs. All he needed now for his happiness to be complete was for Margot to stay in Sydney until her plane left for wherever it was that she decided to take herself off to.

<h1 style="text-align:center">68</h1>

After the early morning start and over three hours of mostly fast riding, the hunt was breakfasting in the homestead's cobbled courtyard, which was decorated with miniature fruit trees in large pots. The property near the historic town of Braidwood where they had gathered had its own unique history, not the least part of which was the National Trust listed Georgian style homestead, dating back to the early 1840s.

Leila leaned against the wall at her back, her hunger sated with Gill's spinach pastries and a slice of pear and caramel tart. She smiled at Lillian Bickham's toast to 'our new lady Field Master', and then her overheard comment that the position was a poison chalice and she wouldn't touch it with a bargepole herself.

'In other words, she's jealous that it's you not her that got the job,' Gill said to Leila.

The talk around the table moved to the ball. Hordes were coming. The Burragong Arms and the local B&Bs and everyone in the Highland Hunt's spare rooms were full. Blooming Beautiful was not only doing the flowers but two christenings and despite her cast, Gill would be at the shop every day with Julie. The Bombay Duck had organised extra staff and rented an empty cool room in the Burragong Arms. Someone said that Vivienne had been offered a thousand dollars for an appointment and turned it down. Lillian scoffed at this. She and Julie had gotten appointments yesterday morning. When Gill reminded her about her threat that she wouldn't set foot in A Cut Above until Hazel got another horse, Lillian just shrugged.

She wouldn't be trying for a last-minute appointment, Leila thought. She'd just be pulling her hair back off her face and into a ponytail as she did every morning. The "do" made the wonky line of her nose more prominent, but who cared? She was looking forward to the ball about as much as she looked forward to a visit to the dentist.

She glanced at Donnacha, seated at the next table with Lesley and her husband and their pig farmer friends who had followed the meet on foot. The slight tilt of his head told that he had felt her gaze, but his eyes remained fixed on Lesley, who, from the movements of her hands, was in the middle of an involved tale. Cold bastard, she thought. He had even gotten through the long minutes of BlueBuckle's castration without once acknowledging her.

Simon was describing his and Lucien's jaunt to New York for the jaw droppingly glamorous Masters of Foxhounds Association Ball and the laughter that punctuated his tale felt like the beginning of a headache. The sun on her face had developed a sting and Scott's arm leaning casually against hers felt as though it could bruise.

She touched Scott's arm to get his attention. 'What time are you planning to leave?'

'In a few minutes,' he said.

'I'll head now then,' she told him. 'I'll make up Elvis' feed so it'll be ready for him when he gets home.'

She extracted herself from the table and raised her hand to tell Simon she was leaving. Simon nodded and continued his story. She walked quickly out of the courtyard, not checking to see if Donnacha had clocked her departure.

Strange that Lucien had not been at the meet, she thought as she went to Scott's truck to check Elvis before setting off. Though he hadn't been around for most of the week. Maybe he'd gone up to Noosa with his mother? Hopefully he had and was planning to stay there until the ball. Everyone, the horses included, was more relaxed when he was not prowling about the place.

Elvis had emptied his haynet and was dozing in the sun next to Scott's horse. He hardly stirred when she knelt and ran her hands down his legs to check for heat or swelling. His legs were fine. She glanced at his smooth scrotum. The image of BlueBuckle's blood dripping onto the grass while Donnacha worked the needle returned. It had not been a good moment.

When Pan had told her about the pending castration and she offered to come over and help, he'd accepted gratefully. Blue-Buckle was still very weak, but Donnacha had balanced that against the fact that stronger, he'd be more likely to damage himself, or them during the procedure. It was crazy to do it out in the paddock with no vet on hand, but the first thing a vet would have done was scan BlueBuckle's microchip and then the questions would have started. Donnacha had brought a euthanizing dose of anaesthetic just in case it all went pear-shaped, but except for the frightening amount of blood, which Donnacha had expected given BlueBuckle's age, the procedure had gone amazingly smoothly. Donnacha's family never having the money for vets and his being the steadiest hands, he had been cutting and sewing up horses and cattle and every other Keough animal since his teens.

The Forrester was parked next to Scott's truck. She got in and called Pan. Hopefully BlueBuckle had not ripped out his stiches or anything equally awful. Pan's phone was engaged. She left a message, started the Forrester and set off for Scott's.

The truck was not yet back, and no one was about. Scott must have stayed longer than he planned, and Stephan gone early to the Bombay Duck. She made up Elvis's feed and stood at the edge of the arena, wondering how much it had cost.

The minutes passed. Still no truck. She set off to look at the fences. Should she go for galvanised posts or the cheaper, plain steel variety? There was such a lot to think about. Scott and Stephan's paddocks had both. She was checking out the watering system when she saw her, or rather heard her – as she trotted towards the gate she was whinnying.

They got to the gate at the same time. Mockingbird almost knocked her over as she let herself through. What was she doing here? Why hadn't Scott told her, or Stephan? She pressed her face into the mare's neck, not knowing whether her tears were bitter or sweet. She filled her lungs with the mare's smell and her heart with the soft glow in her dark eyes.

Some believe that horses are spiritual guides, that their role in the modern world is to offer to those whose hearts are open a way back to their true selves, back to nature. That a particular horse will seek out a particular human …

Did she believe this?

She didn't know. But what she did know was that sometimes when she was with Mockingbird, she had felt nature's breath on her cheek.

Mockingbird raised her head. A vehicle, but not the truck.

A tired looking Stephan was unloading plastic tubs full of white damask napkins from the back of the van.

'Hi,' he said. 'Scott's about half an hour away. A horse colicked as he was leaving and he stayed to look out for the vet.'

'Mockingbird's here.'

Stephan put the tub he was holding on the veranda and straightened his back. 'Donnacha bought her. He asked us not to tell you.'

Leila shook her head. 'Donnacha? Why, why would he do that?'

'You'll have to ask him.'

Donnacha rose from the sofa, his face showing that he'd been asleep.

'Mockingbird,' Leila said.

'Ah.'

'That's it? Ah?'

He shrugged. 'What else is there?'

'Why you bought her for a start. And why you didn't tell me? Why you didn't tell me she was for sale? You know I would have bought her myself.' Leila's anger rose. 'Anyway, it doesn't matter. I want to buy her now.'

'You can't.'

'Why not?'

'Because you already own her. I bought her for you.' His brain fumbled with the words. 'I thought … You know … I was going to … I had this plan, but I focked it up. I couldn't … And … Whatever. The mare's yours.' He'd been going to give her Mockingbird as a way of saying he was sorry for being such a dick. He'd been going to attempt a reasonable conversation about what he'd seen at the opening meet. He'd been going to tell her that he loved her. But he'd done none of it, of course. He shrugged again. 'Joost don't bring the mare back here. Blythe thinks she's gone to someone in Victoria.'

Leila shook her head. Nothing was making any sense, nothing except the fact that she was aching for Donnacha to look at her, to touch her.

She took a step towards him. *Throw your heart over the fence and the horse will follow.* She stepped back. Donnacha wasn't a horse. But her blood was up. She touched his arm. 'Thank you.'

He kept his eyes on the floor but didn't move away. 'I'm a dick, Leila. You don't want to be bothering.'

'We should have gone slower.'

He looked at her, then. 'That's not who we are. We don't do slow.' He covered her hand with his own and made a fist and placed it over his heart. 'The problem's in here. It's black. Any bit of light that comes in gets swallowed up. Look at us, a train-wreck in what, two, three months and all down to me.'

'That's not how it feels to me.'

He smiled sadly. 'But your heart's full of light.'

Returning his gaze, she saw how much she was loved. *Throw your heart …* 'Can we go to bed? It's been a long day.'

It was a long night. And Donnacha was as excited about Yarra as she was. He was going to buy her a float, put in a dressage arena so she could start schooling Mockingbird. But none of this she wanted. It could come later, maybe. First, he had to explain what had made him think she was interested in Pan Villon. He had to learn to talk in a way that didn't turn words into weapons. He had to let some of the darkness out of his heart and let in some light.

And her? She had thrown her heart over the fence and was following it. She was flying.

<h1 style="text-align:center">69</h1>

Pan clicked his tongue and asked BlueBuckle for a few strides of trot. BlueBuckle obliged. He lowered his energy and the lunge rein and BlueBuckle dropped back to a walk. He was healing well; the light exercise Donnacha had recommended was helping. The swelling had gone down and the incision was clean. He had stopped the anti-inflammatories but the morning injection of a half dose of progesterone would continue for another week.

He halted BlueBuckle and gave him a piece of carrot. BlueBuckle crunched the treat and nosed him for another. 'Not until you've done a little more,' he told him, stepping his shoulder away and asking him to walk in the other direction.

He really was an obliging and friendly horse. Aside from his obsession with Pharlap, who, enjoying a break from nursing duties was snoring on the mattress she had ploughed up in a corner of the yard, he was very laid-back. He led calmly and when shown about his new home yesterday, had looked about with interest, and even let the dogs lick his nose when they came to say hello. If he continued to heal as well as he was, both physically and emotionally, he'd be a very handy horse.

Leila had been okay about being an extra pair of hands at the castration. Though obviously rattled, she'd understood there was little choice. They could hardly return BlueBuckle to Whistlejacket. There was no way to explain his disappearance without exposing them to a charge of theft, and even if they were to do such a crazy thing, it was hardly likely that Lucien would have Pharlap, or any other pig, at Whistlejacket.

Though he'd been rattled about the castration as well. Donnacha too, probably, despite his calm, almost wooden expression when Leila was around. So many things could have gone wrong. And still could – the drugs for an emergency euthanasia were still in the feedroom fridge. Looking at BlueBuckle now though, it did seem that the worst was over. But Donnacha still called every morning and every night and Leila in the evenings. Though last night, Leila had talked mostly about the property she was buying. Longer term, she planned to set up a foaling and spelling facility, but in the meantime, she was researching land management. She'd been reading about using different animals along with the horses to keep down weeds and parasites and stop the horses from degrading the pasture and waterways. She had already joined the local Landcare group.

Her excitement was wonderful. What a shame Donnacha couldn't catch a dose of it. Hearing that Leila was coming for the castration, he'd gotten even more dour.

BlueBuckle's lunging session had been long enough. Back in his paddock, he took a long drink from the water trough and then dropped his nose to the grass. Hopefully he was all right to leave for a while. He needed to go into Burragong. The milk had run out three days ago and other essentials were perilously low.

As if reading his thoughts, BlueBuckle raised his head and held his gaze until he laughingly said, 'Okay, I'm off. I'll bring you and your girl back something from town.'

He went inside, made a shopping list, gathered together some bags and checked his phone to see if Margot had called. She hadn't. It was a week since her text and there'd been not a word since. His father's cousin thought she was dug in in some Sydney hotel, five-star and overlooking the harbour.

A black Mercedes was parked behind Grace's Land Cruiser. India must have a visitor, someone come to discuss their portrait, or perhaps even sitting. Pan thought about driving on. Jeffrey would have settled just fine. After Margot's constant harassment he was probably relieved to be back at Mars House. He went to start the vehicle but changed his mind. Now he was here, he might as well stick his head in.

India's eyes took a while to focus. Her hair was pulled back and secured with what looked like the rubbers used to fix horse plaits, and her shirt was smeared with paint.

'Sorry,' he said, 'you're working.'

A familiar voice punctuated by giggles came down the hall. 'If that's Chaz, show him in. If it's not, show him in anyway. Or her.'

'Maddie Vilanders?' he said softly.

India nodded, saying in an even quieter voice, 'Naked.'

Pan grimaced. 'I'll come back another time. I just called in to see how Jeffrey is.'

India opened the door wider. 'He'd love to see you.'

Pan looked doubtfully down the hallway as Maddie Vilanders called again. 'Chaz what are you doing, naughty child?'

'It's all right,' India said. 'She's in the living room. Jeffrey's hiding in my room. First door on the left.'

'I'll just stop for a minute.'

The air smelt of Chanel No. 5 and leather soap and linseed, and although the curtains were open, the camellias crowding the window kept the light low. It took a minute to find Jeffrey who was half-concealed by the rumpled bedclothes of the unadorned oak four poster bed that dominated the room. He raised his head and waved his nose in a vague gesture of welcome.

Pan touched his ear with the back of his hand. 'I see you're okay, fella.'

Jeffrey gave a contented sigh and dropping his head, returned to his slumbers.

Eyes now used to the light he looked around curiously. In front of the door to what he assumed was a dressing room was a red and white check chintz armchair almost hidden by a jumble of Jeffrey's coats, a gown bag and a pair of paint splattered jeans. Pieces of Louis Vuitton luggage were piled in a corner and the rattan table beside the bed held a lamp and a stack of older style photo albums, a small canvas propped up against them. He picked up the canvas and turned it towards the window.

Maddie Vilanders spread her legs even further apart as he appeared in the doorway. 'This is a pleasant surprise, Pan.'

'I need you a minute,' he told India, his eyes firmly averted.

India put down her brush and followed him.

'She won't come after us, will she?' he said with a shudder. 'I hope Charles is paying you a bomb.'

'Is Jeffrey okay?' India said.

'Jeffrey's fine. I wanted to ask about this.' Pan pointed to the painting on the rattan table.

'It's personal,' she said. 'It was a dream.'

He picked up the painting and touched one of the figures. 'Me.'

The figure was taller than the rest and its hair was lit with coppery tints. India pointed to another figure.

'Gill,' he said.

India's finger moved again, and again.

'Simon Sinclair, Eleanor Lonsdale, Donnacha Keogh, Xavier Swift, Lesley Bond, Lillian Bickham, Scott Page. We rode up the big hill with Grace's ashes, right to the summit. That's where she wanted to be freed. Out towards the escarpment, into the wind.'

Tears streamed down India's face. 'I want to go there. Will you take me?'

70

Margot wasn't holed up in a five-star hotel overlooking Sydney Harbour, she was holed up in the five-star farmstay cottage overlooking a lake, ten minutes from Whistlejacket, that Lucien had organised before they left his mother's apartment in Sydney. He couldn't do enough to please her. And please her he did, in every way imaginable. But she didn't tell him how pleased she was, of course. She had quickly realised that uncertainty was a powerful aphrodisiac for her new lover, and as he was very much worth keeping, he must be kept very much in a state of uncertainty.

So far, so good. He called the minute he left for Whistlejacket, and when he was not with staff or meeting his accountant or talking to clients or doing any of the other things his work demanded, he texted sweet or dirty messages, some of which she answered and some of which she did not. While he was away, she pored over Whistlejacket Thoroughbreds' website, familiarising herself with the stallions and the infrastructure, the business terms and calendar of events, the stud's many sale ring and track successes. Of the famed homestead, however, there was only a distant shot. But no matter. She would be walking through its doors soon enough.

They had worked out that one of her uncles had raced a horse bred by his father at the Berkshire Whistlejacket, and this they both agreed, gave them an almost familiar connection. And there was her own history with horses to legitimise her interest in Whistlejacket's operations, not to mention her obvious riding expertise. Lucien was looking for a nice horse for her to hunt. A grey gelding that might very well suit her would be coming onto the market soon. She loved greys, they were naturally elegant and stood out. Being made to ride a scruffy one-eyed pony at the opening meet had been but one of the insults she had endured from Pan.

Gill threw up her hands. 'It's the worst idea you've ever had.'

'Garry thinks it's brilliant,' said a pleased looking Simon.

'Garry? He's never been to a Hunt Ball. To any ball, I'd imagine.'

Simon kissed the top of her head. 'Come on, it'll be fun.'

'It'll be hell. Everyone'll be scratching each other's eyes out. The men especially.'

'That's why we need to keep it under wraps.' Simon sat down next to Gill. She was going to take a bit of convincing about a Fashions on the Field for the fillies and fellows it looked like. But he wasn't surprised. She was totally ratty from constantly fiddling the seating plan as this or that ticket holder suddenly ditched their partner or began feuding with a neighbour or a friend, the friend's spouse or their child or dog, and couldn't possibly now share a table with said new enemy.

Which was why he'd waited until the ball was almost on them before telling her about the Fashions on the Field.

'So, who's this we that's having to keep things under wraps?' Gill asked archly.

'Me and the judges.' Simon giggled. 'Guess who they are.'

'Do I want to know?'

Simon's giggles became snorts of laughter. 'Lillian's judging the fillies and Xavier the fellows.'

'God, Simon, you're an even greater idiot than people think you are,' Gill said, then, unable to help herself, she also started to laugh. She reached across the table and took his hands. 'Thank you, darling. I needed lightening up. You're right. It will be fun. We'd better make sure there're mops about for the blood though.'

Simon slid his hands out of her grasp and reached into the pocket of his vest and placed a Tiffany & Co box on the seating plan.

Gill stared at the robin's egg blue box.

'Open it,' Simon urged.

The carved jade heart was the colour of the deeper reaches of the sea, the gold mesh chain on which it hung so fine it looked like woven ribbon. Her breath caught in her throat.

'I'll be voting for you, of course,' Simon said huskily.

Leaning forward to free up Frenchie's hindquarters as Pan had instructed, India balanced on the stirrups and left the reins untouched. Frenchie took careful step after careful step, ensuring that his nose was never more than a few centimetres from the grey mare's enticing bottom.

After half an hour's climbing, they were out of the mist and three quarters up the big hill. Pan halted the mare, who, although now sweating about the ears and hot to touch, was enjoying the adventure. He gave her shoulder a rub and looked across at India.

'Okay there?'

India nodded.

They sat in silence while the horses got their breath. The air was dense with the scents of eucalyptus, humus and cold stone. Below, the homestead and outbuildings were matchbox size. The recent rain had brought a tinge of vivid green to the paddocks and wisps of remnant mist hung over the dams and wreathed the taller trees.

They resumed their climb, travelling slower now as the way steepened. The track narrowed, turned and cut a sideways course across the summit. The trees were replaced by wind burned grasses and huge granite rocks. India wanted to tell Pan to stop so that she could touch the rocks' eons old skin, but her voice had left her.

The hillside became scrubby, the exposed earth leeched of any colour. A wallaby sat on its haunches and gazed at them and hopped away. Pan gestured at the gaping holes that ran alongside the path. 'Wombats.'

They rounded a bend and a rolling wave of green grey met their eyes. The densely wooded hills stretched as far as the eye could see and where they marked the distant edge of the escarpment seemed to end in mid-air.

Pan got down off the mare. India followed his lead and climbed off Frenchie. The weakness in her legs surprised her, but not the tears pricking her eyes.

Pan pointed to a knot of gums a little further along the track. 'There.'

But she knew that already.

They led the horses towards the trees. An eddy of wind rose and swirled around them, pushing them close.

They stood for a while in silence, India with closed eyes, Pan, in his heart, back at that moment when he had said goodbye to Grace.

'There was a book of Kahil Gibran's works on her bedside table,' he said, after a time. 'She had marked some lines.' They were part of him now.

'"For what is it to die, but to stand naked in the wind and to melt into the sun? And what is it to cease breathing but to free the breath from its restless tides, that it may rise and expand and seek God unencumbered? Only when you drink from the river of silence shall you indeed sing. And when you have reached the mountain-top, then you shall begin to climb. And when the earth shall claim your limbs, then shall you truly dance."'

71

'You proposed?' Lady Blythe said. 'The moment just presented itself … That's exactly what your father would have done … You bought a ring. I'd rather thought she might have had Jonno's mother's, your grandmother's … Of course, my fault entirely. I should have given it to you before I left. It'll be hers anyway … I do trust your taste! It sounds gorgeous. I don't suppose you've talked about children, just a thought. It's way too soon of course. I shouldn't have mentioned it … Oh, you have, she does! I feel like all my Christmases have come at once … I can't wait to see you either. Both of you. And the ring, of course. Not to mention the gown. You haven't seen it yet? Trust me, she'll look utterly divine. We'll have to take a snap of you two together and send it to Paris. I don't need to tell you how happy you've made your old mother … Yes, I am old. Well, perhaps not quite. Anyway, the last thing a child wants is a gan gan with a face like a camel's bottom … Yes, I thought that was funny as well. I'm a bit delirious I'm afraid … How sweet of you, yummy grandmummy, I must tell them at the bridge club. On another matter altogether, Gill Findlay's gotten tickets on herself since Simon's taken her up. She was almost nasty when I asked if she'd mind squeezing Digger onto our table. He's ditched the witch you know. Goodness, I can't even remember her name, isn't that shocking of me? He's not remotely upset. He must know that he's made a lucky escape. It's so nice to have him back in the fold. But darling, mostly I'm so excited about your news.'

72

The ball goers were entering the hall in a steady stream. The night was cold, threatening frost, but there was more flesh on display than on Sydney's famed Bondi Beach.

Gill smiled up at Xavier. 'Sit here,' she said, patting the empty chair next to her. 'You look very glam.'

Xavier's hair was slicked back and in his white tuxedo, white shirt and white bowtie, he looked like he'd stepped out of a 40s nightclub. (He had decided to wear the white tuxedo – in some cultures white was the colour of mourning.) The glitter in his eyes showed that he had already been at the drink.

Seeing the jade heart, he murmured, 'Elsa Peretti. Nice.' Then he said, 'You look squeezable yourself.'

'Thanks,' Gill said. She was wearing the silver and blue beaded flapper dress she had bought for the first ever Highlands Hunt Ball because it was fun, and she loved the way the fabric moved over her skin. But on that occasion, Nicholas had threatened to stay home if she wore it, so it had remained in its cover in her wardrobe. Simon, on the other hand, when she asked his opinion, had slid one hand down the rather low bodice and ruched a handful of the slippery material up around her bottom with the other.

Smiling at the memory, she looked out through the plate glass doors to the atrium. The hunt staff, Simon, Donnacha and Scott in their scarlet tails, Leila in a pale green strapless gown printed with butterflies and Lesley in a black and white Audrey Hepburn number, were greeting the new arrivals.

'Looks like everyone's pretty much here,' she said. 'I wonder where Lucien is?' As Joint Master, he should have been standing next to Simon. Instead, it was Leila, the next most senior of the hunt staff who was between him and Donnacha.

'Who's he bringing?' Xavier asked.

'India.'

'I doubt that.' Xavier picked up Gill's glass and took a swallow. 'My God, what are you drinking? It's not even bottom shelf.'

'Alcohol free champagne,' Gill said. 'It tastes better after a few mouthfuls.' She giggled. 'And it actually gets you quite pissed.'

Xavier raised his hand to attract the attention of one of the drink waiters circulating among the tables. 'I'll get us some of the good stuff.'

'Thanks, but no thanks,' Gill said firmly.

Xavier shrugged. 'More for me then.' He gave the pink-haired young man now standing in front of them a hundred dollar note, requested a bottle of Moët and told him to keep the change.

'Do you think India isn't coming,' Gill said. 'If I'd known, I could have given Kevin her place instead of squeezing another one onto the table.'

'I didn't say she wouldn't be here. She just won't be with Lucien.'

'Lillian and Julie are convinced Lady Blythe's plotting to marry her off to Lucien as a way of getting back at Grace for all the imagined hurts she inflicted on her. I'm worried that Lillian's planning to call her out.'

'Might make the evening bearable if she does,' Xavier said.

The drink waiter put an ice bucket on the table and Xavier gestured at him to fill his glass.

Watching Xavier empty the glass then lift the bottle for another, she asked, 'So what happened to your plus one?'

'Stood me up.' Xavier answered curtly. 'And Leila as well. Not that I mind in her case.' He pointed towards the front door, where, their backs now side on as they turned to leave the doorway, they could see that Donnacha had Leila's hand firmly clasped in his.

'Well, thank goodness for that,' she said, then cursed her tactlessness as Xavier tossed down another glass.

A beaming Simon came towards them. He had wanted Gill to stand at his side for the meet and greet at the front door and her heart had turned over when he'd asked, but she had said no. It was too soon to announce themselves as a couple in such a formal way, for her at least. 'Next year then,' he had said, firmly, reading her mind. 'Olivia has to know some time.'

He said hello to Xavier and, dropping a kiss on Gill's head, slid into the chair next to her. They were joined by Lesley and her husband, Donnacha and Leila and Scott and a proud looking Garry and his date, Whistlejacket's ex-office manager Pinkie. Looking fabulous in a fuchsia satin cami and floor length black skirt slit to the thigh, Pinkie was obviously as rapt in Garry as he was in her. Donnacha filled her glass and Leila began grilling her about what she'd been doing since leaving Whistlejacket.

Topping up his and Gill's glasses, Simon waved at the landowners and hunt members at their different tables about the room. 'Isn't this fantastic?' he said. 'I think this is going to be our best ball yet.'

The chatter and laughter were already raucous. Under the canopy of silver fairy lights webbing the ceiling, the room was seething with colour. Jewels that had not seen light since last year's ball added to the brilliance. Scent from huge vases of Oriental lilies mingled headily with the chosen favourites of the guests. Shoulders and the backs of the replica Philippe Stark ghost chairs were draped with fur and pashmina. Polished to perfection cutlery and glassware and silver rimmed side plates sat stylishly on the dark green damask tablecloths. Next to each place card, a parchment scroll tied with silver ribbon lay atop the beautifully folded white napkins, this the menu and drinks list and the program for the night. After much arguing about the centrepiece, Gill and Julie had found a compromise in white cyclamens and these, potted into glazed pots a similar shade to the tablecloths, glowed with innocent grace.

Suddenly missing Olivia shockingly, Gill looked across at Vivienne's table to see how Hazel was faring. Hazel's chair was empty. Toby's as well. Ultra-sharp in a plunging ruby MLS gown, Vivienne appeared engrossed in the conversation of her long-time partner, Ian Willis. Her eyes, however, kept darting to the atrium.

Vivienne was in fact extremely angry. So angry she was hardly taking in a word of what Ian was saying about a prime piece of real estate about to come on the market in the middle of Burragong. Having returned from Sydney last night for the ball, this morning Toby was gone. At first, she'd thought he'd gone out for an early breakfast. And when she discovered that Hazel was also nowhere in the house, she assumed he'd taken his sister. Naturally, she'd rung, first Toby's phone then Hazel's. When neither picked up she decided they were somewhere noisy, like Pregos. The morning rolled on. She kept calling between clients, while she was driving to and from Le Manoir. Neither child had answered or returned her messages. Then, just as she was about to call the police, Toby rang. She couldn't shout at him because she was with a client and as she was composing herself, he'd said: 'Hazel's with me, Everything's okay. See you at the ball but don't worry if we're a bit late,' and rang off.

How could everything possibly be okay? When she'd told Ian that Hazel and Toby would be coming later, he had pointedly straightened the already perfectly straight ties of his thirteen-year-old twins, sitting at this moment like perfect little soldiers with their heads together over an iPad. Her eyes went back to the atrium. Other than the members of the string quartet that had welcomed the ball-goers and were now folding up their music stands, there was no other sign of life.

Gill touched the back of Simon's hand. 'Did Hazel and Toby come with Vivienne?'

'I didn't see them,' he answered.

'Who cares,' Xavier said.

Simon looked at the nearly empty bottle of Moët. 'Go easy on that, man. You're supposed to be scouting for the Fashions on the Field.'

Xavier leaned back in his chair and making a face like a sullen schoolboy, clasped his hands behind his head and appeared to go to sleep.

Gill caught Simon's eye and drew a heart in the air with her index finger then made a ripping gesture. Simon nodded to show he'd got the message. Gill then laughed as Lillian Bickham, dressed in a tux and sporting a rainbow coloured bowtie, dropped a white card, printed on one side with the Highlands Hunt insignia and the other with the scrolled letters F F, onto the table in front of her.

'How much did Simon bung you to give me that?' she asked.

'Not nearly enough,' Lillian said darkly. 'That chap over there with no hair offered me five hundred to card his daughter. I assume it's his daughter. Don't know who they belong to. Never seen either of them in my life.'

Leila, her hand now openly joined with Donnacha's on the table for all to see, began telling Scott and Lesley about Yarra.

'We'll have to get Leila a housewarming present,' Gill told Simon, checking out the plate of stilton stuffed zucchini flowers the waitress placed in front of her.

'I expect Lesley will give her a pig,' Simon said.

'A house without a pig is like a garden without a rose,' Lesley said, overhearing.

Waiting for Simon to be served his entrée, Gill looked around the tables. 'Lady Blythe's not wearing her happy face. She's got empty chairs as well.'

'Fucking Lucien,' Simon said, following her gaze. 'Should have been with us at the door. Didn't even ring. God, he can be a rude bastard. Learned from his mother I suppose.'

'He'd better show,' Lillian said, having returned to give Leila a card for the Fashions on the Field. 'There'll be rioting if he doesn't.' Dinner with Lucien was one of the auction items.

'It'll be good for the bar though,' Scott said drolly. 'The men'll be celebrating and the women drowning their sorrows.'

'Did you see Lucien this afternoon?' Gill asked Donnacha.

'Didn't see much of anything I'm afraid,' he answered with a smile.

'Except for a great deal of lovely Leila,' Lillian said under her breath.

Donnacha shot her a look then, to everyone's delight, laughed. 'You could be right, there, Lillian.'

The entrée was superb. The main followed soon after: beef wellington with creamed parsnip, smashed peas and a red wine and lavender jus for the meat eaters and a sweet potato and fetta filo wellington with beetroot marmalade and a caraway dressing for the vegetarians, or "vegetables" Lillian was heard loudly calling them as everyone was tucking in.

Simon raised a loaded fork at Scott. 'Your man can certainly cook.'

'And dance,' Scott said, looking over to where Benny's DJ friend was setting up his booth. Hopefully Stephan would not be too tired to hit the floor when things hotted up. But if he was, there were other options. Some of his students had taken a table and looked in the mood for a jive.

Simon leaned across and prodded Xavier, whose beef welling-ton, like his entree remained untouched. 'You're missing bloody good tucker.'

'If I open my eyes the room spins,' Xavier moaned.

'Keep them closed, then,' Scott advised, pouring what remained of the Moët into his glass.

'Most definitely,' said Lesley, reaching for Xavier's plate and scraping the beef onto her husband's.

'Well now, will you look at that!' Simon said.

'And that!' Scott echoed.

But all Gill could hear were the cries of 'mum, mum'. It was Olivia, dressed in a striped frock that made her look like some kind of weird bee. But never mind the frock, it was Olivia! The table rocked wildly as she pushed back her chair, and forgetting her cast, tried to stand. Luckily Simon grabbed her as the force with which Olivia flung her-self into her arms would have brought them both down.

Xavier's eyes jolted open and he promptly turned and vomited beside his chair.

'You look like you need a doctor,' Toby said, dazzling in a twin tuxedo to Xavier's and holding out a napkin.

Xavier tried to stand and sank back in his seat. He picked up his fork and began tapping the empty Moët bottle. 'Ladies and gents, can I have your attention. I'd like to announce the winner of the Fellas on the Field. All eyes on Toby Teo ...'

Despite the racket coming from Simon's table, Lady Blythe could not tear her eyes away from the couple crossing the room. What was Ann India doing with Pan Villon? And wasn't that the ivory silk maxi from the window of Recycle? The boned bodice and Oroton styled silver buckle on the wide belt had even caught her eye. But where was the Chanel gown they had bought in Paris? She gave a little moan.

'Ma.'

Her heart jumped so hard that for a minute she thought she was having a heart attack. The men at the table – Brian, Kevin and Martin, Digger, and Patrick the husband of her dear Sydney friend Jean who'd come down for the ball – were all getting to their feet.

A hush spread over the room as Lucien, gold coloured hair curling over his temples, and in his immaculately fitting scarlet tails, snowy breeches and long black boots looking like he was about to lead a cavalry charge, walked Margot up to his mother. Even Lillian Bickham couldn't help staring.

'Ma, I believe you've met my fiancé, Margot. Margot Apsley.'

Margot held out her left hand, the fairy lights catching the cushion-cut diamond on her ring finger and creating a dazzling fireworks display.

'So pleased to meet you again,' she said in a voice that pinged like Waterford crystal. She withdrew her hand and tucked it proprietarily through Lucien's arm, taking care not to snag the enormous ring on his sleeve. 'I'm one of your biggest fans.'

Digger grinned. 'Hello Lucien. Tasty filly, I must say.' His eyes crossed as they took in the ski slope curve of Margot's brown lower back, artfully bared by her Oscar statuette, gold satin gown. No wonder bloody Lucien was looking so smug.

'Sir,' he shouted at a nearby drinks waiter. 'Moët. A dozen bottles. Let's get this party started.'